# LAURANN DOHNER

*NEW SPECIES*

**ELLORA'S CAVE**
Romantica®
www.ElLORASCAVE.com

An Ellora's Cave Publication

www.ellorascave.com

Slade

ISBN 9781419965517
ALL RIGHTS RESERVED.
Slade Copyright © 2011 Laurann Dohner
Edited by Shannon Combs and Pamela Campbell.
Cover art by Syneca.

Electronic book publication August 2011
Trade paperback publication 2011

# SLADE

ဆ

# *Dedication*

෩

*To my always and forever – Mr. Laurann.*

# Prologue

### ඩ

"Didn't you used to work for a veterinarian, Trisha?"

Trisha frowned, taking a sip of her iced coffee. Her body tensed when she heard the man's voice. Dr. Dennis Channer was a prick. He always tried to go out of his way to harass her by any means possible. The guy just had it in for her.

It was difficult for people to get to know her, she'd come to grips with that, but it still hurt her feelings sometimes. She'd graduated high school at the young age of fourteen and by the time she was twenty-four, she'd finished medical school, had completed her residency, and spent a few years in the trenches of some of the toughest hospitals known for incoming trauma victims. At twenty-eight she had landed her dream job at one of the top-rated hospitals within the U.S.

Most people were either intimidated by her or believed she had to be pretty conceited. She wasn't a snob, didn't think she was better than anyone else, and she definitely wasn't a cold fish. Her social skills just sucked. She had always been a bit shy, led a busy life that hadn't allowed her friendships for the most part, and then there was the fact that few people were friendly to her. It wasn't easy to warm up to people who gave her the cold shoulder.

Dennis Channer was her boss and he resented the hell out of her. He'd been in his thirties, a full decade older than Trisha, when he'd come to work at Mercy Hospital. He thought her too pretty and he hadn't hidden his opinion that her looks had landed the job rather than her skill. She'd worked her ass off to get where she had. She'd sacrificed having a personal life for her career.

"Yes, I did. I worked at an emergency veterinarian hospital through med school."

"No scholarship?" He sneered at her.

She counted to ten silently. "No."

"You're up next." His lined face appeared highly amused, too pleased to suit Trisha. "We have an incoming that is right up your alley." He laughed, obviously making some private joke, targeting her.

Her teeth clenched to prevent her from saying something she'd regret. She dumped her iced coffee and the rest of her sandwich into the trashcan before following Dennis down the hallway from the lounge. *It will probably be another unfortunate soul*, Trisha guessed. Dennis loved to toss drunks, vagrants, or gang members her way. Since he'd mentioned alley, a homeless person came to mind.

An image of a highly smelly, unwashed body that would knock her back with its stench flashed through her brain. It might even be one of the crazy ones who would yell about how aliens from Mars were going to kidnap them all. Trisha had dealt with many of them, unfortunately. A lot of them tended to wrap foil around various body parts to prevent aliens from supposedly scanning them. Removing the stuff to evaluate their injuries usually resulted in at least four of the staff having to hold them down.

Trisha passed Sally, a nurse she had become friends with, as she moved quickly toward the emergency doors. The frightened, grim expression on other woman's face made Trisha tense more. Whatever was coming in had to be pretty ominous since the woman was one tough cookie, having seen a lot of horrendous things in her fifteen years working the emergency room.

Trisha started to worry. There wasn't much that scared Sally. The nurse hadn't even flinched when two weeks before a gang member had been brought in with three gunshot wounds to the back. While they'd been working on the young man, a rival gang had sent one of their members into the emergency room to finish him off. Sally had calmly helped Trisha wheel the unconscious man into a closet to hide him while security cleared the building to locate the armed thug.

Dennis turned, smiling smugly at Trisha. "We have an incoming half man, half dog."

"That's not funny." Trisha sighed. "I dumped my dinner for this? Grow up, Dennis."

He lifted his hands, still smiling. "I wish this were a joke but I'm serious. He's been rescued from some Frankenstein research facility for a drug company. We have incoming to different hospitals to the tune of about sixty-five patients. We're the nearest trauma center and they are flying him to us because he's the worst of the victims. The onsite paramedics and the life-flight crew have confirmed that this man is human with doggy parts." Dennis appeared downright gleeful. "And he's all yours since you know your dogs."

Trisha put her hands on her hips. "You should have saved this one for April's Fool's Day. What is the real story? Are they bringing in a victim wearing a dog suit? Is he a character actor who tripped at some kid's birthday party while playing a mutt?"

"It's true," Sally intervened softly. "It's on every major channel." She didn't play practical jokes on Trisha. Her dark eyes looked anxious. "The cops busted some research facility and they are pulling survivors from the building, saying they are part animal and part people. We do have an incoming life flight with one of them onboard. We called an emergency vet to back us up but he's twenty minutes out."

Shock rippled through Trisha as she struggled to take in the ramifications of what she'd heard. She spun around to stride quickly to the nurse's station to peer up at the television mounted to the wall. Two nurses were already watching, their eyes glued to the set. A news helicopter circled a building while filming ambulances, police, fire and swat vehicles on the ground. In bold lettering scrolling across the screen she read enough to cause her to spin back around.

"Time?" Trisha shouted.

Cory, the male nurse who did incoming control, spoke from his tucked-away position behind a desk at the entrance. "They are three minutes out. He's stable so far."

"Crap," Trisha ground out. Her gaze flew to Dennis and she gave him a grim nod. "What do we know so far?"

"Shaky details at best." Dennis still smiled. "He's got blood loss, he's in shock, and they don't know what is wrong with Dog Boy. They just scooped him and ran when his vitals crashed. Maybe you can give him a doggy treat and he can bark out his injuries."

"You're amused?" Trisha glared at him with disgust. "God, you're a bastard. This is someone's life." She turned her back on him and focused on Sally. "Prep an OR just in case since we don't know what we'll be dealing with. Get everyone woken up. We'll have to cross and match his blood type and I want full panels. We—"

"Don't carry doggy blood," Dennis interrupted.

Trisha whirled around and glowered at him. "I'm working here. I'm a professional. Do you remember what that is?"

His smile died. "Don't speak to me that way. I'm your boss."

"You're only one of them and I'll go over your head if you don't back off me right now," Trisha threatened. "Either help or get out of my way. The life flight should land in under a minute." She spun on her heel, jogging toward the outer door. She yelled instructions on her way outside to scan the sky.

She heard the helicopter before she saw it. Noises behind her assured that her team moved into place as the doors whished open and she turned her head, throwing her arm up as the helicopter lowered. The wind blown up by the blades made her turn her head even more, tucking it under her loose white coat sleeve to shield most of her face. Her gaze fixed on Sally and the other two medical personnel who had rolled a gurney outside with them. She hoped she didn't look as apprehensive as the other three did. The helicopter touched down.

Only years of experience kept Trisha calm. She barely glanced at the large, covered bundle being lifted from the helicopter. She gave her full attention to the attendant while he yelled out the patient's vitals and information. Trisha nodded, listening.

"What's his name?"

"215."

Trisha frowned at the life-flight medic. He nodded vigorously. "It's all we have. It is what they called him."

"Thanks." Trisha pivoted, hurrying after the gurney being pushed inside. She flashed Cory a glance as she stormed past him. "Get me more information on him. Call the police handling that mess, whatever it takes, but I need to know everything I can about this guy. The only name they have for him is 215." She yanked gloves out her pocket and pulled them on.

"I'm on it," Cory promised, grabbing up his phone.

Trisha loved working with him. He was a "can do" kind of guy. He never bitched, never whined about a thing, and did whatever she asked even if it wasn't technically his job. She knew he'd do what he could to help. She rushed into the exam room and watched as her team transferred the victim from the gurney onto an exam bed. She moved to his head and her gloved hands reached for his face.

"Let's go," Trisha ordered. She glanced at the body being revealed as her team began removing his clothing. The victim had dirt smeared on his face and body, some of it dried clumps of mud, making it difficult to make out his features.

"Look at this," Sally muttered. "His clothes have Velcro on the sides instead of seams."

"Handy," Pete grunted. "Help me roll him, Ally. He's a big son of a bitch."

"Possible knife wound to the lower back," Ally noted. "Four inches at least." She probed the wound with her gloved hands. "It isn't deep."

"We have some burns on his right shoulder," Pete added. "Second degree, so not bad. I think someone used Taser darts on him. There are small puncture wounds centered in the affected areas. What kind of weapon causes burns? I've never seen this before."

Trisha had been feeling his head. "He's got a lump but no visible bleeding. Order a CT scan." She released him and gripped her mini flashlight. She gently opened one eyelid, seeing he had beautiful blue eyes. She flashed her light in each eye, checked responses. Her relief was instant when his pupils reacted perfectly. She touched his throat, feeling for anything off. *No obvious broken bones, no swelling,* she mentally ticked off the checklist inside her head. She focused on his mouth next and pulled apart his lips. And gasped.

Her team froze, all focused on her. Trisha shook herself from the stunned moment. She stared at the sharp teeth inside the patient's mouth. They resembled vampire fangs. She carefully reached between his full lips and spread his jaw farther apart to check inside his mouth and get a look at his airway.

"Are those dog teeth?" Pete's voice came out shaky.

"Gunshot wound to the left thigh," Ally announced. "Through and through."

"Bleeding?" Trisha released the patient's mouth.

"Manageable but he's nicked an artery. The medics pressure patched it. His blood pressure is stable at the moment. The fluids they pushed in transit seem to have helped."

12

"Let's move him to OR as soon as we're done. Wrap it up. It should be prepped and waiting for us."

Trisha ignored the other staff who dashed in and out of the exam room grabbing samples from the victim. She had faith in her team and they worked well together. Mercy Hospital had a reputation of only hiring the best staff. They carefully rolled the patient onto his side and searched every inch of his skin.

"Needle marks on his right ass cheek," Sally noted. "He isn't a junky. He would have to be pretty flexible to reach there and with those guns he has, men aren't real flexible."

"He has a gun?" Trisha yanked her hands away from the patient. "Where? Be careful."

Sally laughed for the first time. "Not a real gun. *Guns*, Trisha. Don't you know that means big, buff muscles? The guy is total beefcake. Didn't you notice?"

Trisha shook her head, relieved the guy wasn't armed. "Let's get him into the OR and check out that thigh. It's still bleeding." She examined the gunshot wound. She prodded the holes on each side where the bullet had gone through.

"Let's move, people," Ally ordered.

Trisha headed for the door. "I'll scrub up."

She made it to the hallway before she was brought to a stop where Dr. Jose Roldio blocked her path. He looked pale. "I have this one, Trisha. Thanks." He shoved past her.

Trisha stood there stunned for a few seconds that Jose had just taken over her patient's care without her asking for a consult. She leaped out of the way quickly though when her team wheeled the unconscious man from the exam room. She stared at the patient's face now that she had time to think, her mind allowing impressions to register. He had long, thick, brown hair with blond streaks threaded through it. His eyes had been unusually colored—dark blue with lighter blue streaks swirling in the irises, making them really beautiful. She tore her bloody gloves off and stormed to a trashcan. It irritated her badly that she wasn't the one who'd operate on him.

Trisha found herself back inside the doctor's lounge six patients later. She sipped another iced coffee and tried to cool down. Jose Roldio was one of the leading trauma surgeons in the country and the patient was important, newsworthy. It shouldn't bother her so much that he'd come running from wherever he'd been to take over the man's care but it did. Her shoulders slumped. She always wanted to follow through with her patients.

The door behind her opened, drawing her attention. She met the gaze of the devil himself as Dr. Roldio walked in looking worn out. He nodded at her, moving for the coffee machine. Trisha twisted in her chair to face him.

"Did he make it?"

"Yeah. I had to repair an artery but that was the worst of it. The bleeding wasn't as bad as we thought. The vet guy showed up but he was too afraid to touch our patient. He just took up space inside my operating room. You saw the patient's abnormalities. That's not from plastic surgery. I checked while he was on my table. They somehow made that guy. He's got enough anomalies that I'm convinced he's not totally human. Can you believe this shit? I mean, Jesus."

"Were we able to match his blood?" That mystery had bothered Trisha's thoughts for hours.

"No. We gave him universal plasma and he didn't reject it. He's stable now but I had to send him up to ICU, considering we have no idea what we're dealing with. We got word from the division handling this nightmare that some of these people are kind of dangerous. We had to put guards outside his door for his protection and ours. I guess there are news crews camping at reception trying to sneak inside too." Jose slumped into a chair as he met Trisha's gaze. "I didn't mean to step on your toes. I think you're a great doctor but this one was over my head. The big guys were afraid he'd die so they called me in. The shit is going to hit the fan worldwide over this."

Trisha shrugged. "I understand." She smiled. "It made me mad at first but I calmed down. It's your specialty."

"I left your name with security." He smiled back. "I figured I owed you and thought you might want to look in on him. I know you always do that with your patients."

She sipped her drink. "Why would you have to leave my name? My hospital badge will be enough to get me into ICU to check on him."

"The guy is a medical freak." Jose sighed. "We're having a problem with everyone on staff wanting to gawk at him. They are worried someone will take pictures of him to sell to the media too. Someone spread it around that he's got vampire teeth."

"Canine. There's a difference."

"Whatever. He's a freak and the hospital is terrified of breaking confidentiality. We've got a great rep for protecting our patients. We've had to restrict access to him but you are authorized to check on him." The doctor stood. "I have to get home to my wife. We were on our way to dinner when they paged me and she didn't take it well. It's her birthday."

"Hit the gift shop to buy her chocolate on your way out." Trisha winked. "I'd forgive anything for a few pounds of that."

Jose laughed. "My wife isn't so magnanimous. I think I need to call a jeweler. Please check on him for me so I can get some sleep. They'll page me if needed." He saluted her as he left.

\* \* \* \* \*

Trisha yawned. She'd been on shift for far too long and it was time to head home. She thought about her soft bed and she couldn't wait to throw herself onto it. She flashed her badge at the security officer.

"I'm Dr. Trisha Norbit. Dr. Jose Roldio asked me to check in on a patient of his."

The guard read his clipboard. "Go on in, Dr. Norbit. You're cleared."

Trisha walked into the ICU and nodded at a nurse monitoring from the station, someone Trisha had spoken to a few times. She didn't know many people who worked the day shift and there had just been a shift change. She glanced at the ICU board and knew which room he'd been assigned immediately. The numbers 215 were written on the board. She turned, going to room three.

Trisha eased the door open slowly. The man sprawled on the bed had been cleaned up and his hair washed. It flowed down over his shoulders and she couldn't help but notice the way it looked, as though streaks of golden sand were running through lines of wet, darker sand. He looked a lot different without dirt and mud clumps smeared over him. He was handsome. He had a very masculine, strong face with beautiful bone structure.

She reached for his chart to study it. Her gaze lifted to him again, her attention going to his bare, broad chest where taped-on leads that connected him to the monitors marred his skin. She gawked a little at his thick, toned arms. *Guns.* She hadn't heard that term before but he was extremely muscular. *Maybe he is a bodybuilder.* Her gaze lowered to his drug screen panel as she thumbed through his chart. She looked for any known drugs that bodybuilders used but he'd tested negative for them. He was only positive for a well-known sedative.

Trisha returned his chart to the holder and walked closer. She stopped at the side of his bed and put her hands on the raised bedrail bar that prevented him from rolling out of bed. She studied his face closely, fascinated. His cheekbones were more pronounced than a typical human and his nose wider and shaped…different. She bit her lip as she leaned closer to get a better look at the generous lips that hid his canine teeth well, until they were pulled back. She only hesitated for a second before digging into her pocket to slip on a glove before she reached for his mouth, intent on getting a second look at those teeth while she had the opportunity.

His full lips were soft, perfectly formed, and warm. She hadn't noticed that last night but she'd been too busy assessing injuries, not facial traits. She gently used her gloved fingers to pull down on his lower lip. His bottom teeth appeared normal except his side teeth were sharp, canine style. She used her thumb to gently lift his top lip as she bent forward to get a closer look and gently cupped his face in her ungloved palm. She opened his jaw wider and held his mouth open. She had to stretch over his chest to get a better look, studying what she saw.

She visually examined the extended teeth, the sharp points, and wished she knew more about dentistry. She leaned lower, realized her hair fell on his bare chest but wasn't concerned about waking him. He'd been heavily sedated during surgery and it would be hours before he woke. Her face hovered mere inches from his mouth while she examined his back teeth, and took mental notes. The upper and lower molars were definitely canine, sharper than human teeth. His abnormal teeth were there for tearing and chewing.

Trisha pulled her finger and thumb out of his mouth to allow it to close, still cradling his chin on her palm. She looked at his face again to study his flatter, wider nose but instead she found herself staring into a pair of wide-open, amazing blue eyes that peered right back into her startled ones.

"Hi," he rasped softly in a gruff rumble.

Trisha jumped. It startled her that the patient was awake when he shouldn't be. She tried to pull away from him but two hands grabbed her arms. Her hip banged the side of the bed when he yanked on her hard, pulling her down on top of him. Pain shot through her hip from the impact with the metal rail when he flipped her into the narrow space next to him. His weight crushed her body into the mattress when he rolled on top of her, pinning her under him.

Trisha began to struggle after a few seconds when she realized what had happened. The patient's hands slid along her arms to grasp her wrists, yanked them above her head, and a loud growl tore from his throat. The sound was surprising, so scary and vicious that it froze Trisha with instant terror. She stared up at the very masculine face hovering inches above hers. His strangely hypnotic eyes seemed to look right into her soul as he studied her intently until his eyes narrowed. His tongue slid from between his generous lips to swipe across his lower one.

"You're new. Didn't they warn you to never cross the kill-zone line?" His gaze lowered to her throat but returned to her face. "And it was really stupid not to chain me down. Didn't they give you the rundown on how to handle us, Doc? You never remove the restraints."

She found her voice finally. "You're in a hospital. You're going to be fine."

He frowned. Trisha was pinned under him, his body pressed tightly against hers from breast to feet. She also couldn't ignore his heavy weight or the fact that his body totally blanketed hers.

"I don't know if I should mount or kill you," he growled softly. He shifted his body over hers suddenly, causing Trisha to gasp when something hard pressed against her. There was no mistaking the fact he had an erection when he settled on her again, pressing his hardened cock right against the seam of her thighs. "My vote is mounting you since I'd hate to kill something so beautiful." He grinned at her. It frightened Trisha when she saw his sharp teeth. "Ever wanted to be fucked by an animal, beauty?"

"I'm Doc—"

"I don't care," he growled softly, cutting her off. "Kiss me, beauty. Then I'll show you what you've been missing. I've decided to mount you. I just can't resist." His nostrils flared as he inhaled and a deep groan rumbled from his parted lips. "I'm so hard for you and you smell so good."

Panic seized Trisha. She screamed. "Help!"

215 stared down at her and smiled. "No one would be stupid enough to come inside this room to try to save you, beauty. You took the restraints off and now you're mine."

He adjusted her, putting both her wrists in one hand by holding them together with his spread fingers, freeing his other hand to trail down her body. His hand hesitated on the curve of her breast long enough to make her gasp before it flattened over her ribs, then inched lower to her hip. He shifted over her enough to slide his roaming hand between her and the bed, took a firm hold on her ass cheek and squeezed.

"Your ass is mine, sweet thing. Don't worry though. I'm not going to hurt you and I definitely won't kill you. I like you a hell of a lot. I just decided I'm going to keep you with me for a few days, Doc. I'm going to do things to you that will make you never want to leave this room. You'll want me mounting you as much as you want to eat or breathe air by the time I'm forced to release you."

A loud alarm suddenly blared inside the room. Trisha stared at the man who continued to smile at her. His hand on her ass gripped her more firmly as he shifted his body, forcing his hips between her legs and spreading her thighs when he parted his. The hard ridge of his cock rubbed against the vee of her pants. Her eyes widened at the feel of him pressed so tightly against her.

"You're going to want me as much as I do you," he promised in a husky tone.

He leaned down closer to Trisha, his gaze leaving hers. He nuzzled her face with his cheek, pushing against her until she turned her head away. His lips brushed her throat, opened, and he licked her skin and groaned. Shock jolted through her when he nipped her skin there, but worse, his hips started to move at the same moment. The rigid length of his shaft rubbed directly against her clit through their clothing. Her body jerked under him, tensed, and he growled, his jaw tightening on her shoulder.

It half horrified her when her body responded to him. Her nipples hardened, her stomach quivered, and pleasure at his rocking hips massaging her clit, even through layers of clothing, made her pant. Being restrained had never been a fantasy of hers but suddenly she couldn't help but be turned on that a powerful, handsome, and very dangerous male controlled her body. She fought it, tried to reason with her physical responses with cold logic but her mind didn't want to work.

He groaned against her throat, his mouth releasing her. "I can't wait to taste every inch of you. I'm going to bury my face between your thighs and fuck you with my tongue until you beg me to make you come, beauty. I know you're going to taste as sweet as you scent." He growled louder. "Then I'm going to flip you over, put your ass in the air, and mount you until you come again."

Trisha arched against him. The image he painted inside her mind, combined with the stimulation of her clit, nearly made her climax before he did any of those things. She knew if he didn't stop moving his hips she would. Her clit throbbed and she bit her lip hard not to moan.

The doors to his room suddenly burst open loudly as at least six people rushed inside. The disturbance may as well have been cold water dousing the flames of Trisha's runaway libido. The man on top of her jerked his head toward them and a loud, terrifying snarl erupted from his throat.

"Sedate him," Trisha yelled, her mind working again.

Orderlies and security guards dived on the patient. He tried to twist to face them with a roar of rage, his intent to fight them clear. His hands released her and he tried to push his body up to throw off the men trying to hold him down. Trisha was terrified he'd get hurt and threw her arms around his neck, wrapping her legs around his thighs to try to help keep him down. He thrashed, his cock rubbing against her tighter, making her more aware of how turned on she was. She saw two orderlies jabbing needles into him as they sprawled across his back to hold him down.

Mean growls tore from his throat but he finally stopped struggling. His body grew lax and his dead weight settled on top her the way a smothering, heavy blanket would until she couldn't even draw breath. She was only able to get free when two orderlies, a security guard and two nurses lifted the big man off Trisha enough for her to scoot out from under him after the side rail was lowered.

Trisha was sweating and panting by the time she rose unsteadily to her feet. The patient was sedated and facedown on the bed. She stared at him, trembled, and was deeply disturbed by what had happened. They'd probably be having sex if she hadn't been rescued.

A hand touched her, making her jump. Dr. Hearsal Morris, looking concerned, squeezed her shoulder.

"Are you all right? Did he hurt you?"

Trisha cleared her throat. "I'm fine," she lied.

# Chapter One
## *One year later*

ဆာ

Trisha sat at her desk, remembering 215. He still haunted her with his amazing blue eyes, how he'd pinned her under him on his hospital bed, and nearly…seduced her. She knew she'd never forget him but he didn't remember her. It really bothered her too.

She had heard that New Species, the survivors of the drug company testing facilities who'd been rescued, had given themselves names instead of the numbers Mercile Industries had tagged them with. He'd picked the name Slade.

It fit him. He was a big son of a bitch, broad-chested, with long, wild hair, and he gave off an attitude of danger. Every time he showed sharp, abnormally long teeth when he flashed a grin, it made him appear predatory. It almost seemed as if he were threatening someone when he smiled. He also had to be the sexiest man she'd ever met and the memories of that hospital bed always made her tingle with arousal.

The New Species had been given a private retreat, of sorts, called Homeland, for the survivors of the testing facilities. The world wasn't completely welcoming of their existence and they needed to live in a high-security setting for their protection against hate groups who believed they were an abomination.

Religious fanatics called them evil, unnatural, and an affront to God because they'd been created inside test tubes by scientists. If they didn't take up the religious excuse to hate, they called New Species two-legged animals who didn't deserve human rights, nothing more than trained pets who mimicked people. It was ridiculous. It irritated Trisha when she heard those crazy rants by idiots on the news. New Species were victims, not a blight on humanity, and definitely not the evil spawn of Satan. They also weren't pets with the ability to speak words.

Two months before she'd heard a private medical center would soon open at Homeland. She'd immediately submitted her résumé, hoping to secure a position as one of the doctors they'd planned to hire. She'd never forget how surprised she'd been when two days before she'd gotten *the* call. They'd chosen her over all the other candidates.

Everyone in the medical community was fascinated by New Species. Their total surviving numbers were unknown but Mercile Industries, a leading drug research company, had been using them as live test subjects. They'd introduced animal DNA into their genes. Rumor had it that they had created them to combat diseases that crossed from animals to humans and to create vaccines and medicines to battle diseases in humans that animals were naturally immune to. Later it was said the company had branched out to physical enhancement drugs to make humans stronger, more muscular, and in better shape just by taking the pills they created.

It stunned her that other doctors and scientists had sold their souls for a paycheck but obviously many had done the unthinkable to the men and women forced to be living experiments. The fact that someone had even figured a way to successfully combine human and animal DNA to create life had set the medical world on its ear. Living proof existed though with the New Species.

Trisha hoped she'd learn more detailed information about them now that she had landed the job but so far they hadn't told her much. She'd been given one file to look over. Some of the information had stunned her but she'd been ready for any challenge presented. Unfortunately, it seemed they'd only hired her to play nurse to the human employees since none of the New Species had stepped into the clinic.

She leaned back in her chair, propped her feet on her desk, and reviewed the facts she had learned. New Species picked weird names for themselves, usually something that had meaning for each individual. They had chosen to call themselves New Species because many of them were not altered with the same animal DNA strands. She'd learned there were three types—canine, feline, and primate species. Then there were a few documented notes on the physical differences discovered about them. Her thoughts instantly fixed on the reason for her aggravation.

*Slade doesn't remember me. He practically molested me, swore to do obscene things to my body, and he just...forgot what he did?* She hissed out air, surprised steam didn't rise from her ears from the anger that burned brightly inside her. She'd just had a confrontation with him and she hadn't seen a flicker of recognition in his eyes. *How could he forget? I sure can't and it's not fair. Just like a man. Turns a woman on, gets her all hot, and then forgets her the second she's out of sight. Jerk!*

He'd been extremely rude to her, adding insult to injury. One of the fully human employees at Homeland and a canine New Species male were living together. Trisha knew they were having sex, despite their denials, and she wanted to study the couple's sex life. Slade had gotten in her face, had been vulgar, and had the nerve to call her nosy!

Any details about the couple's sex life could be important. There was so much not known medically about the New Species. Were they even sexually compatible with humans? Trisha wasn't sure what percentage of males were involved but it had been documented in the few reports that she'd read to prep for her new patients that some of the males swelled at the base of their penises right before ejaculation. Was that painful for a woman? That was a question she'd wanted to ask the woman living with a New Species but Slade had ordered her to stay away from the couple.

She wanted to explore the possibility of humans and Species having children together. She had been told Mercile

Industries had paired the New Species females with their male counterparts for years, hoping to create more of them. They'd never had a single pregnancy result. It might be that none of the New Species were able to conceive children due to something simple that could be medically treated. She might be able to figure it out if anyone would allow her to help but that wasn't going to happen if no one would permit her to run tests on them.

"Dr. Norbit?"

The voice pulled Trisha from her thoughts to glance at Paul as he walked inside the clinic to relieve her shift. He was the only nurse and he seemed nice enough. He was in his early forties and he'd mentioned he had a military background.

"A penny for your thoughts."

Trisha forced a smile. "They aren't worth that much. I'm feeling sorry for myself. I wanted this position to learn about New Species but I'm getting stonewalled at every turn."

"Yeah. The NSO aren't real talkative. I've been here longer and I still don't know much. We're supposed to care for them but they won't tell us squat about their physiology to help us do it."

"NSO?"

"New Species Organization. It's what they call themselves around here. I'm surprised you haven't seen the uniforms they outfitted some of their people with. I don't think they appreciate our security and have created their own teams. I don't blame them. You missed out on the attack that happened here not too long ago."

"I heard something about it on the news."

Paul winced. "It was bad. Those protesters and human rights bastards broke down the front gates and about fifteen trucks full of gun-toting morons came pouring inside. The buildings are thankfully built to withstand attacks and security was able to get most people to safety when the gates were being breached. Those bastards came in here as though someone had declared New Species hunting season. Ever been on a deer hunt?"

"No."

"That's what it reminded me of. There were a total of seventeen fatalities by the time it ended. It was the longest forty-some minutes of my life before I had help. That's why they wanted to hire a doctor. I was swamped with injures that day and in way over my head."

"Seventeen fatalities? I didn't hear that the numbers were that high." The news horrified Trisha.

He shrugged. "Some of them died later from gunshot wounds. The hired security sucked. The New Species guys teamed up to kick some ass when they showed up here to stop a few of those bastards from trying to ram open the medical doors. I was alone, thinking they were going to get inside and kill me since they weren't real picky about who they shot. If you were breathing, you were target practice to those goons. The New Species officers wear black SWAT-type uniforms with NSO written on the front of their vests in white lettering."

Slade had worn a uniform like that when he'd stopped her earlier. "So men who wear those are NSO security guards?"

"They call themselves New Species officers, and yeah. You don't want to mess with those guys. One of them told me he was an experimental prototype at the facility where they held him. The rumor is that some of them were trained to fight and kill just to show off what they could do and how fast they were. I heard Mercile Industries might have had a contract with a few third world countries to sell their enhancing drugs to the highest bidder. The New Species deny it but who knows what the truth is. Either way, they are badass. They aren't denying the fact that they were tortured regularly and beaten to see how much damage they could survive and heal from. Have you seen some of those guys up close? Jesus! They are huge and add in the fact they are fast, have enhanced hearing, sense of smell, and vision, and they just kick ass in general. I was in the Army and I sure as hell wouldn't want to find myself facing off a few of them even with my entire unit backing me up."

Trisha glanced down at her watch. She didn't want to hear any more about how mean and dangerous New Species probably were. They intimidated her enough without listening to the speculation. She'd also learned, since meeting Paul, that he had a tendency to ramble for hours if given the opportunity.

"I am off shift. I guess I'll go home."

"How do you rate the housing? Isn't it great? They gave me a two-bedroom, cottage-style house. My wife loves it."

"They are nice," Trisha agreed. She stood, reaching for her purse. "I'll see you tomorrow. Call if you need me." She tapped her pocket. "My cell phone is on."

"Will do, Doc...uh, Trisha."

Trisha left the medical center and walked down the street. Her house was only a block away inside the human employee area where dozens of cottage-styled homes had been built. They'd assigned her to a cute little blue one. She peered up at the moon, deciding it was a beautiful evening.

"It's kind of late for you to be walking by yourself," a husky male voice rasped from behind her.

Trisha gasped as she spun around, trying not to show her surprise at seeing Slade. He wore his black uniform and her attention fixed on his right chest where the letters NSO were printed clearly over a small patch. Her gaze lifted to the most amazing blue eyes. They were a dark shade that she couldn't help but stare into.

If he was an NSO officer, he had to be pretty tough, a survivor of the worst of the abuse, and possibly had been trained to fight to be one of their prototypes they filmed to show off what horrendous things they'd done to his body, if Paul had his information right. That meant Slade could be super dangerous. She took a deep breath, trying to calm her pounding heart.

"I didn't see or hear you," she admitted.

He flashed sharp teeth when he grinned. "My point exactly. You shouldn't be out walking alone. It could be unsafe."

"This is a highly protected facility with security guards all over the place." She frowned. "I think I'm pretty safe." *Except with you*, she amended silently. *He's way too attractive. Look at those gorgeous eyes and that mouth. I wonder what it would be like to kiss him. Don't go there*, she mentally ordered her thoughts. *He doesn't remember.*

Wide shoulders shrugged. "Are you still interested in learning something about the breeding process between our two species?"

That question had her heart racing instantly. "Did you talk to Mr. Fury and Miss Brower? Have they changed their minds about allowing me access to them?" Excitement at the concept of talking to the couple who lived together was instant and strong. She could learn so much from them. She'd be doing something real instead of sitting behind a desk waiting for people with paper cuts to come see her. "I'd love to talk them into running a few simple tests."

"Nope." He took a step toward her. "They still aren't interested. I was just wondering if you were still hoping to study the breeding process between our species."

Her excitement died. "I'm very interested. Is there another couple that I haven't heard about? I'd appreciate the opportunity to speak to them if there is."

He took another step, stopping just feet from Trisha, making her realize he was a good foot taller than her. Trisha immediately felt intimidated by his size. A memory flashed of him pinning her under his large body on his hospital bed. She swallowed hard and tried not to allow the attraction she felt show in her features.

"I could go home with you." He winked. "You could examine me all you want, Doc." His attention lowered and he stared at her breasts before meeting her gaze again. "I would be more than happy to volunteer to show you personally how we could have sex together. I'm up for an hour of meaningless sex."

Trisha backed up a step, stunned. She knew she shouldn't be since he'd once talked to her worse. He didn't remember it but she did. It hurt her feelings that he'd offer her so little, something so trivial, when he had become a fixation in her thoughts.

"No thank you."

The skin next to his eyes crinkled with amusement while he shrugged again. "It's your loss. You know how to find me if you change your mind. I'll walk you to your door."

"No thanks."

"I'm escorting you home." He kept his amused expression in place. "So walk, Doc. Or we could stand here. Either way, I'm sticking with you until we reach your place."

Trisha spun away from him and strode quickly down the sidewalk. She could *feel* him behind her but he didn't make a sound. For a large man, he could move very quietly. She turned her head as she reached her yard and gasped over how close he was to invading her personal space.

"Home safe," he whispered. "Are you sure you don't want me to come inside, Doc?"

"I'm sure," Trisha stated firmly.

Her hands trembled when she darted to her front door. Would he try to force his way inside her house? Press the issue of offering to have sex with her? She unlocked the door and spun to tell him to leave but he had vanished.

Trisha stepped off her porch and glanced in both directions down the sidewalk but he wasn't within sight. She frowned. *Where did he disappear to so quickly?* He irritated her badly. She hurried inside and locked the door firmly behind her.

Trisha dropped her purse on the entryway table as she headed for her bedroom. She passed the empty guestroom, remembering that she needed to order a desk and some file cabinets to create a home office.

She peered around her bedroom. She hated the large four-poster bed with the thick wooden poles that shot up toward the ceiling. It took up too much space inside the room. The house had come furnished but nothing had been to her liking.

She stripped out of her clothing on her way to the bathroom. *Does Slade remember me? He could be playing some sort of sick game to see if I'll say something.* She just wasn't sure. He was pretty convincing if he wanted her to believe they'd never met in the past. She turned on the shower and waited the few minutes it took for it to heat up.

She stepped under the spray of hot water with a sigh. Why was she attracted to him? She couldn't deny that he appealed to her. Maybe it was curiosity. She wasn't sure of her motives but every time he looked at her she remembered the rough, hot feel of his tongue teasing her throat, the way he'd moved against her with his heavy body while he'd nearly made her come just from rubbing his cock against her, and the memory of the sounds he made. The growls had been sexy.

"Mental brain wash," she sighed.

She threw her head back and washed her hair, shaved her legs, and then stepped out of the shower. She heard a distinctive sound. Her pants were buzzing inside her bedroom where she'd dumped them when she'd disrobed. Trisha wrapped a towel around her middle to dash from the bathroom. She bent down, fought with her slacks, and yanked the black cell phone out.

"Dr. Norbit here."

"Trisha, it's Paul. We have a situation. Can you come back?"

"I'm on my way." She hung up and ran for the bed. She dropped the cell phone on it and spun. She took a step toward her closet before slamming right into a wide, solid body.

Trisha gasped. Two large hands gripped her bare shoulders as her head jerked up. She gaped at Slade's amused expression. Her body was pressed against his, he held her firmly by her shoulders, and his lips curved into a smile.

"You weren't answering your phone. They need you down at medical."

"You are inside my house," she gasped.

"I have pass keys to all the homes. I'm security. You should answer your phone if you don't want someone to check on you. Your nurse has been calling for five minutes and finally called us."

"I was taking a shower!"

His focus lowered. "I see. You look good in pink, Doc. You'd look better though if that towel were on the floor at your feet." His body shivered a little against hers as his attention drifted to her shoulders. "It's tempting to lick off all those drops of water."

Her heart hammered from surprise and probably a little excitement at the concept of him doing just that. The look on his face made her swallow hard. He suddenly released her though and backed away.

"I'll be waiting for you in the living room. Get a move on, Doc. Someone is hurt and we need to get you back to medical right away."

Trisha watched the tall New Species leave her bedroom, pulling the door closed behind him. It took her long seconds to pull herself together from the shock of finding Slade inside her bedroom and from him touching her. He'd let himself into her house and he'd seen her almost nude. She looked down at the small towel that barely covered the tops of her breasts and fell to mid-thigh. She forced her legs to move to the closet to pull on clothes quickly.

He waited for her by the front door. Trisha's hair dripped water but she didn't care. She didn't have time to dry it. She walked outside and turned as the large man closed the door, watching her.

"Up for a jog, Doc?"

Trisha nodded as she headed down her porch steps. She turned toward the medical center, preparing to run but instead gasped suddenly when Slade swept her up into his arms. He had the audacity to flash his sharp teeth as he gave her a big grin and winked.

"Hold onto me, Doc."

He started jogging down the street. Shocked, Trisha threw her arms around his neck to hang on. She couldn't believe he carried her as if she couldn't reach the clinic on her own steam.

"Put me down."

"Almost there, Doc. Shut up and enjoy the ride." He wasn't even out of breath when they reached the building. He slowed to a stop and carefully eased her onto her feet next to the door. He winked at her again before turning away. "I'll see you when you're done," he called over his shoulder.

Trisha still reeled from the shock of his actions when she walked inside. There was a waiting room area that had been separated by a long counter. She saw Paul leaning over someone lying on a bed in the open area. Trisha shoved away thoughts of Slade and what had just happened. She moved quickly.

"What do we have?"

Paul turned. "Severe laceration. He's going to need stitches, Trisha."

The next half hour remained busy for Trisha. One of the human male secretaries of Homeland's director had accidentally sliced open his palm with a kitchen knife while attempting to make dinner. Trisha cleaned the wound, gave him ten stitches, and bandaged the injury. She gave him pain medication and a tetanus shot. The medical center had its own fully stocked drug cabinet and she just dispensed what medicines he needed. She watched him leave.

Paul finished cleaning up. "You do nice work, Trisha. I doubt he'll have much of a scar."

"Thanks."

"I've got this. You go on home. I'll do the paperwork. You're off."

"Sorry I didn't answer my phone. I was taking a shower."

Paul grinned. "I see. You need to comb your hair. It's kind of in clumpy, damp curls."

"Good night," she sighed, walking outside.

Relief hit her when she didn't see Slade anywhere. She walked about ten feet before she sensed him. She stopped and turned to watch him stride down the sidewalk, moving right for her. He smiled as their gazes met.

"Ready for me to escort you?"

"I can find my own way, thanks. I'm thirty years old. I have mastered getting home."

"You can't be too careful these days, Doc. You never know what kind of animals are wandering around."

She shot him a look. *Like you?* She didn't say it out loud but was tempted to. She kept walking. He stayed beside her this time. She had to move quickly to keep up with his longer legs.

They reached her yard and Trisha turned to study the man who peered down at her. She unlocked her front door and opened it only wide enough for her body to fit through. She turned, faced Slade, and backed into the safety of her home.

"Don't ever walk into my house again. What would you have done if I'd still been in the shower?"

He grinned. "Walked in there to tell you they needed you at the center and handed you a smaller towel than you had on.

Maybe a hand towel." His gaze roamed her body slowly and he smiled wider. "Or a washcloth."

She tensed. "You enjoy needling me, don't you?"

He just shrugged, still smiling.

"Is there any particular reason or am I just special?"

His smile faded. "Maybe I'm interested to see how our two species breed too."

"Well, find someone else to harass."

He shrugged. "Fine by me. If you aren't interested, you just aren't. I was just looking for a sex partner but I won't bother you again. You should have taken me up on it, Doc." His eyes narrowed. "I just wanted a few hours to answers all those questions you have. You're pretty enough that I thought it might be worth my time. Night, Doc." He turned away and started to leave the porch. He was halfway to her sidewalk when she opened her mouth.

"Only a few hours, huh? And pretty? Last time you kept calling me a beauty." Trisha allowed her anger to flow. "Last time you offered to have sex with me for days, 215. Should I feel insulted?"

He spun around. She knew shock when she saw it and it etched his handsome features. That answered her question. He really didn't remember her. She glared at him.

"I think I liked you better when you were recovering in my hospital. You were more appealing half dead than you are fully healthy. That's really sad."

She slammed the door closed the second he took a step toward her. She twisted the locks, slamming the bolt into place.

"Doc? Open up the door." He growled the words from the other side of the door.

"Good night, Mr. Slade."

He twisted the doorknob but the lock held. She heard keys jingle. He would try to unlock her door? She bit her lip.

"I'm calling security," she threatened. "Remember them? They were good at stopping you before even though you said no one would come to save me last time."

He uttered a soft curse. "You're the Doc from the hospital, aren't you?"

"Oh, so you do remember me." She leaned against the door.

"Your hair is different."

She touched her damp hair. She'd tried her hand at being a redhead the previous year when she'd worked at the hospital where they'd met. Now she was back to her normal color, a honey blonde. "This is the real me. I decided I didn't want to dye it red anymore."

"Open up the door and talk to me." He growled the order.

"Why? So you can insult me more? Be a bigger ass?"

Trisha tensed when only silence answered her question. Would he try to get inside her house another way? Why would he even care if she were the same woman he'd accosted a year before? She listened but didn't hear a thing on the other side of the door.

"Mr. Slade?"

He didn't answer. Trisha finally moved from the door to rush around the house to make sure all the windows were locked. She relaxed certain that he had gone, and didn't plan to bother her. She entered her bedroom and clicked off the light. She slept wearing sweats just in case he returned and decided to surprise her with another unannounced visit.

* * * * *

Slade pressed his forehead against the door, his eyes closed, and listened to the doctor move away. Shock still gripped him that the woman he'd just insulted and angered was the same woman who haunted him on a nightly basis since he'd been freed.

Dr. Trisha Norbit had changed her hair color, had grown it longer. He'd been pretty drugged when he'd awoken inside the human hospital but he should have recognized her scent or placed those beautiful blue eyes of hers when he'd seen them again. The memory of them made him want to kick his own ass for not making the connection. Had their drugs really affected him that badly?

In his defense, he'd never learned the name of the woman he'd pinned under him on the small hospital bed but everything else about her remained intact. Her plush body pinned under his, the taste of her skin on this tongue, and the scent of her arousal tormenting him. He'd been sure no one would save her, that she'd be his for the taking, and he'd relished the idea of making her want him as much as he wanted her. Then it had turned to hell. Humans had rushed inside the room, drugged him, and taken her away.

He bit back a snarl. He'd royally screwed up. Late in the night before he drifted to sleep, he always thought of *her*, his sexy redhead. He pushed away from the cool wood, snapped open his eyes, and glared at the house she hid inside. He'd fantasized about finding her, getting her under him again, and finishing what they'd started. He'd planned out how he'd charm her, had studied human romantic tactics, in hopes of winning her over if that day ever came.

Dr. Trisha Norbit hated him. He couldn't blame her either. He'd purposely been an ass to her for the most part. It had irritated him that he was drawn to her despite having a fantasy woman stuck inside his head. It had almost seemed as if he'd been cheating on the memory of his redheaded fantasy woman every time his body responded to Doc Norbit.

The cosmic joke was on him since they were one and the same. He stomped off into the darkness. He'd just lost all hope of ever having her in his bed.

He paused to glance back at her house. His anger faded into sadness. *Fantasies are for fools. Learn a lesson and stay the hell away from her.*

# Chapter Two

## ഗ

*Tense.* That's how Trisha would describe her new relationship with the NSO officer. Slade patrolled the human section of Homeland, the area she lived and worked in, and she had to deal with him. Since that night they'd hardly spoken. When they did, both of them seemed to come to the mutual agreement not to mention anything personal. Two months had passed that way.

The guy was likable but she wished he weren't. Slade had a quick smile, a keen sense of humor, and every time she'd had to deal with him, he'd gotten her to smile. He'd made certain they were never alone since the night she'd told him just who she was. She was mostly grateful for that fact.

Sometimes when she walked home at night she would catch a glimpse of him on the dark street. She could sense his stare and knew he shadowed her to make sure she arrived safely. *It is his job,* she reminded herself. She regretted what she'd blurted to him but she'd lost her temper.

There was something wrong with her. She mentally kicked herself over being angry with a guy for the reasons that she was, knowing it just wasn't right. She'd felt insulted that he'd forgotten her. Just over a year before he'd wanted to keep her for days, he'd called her beauty, and now… She sighed. He just thought she was pretty and offered her some cheesy one-night stand. *Not even a night. He only wants me for a few hours.*

"Stupid," she muttered.

"What is?" A deep voice spoke softly from behind her.

Trisha started and spun in her seat to gawk at Slade. She grabbed her heart. "Don't sneak up on me that way again. Would it kill you to make some noise when you move?"

His eyebrows arched as a smile curved his full lips. "Then I wouldn't get to watch you react that way."

She sighed. "I'm glad you at least find it amusing. I sure don't."

She glanced around the room, realized no one else was there, and instantly tensed. *Uh-oh.* This was the first time she could remember them being totally alone since that night he'd walked her home. They'd had some interaction when there'd been some problems between the human, Ellie Brower, and her New Species husband. Fury had been shot during a press conference that had been infiltrated by a few members of a hate group and during his recovery a nurse had drugged him, trying to drive him insane. They'd seen each other during that time but had kept it professional.

"What do you need?"

"Good thing you didn't ask what I want." He smirked at her, crossing his arms over his broad chest. "Justice has to go on a road trip and wants you to go with him." He wiggled his eyebrows. "He said to tell you to pack for two days. I had no idea you and Justice were sleeping together."

Trisha glared at him. "You know Mr. North and I...that nothing is going on between us. He's my boss and he's your leader. My only dealings with Justice are purely professional."

His tongue ran along his bottom lip. Trisha watched it. She looked up slightly into his blue eyes, which were staring back into hers. "I know but I love to see you turn all pink when you grow angry." He suddenly smiled. "Justice wants you ready to roll in an hour."

"But—"

"An hour. Don't argue with me. I'm just the messenger."

"But where are we going? I'm on duty right now and tomorrow. What does Justice want with me?"

He shrugged, still smiling. "I just deliver the messages. See you in an hour, Doc. I'll pick you up in front of your house."

She watched him leave the clinic. A curse passed her lips before she could refrain. He loved to annoy her and he had a real talent for it. She picked up the phone to call Dr. Ted Treadmont, the second doctor they'd hired part-time, to cover some of her shifts.

They really needed more medical staff. Two doctors and nurses weren't enough. She made a mental note to bring that up again with Justice when she spoke to him. He headed the New Species, was their appointed leader, and made most of the decisions at Homeland.

She glanced at the phone, half tempted to call him to say she wasn't going wherever he wanted her to go but then changed her mind. She respected Justice and for whatever reason, he needed her to go somewhere that required packing. She might not want to go but she would.

Trisha had no idea what to pack. She cursed and decided to just take a bit of everything. She grabbed a few pairs of jeans, a few pairs of slacks, and some nice shirts along with a universal black dress, just in case. Underwear followed. She took one pair of high heels, a pair of slip-ons, and decided to wear the comfortable running shoes she had on. She also packed up a few sets of sweats to sleep in.

She walked into her bathroom to pack her overnight bag. Makeup and personal items went inside it. She remembered her shampoo and conditioner in case they were heading for a hotel. She hated samples. Her hair was too long for them to be of any use.

A black SUV pulled up and honked in front of her house. Trisha glanced at her watch to see he'd arrived fifteen minutes early. She clenched her teeth. Slade did enjoy aggravating her. She grabbed her purse, her suitcase, and slung her overnight bag across her shoulder. The weight of all her luggage made her struggle to get out the front door.

No one came to help her. She stared pointedly at the security guard driving the SUV but he just watched her as she closed her front door and fought with the keys to lock the deadbolt. Some of her irritation eased since the driver wasn't Slade. She relaxed, took a deep breath, and turned. She tried not to groan as she moved down the sidewalk. Her suitcase was heavy and the bag dug painfully into her shoulder.

The back door opened on the vehicle and Slade jumped out. He smiled at her, glancing at her bags. With a shake of his head he walked to the back of the vehicle to open up the hatchback. He stepped out of her way, chuckled, and waved her to put her things inside.

"Gee, thanks for the help." She shot him a nasty look.

"I said we were going to be gone two days, not two weeks, Doc. I guess you can stow your own gear if you think you can wear all that crap you have jammed into those bags."

She did groan when she hefted the suitcase up to dump it into the back of the SUV. "I didn't know what to pack and I had to bring different kinds of clothes. It would have saved a lot packing if someone," she glared at him as she tossed in her overnight bag, "told me where I was going and what this is about."

He closed the hatchback. "Let's go, Doc. We don't have all day to stand here chatting."

Trisha was pissed. She gripped her purse in a stranglehold. The door to the back of the SUV still stood open, she moved before Slade could and climbed inside, knowing he'd been sitting there. She shot him a mean smile while getting comfortable in the still-warm-from-his-butt seat. She slammed the door and turned to ask Justice what was going on. The vehicle was empty except for the driver and Slade, who opened the other door across from her and climbed inside. The door closed.

"We're picking up Justice last?" She hated the hopeful tone in her voice.

Slade put on his seat belt. "Buckle up, Doc. Nope. Justice already left. We're meeting him in a few hours."

She sighed, securing her belt. "Where are we going?" She gave her attention to the security guard behind the wheel in front of her. "I'm Dr. Trisha Norbit. What's your name, driver?"

"Bart," he shared cheerfully. He met Trisha's gaze in the rearview mirror. "We're heading up north to a private resort."

Trisha frowned uneasily. "Why?"

"Oh," Bart started the SUV, "Mr. North has set a bunch of meetings up there. They figured it would be remote enough to make the press really uncomfortable if they wanted to attempt to follow him there and camp out to see what he's doing. We're hoping they don't find out about it until after the fact."

Trisha ignored Slade. "What kind of meetings? Do you know?"

"Oh sure." The young guy was really talkative, which suited Trisha. "Mr. North wants to buy some land up there for New Species. He's set meetings with all the officials out there and the guy who wants to sell the land. I heard he wanted you present in case someone has any questions about medical crap." He took a breath. "You heard those stupid rumors about how people can catch parvo and stuff from New Species, right? I was kind of worried but Tiger swore it was bullshit. Do you know Tiger, Dr. Norbit? It's not true, is it? I can't catch any animal diseases from working with New Species, can I? Because that's something I would really hate. I think they should give us hazard pay if that's true. My mom says I should go to a vet and get vaccine shots just in case bec —"

"Shut up," Slade snarled.

Trisha jumped at the tone of Slade's voice and Bart closed his mouth. She swung her head to glare at Slade. He shrugged.

"He talks too much. It annoys me."

Trisha tried to hide her disgust. "I promise you can't catch parvo from New Species, Bart. *Thank you*," she stressed those words, "for telling me where we are going and why." She shot

Slade another nasty look. "Some people don't appreciate someone who is polite but I certainly do."

Slade turned a little, faced her more from his position on the seat, and smiled as he crossed his arms over his broad chest. He openly stared at her breasts and kept his focus there. "I can be really nice when I want to be. I know how to stimulate conversation." His gaze rose and he winked at her. "I'm pretty good with my oral skills when I'm motivated." He glanced down to her lap and his grin widened. "I'm very good with my oral skills."

*You son of a bitch.* Trisha ground her teeth, refusing to say it aloud. He wasn't talking about conversation and she knew it. Why did he always try to annoy her? Maybe he thought he could embarrass her by his blatant sexual innuendos but she was a doctor. She took a deep breath and forced a smile. She'd been harassed by drunk men in the emergency rooms far too often to allow him get the best of her.

"Oral skills are always a wonderful thing to have, Mr. Slade." Her gaze lowered to the crotch of his black pants, lingered there. She slowly allowed her gaze to travel up his body to examine every inch of him until they were staring into each other's eyes. She saw his smile had faded, knowing her actions had wiped the amused look from his face. "I guess you could say I have a real oral fixation myself."

She smiled wider at him, licked her lips, letting her tongue glide slowly over the surface. His jaw clenched as he adjusted his weight. She noticed his interest.

"Good conversation is very important, don't you think? It's so stimulating and pleasurable if done right. As a doctor it may surprise you how much I've learned on the subject. It's been a long time since I've had a really good conversation and sometimes I nearly ache from wishing someone could stimulate me." Her eyes narrowed. "But unfortunately I haven't met anyone yet who I want to really talk to. I just keep meeting jerks who have no finesse."

He growled at her. She chuckled and turned away from him to stare out the window to watch as they left Homeland. The guards at the gate just waved the SUV past. Trisha didn't bother to look at Slade. She was afraid he'd be staring at her still. She turned toward the window and shifted until she found a comfortable position.

"I hope you both don't mind but I'm going to take a nap." She couldn't resist. She turned her head to meet Slade's gaze. He still watched her and his amazing blue eyes looked at her without amusement. He actually appeared angry.

"Have a nice nap, Dr. Norbit. I'll wake you when we get there," Bart offered. "Mind if I listen to the radio?"

"Not at all." Trisha turned back to the window, realizing how tired she really was.

\* \* \* \* \*

"Hurry," a male roared. "Drive faster. He's right on our ass."

Trisha jerked awake as she slammed against the window. She groaned as pain exploded at the top of her forehead. She was half asleep, disoriented, as she jerked her head to glance around the SUV to see what was going on.

Slade leaned forward between the seats and Bart still drove the SUV. Trisha studied their surroundings, seeing they were in a wooded area on a two-lane highway with dense trees on each side of the road. The sun had lowered in the sky and it would be night soon. She held her forehead where it still hurt but then pulled her hand back to look for blood. There wasn't any.

"Step on the gas harder," Slade growled. "They are going to hit us again."

*Who will hit us?* Trisha turned her head to peer out the back of the SUV. She saw a red truck with a metal grill coming fast at the back of the vehicle. She knew her mouth opened as the truck moved closer, realizing it would ram them. She softly gasped as it plowed into the back of the SUV.

The SUV swerved, fishtailing on the narrow road. Trisha's head was thrown forward against the back of the cushioned driver's seat. Her seat belt dug painfully into her lap as she realized she had pushed down the shoulder belt while sleeping.

"Oh my god," Bart sounded as though he were sobbing. "They are trying to kill us."

"Punch the gas," Slade roared. "Our engine is bigger. They wouldn't be able to catch us to ram us if you'd find your balls and put on some speed."

"I can't," Bart yelled. "I'll lose control. The turns are too sharp."

"Next time, I'm driving," Slade snarled.

Trisha experienced fear as she watched the edges of the road. There were trees everywhere and one side of the narrow road rose uphill while the on the other side, the one she sat closest to, dropped off into a vast space of trees. She stared downward. They were on some winding mountain road heading up.

"Call for help," Trisha got out, confused and terrified at waking in a hellish situation.

"There's no cell signal." Slade snarled his words, obviously furious.

He turned his head, looking back. He cursed, throwing himself into the seat next to Trisha. She was shocked by the sight of the weapon he withdrew from his back from under his waistband. It was a black handgun.

"Oh crap," she gasped.

The truck rammed them again. Trisha was thrown against the door next to her but this time she managed not to hit her head. Her hand got smashed instead between the door she gripped and her body. Slade was thrown into the back of the passenger seat before he moved onto his knees and bent into the back section of the SUV. He pointed the weapon.

"Cover your ears, Doc."

She did that just as Slade opened fire. Glass exploded. The sound of the gun going off was earsplitting. The SUV fishtailed wildly as it nearly tipped on two wheels. Bart cursed a blue streak, taking a turn too fast.

Trisha twisted around to face the back. She saw white steam pour out from under the hood of the red truck, not needing to be told that Slade had shot into the engine. He had to have hit the radiator or something else. The red truck slowed and the SUV pulled away. Slade stopped firing. He cursed as he dropped the empty clip and shoved in another full one from his side pocket. They took a turn and the red truck wasn't behind them anymore.

Trisha gaped at Slade. His blue gaze flashed to hers. "Are you okay, Doc?"

She managed to nod. "Who was that?"

Slade shrugged. "My guess is they weren't friends of ours." He threw himself down on the seat sideways, placing the gun down between them. He tore his focus from her to watch out the damaged back window. Wind rushed into the SUV from the gaping hole. He yanked his cell phone out of his pocket. He flipped it open, stared at it for a few seconds, and viciously cursed.

"There's still no signal." His gaze met hers. "Where's your cell, Doc?"

"Mine won't have one either if you don't have a signal."

"You never know. We might have different carriers. Where is it? I don't want to sit here debating. I'd rather try."

She reached for her purse but it wasn't where she'd placed it. She peered down and realized it had fallen to the floor. She pointed. Slade lunged for her purse. His hand practically crushed the bag as he yanked it up. In a heartbeat he'd flipped her purse over, emptying all the contents out on the seat between them with a few rough shakes.

Trisha had to fight the urge to yell at him when her mouth dropped open in shock. Those were her things he'd just strewn all over the seat as thought it were garbage. He shoved his hand into the mess he'd created to find her cell then he flipped it open.

"Damn it," he growled. He threw it to the floor.

"That is my phone! Don't break it."

Her temper flared. She was also scared and really, really angry. She unfastened her belt to reach forward to lean down to check on her cell phone. Slade shoved her back against her seat with his hand.

"It doesn't work anyway," he snarled, glaring at her.

"Throw your phone but not mine. That's rude."

"I'm sorry. I would hate to be impolite when someone just tried to kill us."

"Hello?" Bart shouted. "There's another truck. Could you guys stop fighting? I think we have another problem. It looks as if they weren't alone!"

Trisha turned her head to stare in horror out the back of the SUV. A second truck came at them fast, this one a blue pickup that had a metal grill, almost the twin of the red one. She watched as a man stood up in the back of the truck bed, one arm gripping the roll bar over the cab of the truck to keep on his feet, and lifted his other arm to try to point a gun at them. Her mouth opened to scream out a warning.

Slade reached over, grabbed Trisha's shirt with his fist and yanked her down over the seat. His body crushed down on top of hers, causing her purse and its contents to dig into her stomach. Slade's hand shoved in between the seat and her. He grabbed her breast, squeezed it, and his hand turned. He found his gun and yanked it out from under her none too gently. A loud noise sounded but it was muffled for Trisha since Slade's thighs were against her ears.

*My head is between Slade's thighs.* That meant the lump at the back of her neck… She gritted her teeth. *How can Slade be aroused when someone is shooting at us?* She struggled to get out from between his legs but his massive, bulky weight kept her down. His muscles suddenly squeezed, nearly crushing Trisha's head in the process.

"Stay still," he demanded. "Those are my nuts you're pushing back against."

"Screw you. Get off me," she yelled.

A large hand suddenly slapped Trisha's ass hard, sending a jolt of pain from it to her brain, stunning her.

"My face is right here, Doc. You don't hurt me and I won't hurt you."

Trisha just screamed. She was angry, terrified, and her butt stung from where he'd struck her with his big palm. Something rammed hard into the SUV and it caused Slade to topple onto Trisha. They were thrown forward and Trisha's body slid with his. They both slammed into the back of the front seats together.

"Drive," Slade ordered Bart harshly. "One more hit that bad and — SHIT!"

*Shit?* Trisha felt alarmed by Slade's tone. A second later the SUV bounced wildly. She and Slade were actually lifted completely off the seat. She heard a male scream. *Bart.* Then she was slammed hard back down onto the seat with all Slade's weight coming down on her.

She heard a horrible noise as everything rattled, bounced and shook so hard Trisha wondered if she would be shaken apart too. A loud boom rent the air suddenly a second before the truck tilted crazily and she was thrown again. She screamed in pure terror.

She didn't know what was up or down. She knew nothing but pain, fear, and the feeling of motion. Hands grabbed her thighs, she bumped into Slade's body roughly, then something unforgiving. Glass sounded as if it were exploding. Metal groaned and smashed loudly, in deafening volume. Trisha continued to scream but everything stopped moving suddenly.

She panted, laying on something hard. Her shoulder, ear and hand hurt. She tried to calm down as she opened her eyes but instantly wished she hadn't. She discovered her body sprawled on the roof of the SUV. The broken-out back window was to her immediate right, telling her that somehow she'd been tossed into the back luggage area. She stared at dirt and grass on the ground, just an arm's length away. Close to the back of the SUV stood a thick tree trunk. It finally settled into her mind that the SUV had landed upside down.

Trisha moved and it caused pain to shoot up her leg from her knee. She groaned. She put her hands down and tried to push herself up even though her shoulder ached but only managed to lift her head a little. She turned it to the left to stare at Slade a few inches from her. He lay sprawled on his side with his back to her, his head resting by her hip. His arm moved as he touched his face.

"Shit," Slade groaned. "Doc?" His voice deepened as his entire body jerked. "DOC?" Alarm deepened his tone.

"I'm here behind you. Are you all right?" Trisha cleared her throat. Her voice had broken as she spoke.

Slade twisted his head to look her over. "Fine. Are you injured badly?"

"Hurt but alive. Can you see Bart? All I can glimpse from here is the back of the seats and you."

Slade moved slightly and groaned as he lifted his head. "I see him. He's belted in upside down but moving. I can hear him breathing."

A pained moan came from the front of the SUV. Trisha licked her dry lips, instantly tasting blood. She started to inch toward the dirt, intent on climbing out of the wreckage.

A hand gripped her thigh. "Don't," Slade ordered. "They had guns. I don't know how far we rolled but they could be up

49

there. You crawling out of here could make you an easy target."

"Oh God," Bart sobbed softly.

"I have to help him." Trisha met Slade's gaze.

His nostrils flared. "Fine. Crawl over me to get to him. There's a lot of broken glass under me and I don't want you getting cut up. You stay inside the cover of the vehicle. If you can't reach him through the seats, forget about it until I go out there and scout first. I need to find out if we're safe from them shooting down at us."

"You want me to crawl over you? But—"

"Do it, Doc. I'm not kidding about the broken glass. The windows shattered. Safety-glass my ass. This wasn't one of our security vehicles that have been specially built for us. This is tempered glass but some of it is sharp. Crawl over my body to him first and I'll inch out there to take a look at where we stand once you do. Hopefully we rolled far enough down the hill that they don't have a bead on us but they might be coming down on foot to finish us off. Either way, I don't want to stick around here for long. They know where we are or can find us easily enough. I'm sure we left an easy trail of debris for them to follow."

Trisha turned onto her side. She had just enough space to wiggle under the back seat before she met Slade's gaze. He gave her a grin but it didn't reach his eyes.

"You know you want to crawl on top of me, Doc. Here's your chance."

Trisha frowned at him. "You're such an ass."

He winked. "It's not my ass I'm worried about when you're on top of me. Watch your elbows and knees, sweet thing."

Her mouth opened to tell him that now wasn't the time for him to start his crap but Bart sobbed from the front. Slade's smile faded.

"Move it, Doc. They could be climbing down to search for us and I don't feel like being shot at like fish in a barrel."

Trisha carefully reached to put her hands next to Slade's head. He suddenly moved, holding out his hands to her.

"Put your hands inside mine. There's glass. I'll lift you over as much of me as I can. Then keep your hands on my legs. Watch the knees, Doc. Seriously." He winked at her. "As much as I know you want to see how big I am, I'd prefer you feel me with your hands."

"Bastard," Trisha whispered, not really meaning it.

She gave him a brave smile, knowing at this point he was being an ass just to distract her. She'd be freaking out over their dire situation if it weren't for Slade. They'd just rolled down part of a mountain, men with guns might be on their way to the crash site, and Slade tried to focus her attention on him instead of the danger.

"Thanks," she whispered softly, putting her hands inside his large ones. She curled her fingers through his, their fingers locking, palms together, as Slade took her weight. He started to pull her over his body. Trisha lifted her lower body with her knees. She tried not to notice when her breasts rubbed over Slade's face and how her stomach moved close enough to feel his hot breath through the thin layer of her shirt.

"You might want to consider a diet when we survive this," Slade suggested softly.

"Kiss my ass."

He chuckled. "It's not your ass over my face right now, Doc. That's as far as I can pull you. As much as I enjoy where you are, move it, sweet thing."

Her knees reached his shoulders. She gripped his thighs with her hands, knowing she'd have to either pull her body down his body toward his feet by her hands or crawl over him with her knees.

"Hurry, Doc."

She carefully put her knee on his shoulder. His hands suddenly gripped her hips as he lifted her lower body similar to a pushup off his body. He shoved her forward. Trisha was nearly thrown into the gap between the front seats but instead it was just her head that ended up between them with the center console above her. She squeezed tighter into the narrow space. She could see Bart now. Slade moved from under her legs, which were still on him.

"Stay put, Doc. I'm going outside. It was nice knowing you if you hear gunshots."

"Be careful," she warned.

# Chapter Three

ℬ

Trisha's gaze turned to Bart, studying him. He was still strapped into his seat where the belt held him in place. He appeared to be unconscious now and his hands hung limp against the roof. She saw blood covered his left hand and she reached for it carefully. It was hard to do since it was on the other side of his body.

She inwardly cursed, realizing it appeared to be a crush injury. The skin was torn and she guessed his hand must have been thrown through the window that had been smashed out when they rolled. Her fingertips brushed up his arm, feeling for injuries, and she determined his wrist had also been broken. He'd caught a break there, no pun intended, since the bone hadn't popped through the skin. He jerked awake.

"Bart?" She swallowed. Her voice kept breaking on her. "Where does it hurt besides the seat belt and your arm?"

"My leg," he gasped. Tears drowned out the brown of his eyes when he started to cry.

*Crap.* Trisha couldn't get any farther into the driver's area since his body was in the way and the steering wheel was above. She could have seen better if she'd had a flashlight since the sun was going down, making the interior dim.

"Can you move both feet?"

"It hurts," he cried softly.

"Do it, Bart," Trisha snapped. "Those men could be coming after us. Move your feet. I need you to work with me."

He moaned in pain. "I feel them and I think they moved."

Trisha nodded, looking up at where his feet would be. No drips of blood were coming down to hit the roof she lay curled on. *Another good sign.* She forced herself to remain calm and think. Her head throbbed, her body ached and she was in pain. She still tasted blood and didn't even want to guess the cause. She'd assess her own injuries later but right now it was all about the younger man in front of her.

"Listen to me, Bart. I need to find out if your legs are pinned or if we can get you down. I need you to move your legs to see if they are free. Do you understand me?"

"It hurts," he whined.

Trisha clenched her teeth. "I'm in pain too. Come on. Did you hear me about those men who ran us off the road? They could climb down here and kill us. You need to work with me. I can help you better if we can get you free. I can't do much for you right now since there's not enough room to treat you where you are. I have to assess your injures but I need you out of that seat to do it."

"Okay," he hissed softly, "I'll try."

Trisha strained to listen for any sign of Slade but she hadn't heard any gunshots. *Where is he?* She experienced a little fear suddenly. She and Bart weren't New Species. Would Slade just leave them behind to save his own ass? She really hoped not. *Maybe he's gone for help but wouldn't he tell me first?* She just didn't know and that really bothered her.

"I can move them." Pain sounded in Bart's voice.

"Terrific. I know you only have one usable hand but you need to use your good arm to try the door. See if it will open."

"I can't."

Trisha twisted, looking at the passenger side. The glove box had snapped open and things had fallen out. She inched her way to the small area under the passenger seat. The window remained intact on the passenger side but it was cracked and spider-webbed. She used the paper that had spilled out of the glove box to cover the broken glass that had flown around the interior when the SUV had rolled to protect her body. She reached for the door handle. It moved but the door didn't.

"Crap," she sighed. She looked, realized the door was still locked, and reached up. She had to work to get the push-button lock to release. She tried the door handle again and this time she heard a click. She twisted until she rested on her back and pushed with one hand while gripping the door handle. The door moved open a few inches before it jammed into the ground outside. "Double crap."

"Hey, Doc." Slade leaned down to peer inside the wreckage at her from the passenger window. "Do you want out? I don't see any of those assholes coming down here after us so far."

"Can you get the door open?"

Slade lifted his head to study it instead of her. "I don't know. I'm going to have to push against the side to see if I can lift it a few inches because the dirt is loose here and it's stuck on it." He paused. "Maybe. Get ready to feel some movement."

It sunk in what he meant to do when she saw him turn around and plant his feet by the back passenger door. His back pressed against the side of the SUV. She opened her mouth to tell him he wasn't strong enough to move the SUV even an inch but then the vehicle shifted a little under her. He pushed back enough to tip the SUV away from the ground.

"Push the door," Slade groaned. "This bitch is heavy."

Trisha used both hands to shove hard on the door that was a good half inch off the ground. It skidded on the grass and dirt to open another foot. She pushed harder and got another inch maybe. The ground inclined higher. Slade groaned and the SUV shifted again. The door dug hard into the earth under it.

Slade crouched next to the opening and put his head inside between the door and the frame.

"Give me your hands and I'll pull you out."

It was only just over a foot of space, maybe sixteen inches at most. She cursed. "I don't think I'll fit."

"I was kidding about thinking you need a diet. Let's try, sweet thing. I think you can make it. You women always think you are bigger than you really are. It's more space than you think. Go out sideways."

Trisha grasped both of Slade's hands. He slowly started to pull her toward him with her twisting onto her side. Her knees hung up on the front seats but when she bucked a little, it moved her lower legs. Slade pulled on her again. Her head fit through the tight space as she turned it sideways and then her breasts and back were squeezed. She realized she was stuck. Her breasts were hanging her up.

"This wouldn't be a problem if you didn't have such nice boobs," Slade chuckled. "A flat-chested woman would have slid right through there."

Trisha shot him a dirty look as she stared at him. "Just pull me out! This isn't comfy."

"Take a deep breath and exhale all your air. On the count of three. One. Two. Three."

Trisha exhaled until her lungs felt as though they were being crushed inside her chest. Slade pulled her free. She gasped in a gulp of air as Slade dragged her a few feet from the SUV.

Slade released her hands before he reached for her again as she lay on the ground. He grabbed her arms just above her elbows and slowly helped her to her feet. He studied her critically before his gaze met hers.

"Can you stand on your own?"

Testing her legs, Trisha nodded. "I'm good."

He arched an eyebrow. "You wouldn't say that if you had a mirror. Stay here and let me see if I can get Mouth over there free."

"His left hand is crushed and his wrist is broken," Trisha warned. "Try not to touch it or have him put weight on it."

Trisha looked down since her knee throbbed and saw a tear in her slacks. She bent, fought a moment of dizziness, but it passed. She touched the torn material, stained with blood. She gripped her pants with her fingers and pulled the hole bigger. The material splitting sounded loud to Trisha.

She looked closely at her knee, finding redness and a small laceration that her fingers probed. It was a little bloody but it didn't need stitches. She straightened to limp around the SUV and knew she would suffer from deep bruising.

The SUV appeared in really bad shape. She assessed the crushed side panels and the dented-down roof. The back of the SUV had taken the worst of it on the crushed roof. There was a large tear near the front driver's side door and the engine compartment in the front corner had been mangled badly.

She stared at it while Slade opened up the driver's door. It looked as though they'd smashed into something in the front of the SUV on the way down. Trisha's guess was a tree, maybe even a few of them from the damage to the entire front section of the vehicle. It was a miracle they were all alive.

She turned her head and stared up the mountain. She couldn't see the road from where she stood but she could tell where the SUV had rolled before the debris disappeared into dense trees. Broken glass, ripped-off parts of the SUV, and some clothes were scattered in the path of the crash.

She saw her broken suitcase near a tree. It was smashed and torn as if someone had taken an ax to it. She shivered. That could have been her or Slade if either of them had been thrown from the vehicle.

"No!" Bart screamed.

"Be a man," Slade snarled at him. "You can't hang there all day. On the count of three I'm going to slice your belt and pull you out. Your ass will fall but I have your head. One. Two—"

"Don't," Bart screamed, sounding panicked.

"Three!"

Slade sliced the belt and dragged a howling Bart out of the vehicle. Trisha limped the remaining few feet to the man crying on the ground as Slade released him and stepped back. The look Slade flashed toward Trisha showed pure disgust. Slade shook his head, clenched his teeth, and stormed away.

"You deal with him. I'm going to salvage what we can. It's going to be dark soon."

Trisha lowered to her knees to examine the softly crying Bart. Sympathy welled inside her for the kid who was in his early twenties but was acting much younger. She understood how frightened he had to be. Her hands roamed over his body, the only thing she could do without her medical bag. All she had to assess him with was her touch and vision to try to triage him.

She examined his hips and her hands cupped one of his thighs and inched down his leg to his ankle. He didn't appear to have broken feet or ankles. She wasn't about to remove his footwear to find out for sure, knowing that if he had broken any bones there the shoe would keep it immobile and control the swelling for the time being. She rose and gripped his other thigh, circling her hand around it high up, and inched her way down.

"Do you want a room?" Slade sighed. "You touch me that way and I hope you have a wedding ring to give me, Doc."

"I'm checking for more broken bones." She didn't even glance over her shoulder at Slade. "So far so good."

Trisha leaned back and frowned at Bart. "Where does it hurt?"

"My hand."

She'd explored his stomach and his head until she'd run her hands all over him. "How does your neck and back feel?"

"They are fine. My hand hurts." Bart cried softly with his arm cradled to his chest.

Trisha turned her head to gaze up at Slade. "He could have internal injuries but I won't know without getting him to a hospital. The only ones I know of for sure are his wrist and hand. Can you get my suitcase and pick up some of my clothes? I need them."

A frown marred Slade's lips. "You want to change clothes? Give me a break, Doc. You can't be that conceited."

"You stupid son of a bitch," Trisha ground out, her anger flaring instantly. "I need to tear up some cloth to bandage his hand. The handle of my suitcase is the kind that extends. I can remove it and use it to splint his entire arm to the end of his fingers."

Slade blushed a little. "I'm on it. Sorry." He walked away.

Trisha sighed, allowing her anger to fade. They were all under stress. Slade returned within minutes. He used a knife to slice her nice shirts into strips. Trisha splinted Bart's broken hand. He fainted when she did it, which was a good thing because Slade seemed really pissed that Bart kept crying. Bart wasn't doing that for the moment while he was passed out cold.

Trisha took advantage of it and bandaged his bleeding hand and secured it to the brace. She carefully assessed it, deciding that if they didn't get him to a trauma room soon he'd lose the entire hand. She stated that assessment softly to Slade.

"I'll get right on that." Slade frowned at her. "Right after I sprout wings to fly us out of here. What do you want me to say? We're screwed."

"You could walk up to the road to flag someone down instead of standing there making smartass remarks."

"What about the two trucks up there that tried to drive us off the road? Oh yeah. They did that and they could still come back to make sure we're dead. They did go to all that trouble to try to kill us in the first place. They also have guns."

"You didn't see them coming down here, right?"

Slade's expression hardened with anger. "They might be picking up the jerks from the red truck I shot holes in. There's possibly even more of them coming after us. Maybe they want to make it a party. They might be heading down this way right now. I'll go check while you stay put." He spun on his heel and disappeared around the SUV.

Trisha sank down on her butt. Her head hurt and her knee throbbed. She avoided moving her sore shoulder. Every time she stirred her right arm she wanted to wince. She reached up with her left hand to rub her injured shoulder. It wasn't dislocated and she didn't feel anything broken. She hoped it was just a strained muscle or just a deep bruise. Bruising in soft tissue could be very painful.

Bart came around. Trisha smiled at him. "How are you feeling?"

"I hurt. I don't want this job anymore."

Trisha nodded. "I don't blame you. Why don't you try to sit up?"

"I don't want to. When is the ambulance going to arrive? Did Slade go for help?"

"He went to go make sure those people who ran us off the road aren't trying to come down here to find us. He'll be back and we'll get out of here soon. Don't worry, Bart. I'm a doctor, remember? You're doing fine."

* * * * *

Slade ignored his injuries. Anger helped as he climbed the hillside, every one of his senses on high alert. Gasoline messed with his nose, making it difficult to distinguish smells. Some of it had spilled from the destroyed SUV to leak through the debris he navigated and his gaze darted above for any sign of unnatural movement.

Trisha could have been killed. Rage gripped him at the thought. She'd definitely been hurt. The smell of her blood still lingered in his memory despite the horrible gas smell. He half hoped one or two of the assholes who'd attacked them tracked them. He'd love to kill the bastards for harming her.

A huge mass of rock stopped his progress as he peered up a twenty-foot wall. The SUV had dropped from above. The sight made him realize how lucky they'd been to survive. The front of the vehicle had taken most of the damage but if they'd hit it on the side... He shivered. Trisha would have died.

The memory of trying to grab her, to shield her body with his through the worst of the crash would haunt him. She'd been torn from his hold at the end when his head had smashed into metal. It had dazed him enough to make his body go limp. It terrified him to realize how close she'd come to being ejected when he saw she'd ended up in the very back of the SUV.

The human male at the wheel should have been stronger, tougher, and driven them to safety. Instead fear and panic had gripped Bart until he'd lost control of the situation and crashed the vehicle. He clenched his teeth.

He should have insisted upon driving but Justice had wanted a human at the wheel to draw less attention. The tinted windows shielded the sight of Slade from passing vehicles on the road. He swore that was the last time he followed that certain order again. He'd be the one to drive if Trisha traveled in another SUV.

Gratitude gripped him over demanding he ride with Trisha. The idea of her having been attacked without him there left him cold inside. He continued to scan the area above, watching for any signs of their attackers. Humans would follow the path of destruction to locate them. Perhaps they assumed they'd died.

He relaxed. His people would realize they had met trouble when they didn't arrive soon. It would be dark before help arrived but he could keep Trisha alive regardless of how long it took his people to find them.

A sound reached him and a small rain of dirt trickled to his far left. He instantly honed his senses.

"Fuck," a male voice cursed. "I need gloves."

"Be happy we had some rope. Think they died?"

"I'm not leaving it to chance," yet another male voice stated. "We need to find the bodies to prove we killed those animal freaks. We'll take pictures with our cell phones."

"I hope these hold. Are you sure our combined weight won't snap the ropes?" The man who spoke had a slight accent. "Did they have to go off the road here? It's pretty rough terrain."

Slade spun, moved fast, and hid behind trees to get a better fix on the sound from far above. He spotted six males, all in various states of dress, but the thing they shared in common was the shotguns secured to their backs. His lips parted, his fangs flashed, but he held back the growl that threatened to burst forth at the sight of his enemies.

He could fight them, lie in wait to attack, but what if he failed? He'd lost his weapon during the crash. He couldn't shoot any of them to even out the numbers. It would leave Trisha defenseless against them if he failed to kill all of the men before they took him out with bullets. Humans would have her at their mercy.

A soft snarl got past him as he spun to quickly return to her. He wouldn't take any chances with her life. Bart didn't strike him as a tough enough male to travel with injuries. As he moved quickly but quietly, to avoid alerting the men above him to his presence, he came to a grim decision.

He'd have to leave the human security guard behind if Bart refused to flee. Trisha might protest. She had a soft heart but regardless of what it took, Slade would save her. Even if he had to knock her out and carry her over his shoulder. Determination made him travel faster to reach her.

\* \* \* \* \*

"We have to move now," Slade growled suddenly from behind Trisha.

She jumped and twisted her head, wincing. Her shoulder screamed in protest at the sudden motion. "What's wrong?"

"Six men are on their way down to us. They have ropes and guns with them. I think that's what took them this long to try to come down. It's steep where we flew off the road."

"Maybe it's help." Bart sounded hopeful.

"With shotguns strapped to their backs?" Slade snapped. "Give me a break. They will be here soon." Slade spun. "Get up. I'm grabbing what I found that may be useful for us to survive and we're going on the move. It will be dark soon and that will help us lose them."

Trisha struggled to stand and tried to get Bart to take her hand to pull him to his feet with his good arm. He adamantly shook his head.

"No. I'll stay here. It's got to be those anti New Species people. I'll just tell them I'm human and they'll get me help."

"Have you lost your mind?" Trisha gasped. "They tried to kill us and you think telling them you're human is going to matter to those types?"

"They hate New Species and I'm sure that's why we were attacked. Maybe they even thought I was driving Justice North. They really hate him."

Slade came back carrying Trisha's overnight bag. He moved to Trisha and dropped it over her head and under her arm similar to a sling without asking first. He avoided resting the strap on her sore shoulder. It surprised her that he'd obviously noticed her favoring that side. He looked furious as he glared at Bart.

"We're leaving. I think they will kill you so get your ass up and move if you want to live." Slade snarled the words. "You're going to die if you stay here, kid. I don't have time to hold your hand while you try to find your brain. I won't lose my life or hers standing here reasoning with you. Get on your feet."

Bart glared back at Slade. "I'm human and they aren't going to hurt me. They will call me an ambulance."

"You'll die but I don't have time to argue. You were warned. I tried and that's all I can do for you." Slade turned and cupped Trisha's face in his large hand, forcing her to look up at him. His intense gaze met hers. "We need to move fast and put distance between us and them. You are limping and I'm going to carry you on my back. I'd put you in front of me in my arms but it's rough terrain and I'll need my hands free. Don't argue with me, Doc. They are coming. We'll die if we stay."

Trisha had to agree. She had no doubt those men were dangerous. "Okay."

Slade turned his back to her and crouched down. He twisted his head to peer at her and opened his arms at his sides. "Climb on."

She hadn't gotten a piggyback ride since she'd been a little girl. She didn't hesitate though as she climbed onto Slade's back. She wrapped her arms loosely around his neck, making sure she wasn't about to choke him and he gripped her thighs at his hips as he rose. Trisha stared at Bart on the ground.

"Come with us. Please?"

"They aren't going to hurt me. I'll call Homeland when I reach a hospital. I'll tell them what happened and they'll send help for you."

"Last chance," Slade growled as he turned away from the SUV. "Follow us or die."

He moved quickly through the dense trees, not waiting for Bart to respond. Trisha held on.

# Chapter Four

## ℬ

Slade shifted Trisha's weight slightly. She looped her arms over his shoulders, trying to support her weight and not slide down his back. He had lifted her higher up onto his back, hooked his arms under her bent knees, and locked his hands together at his waist.

"You could put me down. I can walk. My knee isn't that bad."

"You're fine. I want to make another mile before the sun is totally down. We'll keep moving for as long as there is light for them to track us."

The sky filled with pink streaks above them as the sun lowered. The wind picked up and blew chilly air at them from behind. Trisha was cold on her back but was toasty warm down the front of her body where it pressed against Slade. Her arms hurt from holding onto him and she tried to ignore the achy muscles between her thighs. She wasn't used to straddling something for a long period of time.

"You have to be getting tired, Slade. Come on. Put me down. I'm heavy. I know you are strong but this is a bit much. You said that we've covered a few miles so far. At least slow your pace. You're going to wear yourself out."

"Shut up," he ordered. "I'm trying to concentrate by telling myself you aren't there. You screw that up every time you talk."

"Thanks."

"That wasn't an insult but you aren't as light as a feather. I'm trying to forget you are there to convince my brain my muscles aren't aching."

She bit her lip. "Sorry."

"Shut up," he sighed.

She refrained from speaking as she darted a glance around the area. Slade really could move, walking faster than she could jog with his long legs. He only slowed down when they climbed uphill or if he had to get them both over a fallen log. They'd had to do that twice.

"BOOM!" Pause. "BOOM! BOOM!"

"What was that?" Trisha's heart raced.

Slade stopped, tilted his head at a slight angle, and tensed. "They must have found Bart."

"Those were gunshots, right?"

"Three shots. Yeah." Slade started walking again. "I guess they didn't care if he was pure human after all."

Trisha couldn't stop the tears that welled in her eyes. Those men wouldn't have shot something unless they meant to kill it. Bart had been sure they'd care he wasn't New Species. He'd just been a scared kid who hadn't deserved to die.

"Don't cry for him, Doc," Slade growled. "I know this is tough but survive first and grieve later. You can't do anything for him now."

She fought the urge to weep, knowing Slade had a valid point. They would both die too if those men caught up with them. Slade moved faster as Trisha clung to him while darkness slowly fell. Slade slowed eventually but kept moving.

"How can you see?"

He breathed heavily now. "My night vision is better than yours. I can't see really well but I haven't walked us into anything yet."

"You need to rest."

Slade uttered a soft curse as he stopped. His arms slid out from under her knees. Trisha groaned when he lowered her to the ground until her feet touched. Her knees held her weight and she released him but was a little shaky. It was so dark she couldn't even see him. She jumped when his hands touched her waist.

"Walk this way. I'll lead you. We'll lie down for a little while to rest. They could still be tracking if they have flashlights but it would severely slow them down. I also walked on rocks as much as I could to hide our tracks and they didn't have hunting dogs with them. We're also downwind and it will be harder for them to scent us. That's why I kept it at our backs."

He helped her to the ground where she sat on soft grass. She moved and bumped something hard and rough with her elbow.

"They can't smell us, Slade. New Species have that ability but humans don't."

"I keep forgetting that." He paused. "That's a small tree next to you so be careful not to hit it."

"Thanks. I can barely see my hand in front of my face." Trisha peered up at the sky. "I don't even see a moon."

"Too much forest is in the way. The trees are thick in this area. That's good for us."

"Shouldn't we double back and try to find the highway?"

"No." Slade moved, touching her. His fingers brushed her breast and he yanked his hand away instantly. "Sorry. Give me the bag."

Trisha removed it and held it out blindly in the direction she thought he was. The weight of the bag eased from the strap and she let it go, knowing he had it. She heard the zipper before Slade pressed something against her arm.

"It's all we have so just take a sip. I'm hoping we run into water soon."

Trisha uncapped the bottled water by feel and took a sip to soothe her dry throat. She took another tiny sip before putting the cap back on.

"Thanks. Here."

His hand brushed hers as he took it from her grasp. She heard him take a drink.

"Why shouldn't we find the highway?"

"They could have more people searching for us. They could be driving the roads hoping we'll pop up. That's what I'd do if I had prey I wanted to hunt. We're safer lost. All our vehicles have tracking systems. It might take a while for my people to locate the signal since there wasn't even a cell reception this far out but they know where to look. Justice knew our route. By now he knows something happened to us. We should have arrived before dark. He would have tried to call me and when I didn't answer, he would have known we were in trouble. We'll stay out here. My people will hopefully find us before those humans do."

"Do you think we'll be found by your people tomorrow?"

Slade hesitated. "I don't know, Doc."

"I have a first name, you know. It's Trisha. Would it kill you to use it?"

Silence. "It wouldn't kill me."

Trisha took a deep breath. She'd had a hellish day, didn't feel well, her body ached, and hunger clawed at her belly. Her frustration level rose. "But you won't use it, will you? Why do you go out of your way to try to annoy me? What did I ever do to you?"

Long minutes of silence passed. Trisha shook her head, guessing he wasn't going to answer. A hand touched her arm and she jumped, startled. She hadn't expected that at all.

"Let's lie down. We should sleep a few hours while we can."

"What if they find us? Should we take shifts sleeping while one of us keeps guard?"

"No. We're downwind from them. I'd smell them if they were near enough to us for them to reach us that soon. I'm going to lie down next to you. You can use me for a pillow, Doc. You need my body heat to stay warm."

"No thanks."

She heard him either snort or chuckle but wasn't sure which. "It's getting pretty cold and the ground is hard, Doc. When you get tired of both you can curl up to me. Good night."

His hand left Trisha and he stretched out next to her because his body settled against part of her thigh. Her vision adjusted somewhat until she could nearly make out his shape on the ground. The wind blew colder as time passed. Trisha settled down, moving a few inches away from Slade. She turned on her side and used her arm as a pillow. Hunger and exhaustion nagged at her. As she lay there another problem arose.

"Slade?"

"What?"

"I have to use the bathroom."

He sighed. "Fine." He sat up. "Give me your hand and I'll lead you somewhere farther downwind."

"Why?"

He hesitated. "I don't want to smell urine. I really don't want to be downwind if you have to do more than that."

"Oh." She blushed. She'd never thought of that.

He gently pulled Trisha to her feet and she followed him. He walked about twenty feet before stopping. "You can go right here. I'll go about fifteen feet away. I may as well go while you're at it."

"How do I know you won't watch?"

He suddenly laughed. "I'm perverse but that doesn't do it for me, Doc. I'll be back real soon so hurry."

It had been fifteen years since Trisha had been camping. She unfastened her slacks and dropped her pants. Being blind didn't help. She prayed that Slade really wasn't somewhere he could see her. She heard something faintly and smiled. She envied him being a man at that moment. She quickly finished up and righted her clothes. She stepped a few feet forward and waited.

"Hope you don't wipe with your hand," he snorted softly. "Tell me now if you did and I don't take that one."

"I didn't." Trisha sighed. "You are just sick. Did anyone ever tell you that? Who would do that?"

He laughed. "I don't know but I wanted to make sure." He clasped her hand in his and led her back to their resting spot. "Good night, Doc."

"Stop calling me that. It's Trisha. Why won't you say my name? What did I ever do to you to make you not like me so much?"

Silence.

Anger gripped her. "I'll keep talking if you don't answer me. I thought you wanted to get some sleep."

"You wouldn't dare. I saved your life by carrying you for miles on my back today."

"I totally would. Tell me what I did to deserve you not even saying my name. I want an answer. You have no idea how annoying it is. I'm going to start calling you 215 if you don't knock it off or at least explain to me why you feel the need to make me mad."

A growl tore through the silence of the night. Trisha instantly knew she'd gone too far. She had known it the second the words passed her lips but it was too late to take it back. She'd read somewhere that all the New Species absolutely hated being called by their file numbers. She hadn't meant to really insult him. She'd only thought it would annoy him the way he did her by calling her anything but her name.

"I'm sorry. I didn't mean to upset you." Her voice softened. "I just want to know why you refuse to say my name."

Pain lanced through Slade at the reminder of his past. Anger quickly followed. Is that how she viewed him every time she looked at him? As a victim? As the half-wild creature he'd been when he'd awoken inside the hospital room assuming she'd just been new enough to the testing facility to be foolish enough to remove his restraints? Usually, given an opportunity, he would have instantly killed a human male but she'd been female.

He'd never kill a female. He'd grabbed her instead. Even half out of it, he hadn't wanted to harm her. Once he had her body pinned under his, her scent had filled his nose, and he'd peered into those incredible eyes, her pouty lips, and his body had roared to life. He'd wanted her more than any woman he'd ever touched.

He'd wanted to keep her for as long as possible. Enjoy every inch of her and make her burn with the passion he felt. He would have gone days without food or water just to know her body. To possess something so wonderful and forbidden. Any punishment would have been worth the cost of pleasuring them both until they couldn't move. Then and only then, he'd have released her from his arms. The memory of the time they shared could have lasted him for years when his mind threatened to break from the pain and agony he suffered on a regular basis.

Of course it hadn't gone the way he'd planned. He'd been in for a shock when more humans rushed into the room to pin him down, his reflexes slowed by the drugs in his system, and he'd awoken to discover his world changed forever. He no longer was locked inside his cell, no longer chained to a wall, and the scents around him assured him that nothing was familiar. They kept him restrained but he understood why it had been necessary. He wouldn't have attacked them but he would have tried to flee.

Four females in uniforms had leaned against the wall of the hospital room to inform him he'd been rescued, his people freed, and they'd slowly explained he needed to calm down.

They'd shown him videos on a little machine of more of his people, taped footage of the rescue, and sworn no harm would befall him. It had taken time for it to sink in that they were telling him the truth. The shock had staggered him. The females meant no harm, they didn't work for Mercile, and that life no longer existed.

He'd been transferred from the hospital to a remote motel in the desert with dozens of his people. All female military officers had been assigned to protect them at the secured location. Humans had quickly assessed that New Species males wouldn't attack human females and had used that as a way to assure they didn't feel threatened. It had worked. The females hadn't even carried guns except for the ones who patrolled the perimeters to keep humans away.

The U.S. Government had promised them a place of their own, where their people could live safely from the press and from other humans who viewed them as a threat. They'd read books, watched television, and talked to humans who answered all their questions. The months spent in the desert waiting for such a place to finish construction had calmed them, assured them that they had human rights, and his new life had begun at Homeland. He'd gone from being a test subject to a man. The Doc obviously didn't agree. To her, he'd always be 215.

It hurt. All he'd wanted was to have her view him as a sexual male, her equal, and he'd messed that up for good by insulting her by not recognizing her when he met her again. She obviously didn't have forgiveness in her heart. The pain turned to anger quickly. *Damn her. If any male deserves some leeway, it is me.*

The memory of touching her, tasting her skin, and the scent of her arousal flashed. She might not think of him as a man but her body could be persuaded otherwise. Lust and desire gripped him hard. Maybe she just needed to be taught without her mind mucking up the truth. He moved before he could talk himself out of the crazy idea.

Two hands suddenly grabbed Trisha by her shoulders. Slade took her to the ground, flat on her back, and suddenly ended up on top of her. Trisha struggled but she couldn't get him off her. He pinned her down with his body. She opened her mouth but his hand clamped over it.

"Are you going to scream and tell those murderers where we are? Sound can carry a long way."

She had planned on yelling at him. She shook her head against his palm. The hand instantly released her. Trisha pushed at Slade.

"Get off me right now," she hissed.

"Do you want to know why I won't say your name, Trisha?" He spoke softly to her, almost whispered.

She swallowed, surprised that he'd finally uttered her name. "Why?"

"It gets under your skin the way you get under mine all the time. I think it's only fair if I annoy you as much as you do me."

"How do I annoy you? You're the one who's always got some smartass remark to say and who constantly makes some sexually rude comment."

"You're the one I want to fuck so bad you make me ache." He growled at her. "That's more annoying than me shooting my mouth off, Doc. Trust me. I don't make you so hard that you worry about busting out of your pants. You do that to me."

His words left her speechless. She'd never expected that answer from him in a million years. Out of all the things he could have said, those things wouldn't have even made her list.

With his traumatic history she could see him hating anyone in the medical profession. She also thought he might think her a snob because people always accused her of being standoffish. She didn't mean to be but she just didn't know how to relate to people.

"Nothing to say now, Doc?"

She didn't know what to say.

Slade growled. "You're one cold bitch. I wonder sometimes if you ever heat up." He paused. "Do you ever warm up even a little?"

"I'm not cold."

"Really? You fool me all the time."

"That's not fair of you to even say. You don't really know me. We've barely spoken unless it's to insult each other or say something rude."

"Ummm." He shifted. "Warm up for me, Doc."

Trisha gasped when Slade arched his stomach away from her body. His hand slid between them and fisted her shirt. She tried to grab it but Slade moved faster. He yanked the material all the way up her body to her neck and pushed away her frantic hands. His finger hooked the edge of her bra cup and gave it a yank. Trisha's breast was freed to the chilly air that hit her skin.

"Nice," Slade growled before his mouth lowered.

Trisha pushed frantically at Slade's broad chest until his mouth closed over her hardened nipple. She gasped at the shocking feel of hot lips and wet, rough tongue when Slade gently sucked the tip of her breast into his mouth. He growled, causing vibrations. Trisha froze, ceasing her struggles. It was an erotic feeling, something she'd never experienced before, and then Slade suckled on her with hard tugs.

Trisha's stomach quivered and she couldn't stop the moan that came from her parted lips. The sensation of what he did to her felt amazing. She arched her chest upward against his face to give him better access and at the same time realized she wasn't pushing at his chest anymore. Her fingers clutched the material of his NSO uniform to keep him close instead.

Slade sucked harder and his teeth rubbed against her sensitive nipple. Trisha moaned louder. She found his hair and dug her fingers around his scalp, holding his head in place. Her heart raced and she knew her body responded in a shocking manor when desire nearly burned her alive.

Slade's other hand shoved at her thigh when he lifted his body off her enough to put a little space between them. He pushed against it to spread her thighs wider. She gasped as his hand cupped between her spread legs under him. He pressed his thumb against the center of her slacks and rubbed firmly right over her clit. She reacted instantly as the sensation tore through her body.

"Yes," she moaned.

Slade froze, his entire body stiffening over hers. His hand tore away from her sex at the same instant he released her breast with his mouth. Cold air hit her bare, wet nipple as he jerked away from her. Trisha's eyes flew open and she tried to see him in the dark but he was just a dark shadow above her.

"You do warm up," he rasped so softly she almost didn't hear him.

"Slade?" Her voice came out shaky and breathless.

He uttered a vicious curse and rolled away from Trisha. His shadowy form stood. She pushed upward, wincing at the sudden pain that tore through her shoulder. She stared in shock at his fading outline as he backed away from her. She barely remembered her bared breast and reached down to fix her bra. She shoved down her shirt to cover it.

"I'll be back," he stated harshly. "I'm going to make sure no one is near us."

"But..."

Trisha closed her mouth. She trembled and her body ached. *That son of a bitch.* Anger poured through her. He'd purposely turned her on and stormed away, leaving her to deal with the rejection. That's exactly what it had been. She'd practically begged him to take her. She may not have said the words but her body had done the talking for her.

"Bastard," she cursed.

Trisha lay back down. Her body tingled in all the wrong places. Her breasts felt unbelievably heavy and the one he'd touched had become so oversensitive that her bra cup against it nearly hurt. She clenched her teeth. She'd change her underwear if she had a spare set since hers were soaked from sexual desire. She turned on her side and drew her knees up to huddle in a tight ball.

*That bastard!* she silently screamed. He'd turned her on just see if he could.

She attempted to find a comfortable position on the hard, cold ground. She should have gone through her clothes that had been spread out around the crashed SUV to find a long-sleeved shirt but it had been warm during the day. She shivered and huddled tighter. Forever seemed to pass and Slade didn't return.

Eventually fear set in. *Has he just abandoned me here? Has something happened to him? Did those men find him?* Tears welled in her eyes but she fought them back, blinking rapidly to accomplish it. *With my luck he'll come back in time to find me crying.*

He hated tears. She had seen him react to Bart's pain and she had a pretty good idea that most New Species didn't have a lot of patience with weakness. They'd had very harsh lives and it had been instilled in them over the many years of captivity they'd endured that weaknesses were bad. She'd bet her life Slade didn't ever cry.

# Chapter Five

## ಬ

Slade watched the camp grimly. The humans were closer than he wished but far enough away to assure him they wouldn't catch them quickly. He'd keep moving throughout the night but Trisha wasn't New Species. She'd need to rest with her weaker human body.

She hadn't complained but he'd noticed her fatigue. He had to admit to feeling a certain amount of pride at how well she'd taken the stress of the situation. Humans weren't very tough but she'd been brave. It made him want her more.

His cock finally softened enough for him to move without pain. His teeth clenched. He'd nearly taken her body on the dirt. He'd have become the animal she probably believed him to be when he fucked her like one on the ground.

The taste of her sweet kiss and the feel of her plush curves against his body had driven him to near insanity. She deserved more than a quick coupling on the ground. He may be part animal but she wasn't. Human females expected certain things from males. A soft bed, a romantic setting and maybe candles. He'd be damned before he allowed his instincts and desire to drive him to do something else he'd regret.

He needed to stay in control until they were safe. Once they returned to Homeland, he'd seduce Trisha in a bed, inside a home, in a secure location where danger didn't lurk. He'd take his time, strip her slowly, and explore every inch of her until her need grew as strong as his. Then he'd make love to her. Gently, do his best to pretend he could be more human than he actually was, for her sake.

He sniffed the air, the smell of smoke nearly making him sneeze, and slowly withdrew from the area. He'd left Trisha longer than he'd intended to. He'd had to make certain he had his desire under control before he touched her again. Otherwise all his good intentions would be forgotten.

He'd been an ass when her body had curled against his. Restraint wasn't his strongest asset but he'd try for her. She deserved a male who could respect her human needs. Those being a bed to have sex in and to have it at the appropriate time.

They'd have to leave before the sun rose. Trisha being in danger wasn't acceptable to him. Justice would have teams searching for them by now. The humans may have to wait until the sun rose to mount a rescue mission but New Species were already tracking them. He knew that as well as he knew the tempting feminine scent he followed right back to Trisha.

He spotted her huddled form on the ground, a snarl rose in his throat that he had to force down to muffle, not enjoying how cold she appeared. He'd left her for too long. Was there anything he could do right when it came to her? It seemed not. His stride quickened in his need to warm her and make certain she survived the night.

*Calm down*, he ordered his body. *Act natural so you don't frighten her.*

Something rustled, sounding similar to crunching leaves being shifted. Trisha tensed but didn't move as she listened. She only heard the wind in the trees above her. Her fear spiked when she saw something move close to her. It was big, man-sized, and drawing near.

"We're good," Slade announced softly as he settled down next to her.

She wanted to cry over him coming back to her, that grateful that he'd returned safely, and hadn't abandoned her. She swallowed a sob. She blinked hard at the tears that swam in her eyes. Slade stretched out onto his back next to her, just inches away, and he took a deep breath.

"Curl into me," he demanded. "It's cold."

Trisha didn't speak, too afraid something in her voice would give away the fact that she was so emotional. She just lay next to him, listening to his breathing.

"Fine. Don't." He had an annoyed tone in his voice. "Night."

Minutes had to have passed when she heard his breathing change, slowing, and guessed he probably slept. She waited a few more minutes to be sure before she inched forward, closing the distance. His hands were looped together behind his head to form a pillow. She pressed her body against his side, facing him. Her head rested down on his thickly muscled arm.

He was very warm. She shivered, burrowing tighter against him until her body pressed against his firmly. She put her hand on his stomach. Suddenly the body against hers tensed. Trisha froze, her heart pounded. His breathing had changed.

"Cold, Doc?"

She hesitated. "I'm freezing."

He sighed. "See what I mean about how annoying you are?" He pulled down one of his arms and his hand closed over Trisha's hand on his stomach. Then he pushed it lower. Her palm ended up covering a mound. "Feel that?"

Trisha tried to yank her hand away from his pants but his over hers prevented her from doing that. He pushed her palm tighter against him.

"Want to keep warm, Doc?"

She clenched her teeth. "Want to let go of my hand?"

"Rub me."

"Fuck you."

He chuckled. "I'd let you, sweet thing. There are a few problems with that. First off, you are loud. I can't have you screaming out while I'm fucking you since we're being hunted.

You'd let them know where we are. Second problem is that if you want to lie against me and stay warm while you sleep, I want to sleep too. I can't while you could take my pulse by how hard you make me."

"You're such an asshole."

"There's that option." He laughed. "I don't think that would feel good, Doc. I'd rather hear you scream in pleasure than in pain. But that still means there would be screaming. You'd give away our location."

His meaning sank in. Her mouth opened. "You...you..."

"Not a back door kind of gal, huh? Good thing we found something we agree on. I'm not into that either. I've been assured by humans it's tighter but I'm a pussy man. Now, either rub me or move away."

"Release my hand."

He didn't. He moved it against him. "See? That's not bad, is it? I would say that's not hard but it really is, Doc."

Fury slammed into Trisha. "Fine. Do you want me to take care of your problem, Slade?"

He hesitated. "If you hurt me, Doc, well, I wouldn't advise it. I'd hurt you back." His hand over hers eased up and lifted away.

Trisha cupped her hand firmly over the outline of his thick, hard cock, trapped inside his pants. It felt impressive in length and girth. She moved, sitting up, and reached blindly for the front of his pants. His body stiffened next to her.

"What are you doing, Doc?"

"You want touched, right? Well, I'm going to, Slade. I have to open your pants to do that."

"Allow me," he rasped softly. The amusement seemed gone from his voice now.

Trisha lifted her hands. Slade moved and she heard a zipper. She could barely make out his shape. He lifted his hips and shoved his pants down to mid-thigh. Trisha couldn't make out much but she knew when Slade freed his cock from his pants.

She stared, trying to see. She could barely make out anything but it appeared he had nothing to be ashamed of, that was for sure. There was no missing that shadowy shape standing erect and proud. He was long and thick, just the way he'd felt. She hesitated, the idea of that inside her a little scary if they ever did have sex. He was bigger than anyone she'd ever been with. Her past number of lovers wasn't impressive, just a few, but none of them compared to him.

"Doc? We should get some sleep before we need to be moving on." His voice was a soft growl. "I'll zip up. I shouldn't have done that. I'm sorry. I am being a bastard. I was half asleep and just a tad too tired."

Trisha's hands shook slightly as she moved forward. One of her hands curled around Slade's cock before he could cover it. She heard him suck in air. He was hard all right and hot. His skin was velvety soft wrapped over steel-hard thickness. She let her fingers and palm explore him. Slade's breathing increased.

"That feels so good," he groaned.

Trisha's anger seeped away. He turned her on. She hated it but he did. She enjoyed touching him. She bit her lip and curled her other hand at the base of Slade's cock. He shifted his legs, trying to open them wider for her to explore him. He softly cursed when his pants bunched at his thighs and wouldn't allow it.

"That's good, Doc."

"Trisha," she ordered softly. "Call me by my name or I stop." She gripped his shaft more firmly, moving her hand against the crown of his cock to trace the rim.

"Trisha," he groaned. "That feels so good."

"I wish I had lotion."

"Me too, Doc."

She tore her hands from him. "My name is Trisha. Use it."

Slade sat up. "Want me to use your name?"

"Yes. I do."

"Fine." He moved away, shoved his pants and underwear down his long legs to his ankles, and lunged for her.

Trisha gasped when he grabbed her. He yanked her up to her knees as he got to his. His hands left her arms and he grabbed her hips and lifted her, turning her away from him.

"What are you doing?" Excitement and a little fear merged but she wasn't protesting.

"Put your legs between mine," he growled in a rough tone, spreading his bare thighs apart to make room for her.

Trisha twisted her head. "Why?"

"Do it," he rasped. "Now, Trisha."

Her heart started to pound. She had an idea what he would do. He was on his knees and he'd turned her until her back was to him. She shifted and fit both of her legs between his, which were spread apart. Her feet tangled with his pants at his ankles but she lifted them to hook over the material. One of his hands left her hip and his other hand slid to the front of her body. She tensed, her breathing increased, as he unfastened her pants. His chest pressed against her back as he lowered his head until his breath fanned her ear.

"I'm going to fuck you, Trisha." He growled when he stated it. "I'm going to sink so deep into your pussy that you will want to scream out my name but you can't. Do you think you can keep quiet?" He shoved her pants down. Her panties were pushed down to her lower thighs next and all the material bunched together.

Trisha's breathing was shaky. She wanted Slade. "Yes."

He made another growling noise. One of his hands slid up her shirt and pushed her bra cup up. His hand gripped her bare breast and gently squeezed.

"Bend over for me, Trisha. I'm going to fuck you the way I've wanted to since I saw you. I'm going to drive so deep into that wet little sheath of yours until you don't know where I end and you begin. I bet you're going to be so tight that you fist around my dick and I have to fight to move inside you."

She put her hands on the ground. She'd never in a million years have thought she'd have sex with a man in the middle of the night in the woods on her hands and knees. Then again, she never thought she'd want anyone as much as she wanted Slade. Her body screamed for him to enter her pussy and she knew he wouldn't be disappointed with how he imagined she'd feel wrapped around his cock. He was so big it had to be a tight fit.

His hand cupped her between her thighs firmly, massaging her clit first and spreading the wet heat of her desire. She moaned as his fingers explored her from her clit to her anus. He pushed a finger slowly inside her pussy, the sensation amazing as his thick digit pushed in deep, and Trisha arched her back as pleasure tore through her.

"So wet, Trisha. So fucking tight too. I knew you would be." He growled softly while he withdrew his finger and traced the seam of her pussy lips, before moving it away.

"Slade?" She feared he'd change his mind, stop, and her body ached.

"I can't wait, need to be inside you too bad to stretch you more with my finger. I'm sorry but I've got to fuck you right now or I'm going to die." He pressed the crown of his cock right at the entrance of her vaginal opening. His hand left her breast and he gripped her hips with both hands. "Quiet, sweet thing. Be real still. I'm going to be easy with you. You're so tight I'm afraid I'll hurt you and I don't want that."

Trisha bit her lip as Slade pressed the thick tip of his cock against her pussy. She almost panted, aching so much it hurt. His cock entered her slowly when he slid into her an inch, then pushed in more. His shaft was wide and her body stretched to accommodate him. Trisha wanted more and pushed back against him. He gripped her hips, moved his body to match her movements but he didn't allow her to take him inside her farther.

"Slade," she begged.

"Don't move," he demanded. His hand left her hip and he gripped her around her chest. He pulled her up and she straightened. They were on their knees and her back leaned firmly against his chest again. "Ready, Trisha?"

She opened her mouth to tell him she was but his hand gripping her hip jerked away. His palm suddenly covered her mouth just as he thrust into her hard and deep. Trisha screamed out in rapture.

Slade's hand muffled the sound. His hips pumped fast, hard and deep. He drove in and out of her pussy with a wild abandon that drove her insane. Pleasure notched higher, nearly unbearable, and she knew she was going to come. She'd wanted him for too long, dreamed of how it would be and the reality was much better than any fantasy. Just him hammering his cock inside her was enough to draw a climax from her.

His hand around her chest slid down her body and dived between her thighs. His fingers found the magic spot, rubbing against her clit furiously as he pounded into her pussy harder from behind. She cried out again against his palm, panting, and her vaginal muscles clenched around the thick shaft.

"Fuck," he growled softly. "So fucking amazing."

Trisha didn't even care that Slade had his hand over her mouth as long as he kept it clear from her nose to make certain she could breathe. She didn't really care if she could get air or not at that moment. Nothing had ever been so good. The sexual satisfaction became more intense as Slade pounded faster into her body, hard enough that he nearly lifted her from the ground, and she screamed as she climaxed.

Her insides were going insane, muscles clenching and shaking. She screamed again as pressure increased against her oversensitive vaginal canal, sending even more overwhelming ecstasy through her. Slade suddenly bit her shoulder and a muffled, vicious sound tore from between his lips, which were sealed around her skin. His hips jerked violently against her ass, grinding against her, until everything stilled except their heavy breathing. Trisha could feel heat seeping through her from the inside out from his hot semen as it filled her.

Slade opened his mouth and released Trisha's shoulder from his teeth. She felt nearly boneless and didn't care that he'd bitten her. She didn't mind the slight pain in that area. It didn't hurt as much as softly throb.

She was more in tune to the heat that continued to flood her pussy, coming from Slade. He'd continued to ejaculate as her vaginal muscles squeezed around his still-hard cock buried inside her welcoming body. She felt fused to Slade with the way their bodies seemed connected and she really enjoyed the feeling. She resisted the urge to collapse against him and stay there for a very long time.

"Don't move, Trisha." Slade finally got his heavy breathing under control. "It will hurt if I try to pull out right now."

"I know," she breathed. "You swell during sex. It's a New Species thing."

"Every guy swells up for sex." He chuckled. "We swell up at the base of our shafts right before we come and stay that way for a few minutes after."

A horrible thought struck Trisha. "You don't have needles, do you? God. Tell me that little tiny needles aren't stuck in me right now. Some animals have that trait. I know you're canine but are you sure they didn't mix you with anything else?"

He laughed, causing his chest to shake against her back. "You crack me up. No. I don't have needles. That would be a hell of a turn-off, wouldn't it?"

She relaxed. "Kind of."

His hand that had held her mouth brushed across her stomach. He pushed his hand under her shirt and his palm brushed across her skin to her rib cage.

"I love being inside you."

Trisha turned her head against his chest. "I love you being there. Wow, Slade. Just wow."

He laughed. "I'm glad you enjoyed that."

"It wasn't just me."

He licked her shoulder. Trisha started and turned her head toward Slade's bowed one. "Why are you licking me?" His tongue flicked her skin over and over, creating a strange but not unpleasant sensation. Just odd.

"I broke the skin. Sorry. I guess I should have been lecturing myself about keeping quiet. I bit you to keep from howling." He licked her again. "You just felt too good and you're so tight it drove me out of my mind. I had to fight to hold off coming until you did. It was too good, feeling your pussy squeezing me. You taste delicious too. Ummm."

"You think my blood tastes good?"

He chuckled and lapped at her shoulder. "It's an acquired taste. And yeah, you taste really good."

"Stop it. You don't have the urge to take a bite out of me, do you?"

She shifted away from his mouth. There was still a lot she didn't know about New Species. She knew they could eat raw meat, that some of them continued to eat it from years of habit from having it tossed inside their holding cells. *Did they crave human flesh?* She experienced a little fear at that thought.

"That sounds fun."

"You don't eat people, do you?"

It was a nice sound when Slade laughed. "It won't be your shoulder that I'd want to eat, Trisha. It sure as hell wouldn't hurt either." His laughter died. "I think I'm relaxed enough now to try to separate us. We do need some sleep. We need to get away from those men. I climbed a tree when I checked the perimeter of our camp a little while ago. They are two ridges over. The idiots lit a fire. I would go pay them a visit they wouldn't live to regret if I thought leaving you alone would be safe."

"You'd kill them?" She wasn't surprised by his statement.

"Bend over, sweet thing. And relax your muscles."

He had ignored her question. She nodded and bent, forcing her body to relax. Slade slowly withdrew from her. She could feel every inch of his still-rigid cock as he withdrew from her pussy. Her body quivered, still oversensitive. Slade chuckled as he backed away from her.

Trisha turned after she straightened her clothing and fastened her pants. She heard Slade zip up after he righted his own clothing. He lay down on his back on the ground.

"Come here, Doc. Use my chest for a pillow and curl up with me. It will help keep you warm if you snuggle one of your legs between mine."

She sighed as she crawled toward him and lay down with Slade. He was large and warm. "Can't you call me Trisha now?"

His body shook under her face as he laughed. One of his arms slid around her waist. "Nope. I'll only call you Trisha when I'm inside you."

She shook her head. "Jerk."

He laughed again.

*So much for good intentions.* Slade held Trisha tighter against his body. She'd touched him, all bets were off, and he couldn't say he regretted taking her. It embarrassed him how little restraint he had when it came to the sexy doctor. Just her hand on his stomach when she'd pressed against him had his cock roaring to life. The blood had rushed from one head to the other. He'd lost the ability to think. He'd taken her more as an animal than a man.

He ran his tongue over his fangs. The taste of her blood still lingered there and he ignored his cock stiffening yet again from wanting her. He turned his head enough to brush his nose through her hair. Her scent called to him and drove him a little insane. Possessive feelings stirred inside his chest and it scared him worse than anything he'd ever experienced. He'd marked her with his bite and had come so hard, so much inside her, that he'd marked her that way too. He'd never experienced anything like it as more and more semen had jetted out of him into her, the pleasure so strong he'd nearly collapsed under the sheer force of it. Only worry that he'd hurt her had kept him up.

She was a smart human, a doctor by profession, and what did he have to offer her? *Sex? A bad disposition? Crude words with animalistic sex?* His eyes squeezed closed. She deserved more than that from a male. He couldn't ever be the type that she'd be proud to have claim her.

*Damn. Open mouth, insert foot should be my motto in life.* Once again he'd probably made her believe he was a total asshole. He'd earned it after the way he'd demanded she touch him. He just needed her that bad. Wanted her even worse. And having her only made the desire stronger to take her again, to keep taking her.

Her breathing assured him she slept. Otherwise he'd be tempted to roll her, strip her naked, and fuck her for hours. He really longed to have her stretched out bare under him, wanted access to every inch of her skin to lick and taste. To explore until he knew her body as well as his own.

The idea of spreading her legs and feasting on her pussy made him drool. He swallowed hard. The scent of her desire drove him out of his head but to taste it? To have her crying out his name while he licked her to climax sounded heavenly.

His cock began to ache. He was rock hard again, as if he hadn't just emptied his seed into her until he'd wondered if any remained. She affected him in ways he didn't seem to have the strength to control.

He promised that he'd try to be a better man for her. First though, he needed to keep her alive. Rage built inside him at the males who threatened his female. *Mine? Damn. I really have it bad for the sexy doc. I just wish she felt the same.*

# Chapter Six

### ഇ

"Hey, time to get up, sweet thing."

It was still dark when Trisha woke and Slade's body wasn't pressed against her side anymore. A hand took hers and he started to pull her to her feet. She groaned softly and stood, still groggy. She wasn't sure how much sleep she'd gotten but it wasn't nearly enough.

"Walk about ten feet that way and do your thing." He released her hand and turned her.

"My thing?"

"Morning piss," he explained. "Hurry up. I already used the boy's tree."

"I can't see a thing."

"Then it's a good thing I am pointing you in a direction where you won't walk into something. Wake up, Doc. It's an hour or so before dawn. We need to put more distance between us and them. I already climbed a tree on higher ground and saw they let their fire go out but I can still smell the smoke. They are out there. When it's light they will have an easier time finding us. That's why we need to get a move on."

"'Kay," she sighed. "I don't suppose there's anything to eat?"

"Sorry."

She nodded and took a step away from Slade when he released her. She walked about twelve feet before she stopped and dropped her pants. She had to pee but it took her a minute to relax enough to squat. She wasn't awake at all. She'd kill for an iced coffee and even a piece of plain bread. Her stomach rumbled when she thought about food. She hadn't had anything since breakfast the morning before.

She fastened her slacks and walked back toward Slade. She heard a chuckle somewhere to her right before hands gripped her.

"This way. You're going in the wrong direction. You aren't a morning person, are you?"

"No. I'm not."

"I guess you are one of those women who prefer to stay in bed and hit the snooze button on the alarm over and over again until the last minute."

"What's wrong with that? I've gotten lax since I left hospital rotations to work at Homeland. I get way more sleep and I can't say I'm sorry about it."

He laughed. "No snooze alarm this morning."

"Yeah. Just some running for our lives."

"That's a good sum-up." He took a deep breath. "Do you think you can walk for a while?"

"I'm feeling better. Sore but better."

"Are you sore from the accident or from me?"

"Don't flatter yourself." Trisha smiled. "You're impressive but I can still walk just fine."

"Ready to go, sweet thing?"

"Sure, lollypop." She grinned, turning her head so he couldn't see.

"Lollypop?" He almost sounded insulted.

"Because I want to lick you," she replied sweetly.

He growled and gripped her arm. "You're only saying that because you know we have to leave."

"Are you sure about that?"

"Let's go."

"Lead the way."

Trisha couldn't see a thing. Slade kept a good hold on her arm, warning her when to step over something in their path. She stumbled a few times. Slade paused after the fourth time she nearly fell.

"I'm going to carry you until the dawn. We're moving way too slow."

"I'm sorry." She meant it. He could travel much faster if she wasn't with him, knowing full well she posed a danger to his survival.

"Don't worry about it. I know you have your limitations since you're only human." Amusement laced his voice.

Trisha lifted her other hand and gave him the finger. "Can you see this?"

"Maybe later, Doc. I'll take that as an offer. I'm turning around for you to climb on my back and here's the bag. If I have to carry you, you need to carry it."

He carefully put the bag over her head and arm so it rested on her back. He moved until she knew he waited in front of her. He crouched and she climbed onto his back. He lifted her as she gripped his shoulders and started walking.

Finally, dawn broke and Trisha could see. "Put me down."

He stopped and released her knees for Trisha to slide down his back to her feet. They were in a sharp ravine that twisted out of sight. She stared upward on both sides. "That's going to be a climb if this thing doesn't end somewhere soon."

Dark blue eyes met hers. "I waited for you to be able to see but we need to climb now. I want out of this. It was good for carrying you but we're better off on higher ground."

*I had to open my mouth*, she thought but she nodded. "After you."

He shook his head. "After you. I want to be able to catch you if you fall."

That made sense to her. She took a deep breath. Slade pointed and Trisha nodded, turned, and saw a lot of brush on both sides. She grabbed hold of a root and started to climb. The ground became rocky in some places but she kept finding handholds with the vegetation. Slade stayed right behind her. Her foot slipped once and Slade grabbed the heel of her shoe, stopping her from sliding. She turned her head.

"Thanks."

"Keep moving, sweet thing."

"You got it, lollypop."

"Knock that off."

"Right back at you."

She gave her attention to where she climbed and kept moving. Her hands hurt but she tried to ignore it, knowing their lives were at stake. The light got stronger as the sun rose and the chilly air turned into a warm, sunny morning, causing Trisha to sweat.

Trisha knew her relief showed clearly when they reached the top and she groaned. She felt as though they'd been climbing forever. A hand suddenly grabbed the back of her slacks and yanked her down. Trisha gasped as she collapsed to her knees. Slade crouched at her side.

"Stay down," he ordered, flashing her an irritated look. "We're higher, easier to spot, and your blonde hair is too visible."

"Sorry. This stuff isn't my forte."

"Unfortunately, it is mine. Take a break, stay down, and be quiet. I'm going to scout the area."

"Sure. You do that." She was exhausted as she just spread out on the ground, not caring how much dirt she sprawled over. She put her arm under her head. "I won't move."

Slade snorted. "Women."

"Men."

"Smartass."

"Dumbass."

"Doc, knock it off."

"While you're scouting, I don't suppose you could find a local coffee shop and bring me back an iced mocha coffee, could you? Maybe a muffin? Or a donut?"

Teeth flashed at her when he suddenly grinned. "I'll do my best."

Trisha watched him leave. He stayed low. She studied the sky, deciding it would be really hot when the sun rose completely. She could just feel it. She sat up a few minutes later and carefully looked around, spotting ridges below. They were at a high point all right. She lay back down, hoping Justice North had sent out the National Guard to rescue them. She wanted a hot shower, clean clothes, and food. She yawned.

She hadn't gotten enough sleep. She was a pro at taking cat naps. She'd done it since med school. Being an intern could be a sleepless existence. She had learned to sleep under extreme conditions. She just hoped that training helped her survive on so little sleep and the grueling pace they needed to keep to stay ahead of the men hunting them.

\* \* \* \* \*

"Don't make a fucking sound." Something jabbed hard into Trisha's stomach.

Her eyes flew open and she stared in fear at the hairy man wearing fatigues who stood over her. His shotgun shoved tighter against her waist, digging into her stomach, and his feet were planted wide apart above her. She stared right up between his spread legs and couldn't miss the fact that he had a tear in the seam of his pants to reveal a section of red underwear.

"Where's the animal man?"

Trisha met the man's gaze as her heart began to pound from terror. *He means Slade.* Obviously the men who'd tried to kill them were definitely anti-New Species. She breathed hard, terrified. He'd shoot her in the gut if he pulled the trigger and that would be a horrible death. If he fired, she hoped he hit major arteries to make her bleed out quickly. With the gun pressed into her skin at that angle, she figured the hole the weapon blast made would finish her off quickly.

"You deaf, bitch? Where is the animal-man?"

"He abandoned me," she lied. "I slowed him down too much."

The man leered at her breasts. "Stupid fucking animals. I would have at least fucked you first. Get up slow. You're the doctor, right?"

She managed a nod despite her shock that he'd know anything about her. "I'm Dr. Trisha Norbit."

"You a vet or a real doctor?"

"I'm—"

"Doesn't matter," he cut her off. "Get your ass up. One of my boys is hurt and it's your lucky day. Usually we kill traitors of our country but I need you. Guess it don't matter what kind of doctor you are as long as you know how to set a bone and stitch up the skin."

*Traitor of their country?* She gawked at him. The guy was obviously a fanatical freak. *Great.* She sat up when he pulled the gun a few inches from her shirt and he took another step back. Trisha carefully rose to her feet and put her arms up.

"You got any weapons besides your tits?"

"My..." She stammered and glared at him. "No."

The man shifted the shotgun, kept it cradled inside the crook of his arm, but trained on her. "Lift your shirt slowly and show me you don't got a gun hidden in your waistband."

She did it, pulling her shirt up to her ribs and slowly turned until he could verify she wasn't armed. She met his gaze when she'd done a full circle. It took a lot of control not to glance around to see if she could spot Slade but she didn't dare. She prayed he'd see the man with the gun and not walk back to her.

"Let's go. Bill? Tom? You still got my back?"

"Yes, sir," a male called out from the left.

"Sure as shit, Sully." The voice spoke from the right.

Trisha glanced around her but she didn't see anyone but the man in front of her with the gun. He grinned, revealing yellowed, crooked teeth.

"Some of my boys are with me. We usually travel in packs of four. It will be the last thing animal-man ever does if he decides to save you. He won't be back for you though unless he gets an itch in his dick."

Trisha refrained from curling her lip in disgust. He was the lowest form of humanity, in her opinion. From the sound of his voice and the things he said, he honestly thought very little of Slade. He didn't even know him and it had to be his prejudice against all New Species. He might be a moron but unfortunately he held a gun on her.

"Move it."

A plan struck Trisha. She took a step and limped badly, dragging her foot a lot, and made a big production of wincing. The man with the gun uttered curse words that made her wince.

"You're injured? Goddamn it!" He roared the words.

Trisha had to resist smiling at the idiot. He'd been worried she'd make a loud sound but he'd just shouted. Slade would have heard that for sure. *Hell, anyone within a mile heard him,* she guessed. She bit her lip hard and watched him as she paused limping.

"It happened when you guys caused the SUV to crash."

He looked furious. "Tom? Get out here."

Tom probably didn't have to shave yet from the looks of his pink skin and he had the narrow body of a pre-teen. He stood nearly as short as Trisha's height of five-foot-three. He gripped a handgun and a large knife had been strapped to his camouflage clothing, making him appear as if he were a twelve-year-old dressed up as an Army guy for Halloween. The faint lines displayed near his mouth were the only signs that gave away his true age, putting him in his mid-twenties.

"Yes, sir?" Tom's voice came out unusually deep, probably something he did on purpose to sound more masculine. Green eyes fixed on Trisha, lowered to her breasts, and that's where his attention stayed.

She wanted to cross her arms over them but was afraid to move for fear of being shot. The jerk leered at her. She glared at him but he didn't seem to care since he probably didn't notice her anger. He wasn't looking at her face. That would mean he'd have to stop gawking at her breasts.

"How far is Pat from us?"

"A mile, sir." Tom licked his lips and rubbed his free hand on the top of his thigh. "That the animal lover, sir? Bet she did him."

"Shut up," the man in charge ordered. "Look at her. She's pretty. She isn't some ugly no-account who can't find a real man like us. Get on the radio and tell him that we're coming in slow with her because she's limping."

Tom finally dragged his attention from Trisha's breasts to look at the older man. "Sure thing, Sully." Tom appeared anything but happy as he disappeared into thick brush.

"Let's go."

Trisha remembered their names. Sully. Tom. Bill. She could identify two of them so far if she lived long enough to reach the authorities. She really wanted them arrested. She concentrated on that silent plan as she slowly limped along, purposely dragged her foot, and made a show of nonexistent pain. If she slowed them down it would give Slade more time to get away. He could look for help and send back the police to her.

They mostly traveled downhill. She stumbled a few times but Sully never lifted a finger to help her. He kept the gun trained on her, followed close behind, and didn't say a word. Trisha guessed that if Slade didn't get her help she probably wouldn't be alive much longer than the time it took for her to patch up the injured man. They'd probably shoot her the way they had Bart when they no longer had a use for her.

They left the thick brush finally and she spotted a clearing with a tent set up and the fresh remains of a small fire. Trisha smelled food and her stomach rumbled. A coffeepot sat in the dead ashes of the crude fire pit they'd built with stones in a circle. Trisha paused, turned her head, and met Sully's mud-brown eyes.

"He's inside the tent so get your ass in there and help him. Pat, we're here and the doctor is coming in. Don't go blowing her brains out before she can tend you."

Trisha limped toward the tent but nearly screamed in real pain when a fist grabbed her hair from behind and yanked her body back. She stumbled and collapsed to her knees, forcing Sully to release her. Tears blinded her for seconds as she grabbed the back of her head, guessing he'd torn out some of her hair. She looked at Sully in shock when she could see him past the tears.

He had his gun pointed at the tent. "Pat? Call out now."

Trisha shifted her attention to the tent when no one answered. The tent door had been zipped closed. Sully inched forward and leaned down. He unzipped the tent flaps and jumped back, shotgun pointed inside as he eased back a little more.

"Pat? I want you to call out now."

Silence.

"Bill? Tom? Call out now," Sully roared.

"Here, sir," Tom yelled. He stepped out of the woods about twenty feet from where Trisha and Sully were.

Another man, in his forties, balding, with a pot belly, stepped out from the woods across the camp. Trisha guessed that had to be Bill. He nodded at Sully. The three men glared at the tent. Sully nodded to Tom and jerked his head at the tent, keeping his shotgun trained on the opening.

Tom moved forward, shoved his handgun into his shoulder holster, and unfastened the large hunting knife on his thigh. He gripped it firmly and crouched to the side of the tent. He reached out with his left hand and jerked up the zipper, opening the flap to peer inside.

"He's gone." Tom gasped.

"Didn't you raise him on the radio?" Sully sounded pissed.

"No, sir. He didn't answer. I thought maybe he was sleeping or taking a shit. He can still get around pretty good even with his arm all busted."

Sully spun to point his gun at Trisha. "When did the animal abandon you?"

She swallowed. "He took off sometime during the night. I fell asleep with him there but when I woke right before the sun rose he'd abandoned me."

"He's far from here." Bill had a deep voice with an accent that hinted at him being Texan or maybe Southern. It was hard to nail down. "As soon as he stopped carrying her he would have taken off like the wind. They can move, Sully. He's probably put ten miles on us by now. Another team will get him for sure though."

"Son of a bitch." Sully lowered the gun he held. "Let's spread out and find Pat. Think he's delirious? He had a fever this morning."

Bill nodded. "Could be. I told you one of us should stay with him. We've been gone since dawn and he could have made some time. One of us will have to stay here with the woman and she can work on him when we find him."

"We should have carried him out," Tom muttered. "I told you he could die. What if he gets himself killed out there?"

"I ain't going to blow that fifty-thousand-dollar reward because Pat is a fool who couldn't watch where he was going." Sully's tone came out harsh.

Bill nodded as he stared at Trisha were she remained sitting on ground. "I'll stay with the woman while you two split up and search for Pat. I'd guess he would go downhill since it's easier to travel that way. Maybe he panicked and is hunting for another team, thinking someone will pack him out or maybe he thought he could head to the highway to flag down a motorist."

"Fuck!" Sully yelled. "Why don't we just forget him, kill the bitch, and go track our animal? I want that fifty-thousand-dollar reward for one of those animal bastards."

Trisha kept quiet but reeled from shock. *Someone paid a fifty-thousand-dollar bounty on Slade? Who would do that? Why?* She swallowed. She hoped they would forget she existed. She hated Sully for wanting to just kill her outright.

"You forget," Bill sighed, "Pat is Thomas' son. If we don't go find that asshole, he'll never give us any reward money for one of those bastards. We need to keep the woman alive until she can patch him up. We have to find that asshole and catch the animal. The animal has been using the ravines and he'll keep to pattern. We'll catch up to him along the ridges. Look how much time we've gained on him."

"But he had the bitch slowing him." Sully ground his teeth together and uttered a curse. "Okay. Let's do this. Bill and I will split up. You head toward the highway in case Pat headed there. I'll head after the animal to see if I can catch him. Hopefully he'll stay low and I can gain on him using high ground. Tom can stay here with the bitch."

Bill shook his head. "Look at the jerk. He can't keep from staring at her tits."

Trisha turned her head toward Tom. He stood there holding his knife, gawking at her breasts again. He grinned.

"I'll be happy to stay with her."

"See?" Bill cursed. "We want her alive, dumbass. I'll stay with the woman while you two split up to search. Tom, head for the highway."

"Fine," Sully agreed, shooting a glare at Tom. "You better find his ass though. I'll hit the ridge to the west to catch the animal faster."

"But I want to stay with her." Tom wasn't happy and it sounded in his high-pitched protest.

Sully pumped the shotgun. "That wasn't you refusing to take an order, was it? I fucking hate whiners. Your daddy isn't the moneyman on this deal and nobody gives a rat's ass if you get shot."

Fear settled on Tom's baby-face features. He shook his head vigorously. "I'll head out now."

Trisha watched Sully and Tom pack light supplies and then both men took off in different directions. That left Bill to guard her. Trisha studied the man who stared at her. He sighed loudly.

"Hungry? Thirsty?"

"Please," Trisha urged softly.

Bill stormed to the tent and quickly returned. He carried a soda and a plastic zip-lock baggy containing some kind of sandwich. Bill stopped a few feet from her.

"Catch."

She held out her hands. He tossed her the soda carefully. Trisha caught it and set it on the ground next to her knees. She held up her hands again and he threw the sandwich. She gave him a grateful look.

"Thank you so much."

"Shut up," he ordered. "I hate it when I get to know things I have to kill later on. Just eat and be quiet."

Trisha hated peanut butter sandwiches but she didn't complain as she chewed. She was starving and was too hungry to care what she ate. She popped the top of the soda and took long sips. She tried not to scarf her food.

She knew Bill had taken a seat on the ground about ten feet from her and silently watched her every move. She finished her sandwich and tried to save some of her soda. She didn't want to drink it all in case Bill wasn't generous later.

# Chapter Seven

ॐ

"Damn it," Slade growled softly, watching the males from beneath some brush where he hid. His sense of hearing came in handy as he listened to them make their plans. They had Trisha. Rage gripped him and he fought back the urge to leap into the camp to kill them all.

They weren't the same men who'd run them off the road. That meant more humans had joined in the search for him and the doc. It worried him not knowing their numbers. The camp setup alarmed him as well. They'd made a base of it in a short time, it meant they were organized, and the danger increased exponentially.

"Calm," he ordered his mind aloud in a soft whisper.

They outnumbered him, had more weapons than he had, and the gun he had acquired wouldn't be of much use if one of the humans used Trisha as a hostage to make him throw down his weapon and it would work. No way would he allow them to shoot her without trying to prevent it. Even if it meant tossing away his weapon and walking right up to them.

He couldn't reach her in time to assure he took out all the threats. Her safety was paramount to him. He'd have to use his skills and kill them one by one. Attacking the camp with all of them around her would be a last resort. He'd die to try to save her regardless of the bad odds in his favor if they decided to kill her. It would be suicide for them both. A last resort.

He listened as the men planned to go find their missing injured human and track him. A plan began to form. The man with lustful eyes would die first if the other males left him alone with his woman. Slade knew the man would try to touch the doc. It wouldn't happen. Not as long as he drew breath.

They wouldn't find the human they sought. A smirk twisted his lips when they decided the man couldn't be trusted not to molest Trisha. That showed they had some intelligence. When two men left the camp he lifted up, ready to attack, but then paused, watching the scene below.

The male guarding Trisha gave her food and a drink. He didn't appear threatening. They needed her alive, her skills as a doctor believed to be needed, and she might be safer there than at his side while he took out the threats.

Indecision tore at him. He sniffed the air but didn't scent any foreign humans in the area. It didn't mean they weren't near though and could show up soon. The wind played hell on his nose with the dust.

His gaze locked on Trisha. She calmly ate and drank. The guy guarding her wasn't threatening or staring at her body in a way that indicated lustful intentions. He seemed smart enough to know that hurting her when they needed her doctoring skills would be detrimental. The asshole who'd pulled her hair would pay dearly for hurting her. He wanted to kill him first for that offense. The sooner, the better.

For now she seemed safe and if other humans returned to that camp, the male guarding her knew her value. It would be a while before they realized they didn't need her doctoring skills. He couldn't hide her somewhere, leave her to track the males who'd become a threat to her, and not worry that she'd be discovered again. He glared at the male watching the doc.

The guy seemed bored but he didn't appear eager to move either. Slade slid back in the dirt, carefully kept low as he started to follow the older male who'd dared pull the doc's hair, and his blood boiled with rage. The male would pay for causing her pain. Pay dearly.

* * * * *

The silence became awful. The breeze blew and trees whispered in the wind. Trisha heard birds in the distance. She sat under the hot sun wishing for shade. She also needed to use the bathroom. When her bladder was ready to burst she turned her head and looked at Bill.

"I have to use the restroom, please."

He blinked. "Fine. You're too pale to be in that sun anyway. It's too easy to get dehydrated if your skin burns bad. I was thinking of moving you."

"I can get up then?"

He nodded. "See the tree by the tent? Go behind it. I'll break your legs if you try to run away from me. It isn't an idle threat. You don't need them to patch up Pat. You go behind the tree, do your biz, and you can be on this side of the tree under it in the shade. Is that clear enough?"

"Crystal clear. Thank you." Trisha pushed to her feet. Her body had become numb in places that painfully awoke as she remembered to limp toward the tree. She had to duck under one of the lower branches and there wasn't much privacy but she didn't have a choice. She unfastened her pants, bent, and quickly did her business before straightening. She walked back around the tree. Bill stood in her path.

She hadn't heard him moving toward her. She looked up at him. Bill was a beefy man who stood at about five-foot-nine. He had harsh lines on his face from too many years in the sun and his skin was a weathered, soft brown. He frowned.

"I'm tired. I didn't get much sleep last night so this is what we're going to do. Back up to that tree. I want your back to it."

Trisha stared at him with fear. *What is he going to do?* She had a sinking feeling that it would be really bad.

"I'm going to tie you to the tree so I can rest. That's all. I'll sleep a few feet from you to be able to hear every sound you make. You just ate, used the bathroom, and had something to drink. You will be in the shade and it isn't cold. You'll be fine. Now back up before I make you."

It wasn't as though she had a choice. Bill was a much bigger man. He looked to be the sort of jerk no one wanted to end up facing off against in a bar fight. He wasn't overly tall but he had that mean look to him that implied he'd cut someone's throat in a heartbeat. She nodded and slowly backed up against the tree to stare at him with fear.

"Reach up and grip the branches, arms out wide."

"Can't I sit down?"

"I said," he ordered softly, "reach up and grip the branches. I wasn't asking. I was telling and I won't repeat myself again. You can either do what I say or I can change your way of thinking. It would be a painful lesson. Do you understand me?"

She lifted her arms to grip the branches just above her head. She saw the man reach into his back pocket and pull out a bandana he probably used to wipe sweat off him. He stepped very close to her. He used the bandana to tie her wrist, securing it to the branch.

He stank and needed deodorant. She smelled booze on top of it, mixed with the disgusting stench of chewing tobacco too. She held her breath as much as she could while he wrapped something made from a rough cloth on her other wrist. He yanked it tight. He moved back finally and the horrible smell withdrew.

Bill stared at her, nodded, and then turned his back to walk into the tent. Trisha looked up at her restrained arms. He had two mismatching bandanas securing her wrists to the thin branches. She pulled on them but they only moved slightly, proving there was no way she could pull free. She softly cursed and tugged at the bandanas, trying to see if he'd left her enough wiggle room to slide her hand out. He'd tied them too tight.

Bill exited the tent carrying a sleeping bag and pillow with him. He darted a glance at her before throwing the bedding down about four feet from where Trisha stood. She'd thought he was at least decent since he'd offered her a drink and food but that was before he'd tied her, scarecrow-like, to a tree. After a while her legs were going to grow really tired.

He stretched out on his back on top of the sleeping bag, facing her, and settled his gun across his chest. She spotted a hunting knife peeking out from a boot as he crossed his legs. He shoved the pillow behind his head and closed his eyes.

Trisha shifted. Her legs ached and her arms felt as though they were going to fall off. She lifted on tiptoe to level her arms with her shoulders. It sent some blood back into her upper limbs but then her toes would hurt until she'd have to ease back down onto her feet. She rolled her head every once in a while. She tried to sleep but every time she drifted off her legs would start to collapse, causing pain to shoot up her arms from her weight pulling against them. Time crawled by.

Something made a slight noise from the woods. Bill jerked awake instantly, rolled onto his stomach, and leveled his gun in the direction the sound had originated from. Shocked, Trisha stared at him. A bird flew from a tree in that direction. The man on his stomach sighed and rolled back over and glared at her.

"I'm a light sleeper. Quit sighing. I'm getting sick of it." He closed his eyes again and rested the gun back across his chest.

*He can't really be sleeping.* Trisha stared at his chest, watched it rise and fall slowly. The sound the bird had made had been so slight she'd barely heard it but the man at her feet jerked as though something had charged at him. He'd even pointed his weapon toward the right direction. If he faked sleeping then he knew about any sound she made. Her glimmering hope of escape dwindled. She would have been better off if they'd left Tom with her. A man gawking at her breasts seemed an improvement over having been tied so uncomfortably to a tree.

* * * * *

Pain jerked her awake and she groaned. Her body sagged, all her weight on her wrists, and it hurt. Trisha fought tears. She put all her weight onto her feet and rose to her toes. It eased all tension from her wrists and the blood flowed back into her arms while she studied the sky. She'd been tied to the tree most of the day. The sun had lowered in the sky. She looked at the man on the ground to find him staring back at her. She couldn't tell for sure but she thought his attention fixed on her stomach.

"You're awake," she noted softly. "Can I sit down now? Please?"

He sat up and watched her face, frowning until he lowered the gun to the ground next to the sleeping bag and rose to his feet. He walked away from her to the tent. Trisha lifted her chin up to stare at the sky. *Bastard.* He had to know she was hurting and uncomfortable. She needed to use the bathroom again too. She heard him coming back and darted a glance at the walkie-talkie gripped in one hand.

"Bill here," he spoke. "Base?"

"Hey, Bill," a male answered through the small speaker. "Report."

"We haven't found them yet." Bill watched Trisha and he put his finger to his mouth motioning her to be quiet. "We're in section twenty-two. Anyone else have any luck?"

"Not so far," the voice was static-ridden. "You are way out there."

"Aren't there other guys this way?"

"Nope. You're it. How come Tom isn't calling in?"

"He's taking a crap. The kid is green. We'll call back and report in the morning. Over and out." He turned the walkie-talkie off.

"They haven't found your animal friend yet." He dropped the walkie-talkie onto the pillow. "I'm rested now and ready for action. I wanted to make sure no one else was in the area and now I'm sure it's just us."

Trisha's stomach churned as she swallowed. She didn't feel at ease with the way he'd said that or the way his gaze roamed her body. His lecherous look slowly rose until he met her fearful expression.

"You're a good-looking woman. You're one of those bleeding-heart, animal-rights bitches, aren't you? You love animals, little girl?" He reached down and unfastened his belt, his gaze locked with hers. "I didn't want Tom staying with you because the kid doesn't know what to do with a woman."

"Oh God," Trisha moaned, watching him pull his belt free of his pants loops as he fisted the buckle in his hand. Her gaze flew to his. "Whatever you are thinking about, please don't do it."

"Shut up or I'll take this belt to you. I hate screaming. Do you understand me? You don't need a tongue to fix Pat when Tom drags his stupid ass back here. He's an idiot and I'm sure we've got a few hours before they return. He couldn't find his own ass without someone directing him to it. I'll cut out your tongue if you scream."

Bill dropped the belt onto the sleeping bag and reached down. He pulled a long, sharp hunting knife from his right boot. He glanced at it and let his finger trace over one side of the two-sided blade. The back side had a serrated edge. The blade had to be ten inches long. Trisha stared at it in horror. He lifted his head to give her a cold smile.

"Say you're a bitch who is a bleeding-heart, animal-rights moron. Just that way."

She shook with terror. She opened her mouth but nothing came out. She yanked hard on her wrists, frantic, but the bandanas held. She tried to back up but the tree had no give in it.

"Say 'I'm an animal-loving, bleeding-heart bitch who is a moron'," he demanded softly. "Right now."

"I'm an animal-loving, bleeding-heart bitch who is a moron," Trisha whispered.

A smile cracked his lips. "That's a good girl." He took a step closer as he gripped the hunting knife with his fist. He reached and grabbed the waist of her slacks and his head lifted.

"Kick off your shoes."

"I have to use my hands to get them off," she lied. Her voice shook.

"Kick them off now or…" He brought the blade closer until the tip of the knife touched her breast and pushed the knife until it indented the area just under her nipple. "I figure I could slide this in at least three inches before I hit bone."

"Oh my God," Trisha gasped, total panic gripping her. "All right." She used one foot to grip the back of the other shoe and pushed down. Her shoe came off. She switched, using her toes, and got the second shoe off.

"God isn't here, little girl."

Bill suddenly moved, pulling his knife back from her breast and thrust it at Trisha's face. She saw the blade coming at her and a scream tore from her throat. She threw her head to the side. She expected the blade to stab her in the face but it didn't. The expected pain never came. She heard him laugh. She turned her head to see that knife embedded in the tree trunk next to her face. Her ear brushed cold metal.

His hands were brutal as he dug them into the waistband of her slacks. He unfastened them and shoved them down her body. He hooked his thumbs in her panties and pulled them all the way down her legs. When he reached her ankles he just jerked hard to remove them. Trisha's legs were yanked out from under her when he did it and she screamed again. Pain tore through both of her shoulders and wrists as her full weight sagged on them.

He rose and stared down at Trisha as she struggled to stand again to take some of the pain from her arms. She was naked from the waist down and knew he planned to rape her. She turned her head and prayed as a hand fisted in her hair.

"Look at me, animal-loving bitch," he ground out.

Trisha whimpered from the pain he inflicted on her. He turned her head by jerking on her hair until she had no choice but to look at him. He smiled, giving her the coldest one she'd ever seen.

"When the boys come back, this never happened. I will kill you myself if you tell them and it won't be painless. Do you understand me? I'm not going to risk one of those loud-mouth asses getting drunk and popping off so my wife finds out. I'll just tell them you tried to run if you don't do what I say, how I say it. I'll cut you up while you're still breathing. Do you hear me, little girl? You do what I say or you don't live 'til morning. You tell any of the boys what you and I are about to do and you'll be begging me to die by the time I get done with you." He winked at her. "Hell, if you do tell, the boys might want to do it to you too." His hand released her hair as he laughed. "On second thought, the boys can't tell if they do it too. We could have our own little animal-loving-bitch party."

"Please don't. I have money. I could pay you anything you want. Just please—"

He slapped her hard. Pain slammed through Trisha as it exploded from her cheek to her jaw. She groaned. Agony tore through her shoulders as her knees collapsed under her. She fought blackness and won. The world spun though and the metallic taste of blood filled her mouth. She settled her weight back onto her feet.

Hands were on her chest. The asshole yanked her shirt up and over her head. He snagged it on the back of her neck where it would stay hooked away from her chest. He couldn't remove it without untying her or cutting it all the way off her body. Her hands were bound too tightly to break free when she frantically tried to do just that. The shirt did move as she fought and some of the material slid forward, along the back of her head when she lowered it to her chin. Bill cursed and gripped her shirt again to bunch it behind her neck to keep it up. Hands gripped the front of her bra and he yanked hard, causing material to tear. He shoved the cups aside.

"You look better than my wife ever did before the bitch had six kids." He gripped her waist painfully. "I bet you're fucking tight too. You don't have any stretch marks. You haven't had any kids. I can tell by your tits."

The dizziness receded. Trisha slowly recovered from the blow. She spit blood at him. He would rape her anyway. "Fuck you, asshole."

He grabbed her throat. Trisha could only stare at him in horror as his hand squeezed her neck painfully. He looked absolutely livid as he moved closer until they were almost nose to nose.

"You think you're too good for me, little girl? You think you can call me names? I bet you're wishing you had held your tongue about now." He took deep breaths. "Want air? It's good. You're turning blue, bitch." His hand released her.

Trisha gasped in air and choked. She stared at him as he reached down and slowly unbuttoned his pants. He nodded at her and then dropped them to his ankles to reveal he wore tighty-whities. He gripped them and shoved them down to his ankles. He grabbed his protruding dick with his fist and slowly jerked on it. Disgust welled up in Trisha.

"See what you're going to get, little girl? I'm going to know every hole in you. Every one. You think you can call me names with that mouth? Try to call me names when I'm shoved down your fucking throat, bitch."

"I'd rather die. Just kill me!" she screamed at him. "You're a fucking loser. You're nothing but a fucking asshole rapist." She hoped he'd snap and kill her. She'd rather die than live through him touching her. "And *that's* fucking pathetic by the way. I'm a doctor and I've seen a lot of them," she taunted him. "Pathetic!" she screamed.

His face turned red and he roared out in rage as he lunged forward. Trisha tensed as he charged and could only throw her back against the tree while she attempted to kick both feet out at him. Her shoulders and wrists screamed in pain but her feet hit him. Pain shot up both of her legs as she made contact with his body. She'd been aiming for his groin but instead she hit him in his upper thighs.

The enraged man didn't fall but he did stumble back about four feet, nearly tripped on his pants around his ankles, but remained on his feet.

"You fucking bitch!" he screamed. "You want to play rough? You think you can try to kick me in the nuts and not pay for that? I'm going to hurt you so bad you beg me to kill you and then I'm going to."

He charged at her again. She saw him raise a fist and knew she couldn't avoid it. Her last thought was that he might hurt her enough to knock her out so she wasn't aware when he raped her. *If I survive.* She doubted she would. She just didn't want to be conscious when he hurt and killed her.

Laurann Dohner

# Chapter Eight

ဆ

The blow never landed. Trisha saw something large and fast slam into the advancing man just inches from her body. She jerked her head to gape at Slade, who was now on top of the half-naked man. Both men rolled and they leaped apart.

"Slade," Trisha sobbed.

"Kind of busy, Doc." He didn't look at her. "You all right? Did he rape you?" He snarled the words, obviously enraged.

"He was about to." Tears fell freely down Trisha's cheeks and a sob caught in her throat. Slade had come after her.

"Fucking animal," Bill spat. He yanked up his underwear and pants, which had been caught around his ankles.

"You're calling me an animal?" Slade snarled. "That's fucking rich coming from a lowlife woman-beating rapist. Want to call me an inbred, idiot asshole too since you seem to want to call me the names that fit you better?"

Bill pulled a small knife from his left boot and waved it between his body and Slade. "So you came after the little girl, did you? Is she your master or something, Fido?"

"I guess that makes you a really sick bastard if you think she's a little girl."

"I'm going to cut off your head and hang it over my mantel," Bill taunted. "Come at me, Fido. I'll just gut you a bit first if you're lucky and make you watch me fuck her to see how humans do it."

Slade laughed. "Like you know how to be human? And that isn't fucking, shit for brains. It's called rape. The only one who needs a lesson is you. And not to change the subject but Doc is right. The last time I saw something that size I was

114

about eight years old when I was looking down. You're fucking pathetic. No wonder you have to tie women to trees and force yourself on them. A woman not restrained would laugh her ass off if you pulled out that little dinky thing. Did you stop growing when you were eight? I sure as hell didn't. I'm bigger than that soft and sitting in cold water."

"At least I can have kids," Bill yelled. "You're shooting blanks, animal. We laugh about that all the time. All we got to do is wait around for you animal fuckers to die off."

"You think so?" Slade's eyes narrowed. "We may not be able to breed children but we do know how to treat women."

He fought the rage inside him. The human had touched Trisha, stripped her body, bared it to view, and the scent of her blood hung in the air. He refused to look at her, knowing he'd go insane if he actually saw any real damage to her. He needed to keep his head. He wanted the bastard to suffer. He'd just rip the son of a bitch apart if he didn't calm down. He'd die too fast.

Bill waved the knife again. "We're hoping your life span is that of a pathetic dog. That's what you are, isn't it, animal? You don't got the pussy eyes I saw on the television from the pet you put before the news cameras."

"Yeah," Slade growled. "I'm canine." He flashed his sharp teeth. "I'm going to outlive you."

"None of you are going to survive long." Bill backed up a little and switched hands with his knife and wiggled his fingers to motion Slade to come at him. "We're going to hunt every single one of you down. You're going to be sport. We'd have to just bomb you fuckers if you were able to breed before you can create puppies." His gaze slid to Trisha for an instant and then he smirked. "You think she wants you? Think human women would want someone shooting blanks, rutting on them?"

"At least I have the equipment to please a woman," Slade growled at him. "You might have the ability to breed children but all you'd passed down is your ignorance and tiny dick."

"I'm going to leave you bleeding on the ground to watch me fuck her and show you how a woman likes it from a real man. I'm going to have something you can only dream about."

Slade's anger boiled but he kept a tight hold on it. The urge to make him suffer diminished quickly, more in favor of just killing the human. He flashed his teeth again, wanting the human to come at him. It would give him the advantage he needed.

"She's already mine. She knows what it's like to have a real male inside her and she wanted me to fuck her." He smiled coldly. "I didn't have to tie her up and she didn't call me pathetic. She belongs to me."

An enraged yell came from Bill and he lunged with the knife. Slade dodged the plunging, sharp blade. He threw his arm out and Bill screamed. A loud pop sounded. The knife dropped and Bill screamed again, jumping away.

Slade had hit Bill's knife-wielding arm hard enough to break it. Slade smiled, showing sharp teeth, and then he closed the distance. He grabbed Bill's shirt and hauled back his fist and punched him in the nose. The human yelled as blood poured from his face while he stared in horror at Slade.

"This is for hitting my woman," Slade growled. "You're going to know pain and suffering before I'm done with you. You never should have touched her. For every second of her pain, you will know it as well." He snarled. "And then you will die."

"No," Bill gasped, his terror showing in his wide eyes and bloodied face.

Trisha watched in stunned horror as the men locked in combat. Fear gripped her that Slade might be hurt but within seconds she realized he had speed and strength against his opponent. He easily took command of the fight.

Slade kept a hold on Bill's shirt as he lifted his leg and kicked the asshole's right knee. The horrible noise seemed really loud as the leg snapped. The sight was sickening when bone popped through the skin, blood flew, and Slade shoved Bill onto the ground when he toppled sideways as his leg collapsed under him.

Bill sobbed. Trisha was stunned. Slade crouched down, resting on his bent knees while he glared at Bill. Blood poured from Bill's nose and leg. Bone protruded just above his knee where the bone had separated right through his pants. Slade continued to watch him for a long minute.

"The pain and terror you are feeling right now is what you made my woman feel. You were going to hurt and rape her. Then you were going to kill her when you were done using her body." Slade paused. "I might be an animal but I'm more merciful than you. I could leave you here to die slowly." He stood, turning his back on the man. He walked over to the fallen knife, bent and gripped the blade handle. He seemed to be testing the weight of it.

"Bill? Go to hell," Slade growled. "You never should have touched what is mine."

Slade turned and in one fluid motion threw the knife. It struck Bill in the chest. Shock and horror fixed on the horrible man's face as he looked down to see his own weapon buried deep within his body. He fell backward and didn't move again.

Trisha gaped at the lifeless man. She was certain he was dead. He'd been moaning in pain from the injures he'd sustained until Slade had buried the knife in him to the hilt. It took a lot of strength and skill to throw a weapon that hard and hit the mark. Slade moved toward Trisha. She tore her gaze from the dead body and met Slade's dark-blue eyes. They were all she could see as he closed in on her.

"Don't look at me that way," Slade ordered softly.

He stopped in front of her and reached for one of her wrists. He tore the bandana free. A pained sound tore from her when her arm lowered because it really hurt. She experienced that pins-and-needles pain as it stabbed down her arm and shoulder almost instantly. Slade freed the other arm. As soon as he had her unrestrained, Slade reached for her and swept her into his arms.

"You're shaking. Come on, Doc. You're safe. I've got you and it's all good now."

Slade moved to the sleeping bag and lowered them to the ground until she ended up sitting on his lap. He stared at her mouth and pulled his arm out from under her knees where he'd lifted her.

Gentle fingers brushed her lower lip. She flinched from the pain. Slade's gaze narrowed. "Damn. He hit you hard enough to split your lip. Open up for me, Doc. Let's make sure you don't have any permanent damage."

Trisha opened her mouth and Slade touched her teeth. His eyes seemed to darken when he moved his finger out and brushed the tip of it over the injured part of her cheek where she'd been struck.

"All there and accounted for but you're going to have a nice bruise." His gaze studied her jaw and cheek. "Let's be thankful he didn't hit you an inch higher or you'd be sporting a black eye."

Her shock wore off and she began thinking again. "We have to leave. There are more men with him and they will come back."

He shook his head. "No. There aren't."

"There are. One of them is hurt and two of them went looking for him and you. If the missing guy is found they could show up at any moment. We have to leave before they return. They have guns, Slade. They—"

"Are all dead." Slade cupped her face with both hands. "I killed them. There were three of them and they had me blocked from reaching you before they did. I heard them state they were bringing you back to their camp. You did good, Doc. You slowed them down and gave me time to come back here. I found the first one inside the tent. I killed him and carried his body away to prevent them from finding him."

"But—" Slade gently put his finger over her lips and she closed her mouth. "I knew they wouldn't harm you as long as they thought he was injured and in need of your help. I hid his body, hoping they'd think he walked off to piss and got lost. I followed the younger one and took him out. I had to backtrack the loudmouthed one for a ways. He was smarter and harder to get the drop on. Then I came back here in time to hear you scream."

"They are really dead?" Shock tore through her that Slade had killed them.

"Yes. The men they are with killed Bart and they were going to kill you. They would have done the same to me too. Trust me. They tried to kill me when I found them. I never would have left you alone if I didn't think you would be safe. I'm so sorry. I swear I never thought you'd be harmed. When I left he was feeding you and giving you a drink."

She saw sincerity in his eyes. "I didn't expect him to attack me either."

Slade cupped her face and studied Trisha. "I'm really sorry, sweet thing. Do you forgive me?"

She nodded, still stunned that he'd really killed those men to save her.

He took her wrists in his hands and peered at them, frowning. "You will have a lot of bruises. Are you hurt anywhere else?" His gaze met hers. "Tell me. Did that bastard hurt you worse?"

"No."

119

"Trisha? Tell me. Did he do anything to you besides the wrists and your face? Did he assault you sexually in any way before I arrived? Did I reach you in time or did he molest you earlier too?"

Tears blinded her. "You got here in time."

"Then why the tears?" He brushed at a few of them with his thumb, eyeing them as though they were something foreign.

Trisha laughed, partly from hysteria and partly from his comical look. "You don't ever cry, do you?" She sniffed, her laughter gone. "I was terrified. I'm crying because of what he planned to do to me."

"No. I don't cry."

Trisha wasn't surprised by that admission. "Well, I do. Crap. I'm naked. See what a mess I am right now? I forgot I wasn't wearing clothes." She gripped her shirt from behind her neck and yanked it down her body to cover her to her lap. She glanced around the area and found the rest of her things before she looked back at Slade. "I should get dressed."

"Don't move. You're still shaking." He put his arms around her. "Just relax, Doc. They are dead and you're safe. There isn't anyone else around for miles. I made sure of it."

She turned and relaxed against Slade, putting her arms around his waist and just clung to him. She fought the urge to cry when both his arms wrapped around her. It was a given that she would have been in some serious hell if it weren't for Slade holding her. He made her feel a little better.

"By the way, don't ever do that again." Slade sighed.

"Do what?" Trisha lifted her head, peering at his tense expression.

"Provoke a man into hurting you." Slade shook his head a little at her. "What if I had arrived later? I wouldn't have been able to reach you before he'd killed you. I would have come to recover your body from his dying, bloody fingers, Doc. Next time you do anything in your power to stay alive. You can survive anything as long as you keep breathing."

"He was going to do horrendous things to me. I would rather die than suffer through that."

Slade growled at Trisha, showing his anger. "No. You survive any way you can but you cling to life. It would have been hell for you and it would have hurt you badly but as long as you are breathing, you have life left to fight for."

"You don't understand. That asshole didn't tie you to a tree and tell you he would rape you in ways that would have left you screaming."

Slade breathed harder now, angry, and glared at Trisha. He gripped her arms, turning her to face him. "I have suffered many harsh things, Doc. You have no idea of the kind of pain and agony I have endured in my lifetime. I watched them kill my friends and they were all I had. I've suffered pain that would have driven most males insane but I am here still. I fought. I bided my time in hopes that one day I might have one like today. I'm free. All the pain and agony, all the hell, all the indignity and humiliation is behind me. I'm here sitting with you on my lap and I'm grateful, Doc. Do you understand? You survive any way you can but you don't give up. Never provoke a man into killing you again." He took a ragged breath and his handsome features softened. "Please. I can't save a corpse."

Trisha nodded her understanding, her anger gone. He had suffered and she had no idea how deeply that anguish had gone. He'd spent year after year being a test subject. He'd seen many people he had to have cared about being tortured to death. One really horror of a nightmare day she'd had to undergo paled in comparison to Slade's entire life.

"I promise."

The tension in his body eased. "Good. We'll eat their food, take their supplies, and get out of here before someone comes to check on them. I'm sure teams of my people have reached the area and are searching for us."

"But those men have hunting parties out there looking for you, Slade. They were talking about a fifty thousand dollar reward."

Slade cursed. "On capturing me or killing me?"

"I don't know but I'm pretty sure it didn't matter as long as they killed you. They just said it was fifty thousand dollars. They mentioned someone named Thomas who wouldn't pay them if something happened to his son. That was the first guy you killed inside the tent." She gave him a smile. "I guess Thomas won't be happy when he finds out his son is dead."

"My bad." Slade shrugged. "He's definitely dead and I hope none of them get paid their blood money. Did you hear anything else?"

"Bill, that's the dead guy over there, used a walkie-talkie to talk to a base camp. I'm assuming they set up a few of them around here. There are more teams out there hunting for you but I guess we're a few miles from them. Bill was supposed to check in with them first thing in the morning."

He smiled. "He won't be."

"They knew I'm a doctor when they found me."

"Your things were at the crash site. It was probably easy to figure out who you were and they can communicate and share information. I'm sure there is a search going on for us. Justice would have publicized our faces to help find us."

"Oh. Sorry. I thought that might be important."

"It was a good catch on detail." Slade winked at her. "Hungry? I am."

She nodded. "I have to pee first though."

"You go find privacy while I find you some clean clothes. They have water. I see the bottles from here. Take one with you and wash, Doc. I'll take care of the body over there and start sorting supplies."

"Thank you." Trisha suddenly cupped his face and leaned closer to him. "You saved my life, Slade. Just...thank you."

A slow smile curved his lips. "Since I saved your life does this mean I'm guaranteed to get lucky tonight?"

Trisha laughed. She couldn't help it. It was the amused look on his face. "I can't believe you said that."

Sturdy shoulders shrugged. "I always want you, Doc."

She climbed off his lap and stood. Slade rose to his feet as well. Her body trembled from the stress and tired muscles but she ignored it. She was more concerned with the fact that she was naked from the waist down. She knew Slade couldn't help but see that as she moved away from him. She walked over to retrieve a bottle of water.

"Tease," Slade growled as she bent over and retrieved one of the bottles her for a sponge bath.

She straightened and shot him a look over her shoulder. "Aren't you supposed to be finding me some clean clothes instead of watching me bend over?"

"I'm doing both." He headed for the tent. "Do you want to lean over and pick something else up before I go inside? I could throw things in your path for you to have to move."

She laughed, walking toward the clump of bushes that would give her privacy. "No thank you. I'm good."

She quickly attended to her immediate needs and then removed her shirt and torn bra. She stood naked in the shade as everything hit her at once. Trisha fought tears as she examined her injured wrists. Her mouth hurt and her cheek throbbed hotly and ached where she'd been struck. She also felt really, really dirty. Bill had touched her and just the thought of what he had wanted to do to her body made her want to throw up.

She crouched, attempting to open the water. She wasn't strong enough to twist the lid off and her trembling didn't help. She made a soft sound, fighting the urge to start sobbing, and hugged her body as she stared at the bottle.

"Doc?" Slade's voice came from right behind her.

She didn't move. She huddled naked and kept her back to him. It embarrassed her to fall apart the way she was and remembered he wasn't fond of tears. She knew if she looked at him he'd see how close she was to completely losing it.

"I found clothes for you," he said, his voice soft as he moved closer.

She hugged her chest tighter. The urge to break into sobs grew stronger. The past events of the last twenty-four hours were just too much. She wasn't used to people trying to kill her or men attacking her.

"Trisha?" Slade crouched down behind her and his arms wrapped around her. "It is okay, sweet thing. I'm here. You're shaking."

Hot tears streamed down her face. She heard Slade softly curse and then he sat on the ground, pulling her into his arms. She didn't look at him. She wrapped her arms around his neck instead, held on tightly, and buried her face against his chest.

Slade's arms hugged her harder and his fingers dug into her hair. He cradled her against his chest and rested his chin on the top of her head.

"You've been very brave," he rasped softly. "I've been trying to keep you mouthy and fighting but it's been too much, hasn't it?"

She nodded against his chest. "You hate tears. I'm sorry."

His hand stopped rubbing her scalp and he sighed. "I don't hate tears on you. Don't be sorry. You deserve to cry. It's actually been a bad two days. I'm so sorry I left you here. I would have killed him first if I thought he would hurt you but I made a mistake. I was certain he would treat you right until I got back and I thought it was best to leave you here with him in case more men came. My reasoning was that they already had you and wouldn't hurt you because they had a need for you to treat their team member."

"It's not your fault." Trisha used her forearm to wipe her tears. "You saved me. Thank you, Slade. I know you didn't have to and you risked your life fighting that man to do it. You killed him for me. You killed all of them to rescue me."

His fingers brushed her hair again. "You're mine, Doc. I'd fight anyone to get you back and I'll kill any man who touches you."

His words sank in. Trisha lifted her head, stared at Slade. His blue eyes met her shocked ones. "I'm yours? What does that mean?"

He hesitated. "Now isn't the time, okay? We'll have this discussion later when we're home. Let me help you get cleaned up. We'll eat, salvage their supplies, and get out of here. I'm hoping we are back at Homeland by tomorrow."

Trisha studied him. "Okay." She wanted to ask him a hundred questions but let it go. *For now. His?* Her heart raced a little. She wouldn't mind belonging to Slade. *Not at all.*

His hand eased out of her hair. "Stand up and I'll help you wash. Then we'll get busy. I don't want to hang around here. The camp is known to their men and besides that, I hate their smell. The camp reeks of their stench."

Slade helped Trisha to her feet since she wasn't steady. Slade wet her shirt and started at her back, rubbing her skin. Trisha held her hair out of his way. Slade's hands were gentle as he washed her down and then ordered her to turn to face him.

Trisha met his steady gaze. She stood naked in front of him and she watched as Slade slowly raked his gaze down her body. His mouth pressed into a firm, grim line. He looked furious. More tears threatened to spill and she had to blink them back.

"Why are you angry?"

His gaze met hers. "No one should touch you the way he did. You have bruises. I'm furious. Anyone who marks your beauty pisses me off. I'm not upset with you. I'm just enraged that I wasn't able to protect you better."

She understood. Slade washed her arms and shoulders but his hands hesitated at her breasts. Then he quickly and efficiently wiped them down. Her body responded to the water and air as her nipples tightened. Slade growled and dropped down on his knees in front of her.

"Don't look at me that way." He sighed loudly. "Please."

"What way?"

His gaze narrowed when he looked up at her. "You have no idea how badly I want you, Doc. You're hurt and you were nearly sexually assaulted. I tried to tease you into thinking about anything else earlier when I asked if I'd be getting lucky later. You have an expressive face. I appreciate that I can tell what you are thinking most of the time but right now I'm trying not to think what you are. Don't look at me while I touch you. I'm honored that you trust me enough to want my touch on your body after your attack. It means a lot that you would face your fear for me." He took a deep breath. "We need to get you dressed and leave here. I want you too but it isn't the time."

Trisha blushed at how transparent her thoughts were to him. She did want him. His touch would make her forget what had almost been done to her. She longed to wrap around his body and get as close as humanly possible to him.

Slade took a deep breath that drew her full attention. He washed the front of her, down her thighs to the top of her feet, and stood. Her gaze met his and she knew at that moment that she needed to feel alive, had come close to death, and she wasn't going to be denied the one man who made her feel.

Slade attempted to cool his heated body. Touching Trisha always made him hot, ache to have her, but now wasn't the time. She stared at him and suddenly lifted her hands, placing them on his chest. The air froze inside his lungs.

"Make me forget. Please? I want you."

He had to force himself to breathe. His dick instantly responded, going from semi soft to rock hard in the space of a few racing heartbeats. The feel of her fingers sliding downward to his waist made him bite back a groan. His fists clenched at his sides to prevent him from lunging at her, hauling her against his body, and taking what she offered.

*She's traumatized. She'd never forgive me if I take advantage right now.* He tried to be logical. She'd just survived an ordeal, had nearly been raped, and while he could understand her need to be distracted, the repercussions of it could ruin any future he might have with her if she regretted it later.

"Please, Slade?" Her voice lowered to a husky tone. "I know what I want and that's you."

He unclenched his hands, gripped her waist gently, and loved the soft feel of her bare skin. Instead of glancing down at her tempting body, he kept his gaze locked with hers.

"I want you, always, but I'm not sure right now would be the smartest thing we could do. You should calm first."

A smile curving her lips drew his focus down to her mouth. He wanted to kiss her so badly he actually lowered his face but paused inches from her mouth. He swallowed hard and jerked his gaze back to hers.

"I'm a doctor who has worked emergency rooms for years. I know all about adrenaline rushes and my life has been on the line before. I've faced off gang members, crazy idiots with weapons, and once an old lady with a switchblade who really didn't want stitches. I want to live right now and I want to do it with you. I survived and now I want to celebrate that. I can't think of anything better than getting you out of those pants."

*Good enough for me,* he thought, knowing he should question it more but Trisha stood in front of him naked and offering him something he desperately wanted. His mouth swooped down and took possession of hers. She opened up to him, her lips soft, and he growled when their tongues met. She was addictive as hell and his.

The feel of her tearing at his shirt, pulling it from the waist of his pants, and going for his zipper dissipated any hesitation he had. She needed him and he was going to give her whatever she sought. He'd wipe away her tears, hold her, or use his body to comfort her. There could be no wrong between them.

His hands slid down to her hips, one of them delving between her thighs to seek her clit to massage. Trisha opened his pants frenziedly, freed his cock, and her hand wrapped around the rigid length. He had to lock his knees to remain standing. He wanted to drop to his knees before her as she stroked him with her soft, tender hand. His wasn't so gentle as he furiously located the hot spot he knew would make her burn for him.

Trisha moaned against his tongue now, her grip on his cock tightening into a fist, and he cupped her ass while he noticed how wet his hand became from her desire, from the way he manipulated the bundle of nerves. He breathed in the scent of her growing arousal, another snarl catching in the back of this throat, and dragged her closer to his body.

He wanted to lift her up, demand she wrap her legs around his waist, and impale her on his dick. The image of it only drove him more insane. He wouldn't last long, was too excited, and knew he'd have to bring her to climax first. He adjusted his fingers and two of them played with the slit of the entrance of her pussy. She wiggled against him, rocked her body, and the hand on his chest frantically reached up to grip his shoulder. Trisha tore her mouth away, threw her face against his chest and moaned.

He drove both digits inside her hot pussy. The incredibly soft and silky feel of her channel tightly hugging his fingers nearly undid his control. He wanted to fuck her fast, hard, deep, and come so bad he knew it would blow his mind. The sexy doctor could do that to him.

She bucked her hips, helped him delve deeper inside her snug pussy, and he envied his damn fingers. He stroked her inside, pressed his thumb against her clit, and began to rub it in short, sure strokes. Trisha moaning his name spurred him on. The catch in her breath as she said it was the last straw. He tore his hand away, dropped to his knees before her, and his mouth latched onto her nipple.

The move had torn her grasp away from his dick, which throbbed painfully, but he was too turned on. He didn't want to come in her hand. He wanted to be inside her, buried deep, when he found heaven. Trisha tugged at his hair, her nails digging into his scalp as she clutched him closer against her chest. His hands grabbed her ass and pulled her tight against his body, urging her to sit on his lap. She easily complied, sliding down him until he'd angled her spread thighs over his. The crown of his cock brushed her pussy, soaked now with need, so warm and ready. He pulled her down more, making her take him as he guided her to sheathe him inside her.

He threw his head back, had to release her breast to avoid biting into her nipple, and snarled as her vaginal muscles squeezed tightly around his shaft. *Fuck, I'm going to come. Hold off. She feels too damn good.* The sounds she made as he filled her, gave her all of his cock, were damn near his undoing.

His ass tensed, he took a ragged breath, and he began to move, rocking his hips. One arm hooked around her back to keep her pressed against his chest while he wiggled his hand between them, located the swollen bud of her clit, and furiously strummed it. Her muscles squeezed him and then she cried out loudly, he could feel her climax—a warm gush of her release coating his cock and flutters against the head of his dick. He buried his face in her neck as sheer ecstasy made his body quake. His balls were drawn up tight and the first burst of his semen shooting into her nearly made him roar out. He clutched at her, held her tightly, and rode out the overpowering pleasure gripping him.

*She's everything to me.* His hold eased slightly as his body began to relax, the aftermath of such intense sex beginning to fade, and he held her tenderly. He kissed her skin, nuzzled the side of her face, and smiled. He'd held on long enough to make sure she'd gotten off first.

"Wow," she panted.

He softly growled. "Feel alive, sweet thing?"

"Oh yeah."

He'd do anything to protect her, to have another moment like the one they shared—her on his lap, their bodies connected, and his arms wrapped around her. She played with his hair, her fingers running through the locks, and he wished he could carry her to bed. He could spend hours exploring her body and making her come over and over. His dick began to harden, his need to take her returning, and he forced it back.

She was in danger. He needed to get her away from the camp, put her somewhere safe. *Mine to protect and I'll kill anyone stupid enough to try to take her from me.* He cupped her face, noticed a little blood where he'd nicked her with his teeth during sex, and used his thumb to wipe it away. The injury was very minor. The sight of her blood on the pad of his thumb made him long to taste even that but he resisted the urge.

He didn't want to break the connection they had, hated that he needed to bring her back to their grim situation, but the enemy couldn't find them in such a vulnerable position. He lifted his head and their gazes met.

"We got to go, Doc."

The sweet smile on her face faded and he hated to be the cause. "Right."

He refused to release her just yet, clinging to her to keep her in place. "We'll do this later, longer, and I'm going to kiss every injury you've suffered. Once we're back at Homeland I'll make this up to you."

"There's nothing to make up. Thank you."

He growled, anger stirred a little at the distance he saw in her beautiful eyes as though she were trying to put up an emotional barrier between them. "We'll talk about this later. Right now we need to get you dressed and leave."

"Okay."

Trisha allowed him to separate their bodies, regretting that the moment was over. He helped her to her feet, fixed his pants, and glanced around the clearing. His hair was messy from her fingers and she hid a smile, more than a little amused at his appearance. Slade had been in a fight and afterward had still looked nearly perfect but hot sex on his lap had left him looking wild and disheveled.

"Stay right there."

Slade found a pair of jeans and used a knife to slice off some of the legs to fit Trisha better but the waist remained a little baggy. He used shoestrings from a pair of men's shoes as a belt to keep them up on her hips. He'd also found her a black T-shirt two times too big but she was grateful for how baggy it fell since her bra had been destroyed.

Slade searched through the men's supplies and packed their acquired things inside a backpack that one of the men had brought with them. He took a sleeping bag, food, and he kept the men's weapons. They also took water and soft drinks. Very quickly, Slade was ready to go. Trisha studied him.

"I'm not playing around with them anymore." Slade wore a determined expression on his face. "You got hurt. I'm not going to be the hunted anymore, Doc. I'm going to find you a safe place to hole up and then I'm going to take the rest of these bastards out."

Trisha just studied him. She knew he could be dangerous and had the ability to kill. She'd seen it firsthand when he'd saved her from being raped. She nodded.

"All right."

# Chapter Nine

ℬ

The sun hung low in the sky when Slade glanced back at Trisha. He'd found a dugout area of earth inside the side of the hill. A large boulder had once taken up the space but time and gravity had caused the large rock to roll down the hillside into the ravine below. It had been really hard to reach the area. It was so steep that Trisha had nearly fallen three times, and if not for Slade, she would have. He'd climbed behind her, one hand on her, and had caught her each time she'd lost her footing.

"You are safe here." Slade crouched down in front of her and his hand brushed her uninjured cheek. "You will hear anyone coming from below and it's too unstable above for them to use their ropes to try to climb down to this place."

"Okay."

"I want you to wait here where my people will find you if I don't come back. It might take a few days but some of the males they send were trained with me from before we were freed. They know how I think and they will realize what kind of hiding place I would look for to stash you. Don't shoot them when they do, Doc." He gave her a tight smile. "It is considered rude to injure or kill someone attempting to rescue you."

Trisha didn't smile back, knowing he tried to use humor to defuse the stress, but she was too worried about him. "Come back to me."

His smile faded. "I can't guarantee that, Doc. I won't make promises I can't keep."

"Then stay with me where we're safe. Please? We could just wait right here together."

Slade hesitated. "I didn't realize there would be so many of them hunting us, Doc. Those men I killed are not the same men who followed us down from the road when we crashed. They obviously have different teams out there searching for us. You know this from hearing them. That puts you in extreme danger and there's only one way to handle this situation. I need to hunt the hunters and turn it around on them." He paused again, staring intently at her.

"But—"

"They won't expect that from me and their numbers need to be thinned out. It could take some time for my people to reach us and I need to help us survive. It will confuse those assholes when they find themselves under attack. Some of them will flee when people start dying. It will weed out the cowards from the truly deadly ones. Those are the ones who need to die. It's the only way to protect you, Doc."

"But this is a really good hiding place. Just wait it out here with me, Slade. Please? I'll beg you if I have to. I'm terrified they will hurt you or worse. You're just one man and there are too many of them out there. Those are your words."

Slade's head slightly tilted and his mouth tightened into a grim line. "I'm not just a man, Doc. I'm something far worse with the advantage, whether they know it or not." He hesitated. "This is what I am. I'm a New Species and I have something important to me to protect. But this isn't just about you and I don't want you to feel guilty if something happens to me. My people will be coming and I don't want them walking into a trap of any kind, which is a possibility. I need to take out as many of these assholes as I'm able to. I'm a predator beneath my humanity. I may try to hide it but it's still there. I'm also a survivor who has had to kill in the past to remain breathing. Mercile trained me to fight to show off their drugs and it's one lesson I'm grateful for at this moment."

"You don't have to fight them. You aren't locked inside a cell anymore and we can hide. From what I understand, you were never really meant to be placed into a real battle zone, which makes that training not count. They just taught you enough to show what you could do but this is real, Slade. I don't want you to die."

He took a deep breath. "It was always real. Not all of my people survived their cruel tests or the shows they forced us to participate in to demonstrate the results of their drugs. I am dangerous, even though it's never what I wanted to become. Whether you accept it or not, that's the truth. They trained us too well and made us less than completely human. It wasn't their intention to ever see us free but we are. I'm New Species. You're a doctor but just because you aren't inside a hospital doesn't mean you stop being what you are. You'd help any injured person if you could regardless of being on the clock or off, wouldn't you?"

Trisha hated his logic. "Yes, but I don't want you to go. Stay with me. Chances are, when your people arrive, it will scare those assholes off. I'm sure they never planned to have to search for us."

"Don't tempt me, Doc. Holing up with you inside this small space for a day or so..." He winked. "I would enjoy the hell out of keeping us from growing bored."

"Stay with me." Hope soared inside Trisha. She just wanted him safe, with her.

"It's too big a risk if I were to stay with you and do nothing. There's too many of them and they can spread out to search a lot of places. If we're found they could surround us." He glanced around the cave and then back to her. "You could be struck by a bullet if there's a shootout. There's too many rocks buried into the walls that something could ricochet off and strike you. I won't allow that to happen. We also don't have enough bullets to hold them off. They could also start a brushfire and smoke us out. It's better if I go after them than risk them trapping us here. I'll make certain that anyone who comes close to you is no longer breathing."

She bit her lip, forgetting her injury, and winced from the instant pain. Slade brushed his finger over her mouth, staring at it.

"You will need to stay low, no standing or moving around much. That blonde hair of yours can draw attention and doesn't blend well with the hillside. Remember to stay out of sight. I'm leaving you all the guns from the camp just in case some of them get past me or they take me out. This handgun is all I need. You only fire when they are close enough not to miss and you have no other choice. The noise will carry far if you shoot and bring more of them this way. That would be bad."

Trisha stared into his eyes when he met her gaze. She did what she really wanted to do most. She leaned forward, gripped Slade's face, and watched surprise cross his features a second before her mouth brushed his. She tested the soft texture of his full lips, heard the sound Slade made deep inside his throat, and then he took control of the kiss.

He deepened it, his tongue meeting hers. She ignored the pain of her cut lip, even the taste of her blood mingling with Slade's taste, just wanting, needing to get lost in that kiss. Her arms wound around his neck and he lifted her weight when his arms slid around her waist, gripping her hips to pull her close, pressing them chest to chest. Slade suddenly growled and tore his mouth from hers, breathing harder.

"Trisha," he groaned. "You're making this difficult for me and if you sat on my lap, you'd know how hard you actually are making it. I have to leave now. Please don't make this worse. This needs done and I have to go while I have enough daylight to move quickly. My night vision is not as good as normal sight during the day."

She knew she'd lost the argument and he had his mind set to hunt down those men. He planned to go out there and risk his life trying to save hers. Hot tears threatened her eyes but she blinked rapidly to hold them back.

"Okay. Just come back to me, Slade."

A smile suddenly twisted his lips. "What are you going to give me when I return, Doc?"

"Anything you want."

His eyebrow arched and the smile widened. "Anything?"

"Anything," she repeated firmly. "Just don't get killed."

Slade nodded. "Stay low, be quiet, and keep those guns ready. Use them only if you have to and hold them off as long as you can. I'll hear if you have to fire at anyone and I'll be coming. No more provoking jerks trying to get them to kill you. Remember to just survive and I'll have something to save. You promised me that, sweet thing. I'm holding you to it."

"I remember and promise. Swear to me that you won't take too many risks. Survive, Slade."

Slade nodded again, studied her intently as if trying to memorize her face, and then he backed away, releasing her completely. He forced his gaze from hers before he quickly took some items and shoved them into his pockets. He gave her one quick glance and then started to climb down from her hiding spot. He was gone in seconds. Trisha had to bite back the plea to beg him to come back, certain that regardless of what she said, he wouldn't change his mind.

She unrolled the sleeping bag on the hard, unforgiving earth to keep busy. The dirt floor was embedded heavily with tiny rocks and hard clumps of dirt. Even with the sleeping bag she could still feel the uncomfortable ground beneath the thick material when she sat to assess what items she had.

Slade had acquired two sets of binoculars and he'd left one behind inside the backpack. She found them and inched to the opening. She used them and it didn't take long for her to spot Slade. He moved amazingly fast without her.

She turned the binoculars, scoping out the area, but didn't spot anyone else. She could see for a long ways with the help of the powerful glasses. She turned her focus back to Slade, knew when he had reached the bottom of the ravine to her left.

He turned and examined the area where she hid and then started to jog away. Trisha kept her focus trained on him.

Darkness crept up too quickly for Trisha's liking. She had lost sight of Slade through trees but sometimes she'd spotted him through the dense foliage. He moved fast, showed no signs of slowing, and he seemed to be heading in one direction. She wondered if he'd caught someone's scent with his amazing nose.

She scooted back into the dark hole and had to feel her way to the backpack and unzipped it. She'd watched Slade take all the beef jerky but he'd left her the breakfast bars they'd found. She ate two and drank a soda before crawling back toward the opening. She glanced at the darkness below her and then gasped. In the distance she spotted a tiny sparkle of flame that came from the same direction Slade had been heading.

Trisha could see what had to be a camp. Flames showed through thick trees, not more than distant flames even with the binoculars. She had a sinking feeling that's where Slade headed.

Trisha sat up and dragged the sleeping bag to the edge where she got comfortable, grateful she at least had somewhere to try to catch a glimpse of Slade. He was out there somewhere and she worried.

If Slade could smell their fire and he planned to attack, that's where it would happen. Forever seemed to pass to her but no distant sounds of a fight reached her ears. She got more comfortable by stretching out on her stomach and propped her elbows on the sleeping bag while she continued to catch snatches of the flames.

More time passed and she lay down flatter onto her stomach. A yawn passed her parted lips, reminding her of her exhaustion. She drifted to sleep until a single gunshot jerked her awake.

Trisha scrambled to sit up while frantically aiming the binoculars toward the campfire. She spent seconds searching the darkness until she found the flickering light.

Her attention remained focused on it until it died out, disappearing in the darkness. No more shots rang out. It gave her hope that he might have survived if he'd attacked the camp.

She fought the urge to shed tears over Slade being out there alone. He could be dead if one of them had gotten off a lucky shot. She dragged the sleeping bag away from the edge and huddled into a ball on top of it. She needed sleep and she had no chance of trying to spot Slade until the sun rose.

\* \* \* \* \*

Slade kept low, watching the four men in the camp with hatred. He could hear their words and it made his blood boil. The smell of the deer they'd shot and cooked faded with the firelight they allowed to slowly burn out.

"Think the animal will beg for his life when we find him?" The one in the jeans jacket asked the one in the black shirt.

"I hope so." He laughed. "I brought along my video camera to tape it all. We need to show all the decent folks that they aren't men."

Jeans jacket snorted. "Damn two-legged animals. Not only do we have to protect our country from them but our women too. First they'll want to vote, then they'll want to get married. If their women look anything similar to the men they will be after our sisters and daughters. It's just sick. I figure they hide how their women look for a damn reason. They probably mixed them with mules and they have jackass faces."

One of the men laughed. "Butt-faced ugly. Forget the coyotes."

"They never should have been set free. We don't go around freeing monkeys they test makeup on. Hell no." The black-shirted man leaned back against the log, putting his boots closer to the fire. "They are dangerous and probably nuttier than fruitcakes."

The blond man who'd kept silent suddenly frowned. "Does fruitcake actually have nuts in it? I won't taste that junk. It looks bad." He paused. "Do they really use cute monkeys to test women's face crap on? Monkeys are cool. I always wanted one for a pet when I was a kid."

"Hell if I know." The guy in the black shirt shrugged his shoulders. "It's a damn saying. My point is that they have to be completely whacked out of their minds. You don't set caged animals loose and let them run around free. It's dangerous and that's why they all need taken out. They sure aren't cute and I wouldn't want one for a pet. It would probably try to hump my wife."

The blond laughed. "I've seen your wife. I doubt it."

The guy in the black shirt threw his can at his friend, tagging him in the arm. "Fuck you, Mark."

"Knock it off," the guy sitting farthest from the fire sighed. "We haven't found our target and every hour that passes means he could somehow slip out of the area. The roads are locked down by our teams. They are trapped in the area, but that woman he's with is some kind of doctor. That means she's smart and is probably thinking for him. They might have found a hole to hide in. That's what I'd do. We need to cover a lot of ground tomorrow at first light, find them, and kill them. I didn't come out here to bullshit and insult each other. I want the reward."

"I'm not mounting that head on my hunting wall." The blond shuddered. "They look freaky and just plain ugly. Of course it would be cool just for a conversation piece. I could charge admission and show it off."

Slade had heard enough. He wasn't about to allow those men to leave the camp. They were too close to Trisha and they were looking for sheltered places. He eased around the camp and waited until the men began preparing to sleep. The blond stood, stretched and walked into the darkness to take a leak.

The man never heard Slade come up behind him until his hands were on him. The smaller man only gasped when a palm slapped over his mouth, he was jerked off his feet, and the knife on his thigh was yanked free and pressed to his throat.

"Be quiet," Slade ordered.

The blond panted but didn't try to cry out.

"Are there more of you nearby?"

The guy hesitated before he slowly nodded.

"More than the other three at your camp?"

The blond nodded again. The news angered Slade. He needed to find the other camps, take out the threat to Trisha, and get hold of their cell phones. Hopefully one would work. He could call Homeland to help them locate Trisha faster. She needed to be taken out of this dangerous mess quickly.

"I'm going to tie you up and go after your friends. If you don't fight I won't kill you. I'll secure you until my people come. Do you understand me?"

The blond nodded. Slade wanted the humans dead but he wasn't at Homeland. He wasn't sure where he stood on the law. Self defense was one thing but the man he gripped posed no current threat. He hated them but he wasn't a cold-blooded killer despite their low opinion of Species.

He loosened his hold and the blond suddenly struck. The guy tried to twist out of his hold and twisted his head. He gasped in air to give the alarm but Slade was faster. He snapped the man's neck. The sound of the bone breaking sickened him as he allowed the body to slump to the ground. He turned to face the camp but suddenly spotted movement. Another human came at him. The guy didn't seem to see him in the darkness until the last second.

The human's shock was apparent as he frantically grabbed for the handgun strapped to his chest in a holster.

Slade threw the blade in his hand and lunged forward to grip the man's arm and throat. The human went down without putting up too much of a fight. He lowered the dying body to the ground, staring into his enemy's eyes.

"We're going to kill you and that bitch who owns you," the man hissed before he died.

Slade released him, his rage heightened by the stench of blood and death. His instincts gripped him hard. *Protect Trisha.* These men weren't compassionate. They weren't worthy of receiving what they didn't posses. They were hunting a helpless woman and a Species in a death sport for money. He snarled softly, releasing his human side and embracing the instincts of the predator that was part of him and came so naturally.

*Kill them, make sure they aren't a threat to my woman, and show no mercy.* Memories of the years he'd been locked up flashed inside his mind. These men were as bad as the ones who'd kept Species prisoner. They didn't see his people as anything but rabid animals. A soft snarl tore from his throat as he jerked the knife out of the body, and rose to his feet. The only way to stop them from reaching the doc was to kill every one of them. He could do it. He'd do anything for Trisha.

His gaze drifted toward the camp as he stealthily moved forward. The humans would die but Trisha wouldn't. He'd make certain of that regardless of how many he had to kill.

\* \* \* \* \*

It was light outside when Trisha woke next. She inched to the entrance on her stomach, gripping the binoculars to scan the area. She was careful to go slowly and tried to use a grid pattern not to miss any sections. She didn't see anyone or anything. She finally gave up after an hour and tried to get some rest on the sleeping bag again. She drank half a soda, saved the rest, and ate one more breakfast bar.

She worried that Slade might not return to her, knowing he could have been killed. She lay there with her eyes closed, his image haunting her thoughts. She wasn't sure what kind of relationship they'd have if they survived. Did they even have one? He'd called her his. *That has to mean something*, she decided. It gave her hope that they had a future awaiting them if they could avoid being killed.

A sound jerked her from a light sleep a little while later. Trisha listened until she heard the noise again. She sat up, her heart hammered, realizing it sounded similar to…she wasn't sure, but it was familiar for some reason. The noise came again. *Crap.* It sounded as though rocks or something equally heavy were falling. She moved and gripped the handgun since it was a smaller weapon, easier to hold than the two rifles Slade had left behind.

She crawled toward the opening on her belly to peer down and jerked back hard when she saw someone move below her. She moved backward, still on her belly, and grabbed one of the rifles too. She fought down fear and inched forward to reach the opening.

She kept on her stomach when she drew closer to the edge, laying the rifle at her side to keep it within easy reach. She stayed as low as possible to peer over the edge again until she saw them. Two men were about twenty-five feet below her, climbing up the hillside were she hid. She ducked down.

Both men wore camouflage green clothing and headed directly toward her hidden spot. She hoped they hadn't seen her, assumed not, since they hadn't called out. They'd reach the opening soon enough if she didn't do something. She wondered how they had found her and if they were New Species. They usually wore black uniforms but did they wear them away from Homeland too? She didn't know.

She could sit there waiting for them to discover her or keep them below her. She didn't know what to do. She frantically wished Slade hadn't left her because he'd know how to handle the situation. At least Slade would be able to smell them to know if they were his people or the enemy.

Indecision sawed at her. She uttered a silent curse and then decided she had to hold them back. If they reached the opening she wasn't sure she could shoot them before they shot her since they outnumbered her. Slade had told her to hold them off with the weapons and he'd hear it. She wondered how these men had gotten past him but it didn't really matter since they had. She moved again quickly and grabbed the last weapon. She wanted all three of them available.

She crawled on her stomach and peeked out over the edge again but couldn't see their faces. She gripped the handgun and waited until one of them looked up. He appeared to be in his mid-twenties. Trisha leaned out more to aim the gun right at him. His gaze widened in surprise when he saw her.

"That's far enough," she called out. "Don't move or I will shoot. Who are you?"

The man next to him jerked his chin up until she could see his face too. He was a little older than his companion, in his early thirties, with facial hair, and a cold look. Trisha kept glancing back and forth between them. They climbed in a steep area below her, she remembered vividly how difficult it had been, and both of them had to hold on not to fall. It would be a painful fall if they lost their holds, if not deadly. They were a good fifty to sixty feet up the incline.

"We're New Species," the younger man stated evenly. "We've come to rescue you, Dr. Norbit."

She bit her lip, studying their features. He looked a hundred percent human but so did the other man. Most of the New Species had distinct facial anomalies similar to Slade's with his flattened nose and pronounced cheekbones. Justice North had those feature anomalies but he had cat eyes. Every New Species man she'd ever seen had long hair that fell at least to their shoulders but these men had crew cuts.

"I don't believe you." Fear gripped her, knowing they were trying to fool her.

"It's true. Justice North sent us." He smiled but it didn't reach his eyes.

*Crap.* How could she tell for sure? She'd hate to shoot the wrong men but an idea came to her suddenly. "What do you smell?"

He blinked. "You're too high up to do that," he responded after a few seconds. "We're primate species."

Those were rare, she'd only met one, but she'd been able to tell what he'd been because he'd had feature anomalies consistent with an ape—a flattened nose and rounded eye sockets. Her suspicion grew that they lied to her. Was she willing to shoot them though, one hundred percent certain they lied? *Not yet.* She'd hate to be wrong since she'd only seen one primate species.

*I have a medical degree,* she reminded herself. *I'm supposed to be smart.* She thought for a second and then smiled. "What's today's password? New Species know about the code system in place and I want you to tell it to me," she bullshitted.

He paled slightly. "It's Noose."

*He's good.* She'd grant him that. He hadn't missed a beat in finding an answer to give her. She smiled. "Wrong answer."

"It was changed after you were run off the road," the other man stated quickly. "It's noose today. Justice changed the password because he was afraid it would be compromised if his man was forced to talk."

*Maybe they actually use code words.* That thought made her hesitate. She'd been guessing but it was reasonable that they'd have secret passwords or codes. They were learning from humans since they'd been freed. She decided it wasn't proof enough since it was a possibility. She needed more proof before she could be sure either way if they were full of crap or telling her the truth. It would be horrible if she shot a real New Species. Slade might not ever forgive her and she wouldn't ever recover from the guilt. She'd sworn to save their lives, not take them, when she'd taken the job at Homeland.

"If you are who you say you are then you'll know the name of the man Justice sent to escort me to where he wanted me to be. Tell me the name of the New Species, not the human escort."

The second man spoke. "His name is Slade."

She wavered for a second but then remembered how Slade had told her that Justice would probably have their names publicized to make it widely known they were missing in an attempt to get people to help find them. Slade's name might be in the press right along with hers. She dropped that line of questioning.

Trisha's finger tightened on the trigger. "What was the password for yesterday then?" She wanted to know how far they'd take it.

The men glanced at each other nervously. The younger one looked up. "Yesterday was my day off. I'm not sure but today it's noose. We're coming up to get you, Dr. Norbit. We have a team standing by about half a mile from here and we're going to take you back to Homeland. You've been rescued."

If there was a code system, the guy would know it, especially since he was a supposed member of a rescue team going after a New Species out of contact with his people. Since he didn't, she figured her bluff had worked.

"There is no password, asshole."

She saw both men glance at each other again, their alarm clear. One of them moved his hand and reached for something at his waist. "I'm getting my ID," he warned loudly. "We do use passwords at Homeland. All security guards do."

"So you're New Species security guards? And you're New Species? Is security guard your job title then?"

They both nodded. She couldn't believe how easily both men lied. Paul had told her New Species never called themselves security guards, instead preferring the title of officers. They hated the other term. She watched him as he removed something from behind him. She wondered if he'd pull out his wallet and try to bluff her by showing his driver's license. Instead he pulled out a gun.

Trisha panicked at the sight of it, jerked the handgun in his direction, and fired. Two bullets deafened her unprotected ears before he fired back. His bullet flew wide and struck the dirt above her, making it rain down over her back. The third bullet she fired hit him.

He screamed as he lost his hold, fell back, and tumbled down the hill. She turned the gun on the second man who struggled to pull out something from the back of his waistband, one-handed, while trying not to lose his grip on the rock he held onto. She saw black metal when his hand came into view. *Gun!*

Trisha fired at him and struck him with one shot, getting better at aiming. She saw a part of his face where his cheek bloomed red and he screamed out. He released the handhold he had and fell straight back. She heard a horrible crunching sound when he hit bottom.

Trisha inched forward to stare down below at both men who lay at the bottom. One of them had landed on his side unmoving with bright red liquid spreading on the ground near him. The other man, the first one who'd fallen, sprawled face up. He moved an arm and she heard him groan even from where she hovered. Blood covered his face and his shoulder area.

She watched him as he lay there moving his leg and then he reached for something inside his pocket. When he pulled out a walkie-talkie she realized he would radio in her location. More of those assholes would come if they hadn't already heard the gunshots. She had to stop him, knowing she couldn't hold off more of them if they converged on her location.

She crawled out more until her body partially hung over the edge. Fear gripped her from how far away the ground appeared to be below her. She could plummet to her death if she slipped from her wobbly perch and was unable to stop her tumble. She aimed and pulled the trigger, watching him jerk as the bullet tore through his chest. The radio clutched inside his palm dropped to the dirt below him. He stared wide-eyed up at her but she knew he had died when he didn't blink, didn't move, after a good minute passed.

Trisha fought the urge to be sick as she assessed both men, determined they were certainly dead and that she'd killed them. She pushed and wiggled her upper body back inside the small cave, still gripping the handgun painfully with her fingers. She stared at it and then dropped it as tears blinded her. The reality of what she'd done slammed home hard.

The shock she experienced left her feeling icy cold inside. When she'd become a doctor she'd sworn to save lives but she'd just taken two. *It was self-defense!* her mind screamed. *Self-defense. I had no choice. None.*

She forced a few calming breaths through her lips and remembered Bill. What he'd threatened to do to her and how he'd hit her wasn't something she'd ever forget. Those men were part of Bill's group and they would have done bad things to her too.

She remembered how all three of those men had only kept her alive to tend to their injured friend. She had no doubt the men she'd shot would have killed her just the way they'd killed Bart. She forced herself to breathe deeply, calmly, and finally regained some control of her shaky emotions. She wanted to cry but Slade's words came back to her from when they'd heard the gunshots after leaving Bart at the crash site.

"Survive first and then grieve," she whispered aloud.

Trisha wanted Slade with her so bad it became an ache that painfully wouldn't subside. She would be safe with him. She knew he'd hold her and say something to make her feel better, distract her from the anguish she suffered. She hoped he was on his way to her instead of more of those men.

She glanced at the handgun she'd dropped and pulled her emotions together. Slade would order her to survive and she'd promised him she would do anything, suffer anything, to stay alive until he could rescue her. He wouldn't want her feeling sorry for herself. He'd expect her to use her head.

# Chapter Ten

**ဆ**

"Calm down and think," Trisha muttered aloud. "Great, I'm going to be one of those people who talk to themselves all the time when this is all over."

She crawled to the backpack to reload the gun. There was a box full of bullets that Slade had salvaged from the camp. She crawled back to the opening on her stomach and gripped the binoculars to study the area in a grid pattern, searching for any movement. She stayed low. Both rifles were at her side and the handgun was placed inches from her hand along with the box of bullets in case she needed them.

Movement caught her attention to her right. She didn't know the distance but it wasn't too far. She spotted three men and then a fourth as they marched through the thick trees. They were dressed in camouflage green, similar in style to the men she'd just killed, and worse, they headed directly toward her.

Three of them had long guns in their arms or resting on their shoulders. One of them had holsters at his hips and on his chest to hold handguns. *Crap.* They were heavily armed. It scared Trisha badly. They weren't going to be happy when they found their dead friends.

She scanned the area, looking for Slade, but didn't spot him. Ten minutes later she spied more movement. She stared at the two advancing figures and hope soared. Neither man was Slade though. One of the men had reddish hair while the other one had jet-black but they were dressed in all black clothing and moved quickly.

Slade had told her that his people would come and she prayed they were New Species. They had to be Slade's men or

150

she was in deep, horrible crap and knew it. Trisha turned her binoculars back toward the area where the four men were.

They had made good progress since she found them a lot closer than they had been. She turned the binoculars back to the two swiftly moving males in all-black gear. It appeared they were headed right for the four hunters. She bit her lip as she tried to estimate if the two possible New Species would reach the four before they made it to where she hid. The chances were good.

The four men coming her way were definitely going to be able to find her. The two dead bodies sprawled on the ground below her were a good indication of where she hid. She softly cursed and prayed that the New Species would reach her first.

Trisha settled flat, hugged the ground tighter, and shifted her binoculars to watch the progress of both oncoming groups. She prayed the two New Species—if they were New Species— were aware of the four-man hunting party and prayed they'd pick up the scent of those men. They would unless they were upwind.

She really wished that thought hadn't come to her. If those two men were New Species trying to save her and Slade, the last thing she wanted was to watch them be surprised by the hunting party. They didn't appear as well armed as their opponents.

The tension inside Trisha rose so high her hands hurt from gripping the binoculars while she watched them draw closer. They weren't moving nearly as fast as the two who she gradually became certain were New Species. She could now make out their shoulder-length hair and their uniforms seemed right, although they were too far away still to make out the NSO patches if they sported them over their chests.

The four hunters had nearly reached the dead men below Trisha and she knew she'd lose sight of them soon. She wasn't about to inch out farther where she could look straight down. They'd be able to glance up and find her too easily. She also didn't want to give them a target to shoot at or give away her exact location.

The two New Species slowed, not jogging anymore. They stalked slowly toward the hunters, obviously aware of their presence by their cautious behavior. Relief swamped Trisha as she watched the New Species duo make hand signals to each other before they separated. One of them sneaked up behind the hunters while the other one moved to attack from the side.

Voices started to carry up to Trisha until she knew without looking they were scary close. She continued to use the binoculars, hoping she was low enough on the cave floor to make a smaller and harder-to-see target with her chin on the sleeping bag. The four hunters were nearly out of her lens range.

"I know those shots came from this direction," a man with an accent stated firmly.

"Buck and Joe Billy said they were going to climb to high ground to take a look-see." The deeper voice had the same Southern accent. "Do you think they killed that two-legged animal?"

"I don't know," a new voice without an accent answered. "But they aren't answering their radio. Look sharp, guys. Those animals have minds the way we do and sure aren't as easy as shooting elk. Wild animals don't talk back or carry weapons the way we do."

"Fucking James," another man without an accent laughed. "Elk? Come on. Let's compare them to something at least similar. Maybe they are closer to apes. Those think and walk on two feet, don't they? For all we know, Joe Billy and Buck are screwing with us. Remember that time last year when they ambushed us just for the hell of it to see if one of us would piss our pants? I'll bet you twenty bucks they will spring out at us any second."

"You're on," a man without an accent said and laughed.

Trisha moved her binoculars from the four men to where she'd last spotted the two New Species but couldn't find either of them. She continued to scan until she finally spotted one but was shocked at where she located him.

He jumped from one branch high inside a tree to another branch in the one next to it. The jet-black haired New Species amazed her with his sense of balance and grace. He stopped practically on top of the four hunters who didn't even realize he watched them from above.

Trisha's heart raced while she kept her binoculars glued to the black-haired New Species as he jumped again to land in the top branches of the tree directly over the moving hunters. He gripped the trunk and seemed to be studying the men below him. He withdrew a handgun from the holster strapped against his chest. Every fiber of her body told her he would attack.

The black-haired Species suddenly dropped to a lower branch. It was the most graceful thing that Trisha had ever seen. He obviously had done it very quietly because the men below him never glanced up. He stepped down to another lower branch, walking it as though it were a balance beam, and moved with the men. He suddenly jumped out of the tree and landed hard on two of the hunters below him.

Trisha gasped but kept her binoculars trained on the three fallen men. She saw movement as the two other hunters spun to look at what had happened behind them. She saw a flash of black and the redheaded New Species seemed to appear out of nowhere as he rushed the two men from behind.

He leaped, tackling them as if he were a football player taking down two rival players. She was close enough to clearly hear the grunts of pain. In seconds the four hunters on the ground lay motionless and the two New Species stood over them silently.

Trisha got a really good look at both men and was assured they were definitely Slade's men. They had the distinct facial anomalies that most of the New Species had. The black-haired Species had a smaller nose than most and his features were telling. She suddenly had a feeling that he had to be part primate. The redhead had cat eyes similar to Justice North, indicating he had to be feline.

The two men withdrew something from the lower pockets of their pants that resembled thick plastic ties and secured the downed men's hands behind their backs. When they'd handcuffed all four of their prisoners, they yanked their ankles up and bound them with more white ties until they had them hogtied. The black-haired Species give a thumbs-up sign to his redheaded companion.

One of them laughed and Trisha moved. Her body was sluggish because she'd lain in the same position for too long but she was able to carefully rise to her feet. She leaned out a little, staring down at the men who were about sixty feet from the area where the two dead men lay.

"Hello," she called out.

They didn't jump or seem surprised when they turned their heads to gaze up at her. She let that sink in. *Did they already know where I was?* She decided they probably had. One of them, the redhead, nodded at her.

"We'll get to you after we dispose of the dead bodies. Your kills?" He jerked his head toward the two men who lay far below her. "Two of them, right? I smell two different scents."

Shocked, Trisha just gaped at him. There was no way they could have seen the two dead bodies from where they stood. They would have had to walk around a few more trees and a huge boulder. She finally nodded.

The black-haired Species pushed his hair away from his face as he peered up at Trisha. "Where is Slade? We caught his scent but it's faded as though he's been gone for hours. Why did he leave you, Dr. Norbit?"

"He said there were too many of them." She paused. "He wanted to cut down their numbers. He seemed certain if he started hunting them that some of them would get spooked enough to leave but he should have been back by now. He said if I fired the guns he'd hear and come running."

The redhead nodded. "That is a good plan. It accounts for why we found two empty camps with the scent of blood but no men."

*Two camps?* She wondered if they'd found the one where she'd been held or the one Slade had attacked the night before. She didn't really want to know. She just worried about Slade. He's promised to come if she needed help and he had to have heard the gunshots but he hadn't arrived yet. Two of his men had to rescue her instead. *Is he hurt? Dead? Maybe he is still on his way.*

"Is there any way you can tell if Slade is close?" Trisha silently hoped they could.

The redhead lifted his head and sniffed. He shook his head. "I don't scent him and if he comes, it's from afar. We will get you down from there when we are done. Sit and stay put. You're safe now, Dr. Norbit. Our people will send a helicopter here to fly you to safety and we will find Slade if he does not return within a reasonable time. We have teams spread out for miles searching for you both. I would track his scent but I'd rather wait until you are secured on the helicopter. You were our primary concern since Slade can take care of himself."

Trisha was speechless over being told she was the New Species' primary concern. She worked for them, sure, but Slade was one of their own. She was glad the man below her had so much confidence in Slade's ability to take care of himself though. He must be really good at survival. Slade had told her that he'd trained with most of these men and they had to know him really well.

The black-haired Species leaned down and pulled something from his bottom pocket. Their pants seemed to have a lot of them. Trisha crouched down but watched what he did. It looked as though he had some kind of bulky cell phone he spoke into. She saw his lips move but didn't hear his words.

She quickly realized he spoke into a satellite phone. She'd seen a few of them a time or two. He hung up and replaced the phone into his lower pocket.

Trisha moved back away from the edge, not wanting to watch them remove the bodies from below. She wondered what they would do with them but didn't ask. She sat on the sleeping bag and hugged her arms to wait.

"Where are you, Slade?"

The silence squeezed at her heart at not knowing if he was okay or if he'd never come back to her. They had some things to discuss if both of them came out of this alive. Did what had happened between them mean anything or was it just one of those trauma-induced moments? She uttered a curse word. What if he had only slept with her and treated her the way he had because of the situation they were in? She pushed those thoughts away. It was too painful.

\* \* \* \* \*

Slade sniffed the air, could scent his own kind, and pure rage gripped him. They'd prevent him from killing all the humans who meant to do harm. The distant sounds of gunfire had come from Trisha's direction. His heart raced as he jumped over a fallen log, used it to kick off, and leaped over a small ravine. He landed hard, crouched, and then rose up.

"Easy," a male called out. "Stop running."

Slade snarled, his head jerked up, and he spotted a familiar face from his perch on a tree limb twenty feet in the air. "She's in danger."

"No, she's not. Smiley and Flame have her. They spotted her perch and are intercepting the males in her vicinity. She's well taken care of." The guy jumped, landed on a pile of dead leaves, and straightened. "You can't be seen by humans right now."

"I must go to her, Ascension."

"She's safe. We have her, my friend." The other male's gaze swept down Slade's body before he met his eyes. "You're soaked in blood and gore. You'll terrify her if she sees you this way. It's a pretty horrific sight even for me. How many did you kill?"

"Many." Slade's body began to relax. Trisha would be safe if Flame and Smiley were near. Both males were very good. "She's safe? You're sure?"

"You found her a secure location. No human is going to reach her before our males do. She is safe. Calm. May I approach? You're injured and feral at the moment. You have that caged look we know so well."

Slade crouched, breathed heavily, and tried to catch his breath. "I won't attack."

"I'm glad to hear it. I wasn't sure how far you'd gone or if you'd lost it." Ascension stepped closer, slowly, and crouched in front of him until only feet separated them.

"I'm fine." Slade stared into the other man's eyes.

"Good. We knew you'd survive but weren't sure of your state of mind if you had to kill. We found some of the kill zones. Why didn't you just stay with the doctor?"

"They were closing in on us, there were too many, and one group of them found her the first time I left her alone. She has no survival skills and allowed them to walk right upon her. I had to turn the tables to make sure no more could harm her."

Ascension watched him silently, frowning. "I smell her on you. It's hard to pick up over the stench of blood and death but it's there."

A soft growl rumbled from Slade. "And?"

Ascension reached over and clasped his shoulder. "She's human, soft, and a doctor. They take oaths to save lives. I don't want to see you harmed."

"I need to go to her." Slade tried to straighten but the other male's firm grasp on him only tightened.

"Listen to me."

"What?"

"You're feral right now. Your mind is calmer than we feared but you're walking death. You don't have a mirror. Your features and eyes have the wild look we tend to get when it happens. She can't see you this way. You'd only terrify her. I'm under orders to find you and bring you back to Homeland. Allow me to take you there."

Slade growled. "No. I'm not done here. There are more of them."

"Orders are—"

"They attacked her, one of them beat her and tried to rape her. She could have died when they forced the SUV off the road. They declared war on us and I want it finished. Any that get away could attack again at a later date."

The hand eased and released. "I can't bring you in if I haven't found you. I understand but you must stay away from her until you regain your ability to suppress your rage. At least wash before you rejoin us. There's a stream to the east. I can smell her on you and they will too. They may fear you forced her into sexual submission in your current condition. I don't believe that. I know you too well and I've seen you watching her while we're on duty. You must have purposely rubbed her scent on you to keep it."

Slade remembered biting Trisha and wiping her blood behind his neck. He hadn't meant to do it at the time but he acknowledged that he hadn't rectified it either. Having her scent had kept him sane when he'd killed to protect her.

"Finish what you started if you believe they will be a continued threat to your female. I never saw you and this conversation never took place. Just swear you'll wait twenty-four hours before you approach her after you're ready to be found. There are three dozen of us inside the woods. We're doing a grid search for the humans. We brought along five primates so watch the trees. I knew you wouldn't expect it and I waited from above to find you."

"Smart."

Ascension grinned. "I know you, my friend. We've been together too long since we were freed." All emotion wiped from his features. "And don't forget to find that stream. I'd do it now and then continue your hunt. Just wash after you find them so you aren't covered in their blood when you come in."

"I won't forget. You swear she's safe?"

"My word."

It was good enough for Slade. "I want to kill them all for risking her life."

"That causes me to feel fear. Find the humanity inside you. I'll say I searched this area without result." He stood. "Go, and watch the trees from now on. I'm not the only one who will think to hide there to seek you out."

Slade rose and took off into the thicker forest, keeping his attention up as well as on his surroundings. Primates kept to the treetops when possible, their scents harder to catch, and he didn't want to be found until he cut down some of the numbers of the humans who had tried to harm his Trisha.

Regret gripped him as he replayed Ascension's words. Trisha was human, she was emotionally soft, and as a doctor, she might hate him for the lives he'd taken. Later he'd think about that, but for now, he had threats to take care of.

# Chapter Eleven

ജ

"I'm coming up, Dr. Norbit," one of the men called out about an hour later.

Trisha stood and walked to the edge. The first thing she noticed was that the two dead bodies were gone and she couldn't even spot blood on the ground. It looked as though someone had dumped dirt over the stained areas to completely conceal the deaths.

Trisha watched the black-haired Species climb up toward her easily without any trouble managing the steep terrain. She almost envied his agility and speed as he approached her. Slade had to shove and push her to get her to the top. He came up it as easily as a leisurely stroll on a flat surface.

He had to be about six feet tall with wide shoulders. Up close Trisha was sure the man was part primate. He was really cute with his softer-than-normal features. New Species were usually handsome in a tough-guy, attractive way. He had the muscular, large frame of a New Species though when he stood before her. His features were nearly adorable with his rounded, pretty almond-colored eyes and his animated features — primate cute.

"I'm Smiley. Hello, Dr. Norbit," he crooned softly as he crouched at the entrance, balancing on the balls of his feet. He was too tall to stand inside the hole. He smiled at her. "The helicopter should arrive here really soon. They have been pretty busy today transporting all the humans we caught. We tried not to kill any of them but..." He shrugged. "Some of them were just too stupid to live. How are you doing?"

"I'm fine. Is there any word yet on Slade?"

He slowly shook his head. "I'm sorry but there is not. He is one of our best and there's no need to worry about him. He can take care of himself in any extreme situation." His gaze raked up and down Trisha but there wasn't anything sexual in the way he studied her at length.

"Who beat you?"

"I was captured yesterday morning but Slade rescued me. Unfortunately before he did, this happened." She pointed to her still-throbbing cheek and her swollen, busted lip. Slade kissing her crossed her mind in a flash but she pushed that memory back. "I'm fine. A few cuts, some bruising and some pulled muscles are the worst of it besides what you see on my face."

"Slade allowed you to be caught?" He looked highly amused as he laughed. "I'm shocked."

"He didn't let me. He got cut off from me while he left to look for a place to stash me like this hole I'm in." Trisha frowned. "Slade has saved my ass in the biggest ways that you can imagine. Please don't laugh about this. He killed men to save me."

His smile faded instantly. "I apologize. There is nothing amusing about this. Let me help you down and we'll wait for the helicopter. You will be flown to a hospital to be checked over and afterward, returned home. Justice was very adamant about securing you and getting you medical treatment before we return to Homeland. He's waiting there to talk to you."

Trisha glanced around the small area but didn't see anything that she should take with her. Her attention landed on the guns. "Should we take those? I'd hate for kids to climb up here in the future and find them. They are all loaded."

"We'll take care of all that." He turned, almost brushing his head on the dirt roof. "I'm going to help you down. Do you need me to carry you on my back? I'm a very good climber and I promise I won't allow you to fall."

"I think I can manage if you just help me down. Slade had to catch me a few times. I'm afraid I'm not as coordinated as you guys are."

He nodded, smiling. Trisha had a good idea why he was named Smiley. He seemed to do it easily and often. "It's a gift we have."

Trisha slowly walked toward him and studied the ground below when she reached the edge. She wasn't big on heights and it was a long way to fall. Smiley moved, climbed out first, and looked up at her.

"Just turn around and start down. I'll be right here below you. I'll catch you if you fall." He winked. "I'm strong. I promise not to drop you."

She was scared but she turned and tried not to look at the ground below. Climbing down was worse than going up had been. She slipped twice but Smiley's hands always gripped her, kept her in place, and finally they reached the bottom. Trisha had the urge to kiss the ground but resisted to prevent her rescuers from believing she'd lost her mind.

The redhead glanced at Trisha and nodded. She saw his nostrils flare and he frowned. He moved closer to her, sniffed again, and looked grim.

"I'm Flame. What happened to you?"

Trisha stared back at him, unsure exactly what he meant. He was about six-foot-three, a good foot taller than her, and obviously New Species with his wide-shouldered, muscular body. He looked as though he could easily kick some serious ass. He was more frightening to look at with his pronounced cheek bones and the sharp teeth his lips barely contained.

"I was captured and beaten. I was also in an SUV that rolled down the side of a mountain and we hit a few trees along the way. It's been a rough few days for my body."

Flame sniffed again. "You have Slade's scent on you but I also smell two human males. You smell of blood, fear, and sex." He looked even more dangerous. "You were raped by the humans?"

Her mouth dropped open but then Trisha closed it. "Slade saved me."

She was a little freaked out. She knew their sense of smell was amazing but it was downright eerie that the man could pick that much up just by sniffing at her. It left her really uncomfortable to know they had heightened senses to that degree.

"I'll track the two humans down and kill them." Flame blinked. "I swear this to you. They won't live for what they have done."

Trisha's heart pounded. "They're dead. Slade took care of that."

A quick jerk of his head and Flame turned away. "Good. I'm going to go babysit the four stooges we captured, Smiley. Don't allow her out of your sight."

"I won't." Smiley turned to Trisha and examined her face. "Why don't you sit down? The helicopter will be here soon."

Trisha sat. She was already coated in a layer of dirt and didn't care if she got more of it on her. "Where will it land?"

He hesitated. "It won't. It will hover. We'll hook you up and they will lift you out. The trees in this area are too dense for a landing and we don't want to risk hiking you out. You've already suffered enough trauma without that. It will be a piece of cake."

"Great." Dread gripped Trisha. "Did I mention I'm afraid of heights?"

Smiley grinned. "It's a good way to face your fear."

*Just great.* Soon enough she heard a helicopter in the distance that grew louder as it approached. Smiley kept silent as he regarded her, something he'd been doing the entire time she'd sat there. He finally turned his head and glanced at the sky.

"They are here. It will be loud. They will drop down a harness and I will hook you up. It will lift you and someone inside will pull you in to belt you into a seat. You will be flown to a hospital and two of our men will be with you until you reach home. You now know what to expect."

"Thank you for everything. Could you please tell Flame that I said 'thank you' too?"

He nodded. "You are welcome from both of us. We are glad you are alive."

"Could you tell Slade to contact me as soon as he's found? I'm worried about him and I won't stop until I know he's safe."

"I can do that." Smiley's gaze returned to the sky as he turned his back on Trisha. "Here we go. Cover your ears. Those things are very loud. They give me a headache but some things can't be avoided."

Trisha stood when the helicopter hovered above the treetops at just enough distance to avoid hitting anything. The wind kicked up debris on the ground that swirled around her until it forced her to cover her eyes. She completely understood when Smiley swore—a loud, foul word. She really wasn't looking forward to the next few minutes.

Someone touched her arm. Smiley gripped her and moved her to where a harness dangled nearby. He gently pushed her toward it and indicated for her to step into the openings of the thing. He lifted it up her legs and two belts were pulled over her shoulders and the last belt snapped closed around her waist. Smiley winked before he stepped back. Trisha gripped the harness in a death grip when Smiley gave the helicopter a hand signal. The harnesses tightened as it lifted Trisha off her feet.

She closed her eyes tightly and tried not to panic when the wind swung her around. She didn't open them until someone grabbed her around her waist. She stared below and saw Smiley had covered his face with his own arm, not looking up. Dirt and dust swirled furiously near the ground from the massive helicopter blades. The person holding her waist hauled her inside the doors until she couldn't see below anymore.

The two men in the back of the helicopter were New Species. They were canines and she'd seen both of them at Homeland. Brass appeared grim and she couldn't remember the other one's name. They wrestled her out of the harness, slammed the helicopter door closed, and secured her onto one of the seats on the bench. Brass handed her a set of noise-cancelling earmuffs and pointed to his headset to show her how to wear it.

The loud noise of the helicopter muted. She nodded at Brass gratefully, thinking that his name didn't fit him. He had brown hair, was huge with wide shoulders, about six-foot-three, and had really dark eyes. The other man was a brunette with dark eyes. He was nearly a twin, body-wise, to Brass. Brass took a seat next to her and the other man seated himself on the bench across from them.

The ride wasn't long until the helicopter touched down on a helipad at a hospital. Medical staff rushed out with a gurney and she had an instant flashback to the night Slade had been airlifted into her life. She was in much better shape though than he'd been.

She let them strap her to a gurney without an argument since she was more than aware of hospital policies. She knew doctors made the worst patients, having treated a few, and tried to forget she was one when the staff rushed her into an exam room. Brass and the other man followed, keeping close.

The doctor on call was in his late thirties, attractive, and appeared, with his golden tan, to have spent a lot of time on a golf course. He smiled at Trisha.

"I'm Dr. Evan Tauras. What's your name?"

"I'm Dr. Trisha Norbit." She saw him flinch and grinned. "I swear I'll be good. I was in a roll-over SUV accident a few days ago, minus a seat belt. It's a long story. I know I should have been wearing one and I was right up until a minute before the crash. I rolled inside the SUV but I wasn't ejected. Then I was physically assaulted yesterday by a jerk who hit me in the face a few times. I have no back or neck pain. I'm not showing any signs of internal injuries." She paused. "I have no medical allergies and no outstanding medical history except I had my tonsils out when I was ten. I'm not on any medications, don't smoke, drink, or take drugs. I'll shut up now and let you do your job."

The doctor nodded. "Thanks. You're making this easy, actually. Have you exhibited any symptoms of a concussion?"

"Somewhat. It's mild if I have one. I was dizzy after the crash and again after getting my bell rung yesterday when I was hit in the face twice. No blurry vision and no nausea though."

"Did they catch the guy who did that to your face?" The doctor examined her head.

"You could say that. He's dead."

The doctor studied her for a second and nodded. "You're the woman who was on the news. I'm glad you were found."

He moved and opened his mouth at Trisha. She opened hers to mimic him knowing what he wanted her to do. He examined her for oral injures, then her face, feeling the bruised area. Trisha flinched a little but held still. The doctor moved lower as he and a nurse visually examined Trisha. She was grateful they didn't strip her naked. Brass and the other man stood inside the doors to the side of the exam room watching every move made since they guarded her.

The doctor gawked openly at the two Species a few times, looking slightly annoyed and alarmed. Trisha understood the reasons and wanted to assure him things were fine.

"An attempt was made on my life and they have to be here. I'm sorry if it bothers you to have an audience."

Dr. Evan Tauras nodded. "No problem. They are just big." His voice lowered to a whisper. "I've never seen them in person but they look smaller on the news. They are very physically fit."

Trisha whispered back. "Yes. I know. They also have exceptional hearing. Whisper 'hi' to them."

The doctor jerked his head to stare at both men. Brass winked at him and flexed his muscles. The other New Species looked grim but waved. Trisha had to fight a laugh as the doctor's face blushed slightly before he turned his attention to his nurse to rattle off a list of tests to run. He wanted X-rays. She didn't think she needed them but she didn't protest. It was his exam room, his call, and she didn't want to be a pain in the ass.

\* \* \* \* \*

Two hours later they released her with some anti-inflammatory medication for her knee, some pain pills for her face, and some antibiotics because she had a few open cuts. She'd considered asking for a morning-after pill but wasn't worried about what had happened between her and Slade. Without medical help she was pretty certain she couldn't get pregnant though they hadn't used protection. There hadn't been a liquor store nearby to buy condoms and since Trisha wasn't sexually active she wasn't on anything.

Brass and Harley—that was the name of the other NSO officer—escorted her to the pharmacy to fill her prescriptions. The helicopter picked them up five minutes later.

No one had heard from or found Slade. Trisha dozed off when the pain medication overwhelmed her. An hour later they touched down at the New Species Homeland and when Brass lifted her into his arms to carry her off the helicopter she awoke.

"You're safe. Just relax."

She didn't ask to be put down. He seemed to effortlessly carry her the way Slade had. They were super strong. "Thank you."

Justice North waited at a Jeep nearby. He darted a look at Trisha and actually flinched. Brass refused to put her down until he sat her in the passenger seat of Justice's open Jeep. He and Harley climbed into the back and Justice drove toward her home.

"I can't begin to apologize enough for all that has transpired, Trisha. This was purely an attack against New Species and you were involved by association."

"It's not your fault. You aren't the idiots who ran us off the road or decided it sounded fun to try to hunt us as though we were deer. Thank you for the helicopter and for having Brass and Harley take such good care of me. Is there any word on Slade yet?"

Justice shook his head. "Our teams are still out there and they have rounded up eight more of those assho— Men who were out there looking for you. We are handing them over to the local authorities as soon as we find them. We were thrilled to get authorization to send our own teams into the area."

Brass snorted. "They were very happy to allow us go in instead of them."

Justice nodded. "There was that. We were more equipped to search a large area of woods than they were and with a much smaller manpower force."

"They didn't want those crazy fanatics firing at their asses," Harley ground out. "They gave us jurisdiction to go in and clean up the mess. We won't get any credit for it, they'll take that, but the local police force wasn't in danger."

Justice glanced at Trisha and frowned deeply as he sniffed. He didn't say a word but Trisha noticed when he did again. He suddenly looked very angry when he parked the Jeep in her driveway. She saw a Homeland security guard standing on her porch but he wasn't New Species.

"Sit right there," Justice ordered her. "I sent him ahead of us because I knew your keys were lost to you after the wreck. We recovered your purse and keys. We returned what could be salvaged to your home. Your clothes that weren't torn or damaged have been cleaned. What wasn't salvageable will be replaced with our funds." Justice rounded the Jeep and lifted a surprised Trisha into his arms and walked to the front door. "I was given a full briefing of the injuries you sustained. The doctor told you to stay off your feet for at least two days."

The security guard nodded at Trisha while he opened the front door. Justice walked into the house and gently placed Trisha on the couch. He hesitated and turned to study Brass and Harley. The security guard had also stepped into the house.

"Could you please give us a few minutes? I'd like to talk to Trisha alone. She's been through enough without the added trauma of having to tell me what happened with an audience of males."

The three men left quietly and the door closed firmly behind them. Justice moved to the loveseat where he sat down. He looked tense. His cat-like eyes met Trisha's.

"I smell fear, dirt, blood, and sex on you. There was no mention in the briefing from the doctor that you were sexually assaulted. Did one of those fanatics abuse you? I was told your face injures are a result of one of those assho—" He cleared his throat. "Fanatics."

"You can call them assholes. I do." She met Justice's gaze without looking away. "I wasn't raped but it was close. I don't really want to talk about the specific details but Slade got there in time. He stopped the guy before he could really hurt me." She paused. "He had to kill him."

"You had sex with someone before you left here? I wasn't aware you were seeing anyone."

Trisha frowned. "My sex life is none of your business, Mr. North."

"I meant no offense. I'm going about this wrong. Excuse my poor wording but I'm trying to figure out if you are lying about the rape. You work and you don't leave Homeland. I am aware of everyone's comings and goings inside these walls. You had sex with someone because I am getting scents off you. Of course I smell Slade and there are two human males. You also now carry both Brass' and my scent as well but they are faint because we both carried you. I know Smiley touched you to help you down the side of a hill."

"How do you distinguish between human and New Species so well?"

He watched her closely. "New Species... It's hard to explain. I just can tell the difference. One male's scent is familiar. I just want to know the truth if you were sexually abused."

"I wasn't. The familiar scent you might be picking up is probably the driver of the SUV, Bart. I don't know his last name. He was injured in the roll over and I touched him quite a bit to check him for injures. He's dead, right? Slade and I heard three gunshots after Bart refused to leave the scene where we crashed. He thought those men wouldn't hurt him because he was human. We tried to tell him they would kill him but he refused to listen to us. We had no choice but to leave him behind."

"He's dead." Justice nodded. "He was shot in the groin, stomach, and head after being tied up and tortured. We assume they tried to gain information from him on where you and Slade had gone. His body was located next to the destroyed SUV. The coroner stated he was killed soon after the crash."

# Chapter Twelve

**ဢ**

Trisha had suspected Bart would die, had been sure of that when they'd heard the gunshots, but hearing the words of what had been done to him leveled her inside. His face flashed through her memory, how afraid he'd been, and he'd just been a boy. One with a mother who worried enough about him to want him to go to a vet to get vaccines against animal diseases.

"Jesus," Trisha gasped. "The groin?"

Justice hesitated. "What they did was vicious and cruel. It's one thing to kill a man in cold blood but another to castrate him before death."

Her stomach roiled just a little. "Castrate?"

"They used a sawed-off double barrel shotgun at close range. We were told by the coroner that they must have put it right against his groin before they pulled the trigger. Those bastards are the animals and yet they have a problem with us. Species would never be that inhuman."

Trisha stumbled to her feet. "I need a shower. I know you have questions but I'm tired, hungry, and dirty." She bit her lip and flinched, forgetting how sore it was. She met Justice's gaze as he stood. "I'll probably have a good cry too. I wasn't raped, I swear. Slade stopped my attacker before he could. I am grateful that you care about my well-being but my sex life is personal. I do have a favor to ask though."

"Anything."

"When you hear word about Slade, I don't care what time it is, please have someone call to let me know. He saved my life out there over and over again. I don't think I'll rest well until I know what happened to him."

"I am going to have Brass stay here. I will have food brought to you and it will be waiting after your shower. I swear that when I know something, I will call Brass and have him relay the information to you. We'll talk about what happened tomorrow."

"Brass is staying here?"

Justice nodded. "Yes. It's just a precaution. It seems that some deaths have occurred with the assholes. Some of their associates are pretty pissed they died instead of doing all the killing. You will have around-the-clock protection until we feel there is no longer a threat. You are familiar with Brass and it's been pretty traumatic for you. He'll take the first shift. I want him inside your house. He can sit on the couch if that's acceptable. He'll be here to accept the food deliveries and relay any information I get to you."

"But we're at Homeland and it's safe here. Those jerks can't get through the gates to reach my house. I'm sure—"

"Someone told them of our movements," Justice cut her off. "They knew the route we planned for your SUV, which tells us they have inside information. Only our human security teams knew where we were going, what time, and how we were getting there. You will have round-the-clock New Species officers to protect you until I am assured of your safety and that won't be until whoever is responsible is found." He took a deep breath. "I have to go but food will arrive shortly. Eat and rest."

She was stunned that someone working at Homeland had betrayed the New Species but she believed Justice and his grim expression. "You don't have to send me food. I can fix a sandwich."

"No. You need a nice hot, home-cooked meal. I'll call it in right now. I'll have them send you a few dishes. I'll see you in the morning. Just call me when you are up and about."

"Thank you. Please don't forget to contact me about Slade."

"I swear I won't. As soon as I know, you will." He left the front door wide open and Trisha heard him softly talking to the men outside.

Trisha slowly walked into her bedroom and grabbed oversized comfortable sweats and a baggy T-shirt. She walked into her bathroom. She got a load of herself in the mirror and wanted to burst into tears. She looked like something a cat had dragged around a backyard before it threw it away to find something else to tear up.

She had bruising from ear to lower jaw that extended inches along her face. Her lower lip was swollen badly on one side where the skin had split. It was red and puffy. Her long blonde hair had matted and tangled hopelessly. On top of it all, dirt covered her in a fine layer.

The clothes she wore were just as bad. She stripped and flinched more over the painful bruises on her wrists where she'd been tied to the tree. She had more of them on her back, hip and shoulder blade from the SUV roll over and then spotted another large bruise on her thigh from the accident. She knew she must appear hellish.

Trisha moved under the water spray and just stood there for a long time then she washed her injured skin very carefully. It hurt despite the pain pills. The tears began to flow hard until she sat down on the floor of her shower and covered her face with her hands. She knew her life had changed forever. Two men were dead and she'd taken their lives. How could she ever go back to being the person she once was? She didn't see one single way.

A light tapping on her door finally made Trisha stop crying. "I'll be out in a minute."

"Do you need help?" She recognized Brass' voice. "I'm safe, Dr. Norbit." He paused. "I'm coming in."

*Crap.* She tried to get to her feet but her body refused to respond. She had the shower doors to hide her body but they were frosted glass. She could make out Brass' shape inside her bathroom when he moved toward her.

"Dr. Norbit?"

"I sat down and now I'm kind of stuck," she admitted. She hated being this weak and in so much pain. "I'll eventually get up when I'm feeling better. Could you just toss me a towel?" She shut off the water faucets next to her to kill the shower. "Please?"

A large bath towel dropped over the top of the shower doors. Trisha caught it and used it to cover up as much as she could. Two seconds later Brass stunned her when he opened her shower door.

"I won't look at you as though you are a woman. Allow me help you, Dr. Norbit. I would never harm you in any way." He bent, reaching for her. His hands carefully gripped her ribs and lifted her gently to her feet. "Let's get you into bed. The food arrived and I'll also get you some more pain medication."

It humiliated her slightly knowing she needed the help. She didn't struggle as the large man guided her to step out of the tub. His arm kept her on her feet and she needed it. She clutched the towel around the front of her but there was no helping her back being totally bare. Trisha knew her face must be flaming pink. Brass suddenly gripped her towel and pulled it from her grasp.

Trisha's mouth hung open. Her focus flew to the man holding her towel. He kept his gaze locked with hers. He released her arm and then opened the towel to wrap it around her body securely before he reached for her again. He just scooped her up into his strong arms and gently placed her on the counter. Brass turned, grabbed another towel, and without a word went to work on her dripping hair.

"Thank you."

Brass nodded. "You've been very strong. For someone so little, you have my full respect, Dr. Norbit. You have been very tough but now it is time for you to allow someone to take care of you."

"Please call me Trisha."

He flashed a smile. "I'm going to pick you up again now that your hair won't soak your bed and put you on it. I see you have pajamas but I've suffered enough injures to warn you from past experiences that you are better off without anything on while you heal. Up you go."

He dropped the towel from her hair into the sink and lifted her up into his arms. Brass gently carried her out of the bathroom and to her bed where someone had already lowered the blankets. Brass eased her down onto the mattress and removed his arms from around her. He held out his hand and closed his eyes.

"I'll take the wet towel into the bathroom to hang while you cover up."

Trisha handed the towel over and pulled up the blankets to her chest. She watched Brass return to her bathroom where he stayed for a few minutes cleaning it. Then he walked out, flipped off the light behind him, and gave her a nod before he disappeared out of her room. He immediately returned, pushing a food cart that had three shelves with multiple covered dishes. Trisha gawked at the sight.

"That can't all be for me."

He shrugged. "Justice didn't know what you wanted to eat so he ordered six dishes to be prepared. The Council has its own personal chef. Justice placed a phone call for food to be prepared when he knew you would be arriving. There are also desserts. Again, Justice didn't know what you would eat so he had them send a little of a lot."

Brass removed a large tray. He placed it over Trisha's lap and smiled. "I'll open up the dishes to show you what you have to choose from."

"You will help me eat all this, right?"

Brass chuckled. "I was hoping you would ask. I'm starving."

Trisha's stomach rumbled loudly. Her face blushed warmly when Brass chuckled again. He'd obviously heard it. He started removing the covers while he listed the food that had been prepared. He didn't touch the desserts.

"I'll take the prime rib and the tri-tip dinners. Is that all right?"

He grinned. "That's fine. I'm grateful you didn't want the ribs. I saw those and my mouth began to water. You are hungry, aren't you?"

"I'm starving."

Brass set both dishes on the tray. He left the room and returned minutes later with a few sodas. Trisha took a cherry-flavored one. She kept three kinds in her fridge. Brass hesitated.

"I'll go into the living room and eat. Call out if you need anything." He lifted the pork-rib dish.

"You can sit there." She pointed to the chair next to her bed. The nightstand was cleared on that side so he'd have a table to eat on. "I was going to turn on the TV. I'm sorry there isn't one in the living room. I planned to buy a few things for the house but I haven't gotten around to it yet. You could stay in here to watch TV and I'll even give you the remote if you promise no history stuff or sports."

He laughed. "You pick the channel." Brass sat down and put his plate on the table. He opened up one of the sodas. "Thanks. What are you planning on changing? It's a nice house."

"I hate this bed and I want to turn the spare bedroom into an office." She motioned toward the corner where she had a desk set up. "I don't want my office in my bedroom. I need to relax in here and every time I glance at it, all I think about is work."

Brass turned his gaze to her. "What's wrong with the bed? I enjoy a big four-poster and that one looks solid."

"It's too big. I feel as though I'm five years old every time I climb into it and I do have to climb." She glanced at the floor. "See that stepstool?" She shrugged.

Brass darted a look down and started to chuckle. He tried to stop but he looked too amused to hide it. "You are short, in the bed's defense. You're a few inches shorter than average for a woman."

"Yeah, I know." She cut her prime rib and took a bite. She moaned. "So good."

Brass choked on his soda. Trisha turned her head to find him staring at her and he thumped his chest.

"Are you all right?"

"Fine." He nodded. "I take it from that sound you made that you're enjoying it and the Council chef is worth the money they pay him?"

"He's worth every penny." She cut into the tri-tip and took a bite. She moaned again as she smiled. "Perfect. Delicious. Almost melts inside my mouth."

Brass stared at her.

"Do you want to try some? They gave me large portions."

"No thank you. It's all yours. I love the ribs. I might hit up that roast-beef plate though after I eat this if you don't want it. We tend to eat a lot."

"Help yourself. I'll never finish all this."

They ate. Trisha found an action movie they both agreed on. Brass managed to eat three dishes and found room for dessert. He gave her two pain pills. Sometime during the movie she drifted off to sleep.

\* \* \* \* \*

"Trisha?"

She woke feeling fuzzy. She stared up at Brass, seeing his face about a foot over hers in the dim but not totally dark room. She blinked up at him, letting memory return. He was staying inside her house to guard her. He smiled at her.

"Those drugs really hit you hard. I've been trying to wake you for a few minutes. I just got word on Slade."

Those words shoved all lingering sleep away and she tried to sit up. Brass suddenly shoved her down. His hands gently gripped her shoulders and he grinned. "Watch your blankets, Trisha. You almost flashed your breasts." His hands released her.

*Crap.* She'd forgotten she wasn't wearing clothes. She gripped the blankets to keep them in place. "Sorry. Is he all right?"

"He is fine. They are bringing him in right now to Homeland. He ran into one of our teams about twenty minutes ago. He has been shot but it's just a flesh wound. They are taking him to a hospital to have him checked over but he should be returned to Homeland within a few hours."

Tears welled but she blinked them back over hearing the news that Slade was safe and alive with only a flesh wound. He'd been shot. All that registered. She'd seen firsthand how tough New Species could be and how quickly they healed. She wasn't too worried that the injury would be life threatening if they expected him at Homeland soon.

"Thank you."

"Go back to sleep. I hated to wake you but Justice said you wanted to know when he knew. I'm sure Slade will come here as soon as he returns to personally check on you. Just rest. You need it."

"Thank you." She smiled at him. "Can you tell Justice I appreciate everything?"

"Sure." Brass backed away to return to the living room.

Trisha studied the bedroom. Brass had closed her drapes but weak light peeked between them. She glanced at the clock, surprised to realize it was five minutes past six in the morning. She rolled over and the drugs lured her back to sleep.

*Slade is safe.*

* * * * *

Slade didn't want to sit on the chair or even be at the meeting. He needed to go to Trisha. He wouldn't truly feel calm until he could look into her eyes, inhale her scent and hold her in his arms. He planned to do a lot more than that once he touched her but he refused to allow those thoughts to flow since every male clustered inside Justice's office would smell his arousal.

"I'm very grateful you are safe." Justice sat on the corner of his desk, his gaze roaming the fifteen officers crammed into the room either sitting or standing, and sighed loudly. "We have answers. The assholes responsible for this attack who were arrested have spoken to the police. I just ended a conference call with the lead detective on the case."

"They hate us," Tiger stated. "That's why they did it. It's why we've been attacked in the past and for the same reason they will do it again."

Fury growled from his position near the closed door where he leaned against the wall. "Every time we believe the threat lessens, something happens."

"Calm," Justice demanded, meeting each gaze in turn. "It's because we hired the doctor and word got out."

Shock stiffened Slade's spine. "Why would they care about her specifically?"

"She did a two-year residency in gynecology." Justice ran his fingers through his loose hair. "Someone printed her résumé in the newspapers. Those assholes have gotten it into their brains that's the reason we hired her." He focused on Fury. "They believe she's here to help you figure out why we can't have children. I've issued a statement that it was her years as a trauma emergency doctor that was the deciding factor for choosing her above the other applicants. I'm afraid they don't believe the truth. They are certain we are trying to find a way for you to impregnate your mate, Fury."

He snarled. "Ellie and I aren't test subjects. We haven't taken any measures to do such a thing. We want a baby but we both agree it's not worth the painful agony of allowing doctors to destroy our lives with the taking of blood and their needles and scans."

"I know this." Justice shifted on the desk. "If Mercile wasn't able to discover what went wrong, I'm certain there's no fix for the problem. They had specialists in fertility nearly torturing our females to death. We're just flawed that way. I wouldn't have hired Dr. Norbit for that purpose even if anyone were willing to volunteer to have tests run on them. I'd have hired someone else who solely dealt in that branch of medicine."

"They put a bounty on my head." Slade spoke.

"That's how they got most of those assholes to agree to go after her." Justice's gaze met Slade's. "You were the incentive for killing her and they offered money as well for the one who brought your body to the man who leads them. They know it's only a matter of time before we die of old age and as long as we're sterile, they are comforted that Species won't thrive." Anger deepened his voice. "The idea of us being with human women really pisses them off too."

"I hate humans." Flame grumbled the words. "Males." He flashed an apologetic glance Fury's way. "The females are sweet. Your Ellie is a wonderful human. I wish her no ill will but those males anger me."

"It's not all of them," Fury corrected. "It's just the ones who hate us."

"The point is," Justice continued, "the idea of us having another human female at Homeland, a doctor, has stirred up their rage. I considered hiring someone to replace Dr. Norbit but I happen to believe she is a valuable addition to us. She's a good doctor who can handle anything, as we've seen." He met Fury's gaze. "She saved your life. She holds no malice toward us. I trust her and that is worth the added annoyance of making us a bigger target because of her experience." He pushed up from his desk. "Thankfully she never hooked up with one of our males. That would really send those lunatics over the edge."

Slade tensed and his mouth parted. Before he could speak, Brass did.

"She may hook up with one of us. She's a very attractive female."

"Any male who cared about her would avoid doing that," Flame warned.

"Too true," Justice agreed.

Flame spoke again. "We're trying to open up another home for our people. We're going to need her to travel often to help us set up the medical facility there and every time she leaves the gates it's going to put a target on her back. Hell, we can't even trust the humans who work here at Homeland. Someone gave away her traveling agenda and the precise route. We've got Brass and Wager guarding her around the clock. There's no way the human hate groups wouldn't make her a prime target. She'd be in as much danger as Justice is if she were with one of our men. It would only make them want to kill her twice as much as they already do. She's keeping us alive if we need a doctor and then she'd be sleeping with one of us. They'd assume that she'd make fixing our fertility problems a priority since they'll assume most females wish to have babies."

An icy-cold fear gripped Slade's heart. Justice received death threats daily. He had to have a full security detail escort him everywhere. Being the leader of their people put him in a deadly position. He could mingle freely with only a few trusted humans and even then it was a risk.

Trisha was the Homeland doctor who treated any human who needed her help. The traitor could just cut his hand and walk right up to her. She'd die before anyone could reach her even with guards. The males who belonged to those hate groups were insane. He had no doubt that one of them would take on a suicide mission to take out the enemy. That would be his Trisha. And they would die if they touched her.

"True." Justice shook his head. "It's a good thing none of our males are interested in her. I'd have to fire her and hire another doctor. She'd have to be as guarded as Ellie is. Ellie is only allowed to work with our females since they pose no threat to her."

Slade's eyes closed and the pain inside his chest became sharper, a near-stabbing agony. Trisha loved her job, being a doctor was what she was, just as he was New Species. That couldn't change and trying would be a fool's errand.

She'd grow to hate him if he made her chose him over the life she led. She'd resent him in time. He wasn't even sure if she cared enough about him to even be tempted to lean in his direction if offered a choice.

"We're going to have to tighten security. Dr. Norbit will have around-the-clock protection until the threat lessens. We need to find the traitor who betrayed us. In time those assholes will realize nothing will help us have children and they will cease having the fear that we'll reproduce and blow their dreams of watching us eventually die out."

Justice continued to speak but Slade stopped listening. Being with Trisha could get her killed. It would put her in too much danger. He got a tight rein on his emotions, afraid someone would smell his strong pain, and knew he'd grieve later, privately. He couldn't put her in that much danger or ruin her life. She meant too much to him.

# Chapter Thirteen

**ஐ**

Sweat beaded Trisha's forehead and she wondered if she would be violently ill. She nervously sat inside the reception area of Justice North's office and fought the urge to throw up. She glanced at her watch. She'd arrived a little early and been informed that he was on the phone.

She'd called the meeting but she'd had no choice, knowing she had to be responsible about the dire situation. It wasn't just her own issues she had to deal with. It would be a huge deal and she had to do the right thing. That meant discussing it with Justice. It involved New Species and he had a right to know. She just hadn't expected to feel sick to her stomach about it.

The tall woman behind the secretary desk closely watched Trisha, appearing slightly concerned. "Do you want some coffee or water, Dr. Norbit? You are really pale."

"I'm fine." Trisha forced a smile. "Nerves."

The woman nodded and focused on her computer screen. "It should only be a few more minutes. Justice is on a long-distance call with the newly acquired New Species Reservation. They are opening up soon and it's been really hectic here. Isn't that where you were heading when your vehicle was attacked? I hope you are all better now?"

"I'm fully recovered. Thank you for asking. And yes, that's where we were traveling to when we were attacked."

Trisha had never gotten to go see the place. She only knew what she'd heard on the news. Brass had told her a bit about the project. Four hundred miles to the north in the woodsy area of Northern California, Justice had bought up thousands of acres of land—an old resort that had closed down years before and abandoned. The owner had sold it cheap to avoid paying taxes on the property. Justice planned to turn it into a home for some of the New Species who didn't want to "get along with others".

A smile curved her lips at the memory of Brass saying those exact words to her. He'd explained that some of the New Species were less human-looking than the ones she saw at Homeland. They didn't want to be integrated with humans, instead just wanted to live in peace within a safe place. They currently resided in an unspecified location far from human contact but with the hate groups, everyone feared for their safety if anyone ever discovered where they'd been placed by the government.

Justice had bought the old resort to bring them closer to their own kind and to be able to protect them better. They'd decided to rename it New Species Reservation. She'd been assured that it was an appropriate title since it was anything but a vacation spot. It would be run the way Homeland had been set up, totally under New Species law and control. It would also have high-level security to protect the New Species who chose to live there.

Brass had become a good friend to Trisha while he'd stayed at her house for the first two weeks after her ordeal. He'd made her laugh a lot and become important to her. She'd worried a little that he might be attracted to her but he'd never done anything out of line. When the threat assessment to her had been lowered, she had actually missed her constant companions who guarded her.

Brass still checked on her and stopped by often with a few action movies and she supplied the popcorn. Sometimes he'd bring a few of his friends with him. Trisha had gotten to know some of the New Species that way. They treated her as though she were a little sister, as if she were one of them, and she'd been grateful for it. It had kept her from feeling self-pity.

Slade had never called or come to see her. As a matter of fact, he'd dropped off the face of the Earth for all Trisha could tell. Several weeks ago one of the men had mentioned that Tiger and Slade were working at Reservation. He wasn't even living at Homeland anymore.

The silent message of actions speaking louder than words had been clear to Trisha. The sex they'd shared had been nothing more than casual sex to Slade. That reality hurt deeply but she was recovering and determined to pretend it never even happened. That was until earlier that morning. She was afraid she would be sick again.

"Dr. Norbit?" Trisha glanced up at the secretary. "You can go in now."

"Thank you."

Trisha rose to her feet even though her knees grew weak. She had the urge to flee. She could leave, quit her job, and move to another state just to avoid the entire mess. She'd been tempted to listen to that panicked voice inside her head. She even hesitated as her gaze flickered to the door that led out of the reception area. She swallowed instead though and forced her legs to walk toward Justice's office. *I'm a doctor and I know what needs to be done regardless of the personal consequences I'm facing.*

Justice wore his usual jeans and sported a tank top and bare feet. It always amused her that the leader of an entire race could always be so casual unless he planned to stand in front of media cameras. He wore dark suits then, would pull his long hair back, and even put on shoes.

As she entered his office, he strode toward her with a smile curving his generous lips. She always noticed how good-looking he was with his fit body, his handsome features and those sexy cat eyes. The fact that he was really nice also added to his appeal. She forced a smile.

"Welcome, Trisha. It's hot today, isn't it?"

She nodded. She'd overdressed in a long navy skirt and business-style button-down shirt, intentionally going for the professional look as a means to calm her nerves. She'd even taken time to pull her hair up into a nice bun. It had distracted her from the upcoming meeting she'd requested with Justice as soon as he had time to see her. She'd specified the urgency of needing to talk to him. He'd made the time.

"So, what is so important? Debra, my secretary, informed me that you needed to speak to me about something right away. Is this another request for more nursing staff? Are the two additional ones we hired not enough? Do you have a request for more medical equipment?" He waved her to a take chair while he walked around his desk. "Have a seat."

Trisha collapsed into a plush chair. Justice kept his smile in place as he took his seat. He leaned forward to brace his elbows on his desk, resting his chin onto his hands. He looked amused.

"You look so serious. Don't be. I told you before that I'm very willing to get you whatever you need for the medical center."

"This isn't about that." She had to slow her pounding heart. "This is about a personal matter."

The smile slowly faded as his gaze narrowed. "Please tell me you aren't resigning. We need you." He lifted his head, removed his elbows from his desk to fall back against his chair, and looked suddenly tense. "I'd be more than happy to discuss money with you if this is a salary issue. We really want you to continue working with us. You are an excellent doctor and my people have grown to trust you. You have no idea how much we value that and you."

She shook her head. "It's not about money and I don't want to lose my job or quit, though you might not want me to work for you after this meeting." She took a deep breath, studying Justice. "I'm sorry. I'm scared to death right now."

"Of me?" He looked surprised.

"Of the situation. I don't even know where to begin. Something has happened and it's pretty serious. If anyone realizes how severe this is, it's me."

"All right." Justice took a deep breath. "Tell me what is wrong."

"I've been given access to a lot of the medical files that contain some of the recovered research data from Mercile Industries. They tried to breed New Species men and women. I know you are very aware of this."

His face tightened. "Yes. I was personally subjected to a lot of their breeding studies." His voice had lowered to a growl.

"From what I've read, from the files I've been given, all their testing was between two New Species pairs and it always failed. They never attempted to breed New Species with pure humans."

"No. We were considered too dangerous and they were afraid we'd kill any of the staff who attempted to lure us into having sex with them. You can't blame us."

"I don't." She hesitated.

"They severely abused us."

"I know that. I— It's happened," she stated very softly.

"I don't understand. You found a file where they held those studies on some of my people? Some of them agreed to have sex with humans while we were prisoners?"

She fought the urge to burst into tears. "No. I'm sorry. I'm not being very clear. A full human has conceived a child with a New Species."

*There. I said it.* She watched the shock transform Justice's face. His mouth opened and then closed. He finally found his voice.

"That..." He looked dazed. "You're sure?"

"Positive. I ran the tests myself this morning and preformed an ultrasound. The fetus has a strong, well developed heartbeat and it looks perfect. I won't lie. This pregnancy isn't normal. The heartbeat is that of a much more advanced fetus and the measurements are off on the size. It appears the growth rate and fetal development are farther along than a typical pregnancy. It's alarming, Justice. The baby is growing faster than it should be and the pregnancy symptoms are premature for the gestation period." Her fingers dug into the chair she sat in. "For the first time, according to what I know, a New Species has been able to help conceive a baby. I know you believed all your males were sterile but at least one of them isn't."

Justice suddenly stood. He turned to the window and presented Trisha with his back. He remained silent. Trisha watched him with fear. She had no idea how he'd react. She had a television, watched interviews with hate groups, and knew that it would only bring New Species huge trouble when word spread that they could not only have children, at least one of them wasn't sterile, but that the mother wasn't New Species.

A lot of idiots believed cross breeding of that sort would be a grave offense. They'd compare it with an animal and a human breeding. Their prejudices disgusted Trisha but she couldn't change their narrow minds. Justice finally turned with a huge grin.

"That's wonderful!" He dropped into his chair. "And we're sure it was definitely a human and New Species breeding?"

"One-hundred percent sure."

He laughed. "I never thought I'd be able to have children. None of us did." He stood again and almost leaped across his desk to grab a gasping Trisha. He yanked her out of the chair, into his arms and hugged her. "This is the best news ever, Trisha. You're a genius! You did it!"

Trisha pushed gently away from Justice until he released her. She looked up into his grinning face with a horrible feeling. He obviously thought she'd done something as a doctor that resulted in the pregnancy. She knew she needed to set him straight immediately.

"This wasn't something I did on purpose. There was no medical intervention. This just happened. It's a completely unplanned and natural-occurring pregnancy."

"That's even better! You've made my day. Hell, my year." Then his smile faded as he tensed. "We have to keep this under wraps. We're going to have to shield the couple. There could be a firestorm of threats directed at us if the press finds out and reports it. Who knows?"

"Just you and me so far."

"The couple doesn't know?"

She realized he didn't understand what she attempted to tell him. She opened her mouth. Justice backed up.

"About that—"

Justice cut her off. "The press will be all over it if they find out. We need to keep this classified. You are going to have to care for the pregnant female. No one, and I mean *no one,* can find out about this until after the baby is born. We'll get the pair secluded to protect them and any paperwork you did on this needs to be destroyed. Can you imagine what those terrorist groups will do and how dangerous it will be when they learn we can breed with humans? It's one of the things they've tried to use against us to drag more idiots into the fight for their cause. They believe it's vile for Species to touch someone fully human and it's going to really piss off the ones who are looking forward to our demise once our generation dies out."

"Justice—"

"You and I will work together to protect them at all costs, Trisha. We have to keep this top secret. I'll call for a helicopter transport immediately to fly them out of here within the hour. The Reservation isn't fully operational but it's very secure and it's the safest place to stash them. You'll have to go there too." He stared at her. "I know your life is here but you need to be protected." He grinned. "This is more important. I—"

"Shut up!" Trisha finally yelled.

Justice frowned at her. "What—"

"Quiet," she ordered him, lowering her voice. "I've been trying to tell you something and you keep cutting me off."

He nodded. "Go ahead. I'm listening."

She hesitated, staring into his beautiful, exotic eyes. "I'm the mother. It's me, Justice. I'm the female carrying a New Species baby. There's no paperwork since I ran all the tests when I was alone at the clinic. I realized I had missed my period but I had chalked it up to stress when I was late. Then I started feeling morning sickness and I took a test when I got out of bed this morning. It was positive. Right after that I went to the medical center and gave myself an ultrasound." She blinked back tears. "There's definitely a baby growing inside me and it's growing at an accelerated rate. The only explanation for that abnormality is perhaps because the baby is half New Species and the pregnancy will be shorter due to the father's altered DNA." Her hand rested over her stomach. "I'm the mother," she repeated.

Justice gaped at her, completely stunned. She collapsed back into her chair while she fought more tears. It was tough but she managed not to burst into sobs. She lifted her gaze and realized Justice mutely gaped at her. Seconds seemed to drag for an eternity before he found his voice.

"You're sure the father is New Species? I know you were seeing someone and I believed him to be human."

"The last time I had sex was about two years ago. I've had sex once since then and it was with one of your men. There is no doubt whatsoever that he's the father."

Justice sat on the edge of his desk. "All right. This is good news, Trisha. You look so miserable but don't be. You have no idea what this means to my people." He gave her a sad smile. "We can have children after all. If one of us is able, perhaps others can as well. I know you are probably scared but this is going to work out somehow. We'll make it. Can you handle your own medical needs until we can secure someone we can trust to take over? You obviously can't deliver your own child."

She blinked back more tears. "I'm still in shock but I want the baby. I'm mostly scared. I never thought I'd be a mom and I know that my baby is in danger because of what this means. It's going to be the first known mixed species baby between our races. I'm afraid of what kind of life he or she is going to be facing. I did the ultrasound and everything looks right but it's so hard to tell at this stage. I'm worried about the size of the baby though because it measured bigger by far than what it should be. I have to run a ton of tests. Something could be wrong with the pregnancy. We just don't know what to expect because this has never happened before. I'm terrified."

"We will get through whatever happens together. You will never be alone, Trisha. We considered you one of us before but you truly are New Species now. Your child is one of us and as the mother of that child, you are officially a part of the NSO. I extend all rights to you as such. You will have our full support, we will take very good care of you, and you will be protected at all times." He rose to his feet and rounded the desk, grabbing his phone. "Get me Brass right now and send him to my office."

Trisha relaxed. This could have gone really badly. She'd expected the worst, maybe him blowing up at the news. The baby put his people in jeopardy. Justice getting very excited and being happy about her baby was a hell of a lot better than anything she'd imagined.

"We'll send you with Brass to the Reservation. He'll protect you with his life and he'll have a lot of help, Trisha. I know how much trust you have in him to keep you safe. I'll tell everyone that I want a doctor out there and you volunteered to go. No one will become suspicious about that. That was what I'd planned to do before your attack. I had wanted you on hand when the medical center there was built. I'll have some of my men pack up your home for you and move your things. I don't want you lifting a finger." He chuckled. "You're going to be very spoiled so get used to it."

Justice sank back into his seat while Trisha watched him speed dial. He told people he had decided they needed a doctor at Reservation and Trisha had been kind enough to agree to go. He set up a flight for her in less than an hour and then called there to let them know a team headed their way. Someone finally knocked on the door and Justice hung up.

"Enter," he called out.

Brass walked into the office and closed the door behind him. He'd obviously been on duty since he wore his uniform. He grinned when he saw Trisha and winked before his attention fixed on Justice.

"I was told you needed me."

Justice grinned. "I'm sending you with Trisha to Reservation. They will be expecting you. I'll let you pick two of your closest friends to take with you to help protect her." Justice stood and chuckled. "Isn't this the best news? Congratulations, Brass!" Justice suddenly strode forward and hugged the surprised man. "You're going to be a father!"

Trisha felt sucker-punched but it was nothing compared to the expression on Brass' face. His eyes widened and his mouth fell open.

"Uh, Justice?"

Justice released Brass and grinned at Trisha. "Yes?"

She shook her head at him. "It's not him."

"What is going on?" Brass had a confused look on his features.

Justice ignored him and kept staring at Trisha as his smile died. "But he is at your home at night. I told you that I'm aware of everyone's movements inside Homeland. You are dating him."

"We're just platonic friends who watch movies together. He's not the father of my baby. I've never slept with Brass."

"Baby?" Brass gasped. His attention flew to Trisha. "You're pregnant?"

She nodded. "I'm sorry about this. I thought Justice called you to be my bodyguard because he knows we've become friends. I never guessed he might believe you were the father of my baby."

"You're pregnant?" Brass suddenly growled viciously. He backed up and crossed his arms over his chest as his focus fixed on the floor.

Trisha noticed his dark reaction and it left her speechless.

"This is dangerous for her and for all of us," Justice warned softly. "You are her personal bodyguard. No one finds out about this pregnancy. Clear, Brass? Is this going to be a problem for you?"

Brass met Justice's gaze. "I'd protect her with my life. No one will know about this from me. What are my orders?"

"There's a helicopter leaving with her in an hour. Pick two males you trust with her life and tell them they are part of your team. This will be an extended assignment. Don't pack a light bag. I'll use the cover that I'm assigning her to oversee the medical center at Reservation for now."

"Understood." Brass didn't even glance at Trisha when he walked out of the office. The door closed softly behind him.

Confused, Trisha frowned.

Justice studied her. "You didn't know he had feelings for you? You might have thought of him as a friend but I think he was slowly courting you."

"I didn't know." It stunned her. "I thought he might like me but he never asked me out so I dismissed the idea."

"We're sometimes hard to read. I've noticed with our kind they either come straight at what they want with the aggression of a pit bull or they try to ease upon something they want until they can pounce on it when it is the last thing you would expect." Justice sighed. "So who is the father?"

Trisha lifted her chin in defiance. "I won't tell."

Justice's eyelids narrowed. "What?"

"It was just sex. It didn't mean anything. This is my baby."

Justice looked slightly angry as his arms crossed his broad chest. "Who is the baby's father, Trisha? You need to trust me. Casual sex or not, a Species would want to know if he were about to become a father."

She bit her lip. "I don't think so."

His arms tightened against his chest. "You admitted you've had sex one time in two years. I smelled sex on you once." He studied her face carefully. "You had my scent on you and I know I'm not the father. You had Brass' scent but you but you obviously haven't had sex together." He sucked in air. "You had Slade's scent on you too. It was strongest but I assumed that was because you'd been alone with him for days and — Of course. Slade is the father."

She let her head drop. "Please don't tell him."

"I'm sorry, Trisha. I must. He'd want to know. He has a right to protect and watch out for you since you are carrying his child."

She allowed the tears to fall when she looked up. "He never contacted me, never called me, never once tried to see me in the weeks he lived here after he returned. Please don't tell him. I can't see him."

Justice softly cursed. "You thought there was more to the sex than it being casual and his actions hurt you."

*Why lie?* She nodded. "Yes. Please, Justice. I can't stop you if you are set on telling him but keep him away from me if you do. Please?"

"I don't understand."

"He didn't want to be with me anymore once we were rescued and I sure as hell don't want him trying to spend time with me now because of this pregnancy. He made his choice."

He studied her for a long time. "I understand but I have to tell him, Trisha. I will make your feelings known to him and I will tell him that he blew it."

She wiped at tears. "Yeah. That's a good way to put it." She stood. "Thank you for taking this so well."

"Thank you for—" Justice moved and hugged a surprised Trisha. "For being pregnant and giving all of us hope of having children. I'm sure everything will work out and that this baby is going to be born healthy. We're a hearty bunch and tough to kill. This baby will be half New Species."

She cried while Justice held her. She hugged him back, admitting she had needed someone to comfort her all day, since she'd realized she was pregnant. The shock had been that great. Justice rubbed her back and pulled her closer, consoling her.

"I'm sorry for the pain you are in. Slade should know how special you are and he never should have let you go, Trisha. I wouldn't have if you were mine. This should be a happy occasion and he has hurt you."

She sniffed and pushed away from Justice. He released her as she wiped at her tears again. "Thank you. That's the nicest thing you could have said to me." She looked up at him. "There is one more thing I want to ask of you."

"Anything."

"I'd request for you to tell Ellie and Fury that I'm pregnant. They haven't conceived but they probably could. I know they want to have a baby. It might just be a simple problem with low sperm count or Ellie just might need a little help with producing her eggs. One round of fertility drugs might help her get pregnant. I can order tests that I'm sure they'll agree to have once they know. They will know they have hope of conceiving. They are the only other full human and New Species couple and they are the only two who need this information. Both of them are trustworthy."

Justice nodded. "That's fine. I'll do that. Don't worry about it. I'll handle it all and I'll have Dr. Ted Treadmont handle their tests. I know it's not his field but he can do some simple testing, right?"

"He's trustworthy. Yes, Ted can handle that."

"Good." Justice handed Trisha tissues from one of his desk drawers. "Here. Blow your nose. You can use my bathroom to clean up. We don't want anyone to get suspicious and you crying would tip off someone that something is wrong."

"Sorry."

"You're emotional. I hear that's normal with pregnancy."

"Yes, it is. God, I hate to imagine what a nutcase I'll be in five or six months." She shook her head. "I already feel sorry for my security detail." She walked to the bathroom door and then stopped, turning. "I feel so bad about Brass. Do you think he'll still be my friend?"

"He will be. He was disappointed but I didn't see real hurt in his eyes. He'll get over it."

She hoped so. She walked inside the bathroom and closed the door.


Justice heard water running. Full humans didn't have their keen senses. He always had to remind himself of that fact, taking his own hearing for granted. He sat down at his desk. He experienced joy and sadness over the fact they were able to breed. He wanted to have a child one day but the fear of how the humans would react if they found out made his gut twist. He dialed the headquarters office at Reservation and asked for Slade.

"Hi, Justice. You actually caught me inside the office. I just had a meeting with one of the builders. The security fence is finished. It will be fully functional by next month with the motion sensors and electronic surveillance. They were grunting and groaning over the deadline for the clubhouse but it's on schedule. In two months they should be finished with it. There's nothing else to report."

"I have news for you, actually."

"All right."

"I'm sending Dr. Trisha Norbit up to Reservation."

Silence.

Justice bared his teeth, showing his anger. Obviously Slade wasn't thrilled with the news. The next sound he heard confirmed his suspicions. He heard a sigh finally.

"All right. Is she going to be here for a reason?" Slade didn't sound happy.

"Yes. Is this a secure line?"

"Of course. Is there a reason it needs to be? Has something happened? Has she been targeted? I thought everything had settled down about that by now. I feel obligated to tell you that I think she would be much safer there if you are sending her up here because she's gotten more threats. There's a hell of a lot of open space for someone to breach Reservation than there is at Homeland."

"There are too many people here who will see her. I think it's best if she is sent there. It's remote and easier to shield her from the public. She is coming so make all the arrangements. I want her put in a remote but comfortable location that is extensively secure. I'm sending three personal officers with her to protect her at all times."

"The danger is that high?" Slade's voice tensed and his tone turned into growl. "Is she well? Has an attempt on her life been made?"

Justice suddenly smiled over the fact that Slade obviously cared. He bit his lip. "She's in extreme danger." He managed to keep his tone cool. "She's fine but she's a bit under the weather. I'm sending her there for her protection and so that she can get some well-deserved rest."

"I'll handle it. No one will harm her here." Slade snarled the words.

"I'm sure she'll be fine. I need to go. I'll have the pilot radio in on their exact time of landing."

"It will be taken care of."

\* \* \* \* \*

Rage poured through Slade hotly until sweat broke out over his skin. The office he sat in had air-conditioning but it couldn't offset the reaction to his anger. He'd done the honorable thing by leaving Homeland to avoid the temptation of seeking out Trisha. He'd sacrificed his sanity at times to make certain she wasn't in danger.

She had to be sent to Reservation due to a threat. The fact that Justice had been so vague on what prompted the move really drove him into a bad mood. Had someone actually tried to harm her? Had it just been threats by phone? Maybe a breach at Homeland? The human who'd betrayed them hadn't been caught. Had he or she gone after Trisha?

He snarled and drew the attention of a few of the people inside the office. Tiger lifted a curious eyebrow.

"What is wrong? Did the crew at the hotel break another water line?"

"No." He glanced at the one human who worked on blueprints and gave his friend a hand signal as he rose to his feet. "We should check on their progress."

Tiger stood. "I'll walk with you."

They walked about twenty yards from the makeshift office before Tiger paused, staring at his friend. "What is wrong?"

"That was Justice. He's sending Dr. Norbit here. She's in danger and he wants her stashed."

"Shit. Doesn't he realize how rough that will be?"

"He didn't seem to care. I couldn't argue with him, knowing everything I said could be overheard."

"True."

"I'm going to see her again."

Tiger's cat eyes widened. "You haven't gotten over her yet?"

"No. I think about her all the time."

"You have to stand strong. We discussed this."

"She's in danger and I've stayed away from her. Obviously that didn't work."

"She'll be in danger regardless. She works for us, and some will hate her for that offense alone. If she's with one of us, with you, and it gets out, whatever threat level against her will worsen. You did the correct thing."

"Did I?" Slade's body tensed. "Why does the right thing feel so wrong?"

"We've suffered enough. It's better not to have her than to risk her being killed because she's your woman."

Pain sliced through his chest. "I'd die inside if that happened. I couldn't live with that."

"And that's why you made the right choice." Tiger shifted his stance. "Work is the cure. We've got enough of it here."

"Right. Work."

"I'll handle her. You don't need to talk to her when she arrives."

"No." He knew it would be stupid but he needed to see her. "Justice didn't give details of why she's in danger but he said she was under the weather. I'll sleep better at night if I can actually see her for myself. I won't rest until I make sure she's physically fine."

"Masochist."

"Shut up."

"I'm just saying it will be painful to see her and not be able to touch her. You'll want to."

"I'm strong. I can deal with this." Tiger shot him a disbelieving stare. "Sometimes I wonder why we are friends."

"I already told you. You're a masochist." Tiger laughed.

\* \* \* \* \*

Trisha walked out of Justice's bathroom. She'd redone her makeup and knew she could pass muster on looking normal. She paused when she saw the pensive look on Justice's face as he watched her.

"I decided to hold off telling Slade about the baby. It's your news to share with him. I'll give you a little time."

Relief washed through Trisha. "Thank you."

"Don't thank me yet. If you don't let him know within the next…" He shrugged. "I will have to. He's in charge of Reservation and needs to know how important it is to protect you. In order to do that he needs to be made aware of the dangers. I think by the way he reacted when he thought you were at risk, he might care more for you than you believe. That's what prompted me to see if you both can work this out on your own before I intervene."

She stared at Justice grimly. "If he cared, as you put it, he would have come to see me. He would have at least called to make sure I was okay emotionally after what happened to us. The way I heard it, he nearly begged for the job at Reservation to get away from Homeland, which probably translates to getting away from me."

"He did not beg for the job. I wanted Fury to go but Ellie couldn't leave our women. She takes her job at the woman's dorm very seriously and she's always under threat as Fury's mate. My next in command is Slade. I asked him and he accepted. I needed someone I could trust handling everything. I have too much on my own plate down here to keep bouncing back and forth. I was getting airsick with the two and three helicopter rides I had to take daily."

"I see."

"I hope you do. Now, Brass should be here at any time to pick you up. I have a conference room meeting with the Council in a few minutes." He stood and sighed. "Sometimes they drive me nuts."

"Good luck with that. I'll go wait for him in the lobby."

"Stay here and relax. The couch is comfortable."

"Thank you."

He grinned as he glanced at her stomach. "I'm very excited about this."

"Me too, when I'm not scared stupid."

Justice squeezed her arm, reassuring her, and walked out of his office. He firmly closed the door behind him.

Fifteen minutes later Brass walked into the room. Trisha stood and studied him. He appeared calm now, collected, and cool. "I'm very sorry Justice misunderstood about you being the father of my baby."

He studied her before his attention lowered to her stomach. "You're really carrying a New Species baby?"

"Yes."

"That's good news."

Trisha noticed he didn't look happy. "Is our friendship all right, Brass?"

"Yes. I'm...wishing I'd met you before you became involved with another male. I hope that doesn't offend you. It's just that I was drawn to you more than I should have allowed. Now you belong to someone else but I'll adjust. We're fine, Trisha."

"I don't belong to anyone, Brass. The father and I aren't together." She rushed on before he could say anything, not wanting to encourage him but needing to be clear she wasn't open to him hitting on her either. "I have feelings for him but he obviously doesn't return them. It's going to take some time but I'm sure I'll deal with it."

He blinked. "You belong to someone. You didn't inform him about the baby?"

"No. Justice has given me some time to contact him and give him the news."

He nodded. "I figured or this male would be at your side. You do belong to someone and he'll let you know that the second he finds out you are carrying his child. Let's go. The helicopter is ready. I chose Harley and Moon to come with us."

Dread pitted her stomach. She really didn't want Slade to find out. That wasn't the way she wanted him back in her life. She'd rather never see him again than have him pursue her just because they'd created a life together. She deserved a guy who cared about her, not one who wanted to be with her out of some sense of duty or honor. New Species seemed to have a lot of both of those traits. She decided not to mention that to Brass. She feared they'd argue.

Trisha had met Moon. He was one of the men who showed up with Harley and Brass at her house to watch movies. The tall man didn't talk much but he had a wicked sense of humor she enjoyed when he decided to break his silence.

"Thank you."

Brass held out his arm and Trisha wrapped her fingers around his forearm. He genuinely smiled at her and escorted her out of the office.

# Chapter Fourteen

෨

Trisha knew she wasn't going to make it to Reservation without being deeply embarrassed. Brass rubbed her back gently while she sat on his lap. She fought the urge to puke all over the floor. She miserably glanced at Moon and Harley.

Both of them gave her sympathetic looks, knew of her pregnancy, and had been sworn to secrecy. They were going to be protecting her, living with her, and they had needed to know the truth. She glanced at the floor and used her hand to motion to them. Both men quickly lifted their feet. Moon grinned.

"Motion sickness is not funny!" she shouted. She wasn't sure if he heard her over the loud helicopter and the headset he wore to keep in contact with the pilots but Moon winked in response, making her believe he had.

"We're almost there," Brass said next to her ear. "Just hang on, Trisha."

She miserably nodded. Her stomach pitched a fit but she didn't want to throw up. She'd be humiliated if all three men got to see her lose her breakfast, not to mention the pilots having to clean it up after they landed. She closed her eyes but it made the sick feeling worsen. She could feel the helicopter lowering. *Thank God. It's nearly over.* The helicopter landed and the pilot started to shut the engines down.

Moon moved first when he opened the side door and jumped out. Harley exited next. They split apart and stood at both sides of the door. Trisha tried to stand on her own but her knees trembled so badly she swayed the instant she put weight on them.

Brass scooped her into his arms where he cradled her tightly against his chest as he bent to carry her out of the helicopter. Harley and Moon gripped Brass with Trisha inside his arms and lifted both of them to the ground. It prevented Brass from jostling her if he'd had to jump down.

Trisha rested her head against the curve Brass' broad shoulder. She hugged him around his neck as the world spun a little. She hated motion sickness. Brass shifted Trisha in his hold, lifting her tighter against his chest, to make her more comfortable.

"Hang on to me," he whispered. "We'll get you settled and I'll put a cool washcloth on your forehead. You'll feel a hundred times better."

"Thank you," she murmured to Brass. "You're the best."

He laughed. "I know. It's a hard burden to shoulder but I'm willing."

She smiled, really grateful to have him as a friend. He always knew how to make her laugh. She heard Harley talking but didn't dare lift her head from Brass' shoulder to see who he spoke to, still fighting the urge to be sick.

"She's motion sick. She will be fine once we get her to a bed and give her some time to recover."

"Is that right?" The male voice sounded furious and was one that Trisha knew too well. She tensed and lifted her head, regardless of the consequences.

Slade stood about five feet from her. He glared as he glanced from her face to Brass, and then back. Trisha knew she'd be experiencing the last seconds of life if looks could have killed and his reaction confused her.

*Why is he so angry? Does he hate me?* He obviously had an issue with her being near him. Their gazes met and held.

Trisha noted that Slade's hair had grown a little since she'd seen him. He wore his usual NSO black outfit, minus the vest though. Instead of NSO stamped onto the breast of his shirt, his name had been printed in the space. He looked fit and handsome. Trisha would have thought he even looked sexy if it wasn't for the murderous rage she saw in his expression. Her heart did a twist from being close to him again.

"Trisha?" Brass whispered against her ear. "That's him, isn't it?"

She turned her head and met his gaze. Brass stared at her for a second and then tensed. "Shit." He nodded. "Let's get you settled."

Brass turned with Trisha and walked toward a Jeep. Slade moved into their path, still glaring at Trisha. "Nice to see you, Doc."

"Hello," she got out.

His focus tore from her for a few seconds as his attention shifted from Brass to Harley, to Moon, and back to her. He finally glared at Brass, locking gazes with him.

"What level of threat is she rated? Justice wasn't clear and I had to watch what I said because I had a human around me during the time of the conversation. He's been in meetings ever since, unable to take my calls."

"Four." Brass frowned at Slade. "She's our prime priority and yours. No one is to have access to her who is not New Species. No humans whatsoever."

That information made Slade blanch a little. "No humans at all? We're in the middle of large construction jobs and we have humans crawling all over Reservation. I have hundreds of them here twenty-four hours a day to complete all the projects we need done as soon as possible. We're doing things in a matter of a few months that should have taken a good year to finish. It took almost four hundred humans three full weeks just to build those security walls to enclose the property. We have them working in two shifts around the clock, seven days a week. We're still wiring the walls for security purposes and I have a hotel being refurbished at breakneck speed. We'll need the housing completed so our people aren't living in tents and a clubhouse is being built still. We have another project going on for the offices to prevent us from permanently being stuck using a trailer. On any given second, on any given day, there are well over four hundred humans here. Does Justice want me to shut down everything so we can't get any work done until the threat is over? He's been pushing me hard to get it all done."

"No," Harley stated. "He just wants her put somewhere safe on where humans aren't permitted. Moon and I have been going over the layout and we believe we should hide her inside the center of the wild zone. No humans would dare go there and they are forbidden in that area. I'm aware that some of our people have already been relocated and that makes it even better since no full human would get past them."

"That wouldn't be safe for her. She's full human." Slade's rage seemed to intensify. "Sure, no humans would ever be stupid enough to venture there and survive it, but it would be baiting them. I believe they would attack if you took her inside their territory. They are very unstable. The second we relocated them, they started marking territory and have been vigilant to make certain no humans breach it."

"We will protect her," Brass promised, his voice firm. "They won't attack her."

"They are insane," Slade snarled. "Some of them will never calm and hate humans to a degree that is beyond what you can imagine. They go into rages just by picking up the scent of one." He pointed at Trisha. "She's seen us but not the failures. Don't you think they would scare the hell out of her?"

"What failures?" Trisha glanced at the men.

Slade glared at her. "We look mostly human but not all of our people were so fortunate. Some appear more animal than human. We have a few dozen who survived. Some of our people were tortured until they were left insane or hold hatred for humans to the point they would kill one on sight. Those are the ones we relocated here. You would not be safe inside the wild zone. It's where we put the most antisocial of them."

Brass bent and placed Trisha on her feet when she indicated she wanted down. He held her waist until she steadied on her shaky legs. He moved back a foot when he became certain she wouldn't collapse. She stared up at Brass.

"What do you think?"

"I think the wild zone is best. They will not hurt you. After we were freed, they used females to help care for all New Species since we don't attack them. I'm sure that holds for the wild ones as well. We will be with you and they will stay back. We can't get lost any better than that, Trisha. It would be smart to put you in the center of the territory since they've claimed it. They are fiercely protective of their domains. They would help keep everyone at bay."

"Damn it," Slade growled. "I'm running this, not you. I will not allow her go in there since I know what I'm talking about and you don't. I'm the one who's spent time with them. I know that she wouldn't be safe. We'll set her up at the hotel where the top floor has been finished. We'll close off all access and keep her there."

"No." Brass crossed his arms over his chest. "Justice put me in charge of her security. I can and am overriding you. No offense but I want her where no humans can get to her, Slade. What if one of those terrorist assholes decides to pose as a workman and sets fire to the hotel? Nothing can happen to her. The wild zone is the answer. Are there any homes there? I am aware we also have some RV's here and we could take one. It would be tight living but it would work. We are to keep her away from everyone but New Species."

Slade was furious. His lips opened and his sharp teeth showed when a deep growl rumbled from him. "Fine. You can have my home. It's only a three bedroom but I'm sure you can manage. It sits away from all other buildings."

"We're taking her into the wild zone. The decision has been made." Brass glared at Slade.

Slade cursed and growled again. His gaze locked with Trisha's. "Tell him no. Listen to me. Those men out there are not stable and you're a full human female. You are a Doc to boot, two things they will want to kill you on sight for being. You will die if you agree to them taking you out there. The wild ones were cared for by females once we were freed but then they were taken to remote locations without them. They have spent months on their own and I'm not certain they'd still resist attacking a woman. I'm also not willing to chance it."

Fear inched up Trisha's spine as she stared at Slade.

"Trust me, Trisha. I would never let you down," Brass promised softly. "I know what I'm doing. The wild zone is the safest place for you to be. They will not hurt you and I would never allow anything to cause you harm."

"Trisha?" Slade shook his head at her, watching her closely. "Trust me. Tell them to put you up at my house while I move into the hotel."

She managed to refrain from flinching. She could stay inside his house but he'd move out. "Brass?" She turned her head and tore her gaze away from Slade's. "I know you will protect me. Whatever you think is best is fine with me. It's your call."

Brass smiled. "We're going to the wild zone."

Slade growled viciously and cursed. "Trisha? Get over here now. We're going to have a private talk."

She tensed as she slowly faced him. "Excuse me? You've known how to reach me for weeks if you wanted to talk to me. You should have tried to tell me before now if there was anything you had to say that I needed to hear." She started to walk toward the Jeep.

She heard someone snarl and spun back around in time to see Brass move quickly as Slade lunged for Trisha. Brass got between them and snarled back at Slade. Slade stopped. Both men were tense as they glared at each other. It looked as though they were going to fight.

"Brass? I really don't feel well," Trisha urged quickly, not wanting them to come to blows. "Can we go? Thank you for your concern, Mr. Slade, but I have total faith in Brass, Moon, and Harley to protect me."

"So that's how it is," Slade snarled. "Fine. There's one empty cabin out that way. You can have it. I'll send someone with supplies immediately. It's a one-bedroom but it sounds as though the four of you won't mind sharing a bed together." He spun on his heel and stormed toward one of the buildings.

Trisha watched him go and fought tears. "Did he just call me a slut in a roundabout way?"

Moon laughed and wiggled his eyebrows. "I wish you were. I'd even be willing to share with them if it meant having you in a bed naked with me."

She laughed, knowing it was meant as a joke. Moon could always make her feel better. "You keep wishing. You guys get the floor if there's only one bed."

Brass relaxed and smiled at Trisha. "Not a problem. You definitely get the bed. You wimpy humans would never survive sleeping on a hard floor. Us males don't mind sleeping on hard surfaces."

Harley chuckled. "Speak for yourself. I love beds so maybe I'll take the night shift and sleep in it when Trisha *isn't* in it."

"I am good at snuggling." Moon wiggled his eyebrows at Trisha again, making her chuckle. "If you get cold just let me know and I'll keep you warm. I'll even behave if you don't make me sleep on the floor."

"I'll have them bring out mattresses," Brass groaned playfully. "When did you guys become so soft?"

"When we were given choices," Harley shot back. "Let's get out of here before Slade returns to snarl at you again. Dealing with all these humans has really made him testy. I don't know what crawled up his ass but I hope he has a need for toilet paper soon."

"Gravity would definitely be Slade's friend," Moon chuckled softly.

Trisha laughed. She loved the guys. She was pretty sure she'd be crying after her confrontation with Slade if it weren't for them. Brass helped her into a Jeep while Moon and Harley climbed in the back. Brass took the driver's seat. He looked at the other Jeep with a New Species man waiting with their bags.

"Do you know what cabin Slade spoke of?"

He nodded.

"Lead the way," Brass ordered. "We'll follow."

Harley handed Trisha her seat belt. She mutely put it on and flashed him a grin. He nodded at her. "Always buckle up."

"Yes, sir."

Trisha stared at the beautiful scenery they passed—lush grass, big, pretty trees and rolling hills. She caught sight of a deer at the edge of some trees. It was such a beautiful place that she was able to push thoughts of Slade from her mind. It was hard to do but she didn't want to break down in tears.

* * * * *

Slade paced inside the forest on the other side of the buildings, hiding from everyone, and knew he hadn't taken seeing Trisha well at all. The sight of her in another man's arms had nearly sent him into a jealous rage.

Brass had carried her in his arms, spoken as if he had a right to speak for her, and she'd allowed it. A snarl tore from his lips. He'd sacrificed his sanity to stay away from her, gone against his instincts to be near her, and she'd defied him when he'd just wanted to protect her.

He stiffened, his fists balled, as his pacing ceased. Pain tore through his chest at the thought that she no longer wanted him. He should have told her why he'd avoided her but he had believed she'd talk him into ignoring her own safety if she felt even a tenth for him of what he felt for her. It would have weakened his resolve, staring into her eyes and if she'd touched him, he would have lost that battle.

A slight noise drew his attention and he turned his head to stare at a Species male seeking him out. "What is it?"

"The architect wants a word with you. There's something wrong with the blueprints for one of the modifications you asked for at the hotel."

Rage burned inside him. Work had taken up all his hours. He barely slept but it kept his thoughts off Trisha for the most part. He needed to keep busy now more than ever. Otherwise he'd jump in a Jeep, drive to the cabin, and...*rip off her clothes and fuck her until she knows she's still mine.*

He pushed back his thoughts, knew he couldn't allow his desire to rule his actions. She was pale and ill. He worried about that. She needed rest, obviously, but then...*damn! Stop thinking about stripping her naked and making her realize I'm the male for her. Now is not the time.*

"Slade? Is everything all right?" The Species male cocked his head, staring at him with concern.

"It's fine," he lied. "Let's go. The faster we deal with these issues, the faster all the work gets done."

He'd deal with the doc later after he had some time to think and evaluate the situation. Her being at Reservation totally changed things. She was in danger regardless, whether he was with her or not. He had to calm down before he decided what to do. It wouldn't be smart to talk to her until he got a leash on his jealousy.

* * * * *

The A-frame cabin had probably been built sometime in the seventies if Trisha had to guess, based on the interior. She grimaced over the wallpaper in the small kitchen and the old shag carpet covering the living-room floor.

"All that is missing is the disco ball."

"I don't get it." Harley stared at her.

"Welcome to the nineteen-seventies, gentlemen. Notice the avocado-green appliances and the orange wallpaper? Another dead giveaway is the wood paneling and that shag carpet went out fashion in the late seventies. It looks solidly built though and I love that fireplace."

"It doesn't have a bedroom. It has that." Brass pointed to the stairwell.

"It's called a loft bedroom." Trisha walked up the stairs to realize the room was actually pretty large. "It's roomy and, wow, there's a half bath up here. That's a nice surprise."

"The bed is too small for all four of us to fit on unless we call a dog pile," Moon stated suddenly.

Trisha started to laugh. She turned and grinned at him, seeing all three men had followed her upstairs. "I get to pile on last if you do. That way I won't get crushed."

"We could all sleep as though we're hot dogs inside a package," Harley offered. "When one of us wants to turn we could all just shout out 'roll' and be like those synchronized swimmers who all move at once."

"Wouldn't work." Moon chuckled. "The person on the outside in the direction we turned would end up falling on the floor."

"More room for the three remaining." Brass winked at Trisha. "I think we should put Moon and Harley on the outside edges, just to be safe."

Moon's smile died and he lifted his head. He turned, sniffed, and nearly leaped down the stairs. "Someone is near," he warned with a snarl.

Brass grabbed Trisha and shoved her onto the bed. "Sit." He rushed to a window.

Harley ran down the stairs after Moon. Trisha heard the front door open. She turned to stare at Brass, fighting alarm.

He had unfastened the handgun he kept strapped to his thigh. He had the curtain open and she heard him softly curse.

"What is it?" Trisha whispered.

"One of the local residents is outside. Shit. What is he doing here? Someone should have warned me they'd transferred him. He must have gotten a whiff of you and came to investigate. Moon is talking to him and Harley is securing the lower floor."

Curious, Trisha climbed off the bed and moved behind Brass. She knew that he was aware of her. He reached behind him and put his hand on her hip to keep her at his back. She hesitated and peered around him. It was still daylight and easy for her to spot the man outside—at least he was mostly man. The sight of his hair and features shocked her deeply.

"He's—"

"Shush," Brass ordered softly. "He'll probably hear what you say. They have better hearing than most of us."

The big male had obviously been altered with feline genes and had an actual mane of reddish-blond hair. His eyes were cat-like, apparent even from a distance. He had a huge, muscled body. He was barely dressed, just wearing cutoff jeans and nothing else. His arms and chest were massive, as if he'd spent his entire life working out. His features were more animal than human with his strange nose and thick cheekbones.

Moon paused about fifteen feet from the man who stood very still at the edge of the woods. He suddenly lifted his head and his strange gaze seemed to immediately locate Trisha. It seemed as if he sensed her somehow.

A roar erupted from the scary guy's mouth when he opened it. It was a loud, shocking sound to Trisha, one hundred percent not human. His entire body tensed and he stormed toward the house. Moon jumped into his path and threw out his arms to prevent the approaching male from passing. Moon spoke rapidly to the guy—she heard his voice

213

but couldn't pick up what was being said. Moon's actions didn't slow the man down one bit.

She watched in horror when the big guy attacked Moon, just reached out a hand, grabbed him by his throat, and tossed him to the side as easily as if he were a rag doll. The son of a bitch moved faster, straight at the house, and quickly out of sight.

A vicious snarl sounded from below and another roar erupted. Something loud crunched as if wood had been snapped in half, followed by a crashing boom. Brass spun around, grabbed Trisha around her waist, and swiftly placed her into the corner. He put his body in front of hers, trapped her behind him, and faced the stairs as his arm rose to aim his gun. Terror griped Trisha as she heard the guy from outside pound up the stairs.

"Stop, Valiant," Brass warned loudly. "Moon, Harley, stay down there. I know him."

"You brought a human here?" the scary guy snarled. "A human? Justice promised us that none of them would ever come here. She's in my territory. Mine. Because it is you, I will give you one minute to get her out of here before I kill her, Brass."

"Calm down." Brass spoke softly now, perhaps trying to soothe the out-of-control male. "She's pregnant with one of ours. She's now one of us."

"You lie. We can't breed."

Trisha edged a little to the left to peer at the terrifying male standing at the top of the stairs. He had to be six-and-a-half-feet tall and his hair was an amazing light-reddish color with thick streaks of blond running through it. It fell just past his broad shoulders. She couldn't help but notice how beautiful and exotic it looked.

Tan skin and thick muscles covered his mostly bared body. He had to be the biggest New Species she'd ever seen. His sharp teeth flashed when his lips curled back and he growled at her. His cat-like golden eyes narrowed and he growled deeper. Trisha would have hit the floor if she had been the type to faint—out cold over the ferocious appearance and actions. She noticed his fingers were tensed, claw like, at his sides and his fingernails looked sharp, the way an animal's were.

"She's carrying a New Species baby." Brass' voice took on a firmer tone. "That does make her one of us. Justice sent her here because she's not safe around humans anymore. No one knows about her pregnancy. It's going to cause all of us a bunch of grief if the world finds out because they fear the idea of us breeding with them. She was brought here to be protected by us."

"Lie," he snarled.

"True," Brass growled back. "Don't call me a liar."

Valiant growled deep within his chest. "Move. I will smell her."

Brass didn't budge. "You can scent her if you swear to me you won't hurt her. She is carrying a New Species baby. She is just over a month pregnant."

Valiant growled again. "Fine. I won't harm the woman. Move so I can smell her."

Brass turned his head. Trisha looked into his intense features. She didn't want Brass to move and she sure didn't want Valiant near her. He terrified her. Brass' gaze softened.

"He just wants to smell you. I know him. We were reared inside the same testing facility and we shared time together right after we were freed before they sent him and the others like him away from all humans. He gave his word and he'll keep it."

Trisha had to fight down panic. She did trust Brass and he wouldn't allow anyone to hurt her. "All right."

Brass stepped a few feet from Trisha, leaving the path to her open. She leaned back against the wall, staring at the frighteningly large man who stared back at her. His

215

dangerous-looking sharp teeth showed and he appeared enraged still. Trisha's heart pounded as he stalked closer, the way a predator would. He *was* one.

"Don't scare her, Valiant," Brass rasped. "It's okay, Trisha."

She nodded but didn't take her focus from the male advancing slowly toward her. His eyes were really beautiful as he drew near but definitely not human-looking in any way. They were cat eyes, comparable to perhaps a lion, because he sure didn't look similar to any house cat she'd ever seen, that was for sure. His eyelashes were a reddish color that matched his hair, abnormally long and lush. He took another step closer. She stiffened but lifted her chin. She was certain Brass would fight to protect her if he thought Valiant posed a danger to her.

Valiant suddenly crouched down on his hands and feet. It looked strange when he inched forward, his intense gaze fixed on her. He drew so close she could feel his hot breath through her shirt over her stomach. Trisha lifted her hands very slowly and pushed the backs of them against the wall near her head to avoid accidentally touching him. She was afraid it would set him off if that happened. He inhaled when he moved closer and nuzzled her stomach with his face, burrowing between the bottom of her shirt and her pants to reach her skin. She made a soft gasping sound, never expecting him to do that.

"Easy," Brass crooned. "You're scaring her and don't you dare shove your nose lower."

Trisha's stunned gaze flew to Brass'. He shrugged. "Some of us...hell, never mind. You have been around enough animals to know some breeds shove their noses in the crotch area to get aquatinted with people."

Valiant suddenly backed away and straightened to his feet. His focus remained on her stomach while he frowned. He looked really unhappy.

"She smells different."

"How?" Brass seemed very calm.

"Not quite full human but not quite us. It's only noticeable when you are against her skin."

Brass hesitated before he looked at Trisha. "Mind if I?"

Trisha shrugged. "As long as you don't sniff lower."

He grinned. "You are no fun, Trisha."

His grin faded when he stepped in front of Trisha and bent until his face pressed against her neck. His nose touched her skin and he slowly inhaled, then did it again. He lifted his head, frowned, and dropped to his knees. He reached for her shirt and pulled it up to reveal a few inches of her stomach. He put his nose against her there and inhaled three times until he moved back and stood. He faced Valiant.

"You're correct. It isn't noticeable unless you are close to her skin over her lower belly. It's that faint."

"She really is carrying a baby from one of us?" Valiant appeared calm now. His voice was deep, kind of rough, as if he'd spent a hundred years smoking or otherwise damaging his throat, but he wasn't growling anymore.

"She is."

Valiant nodded. "I can't believe you would mate with a human. What were you thinking? They are so fragile I'm surprised she isn't broken. You could have at least found a normal-sized one who is sturdier. You must really restrain yourself. What is the enjoyment of breeding if you have to worry about damaging her?"

Brass blushed a little. "The baby isn't mine. I've never bred her. I'm her friend and I'm one of the three men Justice asked to protect her."

Valiant snapped his head toward Trisha and growled. "There is an existing facility for breeding experiments? She volunteered for some doctor to put our sperm inside her?"

"No." Brass moved, stepping between Trisha and Valiant again. "They bred naturally, of their own free will. It was a surprise for all of us that she got pregnant. We didn't think it was possible."

Valiant sighed. "You can move. I won't harm her."

Brass stepped away from Trisha. Trisha met Valiant's gaze. He stared at her but he didn't appear angry anymore. He looked slightly confused. He sighed again.

"You can stay, human. Just you. Don't bring any of your human friends or family. I'd eat them for dinner." His gaze returned to Brass. "I'll spread the word in the zone to make sure no others come to bother her."

"Could you help us protect her? Please keep an eye out for any humans lurking around and make sure they don't get near her."

Valiant smiled, showing his sharp teeth again. "It will be a fatal mistake on their part if any humans are stupid enough to come out this way."

Brass visibly relaxed after Valiant walked down the stairs. He smiled at Trisha but it looked a little forced. Moon and Harley rushed up the stairs seconds later. Harley was bleeding and held a wet rag to his forehead. Moon's clothes were torn.

"No one warned me that Valiant was here. He's the meanest and most deadly of our kind. I would have gone to see him before I brought you here if I'd known. Anyone else we could handle but he's…" Brass shrugged. "One mean son of a bitch."

Trisha moved now that her terror retreated. She walked to Harley. "Bend down and let me take a look at that." She glanced at Moon. "Are you hurt?"

"I'll live. I know how a football feels though when it's thrown and it ruins that sport for me." He turned and headed downstairs.

Harley leaned down a little and removed the wet rag. Trisha examined his wound and softly cursed. "You're not going to need stitches but I need to clean and bandage it."

"Fuck." He blushed. "I mean darn."

Trisha chuckled. "Cuss away. I would have said worse if someone did that to me. What did he hit you with?"

"The door." Harley's gaze fixed on Brass. "You might want to call and order a new one. Valiant tore that one off the hinges and threw it at me. I tried to dodge the thing but the corner of it struck my forehead. The coffee table didn't make it either. On a high note, we no longer have to chop wood if Trisha wants a fire tonight. We can just use the fifty pieces of coffee table on the floor."

Brass sighed. "I'll call for a first-aid kit too so Trisha can bandage your boo-boo, Harley. Do you mind, Trisha? We still don't have a doctor at Reservation."

"Just get me what I need. Do you need me to give you a list of supplies?"

"No." Brass didn't look happy. "I'm sure what we keep inside our first-aid kits will have everything you could possibly need. I guess I'll go downstairs to evaluate the damage and afterward, I'll call the front office and inform them of what we need."

"Thank you." Trisha smiled at Brass. "For everything."

"Hey," Harley groaned. "I took a door to the head. Where's my thanks?" Trisha laughed and reached out to touch Harley's arm and give it a slight squeeze. "Thank you."

"She touched me."

Harley stuck his tongue out at Brass, teasing him, and made Trisha laugh.

"Don't you have something to do?" They could be childlike but she appreciated their playful traits.

"I'm on it." Brass walked downstairs. He muttered the entire way down.

Trisha had Harley sit on the bed. "What did he say?"

Harley grinned. "Something about having to eat crow when he calls and Slade finds out there has already been a problem here when we just arrived."

Trisha walked inside the half bath and grabbed a hand towel. She returned to the bedroom to apply a new wet compress to Harley's bleeding head, holding it there. Brass wasn't the only one who dreaded how Slade would react when he found out there'd already been an incident at the cabin.

# Chapter Fifteen

## හ

"Valiant?"

Slade was so mad he saw red. He stood at the gate of the house that Valiant had been given. Slade heard a door slam and seconds later the mostly naked Valiant casually strode down his porch steps to approach the gate.

"Slade. Why are you out here? You could have called if you needed something."

"What were you doing?" Slade opened the gate and stepped inside. He was ready for a fight if Valiant got pissed about Slade entering his yard without permission. "I was told you didn't hurt the woman but I swear to God if you had, I'd kill you myself. You were out of line going after her," he growled.

Valiant crossed his arms over his chest. "I smelled a human. That cabin isn't far enough away and I was pissed. Justice said that no humans were allowed here."

"Well, you went through two of our people to reach her so you knew very well that she was supposed to be here. That cabin isn't inside your personal territory. You had no authority to attack our own people."

Valiant shrugged, saying nothing.

"I'll kill you if you go near her again," Slade threatened with a snarl. "Are we clear? I know you are friends with Tiger but damn it, I won't permit you to hurt that woman. You stay away from her and don't go near her again. Do you understand me? You are not to touch one hair on her head."

"I won't go near her. I already discussed this with Brass. She's one of us as far as I'm concerned."

Slade glared at Valiant, slightly confused by the other man's remark. "She's not one of us but she's a good friend to Species. She works for us. Justice and I trust her."

"She's one of us now, isn't she? I smelled her myself. She was very brave and didn't even scream when I scented her stomach."

"You what?" Slade exploded. "You got that close to her? You touched her?" He advanced.

Valiant growled and sank into a crouch. "Stop or we will fight."

Slade halted his angry approach but he almost shook with fury. "You touched her?"

"I kept my word to Brass and didn't hurt her. I wanted to scent her when he told me the news because I didn't believe him. They both agreed to allow me to get close to her. It wasn't an attack."

"He allowed you touch her?"

Slade would kick Brass' ass at his next stop, the cabin. Valiant was unstable and anyone with a brain shouldn't have let Valiant anywhere near Trisha. If he'd been there, he would have killed the big Species for even trying.

"I didn't believe she was pregnant. Now I know she is."

Shock tore through Slade. "What?"

Valiant slowly straightened from the crouch. "Pregnant. Didn't someone tell you? The woman is carrying a child. That is why Brass brought her here to safety—from humans."

The anger seeped out of Slade and pain tore through his chest instead. *Trisha is pregnant?* His knees felt as though they were going to collapse under him. His heart pounded and the rage started to seep back into him. *She's pregnant!* A haze of emotions gripped him, mostly murderous ones, that some guy had touched what was his. The idea of anyone doing that nearly sent him over the edge of insanity.

"Justice ordered them to bring her here to protect her from her people. Justice thinks when the humans find out she is carrying a mixed breed they might try to harm her. I have to agree with him. Humans are erratic and hostile for stupid reasons. There's something about her scent against the skin that makes her different. It must be the baby inside her, changing her chemistry."

"The father is New Species? Are you sure?" Slade ground out the words, his bitterness and rage growing by leaps and bounds.

"Scent her yourself. She smells different. Human and of us faintly but enough that I am sure. I have smelled pregnant human women when the military assigned a bunch of them to bring us food and supplies where they kept us. They knew we wouldn't harm them if they breached the territory they gave us. Nothing is as defenseless as a pregnant female. I know the scent of one well but this one smells different. I couldn't detect a difference until I pressed my nose against her skin. It must because she is barely pregnant. When the months wear on it will probably become easier to notice from a distance."

Slade stormed out of the gate toward his Jeep. His anger knew no bounds. Someone should have told him that Trisha had been sent to Reservation because she carried a New Species baby. The Jeep engine roared to life and Slade punched the gas. The tires squealed in protest but he didn't care about the noise. Now things were making a lot more sense. He was killing mad.

* * * * *

"Someone is coming fast," Moon yelled in warning. "It's one of our Jeeps."

Brass threw down his cards and flashed a grin at Trisha. "It's about time they sent those supplies." He glanced at his watch. "They are actually half an hour earlier than they estimated on the phone."

223

"I'm starving. I hope they sent some good food."

"I'm sure they did." Harley winked at her. "A pregnant mamma should eat lots of junk food. I call dibs if they send any candy bars. I love those things."

"I'm the pregnant one." Trisha laughed. "That means I get first dibs on everything."

"Meany." Harley stuck out his tongue, tossed down his cards and stood. "I better help carry things inside. The faster we get it put away, the faster we can get to the goodies they sent."

"It's Slade," Moon yelled seconds later. "He is really coming fast."

"Shit," Brass sighed from the doorway. "He's very angry. I can see his teeth bared from here."

"Why?" Confusion gripped Trisha. "It wasn't our fault that Valiant attacked."

Brass turned at the door. "You might want to go upstairs, Trisha. I think it might get ugly."

Trisha frowned and rose from the couch, walking to the door instead. She pushed Brass out of her way and stepped out onto the porch to watch the Jeep with Slade came to a sliding halt by the cabin. Slade left skid marks as he locked up the vehicle to stop it. It didn't take hyper senses for Trisha to smell burned rubber as Slade turned off the Jeep engine and leaped from of the driver's seat. He reached Moon first and snarled at him.

"Move."

Moon didn't budge. "Is there a problem?"

Slade lunged. He grabbed Moon by his vest and shoved him hard, out of his way, and advanced. Fear grew instantly inside Trisha after realizing Slade seemed beyond pissed. She actually backed up and bumped the cabin wall next to the doorway. Brass sprinted suddenly, going down the porch stairs, and met Slade head-on.

"You allowed Valiant to touch her?" Slade yelled. "He's unstable and could have killed her." Slade decked Brass in the face with his fist.

Brass landed on his ass. He growled and tried to climb to his feet but Slade turned, throwing a kick to Brass' chest. It knocked Brass flat onto his back on the grass. Slade snarled, showing teeth, as Harley inched toward him.

"Stay out of it unless you want me to kick your ass too. This is between us."

Harley stopped, lifted his hands and backed up. "Okay."

"Stop it," Trisha demanded. She tried to rush down the stairs to reach Brass, worried he'd been hurt badly, but Harley grabbed her arm to prevent her from leaving the porch.

"Stay out of it," Harley ordered softly. His arms locked around Trisha's waist gently. "You could get hurt. Sometimes our males fight to blow off steam. This is about dominance and we can't interfere."

Trisha was stunned. It wasn't sane and it sure wasn't something she wanted to stand by and watch. They needed to stop. Someone could get hurt. Harley refused to release her though when she struggled.

Brass rose to his feet. He growled and launched his body at Slade. In horror, Trisha watched the men go at each other. She'd never seen two New Species fight before. It looked to be a combination between a dog fight and a no-holds-barred kickboxing match. It became clear within minutes that Slade was the better fighter. He punched Brass in the face and threw a kick that sent Brass sprawling onto his stomach. Brass groaned but didn't get up. Slade panted, obviously still enraged.

"You thought you could protect her?" Slade snarled. "You can't even protect yourself against me."

Brass lifted his head, looking a little dazed, and blood smeared his mouth. He turned his head to glare at Slade. "Someone had to try to protect her."

"Well, you can't." Slade marched toward the cabin.

Moon had edged around the fighting men until he stood guard at the bottom of the porch steps, blocking Slade's path to Trisha. Harley suddenly released Trisha and leaped down the porch steps to stand next to Moon. Both men appeared tense.

"Move," Slade snarled, stopping just feet from the men.

"Why? You are upset and aren't being reasonable." Harley kept a calm tone in his voice. "You hurt Brass over being angry with Valiant. We didn't know he was here or Brass would have gone to talk to him before he picked up the scent of a human. You are one of our best fighters and you knew you could take Brass alone. You could take both of us one-on-one too. We know that. But you'll have to take on both of us at once if you wish to upset Trisha. Your fight isn't with her."

Slade's dark-blue gaze locked with Trisha's. He panted hard and seemed so enraged that it scared her. She never thought she'd be afraid of Slade, especially after their time alone in the woods, but she'd been wrong. She was terrified of him.

"I knew you were attracted to Justice more than you admitted to me. I would not have avoided you if I had known you were so hot to have a Species male in your bed. I thought I was protecting you," Slade growled. "Being with one of us puts you in danger. You went through too much and I didn't want you to be with me out of gratitude for saving your life. I knew only time would give us a chance." He shook his head. "I could kill you. I told you that you were mine. Mine!" he snarled. "You can stay here and have your bastard but I better never see you again. You don't have permission to leave the cabin while Justice hides you and his love child under my nose."

Slade spun and stormed away. Trisha locked her knees so she wouldn't collapse on the porch. Slade thought she was pregnant by Justice? Her mouth opened.

"Slade?"

He ignored her completely, as though she hadn't spoken, as he jumped in his Jeep.

"Slade?" Her voice rose.

He turned his head and sheer rage showed on his features. "You're dead to me, Doc. Don't ever say my name again. I regret ever speaking to you and I wish I'd never touched you."

The Jeep roared to life and he threw it in reverse.

"Slade? You need to listen to me," Trisha yelled. "It's not Justice's baby!"

He stomped on the brake and turned his head back, curling his lip. "Brass? You should have picked someone stronger, Doc. He just got his ass kicked and I didn't even break a sweat. I bet he says your name though, doesn't he?"

Trisha managed to take a step and grab the porch railing to keep standing. She was mad now. "It's not his baby either. It's yours, you stupid son of a bitch!" She yelled the information at him. "You might have been able to beat up Brass but at least he's here for me. He never abandoned me when I needed him the most and he doesn't lie to me by swearing he'll come back for me but instead runs away as if he's a big coward, the way you did. And that bastard you referred to is a great way to title your own baby. I hate you."

She saw his expression change as emotions crossed his features with rapid speed. Anger, shock, and finally he paled before his expression returned back to rage mode again. He shut off the Jeep and climbed out. His features became unreadable when he stomped toward Trisha. Brass managed to get back on his feet and he staggered into Slade's path.

"Don't."

Slade growled at him. "Move."

"Don't do this," Brass urged softly. "Do you want to upset her enough to make her lose the baby? She's been through enough."

Slade's gaze jerked to Trisha. "The baby is really mine?"

She fought tears. "You mean 'bastard', don't you? Go to hell, Slade. Yes, the baby is yours in the biological way. In every other sense the baby is mine and mine alone. Don't worry though. In the last weeks I've learned exactly what to expect from you so stay away from me just the way you have been. I waited a week for you to call or come see me. When you didn't I was even hopeful for another week. Then you took this job and didn't even have the decency to tell me you were leaving. You just left. I hate you for that, I really do, and I will never forgive you. You lied to me and you just blew me off. Well, I can do that too. Leave me alone and stop beating up my friends, because they actually care about me." She took a ragged breath, fighting the urge to cry. "They don't make me cry. They don't abandon me or break my heart."

She turned and fled inside the house, running for the stairs. She barely made it inside the bathroom before she threw up. When it was over, she washed her face, brushed her teeth, and finally braved opening the door. She was afraid Slade would want to confront her again but it was Moon who sat on the edge of bed.

Slade stood in the yard in absolute shock. A baby. It wasn't possible. Species couldn't impregnate females. They'd been sure of that. Mercile had tried too hard. They would have figured out a way if it were feasible. Trisha wouldn't lie to him though. He knew she wouldn't intentionally mislead him about something that important.

"Happy now?" Brass spit out grass from between his teeth, brushing off dirt. "You upset her."

Slade glared at the other male. "I didn't know."

"You weren't around to find out. You haven't been anywhere near her since her retrieval. I take it that's when you bred with her?"

*Trisha is carrying my baby.* He tried to allow the news to sink into his still-shocked brain.

"You had her and left her. I've heard of stupid moves before but that is one of the worst. You may be able to take me in a fight but never get into a battle of intelligence with me. I'd kick your ass," Brass said before storming toward the side of the house and the water hose.

Slade stood there feeling numb, staring up at the house. He wanted to go after her, wanted to talk to her, and would even beg her forgiveness for the harsh words but he didn't even know where to start. He'd called her child a bastard.

*Why am I always fucking up so bad around her? Damn it!* His chin lowered to his chest and pain gripped him. He was his own worst enemy. Every time he opened his mouth he seemed to push away the woman he loved by saying something that pained or hurt her.

He turned, stumbling toward the Jeep, knowing he needed to cool down and think. He had to figure out a way to make this right. He jumped in the driver's seat but his hand hesitated. He didn't want to leave her. He couldn't. He let his hand drop but then reached for the key again. Anger and pain gripped him. He couldn't seem to do anything right when it came to Trisha. Perhaps he didn't deserve her but he wanted her so badly it made him feel bitter at the concept of losing her forever.

He started the engine and slowly drove away but he'd return. He'd shower, change his clothes and calm down. He'd think clearer and find a way to fix the mess his temper and jealousy had created.

*A baby. Trisha is having my baby.* A warm feeling spread throughout his chest.

\* \* \* \* \*

"He left." Moon studied her. "Are you well?"

"I totally lost it."

He nodded. "I saw and heard."

"How is Brass?"

"Harley is outside, hosing him off with water but he'll be fine. His pride suffered the most at being beaten but Slade really is one of our finest fighters. I told Brass there is no shame in getting his ass kicked by the best. There should only be a sense of shame when you lose to someone weaker."

"I'm so sorry this happened." Trisha wiped at tears.

Moon stood and slowly approached Trisha. "It is not your fault. Slade deserved your harsh words. He had sex with you and disappeared afterward. It is his shame to carry, not yours. You are a gift, Trisha. Any man would be lucky if you cared about him and allowed him to touch you the way he did but he threw it away. He was stupid to do that. Lie down and rest. The supplies arrived a few minutes ago and we will bring you dinner soon. Think of your baby and don't worry about Slade or anything else. We will take care of you. I'm sure once Slade cools down he will return to talk calmly with you. We made him see the good reasoning in leaving you alone until he calms. He didn't want to but his brain started functioning again. I think he was such a dick because he was insanely jealous, believing you had allowed someone else to touch you. He wouldn't have been such an asshole if he didn't care about you and he must care a lot since he was such a big one."

Trisha didn't protest when Moon tucked covers around her after she lay down and he pressed a kiss to her forehead. Trisha smiled at him.

"Thank you. I'm impressed, by the way."

"About what?"

"I think that's the most I've ever heard you say at one time."

Moon grinned before he returned downstairs. Trisha tried to relax. It wasn't easy. She was still upset by what had happened.

*Well, Slade knows about our baby now.* She'd fulfilled what Justice had asked her to do and it had been a disaster. She fought tears. She hadn't dreamed in a million years that she'd end up screaming the news of fatherhood at a man whose baby she carried and she'd called him names on top of it all. *Just…crap!*

Was Moon correct? Slade had been an extreme asshole. If he didn't care he wouldn't have reacted so violently to the news of her being pregnant. It had really hurt when he'd instantly assumed she'd slept with Justice. Maybe he thought she slept around with men regularly. He didn't know her at all if that was the case.

The whole "mine" thing remained stuck inside her head. He'd said she was his when he'd attacked Bill at the camp where she'd almost been raped. Then when they were outside he'd screamed at her that she knew she was his but if he considered her that, why had he abandoned her? He'd said something about protecting her and it was just confusing when she tried to make sense of his words. He wanted to give her time? He'd said only time could have given them a chance or something close to that. *Time for what? For me to feel used and stupid for thinking something meaningful happened between us?*

She heard the stairs creak a short time later and wiped away her tears. Harley walked upstairs carrying a glass of milk and some food with him. A spoon peeked out of the bowl.

"I brought you milk for the baby and soup for your upset stomach. Moon told me you were sick enough to lose your last meal. I'll bring you chocolate-chip cookies if you hold all this down. They sent a large bag of them. I told the guys to at least save you one."

Trisha smiled as she sat up. "Just one?"

"Maybe two. You are eating for two people now." Harley grinned at her. "You be careful with this. It's hot. I don't want you to get burned."

Trisha stared at him with gratitude. "Thank you for being my friend."

"A friend? I thought we could elope to Vegas and have Elvis marry us." His gaze sparkled as he teased. "I had it all worked out too. We could buy some mangy mutt, buy us a rusty old RV, and find some city dump to live next to. I hear it's a great place to find furniture." He lifted up the material on his arm and exposed his thick biceps. "I had a spot picked out here to have your name tattooed on me and I thought I could have my name tattooed across your ass. That way I could actually say I owned your ass."

Trisha laughed. Moon walked upstairs and sat on the edge of the bed holding a plate with a few pieces of buttered toast. He set it down on the bed next to Trisha so she could easily reach it.

"It's not her ass you have your name put on, Harley. You have her tattoo it on her arm so when she forgets your name, it's right there. We all know how memorable you aren't. She'd have to be a contortionist to see your name on her ass."

"If she's a contortionist," Brass called out as he climbed the stairs, "then she'd have to marry me instead. And you never have Elvis marry you. That's a bad omen if I ever heard one. Everyone knows marriage started by a dead guy ends in a dead marriage down the road. And speaking of road, she's high class and don't forget it. You don't buy some rusted-out RV. You buy a fifth-wheel travel trailer and live in style. That way you can unhitch it and not have to remove the patio every time you need to go somewhere."

Trisha wanted to flinch when she saw Brass' face. He had bruising to his cheekbone and jaw, cuts all over, and there was swelling near his eye. He held her worried gaze and winked. "I'm still incredibly good-looking."

She laughed. "Yes. You are."

Moon sniffed suddenly. His gaze turned to Brass and Harley. They sniffed too. Three pairs of eyes turned to the window before they glanced away.

Trisha tensed. "What do you smell?"

"It's nothing to worry about," Moon muttered. "Just a hint of a storm outside."

"Oh. I hope the roof doesn't leak." Trisha glanced up at the slanted wood beams of the ceiling and back at the guys. "The cabin seems pretty solid though, even if it is outdated inside."

"I'm sure it won't, Trisha." Brass motioned to her food. "Eat up."

Trisha ate while the men kept teasing her. She laughed, listening to them get more outrageous about funny marriage scenarios. She saw them glance at the window a few times. It had grown dark outside. The window remained open but she didn't see any flashes of lightning or hear rain.

Trisha finished all of her soup, ate both slices of toast, and finished off her milk. Moon took her dishes.

"I'll bring you cookies and some more milk but I'm going to take a jog first. I enjoy a good run at night. Can you wait for your snack?"

"Yes. Thank you."

He smiled at her and disappeared downstairs.

"I know," Harley chuckled. "You could marry me and we could go live with your parents. I hear that humans living with their in-laws always have a successful marriage."

Brass smacked his forehead with his palm. "Where do you hear this backward bullshit? That's a surefire way to kill a marriage."

Trisha laughed. "You'd run for the hills or worse if you ever met my parents and would probably buy a gun and shoot them. I don't want to be married to a guy who's doing twenty-to-life in prison."

"Yeah." Brass nodded seriously. "Then she'd have to divorce you for cheating on her inside the state pen."

"Cheating on her?" Harley looked confused for a second and grimaced. "That's...just wrong! I am attracted to females."

"It depends on who you ask. I heard once that some men find true love behind bars." Brass winked at Harley. "You do have a nice ass. I'm sure I'm not the only man who will see it that way."

"I'm never bending over in front you again." Harley flipped Brass off. "And that's not an offer. I have way higher standards."

"Enough," Trisha laughed. "You guys are starting to make my stomach hurt. Why don't we give my tummy a break and pick up our card game? I was kicking some serious ass."

"You were not." Harley stood. "I'll get the cards." He strode to the stairs. "We were letting you win."

"He's a sore loser," Brass whispered.

"I heard that!"

# Chapter Sixteen

ഇ

Slade turned when Moon crept up next to him. The wind picked up. Slade hooked his thumbs inside his jeans pockets, having gone home and changed before he'd returned.

Moon took a deep breath. "Are you enjoying standing out here listening to us cheer her up?"

Slade said nothing.

"You really upset her when you made nasty accusations. She treats us as though we are brothers and I can promise you there is nothing between her and Justice. I've been on her security detail for weeks and she just hangs out with us when she's not working. I knew she was sad but I didn't know why until today." He paused. "You shouldn't have left her the way you did. Why would you do it? She's amazing."

Minutes passed. "I was afraid that being with me would endanger her. It made sense at the time but it was all for nothing. I feared for her safety above my desire to be with her. I've put her in much more danger now that she's carrying my child. She'll be a target for the hate groups and I unknowingly put her in more danger by not being there when she needed me." Slade's voice softened. "I also wanted to give her time to make certain how she felt about me but I really needed it myself too. Does she know I'm out here?"

"No. We told her we scented a storm coming. It is hard to want something very much when we have learned anything we value gets taken from us."

Slade silently agreed.

"She thinks you used her for sex and you don't care about her. She is carrying your child and hurting. Do you realize she is a miracle?"

Slade turned his head to glare at the other male. "Of course I know, damn it."

"But you left her alone." Moon shook his head in disgust. "I wouldn't allow anything to stand in my way to be with her if I were lucky enough to find a woman similar to her who cared for me, especially not my own fear. I know all about loss with our shared past. I know how terrifying it is to feel anything because it opens us up to the possibility of deep pain." He took a breath. "I would risk anything for a woman I loved."

"She was attacked for her association with us. I believed being with me would only increase the danger. It wasn't just all about my fear of growing attached to her."

"She knew the risks when she took the job. She is smart, Slade. Homeland had been attacked before she arrived and it can happen again. She watches the news, sees the protestors spew their hatred of us to anyone who will listen when they make their threats, yet she still came to us. She allowed you to touch her knowing what Ellie and Fury faced and still do. She was present when Fury took the bullets meant for his mate. You may have believed you were being honorable but you were wrong. She's already in danger and the degree doesn't matter. What does matter is having a strong male at her side to protect her if someone tries to harm her. You failed in that."

Pain lanced through Slade at the truth of the words. "She won't forgive me."

Moon glanced at the house. "You need to make her understand how much you care and that you've learned how much she means to you."

Slade glanced at the cabin. "Any ideas on how to do that?"

"Actually, yes. I'll go inside and talk to the guys. I'm sure they will do what I say. They care about Trisha and want her to be happy. I believe you can make her understand if you love her as much as I suspect. It might not sit well with Brass though because he is very close to her as a friend. Stop growling. There is nothing between them."

"What do you have in mind?"

"I am going to talk to them and we will camp outside tonight after she goes to sleep. You are going to go in there to get your female back when she is alone."

\* \* \* \* \*

Trisha turned over on the bed and came up against a warm body. Her hands touched hot, bare skin. She gasped as her eyes flew open but it was too dark to see anything. She'd fallen sleep at some point and the men had gone downstairs. She scooted back.

"I guess the floor was too hard for you? You better be dressed from the waist down," she warned the guy sharing her bed. She wished she had their keen sense of smell or sight to determine which of the three she spoke to.

"Mmmm," the voice murmured softly. The body adjusted closer and an arm slid over her waist.

"Hey," Trisha protested and shoved at his chest. "Roll to the other side of the bed. I don't mind sharing but I'm not a body pillow you can curl around."

He didn't put space between them. "I'm trying to get some sleep, sweet thing. You're making it impossible to do with you pushing on me."

Trisha gasped and tried to sit up, her hand fumbling for the lamp on the nightstand. The arm moved from around her waist and she twisted away. Her fingers brushed the base of the lamp and almost knocked it over in her haste. She blindly reached for the switch and pressed. Light blinded her for a few seconds.

She turned and gaped at a bare-chested Slade. Tan, muscular skin was revealed to his waist where the sheet pooled and covered the rest of him. She wasn't sure if he wore pants and didn't want to know. The fact that he was in her bed shocked her.

"What are you doing?" She couldn't believe he was sprawled on her bed. "How did you get in here?"

"I strolled inside the front door I helped fix after you fell asleep." Slade rested on his side. He propped his head on the palm of his bent arm and smiled at her. "Turn off the light. It's the middle of the night and I want to hold you."

Trisha gawked at him. "You leave me high and dry and now you want to hold me? You dare climb into bed with me? Are you for real?"

"Yes."

"Have you lost your mind? I haven't. Get out!"

"Come here, sweet thing."

Trisha tried to scramble out of bed but Slade gently grabbed her, hauling her flat onto her back on the mattress. He pinned her under his big, warm body, careful not to hurt her when he did it. Two things became instantly clear to Trisha. One, Slade was totally nude. And two, he was aroused since she could feel the thick, hot erection bump against her inner thigh. They were skin to skin where her nightshirt had ridden up. She sucked in a breath, beyond stunned that he'd dare pull that kind of stunt.

"I missed you." His beautiful gaze studied hers and his voice came out gruff.

*I want to hate him for sounding sexy and looking so attractive. Remember — he abandoned me. That wasn't hot or sexy. It was mean and cold.* "You knew where to find me." Trisha flattened her hands on his chest, pushed with all her might, but he didn't budge as she glared at him. Her teeth clenched. "I'll yell for help if you don't get off me."

"I hope you have a really loud voice because I sent them away. I wanted us to be alone. This time I didn't want to have to put my palm over your lips."

Memory was instant of the last time he'd done that to keep her quiet while he fucked her. Her body instantly responded when her belly quivered and she hated it, wanting to hate him. She glared into his eyes.

"You left me and now you want me back? Is that what you're saying? For how long this time? Do I wake in the morning and what? Not see you again for weeks? Maybe months? No. Get off me, Slade."

He shifted his weight to make certain he didn't crush her stomach and cupped Trisha's face. "I was scared. You frighten the hell out of me and that's the truth."

"Scared?" She took a deep breath, trying to calm, and resisted the urge to smack him. She was tempted. "So you were afraid? Of what? You're a foot taller than I am and outweigh me by a good hundred pounds or so. What did you have to be afraid of?"

"Being with me puts you in more danger. That was the main reason I stayed away from you. You nearly died in the woods, could have died when the SUV crashed, and I didn't want to be the cause of more assholes targeting you."

She just stared at him, trying to take in his words. It didn't matter though because he'd hurt her. She wasn't about to allow him to do it again.

"It was more than that though. I've had a lot of time to think. I never dared to allow myself to get attached to anything or anyone. I saw too many die and too much pain. I never owned anything, could never count on anyone being there in the next moment, or even the next day. They used it against me if those assholes who kept me prisoner realized I cared about another person at the testing facility. Hell, they used it against all of us to try to control us. I know you can't really understand what a lifetime of that does to a person but I can tell you that it messed me up bad. I'm screwed up. I was afraid of what I wanted from you and that you might not return those strong emotions. I wanted to give you time but I'm the one who needed it. I thought if I walked away that I would stop thinking about you and that you would be safer without me. I said you'd be better off if I wasn't a part of your life. That's not what happened."

His honesty surprised her and some of her anger seeped away. She didn't know how to respond but her heart melted a little at the sincere look he gave her, the obvious pain sounding in his voice, and she had to concede he'd had a really screwed-up past. He admitted that readily, acknowledged he had flaws, and it softened her resolve to remain angry.

"You promised you'd come to me but you didn't. You hurt me, Slade. You wouldn't even talk to me. How do you expect me to stop being angry and hurt?"

"I planned to come to you straight after I returned to Homeland but I had to go to a meeting first. Justice demanded it. I heard them saying how and why you'd been targeted by humans. I started to think about how I'd feel if you were killed because we were together. I freaked out, Doc."

"Stop calling me that. My name is Trisha. Use it."

His fingers brushed her cheek. "And I told you that I'll only call you Trisha when I'm inside you." His face lowered. "And I want inside you in the worst way. I want to taste you and feel you. There's so much we've never had the opportunity to do. I want you to moan my name and I want hear you scream in pleasure. I need to show you how much you mean to me and how much I've missed you. Please let me."

"Please, Slade." She locked her gaze with his. "Don't do this to me. You hurt me when you promised you'd come back for me but you didn't. I had to kill two men and I had faith that you'd come help me but you didn't. Two other men had to save me yet I still had hope that you'd show up. I needed you. I was worried sick until they told me you'd been found alive. I waited for you to come to me when they said you had arrived back at Homeland but you blew me off."

"I did come back to you when you fired at those assholes. I heard the shots but I realized Flame and Smiley reached you before I could. I wanted to save you but you didn't need me." He paused. "I also didn't wish you to see me the way I was at the time. I'd killed a lot of men. I was afraid you'd see the blood, that it would make you rethink being with someone capable of that much violence, and that you wouldn't believe that I'd never lay a finger on you to cause you pain. I'm not fully human and..." He paused, a pained expression lining his handsome face. "It was for the best if you didn't see me that way. Just trust me on that. I want to be a male you'll want, not one you'll fear."

Her resolve softened even more. *He's insecure about what he is and how I see him. He's not such a hard-ass after all.* She took a deep breath. "Slade, I know what you are. I know you're not fully human but I accepted that. I was torn up inside over killing those men. I just wanted and needed you after I killed those men. You just walked away from me as though I meant nothing. I don't know how you could do that if you care about me."

"You were safe. That's what mattered most to me. I was sure I'd scare you in the condition I was in at the time and I decided to go back into the woods instead to find the rest of those assholes and make sure they were no longer a threat to you. I believed it was the right choice at the time. I made a mistake."

"You gave me your word and you lied to me."

"I'm so sorry. It seemed like the right decision at the time. I was also too out of control to hide my possessiveness of you. Anyone there would have known we'd bonded."

"So you didn't want anyone to know about what happened between us?" Anger and pain shot through her. "Well, guess what? Now some people know. I bet that just really humiliates you. I know, it's not PC for New Species to sleep with a human, is it?"

"What is PC?"

"Politically correct. Some of you guys have sworn to never touch humans. It's— Oh hell, get off me. I also hate to break this to you but your guys took one whiff of me and knew I'd had sex. At first they thought I'd been raped. I wouldn't tell them a thing except I hadn't been. I left your name out of it even after I got pregnant but Justice remembered how I smelled that night I was brought back to Homeland. At first he thought the father was Brass but when I told him I'd never touched him sexually, Justice knew it was you. You were the only strong scent left on me."

"Don't speak words that I did not say or even think. I'm not ashamed of you, Doc. I don't care about what is PC. I was trying to protect your human nature. I know human women are very private about their sex lives and being with me put you in greater danger. Ellie and Fury are proof of that. I was also trying to protect you from what Ellie and Fury went through when they got together. Everyone bugged them about their sex life and hell, every time Fury touched her it seemed as though someone accused him of hurting her. That's why I didn't want those men to guess what had happened between us and I wasn't sure if any humans were involved with the rescue who would witness us together."

"I trusted you once and now I know I can't. I—"

Slade's mouth came down on hers and his lips brushed hers. He spoke against her lips. "I'm bad with words, sweet thing, but trust this." Then he forced her mouth open under his.

Trisha tried not to feel but it was Slade kissing her. She wanted and loved him despite the pain he'd caused her. She'd always known her attraction to him wouldn't be easy, him being New Species, her not being. They were worlds apart but when he touched her all those differences seemed to melt away until it was just the two of them. Her hands splayed on his chest, enjoying the warm feel of his skin as she started to kiss him back. Her mouth parted wider, admitting his hungry eagerness to bend her to his seduction. A moan escaped from the back of her throat.

Slade's hands caressed her and his body turned, shifting hers with his, until they faced each other on their sides. His mouth never left hers, his tongue coaxing her passion higher. His hands gripped her nightshirt at the waist and material tore. He freed her breasts to cup them with his palms. Strong fingers kneaded her softer flesh.

Trisha broke away from the kiss, breathing hard. "Slade?"

"Don't tell me to stop. Please? I need you. You have no idea how much I want you, Trisha. I have hurt from how much I've missed you. I'm dying for you."

His head lowered, his tongue rasped over her breast, and all thought left her when his mouth closed over her nipple. He sucked in hard tugs that made her stomach clench, her desire burn brighter, and he nipped her lightly with his teeth. Trisha's entire body jerked from the sharp pinch of pleasure that jolted straight to her brain as a result. She moaned louder, running her hands along his chest to his shoulders, and dug her fingernails into his skin where they curved. Her mind warned to push him away but instead she pulled him closer.

Slade tore his mouth away from her breast. Trisha protested with a whimper. She ached from wanting him and her eyes opened to discover Slade watching her face closely. The passion in his heated gaze turned her on more. He appeared a little wild, ruggedly handsome, and the fangs peeking out between his parted lips did wonderful things to her.

"You're so beautiful." He rose to his knees on the bed, releasing her, but reached for her again quickly as if he couldn't stand not touching her. "I don't want to hurt our baby." He smiled. "I'm happy about us creating one, by the way."

Trisha allowed him to pull her up to her knees. Slade easily turned her body in his strong arms just by lifting her until she faced away from him and her back pressed against his chest. He rid her of the destroyed nightshirt, just throwing it aside. His hands skimmed down over her breasts, before his mouth nibbled at her neck. His lips, tongue and teeth teased and taunted the sensitive skin.

Trisha moaned when his teeth bit down. He wasn't breaking the skin or hurting her but the pinch of his bite felt incredibility erotic. His tongue stroked the skin trapped between his teeth before he moved to other spots on her neck, lightly teasing her with soft nips. His hands slid lower to pause at the curve of her hips.

There was a tug of the material against her skin when his thumbs hooked into the sides of her panties. Slade ripped them from her body easily and tossed them away from the bed. His hands traveled lower and around the inside of her thighs until he gently gripped them.

"Open more for me, sweet thing. I want to touch your pussy. I can smell how hot you are and I want to feel. The memory has tormented me and kept me up every night I haven't been with you." He growled the words.

She moved her knees farther apart. She sucked in air and held her breath when Slade's hands slowly slid up her inner thighs, wanting him to get to the good part right away. She'd wanted him far too long for him to drag it out. She wanted him to touch her, needed it, ached for him to make love to her. She began to breathe heavily and wondered if she'd die if he didn't touch her soon. His fingers found her vaginal lips. They were slick with desire and he parted them with two fingers, rubbed her slit, and homed in on her swollen clit.

Trisha moaned loudly and pressed her head back against his shoulder. "Yes."

"Yes," he growled from behind her, giving assurances that he didn't plan to stop. "I'm never letting you go again, Trisha. Never. You're mine."

His fingers parted enough to capture the sensitive nub between them, rubbing and tugging softly. Trisha moaned louder, ground her ass back against his thighs, and could feel his heavy, hard cock pressed against her lower back. Her nipples tightened until they ached.

"Please? I need you," she whispered. "Do that but I want you inside me too."

"You've got it," he growled, his voice deep and animalistic.

The need that was clear in his voice just made her want him more. This was the Slade who turned her on, the man she wanted and had missed. He backed up a little, put his knees together between her spread thighs, and growled at her again.

"I'm going to fuck you, Trisha. I don't want to hurt you though. I'm going to sit and I want you to ride me so you're in control of how deep you take me."

Slade slowly lowered to sit back on his heels and pulled her slowly down until she straddled him, facing away. One of his arms guided her hips while his other hand continued to stroke her clit until he grabbed the shaft of his cock instead.

Trisha looked down, the sight of him fisting the base of his thick erection made her wetter and more needy to have him buried inside her pussy. She gripped the top of his thigh to help keep her balance, tilted her hips, and eased down as he guided the crown of his cock right against her entrance. Trisha came down over his lap and Slade slowly entered her.

She cried out over how good it felt when he breached her pussy, the snug fit of their bodies as she lowered more, and the slight burn of being stretched open by something so rigid. Trisha turned her face against his neck and her back pressed tightly against his chest. She moaned, feeling his thick, hard cock sliding deeper inside her wet, welcoming pussy as her body fully settled down onto his lap until her ass rested over his thighs. She shivered.

"Slade!"

"Easy, honey. Real slow, even if it kills me." He had released his shaft to allow her to sit fully on him and that hand eased over her thigh, returning to play with her clit. She whimpered, hurting to come.

"So warm, so tight," he growled. "So mine." His lips brushed her shoulder as he growled again against her skin. His fingers continued to tease her clit while he slowly started to rock his hips upward.

"Slade," she moaned.

"I'm here, Trisha," He rasped. His free hand ran up her stomach and cupped her breast to caress her sensitive nipple. "Fast or slow? Tell me what you want."

"Faster," she moaned.

Slade thrust up into Trisha with more force, strummed his fingers against the bundle of nerves between her thighs faster to keep pace with his thrusting hips. Trisha moaned louder. The sensation of him inside her while he rubbed her clit became amazingly intense. She gripped his thighs for something to cling to as he drove in and out of her faster and deeper.

Trisha nearly screamed when the climax struck, her vaginal muscles clenched tightly around the hard thickness of his cock. Waves of pleasure slammed her as he began to swell inside her. He slowed his thrusts to deep, violent jerks, and his entire body tensed. The hand released her breast, his arm hooked around her waist to lock her against his lap, and his body jerked violently under hers as he came.

"Trisha," he snarled.

They stilled and that's when Trisha noticed the heated feel of his semen as it spread inside her while he continued to come, filling her with his warm release. It seemed to go on for a good minute while they clung to each other. Her body quivered as Slade's hands shifted on her body, both of them tightening around her waist, anchoring her on his lap more firmly. He brushed a kiss on the top of her shoulder. They were both panting.

"I missed you," he breathed against her skin. "I won't ever leave you again. Ever, Trisha. I'd rather die than be away from you. I swear to protect you with my life and I won't mess up again. I learned how much you mean to me."

She released his outer thighs to grip his arms at her waist. Part of her was afraid to believe him but she really wanted to. She loved him. *Sometimes you have to take a chance. You'll never know if you refuse to at least give him one more shot.* She bit her lip before blowing out a deep breath.

"This is the last chance I'm giving you. I mean it. I won't give you another chance if you ever hurt me again. You pull another disappearing act and that's it. I'll be stick-a-fork-in-me done."

He chuckled. "I won't. I'll just stay where I am right now. Between the frequent sex and the swelling afterward, I'll be locked into you all the time. I could hold you this way forever."

"I have to eat sometime."

He laughed. "I won't starve you."

"Good to know."

"You're going to need your strength."


Slade held his Trisha until her body started to sag and he realized she was about to drift off to sleep. The swelling at the base of his shaft had receded. He adjusted his hold on her and carefully lifted her off his lap and onto her side. Her blue eyes met his and she smiled softly at him.

Emotions nearly choked him, making him unable to speak. She was so beautiful to him and so fragile. She carried his child within her womb. That fact still stunned and humbled him. She'd given him the ultimate gift. She'd given him her body and a future with her. His lips curved into a smile and he cleared his throat.

"I'll turn off the light. You need plenty of rest, Doc."

"Trisha." Her lips pouted slightly with irritation.

"Sorry, Trisha." He grinned. "Old habits die hard and in my defense, I'm no longer inside you."

"You'll use my name while you're in my bed unless you want to sleep on the floor."

"Fair enough." Amusement and happiness mingled inside Slade. She'd taken him back, forgiven him, and he wasn't sure he deserved it. He'd made a mess of things. Good intentions aside, he regretted his choices. "I'll turn off the light and we'll sleep."

She would have said something to him but instead, when her lips parted, a yawn came out. He turned off the light and reached for his woman. He pulled her lush body against his own, his arm wrapped around her waist and he spooned her from behind. He couldn't get close enough to her, didn't want even an inch of space between their bodies, and she willingly allowed him to settle them onto their sides.

"I really missed you," he confessed softly against her shoulder where he tucked his chin, breathing in her scent. "I thought about you constantly."

"I missed you too and couldn't get you out of my head. I hated it after you abandoned me."

He inwardly winced at the painful tone of her voice. "I'm sorry, sweet thing. It won't happen again. I swear that to you on my life. I made a stupid decision but it won't happen again. I've smartened up."

She lay still in his arms for long moments. "Are you okay about the baby?"

The uncertainty laced in her voice stung. He'd done this to her, made her question the bond between them. "I'm thrilled."

"I am too but I'm scared."

"I'll protect you." A flash of anger shot through him at the thought of her being in danger. "No one will hurt you. They will die if they try."

Her small hand gripped his arm that was around her waist, her fingers tracing his skin. "That's not what I'm afraid of. What if something goes wrong with the baby? Ever since I saw it on the ultrasound I knew I wanted it, Slade. There's so much that could happen. I'm a doctor. I know that—"

"It will be fine." He cut her off. "It's our baby, a miracle, and life has been too cruel to me as it is. I refuse to lose you or our child. Fate has to give us a break."

Her silence worried him but then she sighed. "Happy thoughts?"

He nuzzled her neck. "Yes. Happy thoughts, Trisha. We're together and that's what matters."

He knew when she drifted to sleep. Her breathing changed and her fingers stilled on his skin. He pulled her a little tighter against his body, careful not to crush her, but wanted to wrap around her more. The woman inside his arms meant life to him...and death. He'd do anything to be with her and he'd kill anyone who attempted to come between them.

# Chapter Seventeen

⁊ↄ

"No," Slade growled. His eyes flashed his anger. "I'll stay and protect her. You go do my job at the construction site."

Brass growled back. "I will not deal with all those humans."

Trisha shook her head at the two men who were about to come to blows again. She sighed. "Boys? Could we please not have a fight inside the living room? We already lost a coffee table and I'm partial to the couch because it's comfortable."

"Give it up." Harley chuckled. "They are so going to fight."

Moon had his arms crossed over his chest, looking bored. He nodded at Trisha.

"Want popcorn?" Harley headed for the kitchen. "I love to eat it when I watch a good fight."

"I'll take some," Moon grunted.

"Stop it," Trisha sighed. "There will be no fistfights in the living room. At least take it outside to the yard if you two are determined to beat each other up. Slade? Do you hear me? Brass? Come on, guys. No fighting inside the cabin."

Slade's gaze shifted to Trisha. "I am not leaving you. Tell him to go deal with Justice's projects. He can handle ordering a bunch of humans to build things on time as good as I can. They respond well when we snarl and show teeth. It motivates them to work faster to get away from us."

Brass cursed. "I have no idea what projects need to be done. All I said was that you can leave to do your job during the day and I told you that you can stay with her at night."

"She's mine," Slade growled. "You're telling me when I can spend time with her? Don't even try it. You have no say when it comes to my woman."

"I'm telling you that I can take care of her while you are at work. You have a job, remember? She doesn't need four of us sitting here watching her. She's safe in the wild zone. Valiant promised to talk to the others and that she would be protected by all of them. He assured me no humans would come near her."

Slade didn't appear convinced. "Do you need me to show you who can protect her better? Do you want me to wipe the ground with you again?"

"Enough!" Trisha yelled, finally losing her temper. She realized they weren't exactly normal men but their dominating nature started to irritate her. She glared at Slade. "You, stop beating your chest and threatening my friends." Her attention fixed on Brass next. "And you, stop baiting him." She sighed, lowering her voice as she stared at Slade. "You do have a job to do and I'm fine here. I don't see why you can't go to work and come home to me at the end of the day."

"Fine," Slade snarled. "Choose your friend over me." He stomped to the door.

"Slade? Stop thinking that way," Trisha groaned. "That's not it. Please just—"

Slade spun when he reached the door. "I will see you tonight."

He stormed out and slammed the door. Trisha walked to the couch and threw herself down, cursing softly. She sensed three pairs of eyes on her and she looked back at each of them.

"Why did him saying that sound as if it were a threat?"

Moon grinned at Trisha. "Because it was."

"Yeah," Harley agreed. "You're going to get it tonight." He removed the popcorn from the microwave. "But I doubt he'd let us watch whatever it is he will be plotting to do to you to get even. I do enjoying watching porn movies though. I'm betting that it would be a good show. Too bad."

"Porn?" Trisha sputtered, shooting Harley a glare. "That's not funny."

"He won't hurt you but..." Moon winked at her. "I bet he's going to think up something good to do to you. He'll want to convince you to pick him next time if there's an issue of you choosing."

She frowned. "What does that mean?"

Brass laughed. "We are aggressive and competitive. It's our nature. He's going to probably do something that soothes his pride."

"His pride? I wasn't picking you over him. What do you think he's planning? Come on, guys. I'm a doctor for goodness sake. Stop talking in riddles. What do you think he's going to do to me?"

"My guess?" Moon grinned. "He's going to turn you on until he makes you beg him to fuck you. He'll want to show you who your body belongs to and why he's your male. Then his pride will be fixed where you dented it."

"He's canine." Harley chuckled. "I know what I'd do to a woman if I wanted to show her I was in charge. I'd mount her and—"

"Harley!" Brass snarled, giving him a dirty look. "Shut up."

"What? I was just going to say I'd ride her until she couldn't move." He winked at Trisha. "Us dogs are hornier than hell and we can go for hours."

Brass groaned and wore a disgusted expression as he glanced at Trisha. "Never ask a dog his opinion about sex. Big mistake."

Trisha laughed. "I'm hungry. Is anyone else ready for breakfast?" She lifted an eyebrow at Harley and his popcorn. "That's disgusting to eat this early."

"Breakfast, hell. I had the night shift. I'm going to go to bed after I eat this. This is my midnight snack."

* * * * *

Slade stared at the desk and was certain Trisha had to be trying to drive him crazy. He hated being inside, surrounded by walls, and the temporary office was nothing more than a large rectangular box on wheels. The entire place smelled of humans and although he was adjusting to the scent, he didn't want to be around any, not trusting them completely. He turned his head to watch four of them working at other desks. Two were on the phone, one sipped coffee, and the last one scratched his head while staring at blueprints opened up in front of him.

"Is there a problem, Richard?"

The human dropped his fingers from his hair. "Nope. I'm just trying to figure out how we're going to finish this clubhouse to meet the deadline. I kept telling Mr. North that nobody can build something this size in just a few months. We have all the framing up but we still have a lot to do."

"What will it take?" Slade sighed. He knew the answer already — more money to hire more men to work around the clock.

"I think we'll make it but just pray for good weather. One bad storm front and we're screwed. It will set us back."

"Then what is the problem?"

The human hesitated. "We've been having a few issues of really bad luck."

"Such as?" Slade cocked his eyebrow.

Richard bit his lip. "Someone has been screwing with the site."

Slade tensed with alarm. "What kind of problems? What is going on? Why am I only hearing about this now?"

"I believed at first the stuff going wrong was just accidental. The crews are working seven days a week in twelve-hour shifts. I thought maybe one or two of them made mistakes because they were tired but it keeps happening. I'm beginning to think it's not so innocent. This morning one of the guys got hurt because one of the ladders was messed with. He's fine but we were lucky it broke immediately. It could have killed him if he'd climbed higher or worked on the third level. I inspected the ladder and determined someone purposely damaged it."

"You should have informed me before now." Slade lifted his phone. "I'll send a few officers down there to keep an eye out. That should dissuade anyone from doing more harm."

"Thanks."

Slade nodded. He had been afraid something bad would happen. There were groups out there who would enjoy nothing more than to cause trouble. Having hundreds of humans at Reservation invited a way for some of them to sneak onto the property to give them the opportunity to do harm.

"I'll order more security on all the working sites. I don't want anyone to get hurt or be killed." His finger had barely touched the numbers when the office door jerked open loudly. Tiger rushed inside.

"Slade? We have a problem."

Slade studied Tiger. They had become good friends after they'd been freed from captivity. They had lived and roomed together with other males in a remote motel for the months that had followed until the New Species Homeland had been opened.

"What is it?"

"We're missing human males."

"How many?" Slade grabbed his radio, dropped the phone, and rose to his feet quickly.

"There are exactly fourteen males unaccounted for and we're missing two work trucks. Just as you ordered, we count heads every hour and from last one, that's how many disappeared. I talked to both gates and they didn't leave. They are still here somewhere."

"Son of a bitch," Slade growled. "Attention," he demanded into the radio, rushing for the door. "We have fourteen human males in two trucks unaccounted for. Find them quickly."

Slade sprinted for one of the Jeeps with Tiger following. "Where do you think they would have gone?"

"I don't know." Tiger jumped in the passenger seat. "But we'll find them."

"Slade?" The voice on their radios spoke.

"He's with me." Tiger used his own radio to answer. "What is it?"

"Two trucks passed one of the security guards about twenty minutes ago, heading for the wild zone. It wasn't questioned because a crew had been scheduled to go work on the electrical system along the security walls out that way. We double-checked and they weren't sent out there yet. Whoever was spotted there shouldn't have been in the area without an escort by our officers but the human guards didn't know that."

"Shit," Slade growled. "Trisha is out there."

Tiger groaned. "Why would she be? It's not safe. Have you lost your mind? I thought we'd decided to set her up on the top floor of the hotel and have the access limited."

"Plans were changed."

"Is there a reason for that? A human has no business out there. The males have marked their territory and wouldn't welcome her there despite her being female."

Slade hesitated. "You could say that."

"What is she doing out there? No humans are allowed inside the wild zone. How did you talk them into allowing her into their territory? They've become really territorial and they'd have smelled her pretty quickly."

"Trisha is carrying my child. She's living in cabin six."

"Child?" Tiger gasped.

Slade nodded, punched the gas, and turned the wheel hard. "She's pregnant by me. Justice sent her here to conceal her from the humans during her pregnancy. Very few of us know of her condition."

"Son of a bitch." Tiger seemed stunned. "So you're going to be a daddy. Shit. You got her pregnant. What did she do to make that happen?"

"It was natural."

"Shit," Tiger growled again. "We can get them pregnant? Somebody should have told us that. I guess I better cancel my date with the woman from the city who inspects construction. I sure don't want to be a daddy too. My life is hard enough to deal with on my own but a mate and child?" He shook his head. "Not interested."

Slade shot him a surprised look. "I didn't know you were attracted to humans. I thought you believed they were too fragile."

"Yeah, well, some of them think I'm pretty cute." He shrugged. "What's a cute guy to do? I thought I'd try it. They are too fragile but it might have been fun to allow one to have her way with me a time or two."

"The missing humans better not be anywhere near Trisha. I do want her and our child. Where are these bastards and what are they doing?"

"I don't know." Tiger unsnapped his gun holster to gain easier access to his weapon. "But we'll find them." He stood, gripping the frame of the windshield. "You drive and I'll scent. We'll find them together, faster."

"I'm going to check on Trisha first. We have enough men to search for those assholes. I just want to make sure she's safe."

"Totally understandable. I'll still keep my nose at work. I can at least radio the teams if I catch their scent."

\* \* \* \* \*

"Trisha!" Brass yelled.

Trisha jumped, nearly slipping on the wet tub floor. She grabbed the water handles and turned them off. The bathroom door slammed into the wall when someone threw it open. A stunned and naked Trisha gasped when Brass suddenly yanked back the shower curtain. He pulled her out of the shower by her arm.

"There are a lot of humans coming this way." He released her and shoved her clothes into her arms. "Get dressed now. Be quick about it."

Brass ignored her to step up onto the rim of the tub to peer out the small window. Trisha tried to ignore the fact that she stood dripping wet and naked in the tiny room with him. She fumbled to figure out her T-shirt and yanked it over her head. The material clung to her damp skin. Fear motivated her not to complain about the invasion of privacy. He didn't seem to even notice she was naked...besides ordering her to dress.

"What is going on?" She yanked up her cotton shorts. "Why would humans be inside the wild zone? Are you sure someone is coming? Aren't they banned?"

"I see two trucks coming with many humans inside." He jumped down and grabbed Trisha's arm.

Trisha shoved her shirt down over her lower stomach as Brass hauled her into the living room. Moon and Harley had started to barricade the front door with the couch and they appeared really angry. Brass looked around the room and dragged Trisha toward the fireplace. He reached down, fisted the metal grate that covered it, and shoved it out of way.

"Get inside there."

She gaped at the dirty fireplace. "Why? It's really dirty."

"The fireplace appears to be made solid with rock and mortar. Get your ass inside there now. Bullets shouldn't go through it and it's the best place I can think to put you. We'd flee with you but I'm afraid it's too late. They'd see us and use the trucks to chase us down. Protecting you and your baby is our priority. Get inside there now and curl into a ball."

Trisha cringed but she lowered to her hands and knees. It wasn't a comfortable fit but she sat on her butt in ashes with her knees drawn up tight against her chest. Her forehead rested on her knees and she wrapped her arms around her bent legs. She couldn't lift her head all the way up without banging it into the flue. The interior of the fireplace wasn't tall enough. She watched with growing fear as the three men prepared for the worst.

The cedar chest was pushed in front of the door with the couch. For good measure, Moon shoved a heavy side table against that. Harley ran to the kitchen table and flipped it over onto the floor facedown. The legs were snapped off with a little help from his boot and strong hands. He lifted the heavy, thick wood of the tabletop and ran for the windows near the door. He dropped it in front of the glass so only inches of sunlight showed at the top. He shoved the loveseat in front of it to keep it in place.

Brass rushed inside the kitchen to tear out the fridge from the hole where it sat and shoved it against the back door. It completely blocked the entire opening and he grabbed the stove.

"Gas line!" Trisha yelled.

Brass froze and peered at her. "Thanks. I wouldn't have remembered." He leaned behind the large appliance for a few seconds to remedy the potential problem before he tore the disconnected stove away from the wall. He shoved it against the fridge.

"The top floor should be secure," Moon called out. "There's nothing around it high enough for them to climb up there and they can't leap the way the felines and primates do."

"I have no signal." Harley cursed viciously while he gripped a cell phone.

"Parts of the cabin seem to block it," Brass informed him. "I had to walk around a bit to get service. Try by the base of the stairs. It seemed strongest there." Something broke inside the kitchen.

Trisha watched as Brass tore apart the counter, using his massive strength to just rip off a section, which he slammed over the single kitchen window. He turned, studied the kitchen for a second, before he hurried back into the living room.

"Get your duffle bag," Brass ordered Moon. "Use the top floor to take out as many of them as you can. You're authorized for deadly force. It's my call and I'm making it."

Moon nodded grimly and turned his head to stare at Trisha. "Should I take her up there with me?"

"No. She's safer there, better protected from stray bullets. You'll be drawing fire when you open up on those terrorists." Brass glanced at Trisha and held her gaze. "Do not move your ass no matter what happens. Do you understand me? If one of us goes down, doctor or not, don't move an inch. You think of that baby."

Fear gripped Trisha when the trucks were close enough for her human ears to pick up the sound. Moon dragged out a duffle bag from a closet near the front door and tore it open. He hadn't packed clothes inside the large, long bag. Instead he unloaded two rifles and gripped the hand of the duffle, taking it with him as he hurried up the stairs.

Harley walked to his bag and Trisha watched him unloading handguns and ammunition. He glanced at Brass. "Do you want the front or the back position?"

"I'll take the back. Humans always seem to think they can creep up on us. I think the attack along the back side will be far worse and I'm a better shot."

"Yeah," Harley snorted. "We'll see about that. I bet I can take out more of those terrorists than you can."

"I'm sure they are just lost," Trisha urged, hoping that was the case. "Please don't shoot someone unless you have to."

Brass met her gaze. "There are two trucks of humans trespassing inside the wild zone and Slade would never send them in this direction with you here. They would have a Species escort and Slade would have warned us to move you to keep you out of sight if they had permission. They are here to do harm. Keep your ass where you are." He grabbed a side table and shoved the lamp to the floor where glass shattered as it broke. He pushed the table near her to block the hole and trap her there.

"You move from that spot and I'll blister your ass with a leather belt," Brass growled at her. "Do you understand? You won't sit for a week."

Shocked, Trisha stared at him. Brass suddenly grinned and winked.

"I know enough about human children to know that's an effective threat." His smile died. "And I mean it." He spun away, heading for the back wall of the cabin to a window.

Trisha heard brakes and engines died, letting her know the trucks had stopped outside. She heard male voices. *It just has to be some kind of mistake. The guys are just freaking out and overreacting. They have to be. No one knows I'm in the cabin and no one is coming to hurt me or my baby. It is all just a big misunderst—*

"Are any of you fucking animals inside there?" a male voice yelled from outside. "Come out and let us put you out of your fucking misery."

Laughter sounded and Trisha tensed. *Okay. It isn't a misunderstanding. They're here to do harm.* The men outside weren't looking for her personally but instead were searching for any New Species they found. She locked her focus on Harley by the front window and knew he would be able to see them best. He looked calm to her. She felt anything but. Her terror mounted as the seconds ticked by, praying they'd just leave. She didn't want Brass or the guys to get hurt protecting her.

"Let's go in and get us some animal skin," another jerk laughed.

"We will kill you where you stand if you come any closer. We're heavily armed," Harley warned loud enough for them to hear his threat.

Male voices laughed from outside. "You hear that? One of the animals thinks we'd allow a dog or cat to chase us off. Spread out and shoot the son of a bitch. We're going to show it who the masters are."

Gunfire erupted, the sounds loud and horrible. Trisha's gaze flew toward the loft when she realized that Moon had opened fire. Trisha stared in horror as Harley lifted his gun, pointed it out the narrow opening at the top of the window uncovered by the kitchen table, and fired his weapon. Her hands lifted to cover her ears. She heard multiple gunshots and men shouting outside though she tried to block out the sound.

\* \* \* \* \*

"Fuck," Slade roared.

"We know where they are," Tiger spat, grabbing his radio. "We need help at the wild zone at cabin six. We have active gunfire. Our people are under attack."

Slade snarled at Tiger. "Sit." It was all the warning he gave before he twisted the wheel hard and the Jeep left the road. He had to violently spin the wheel again seconds later to avoid slamming into a tree.

Tiger cursed and grabbed hold of anything he could. Slade had left the pavement and drove at a dangerous speed through the woods. The Jeep bounced roughly, the ride nearly terrifying as they dodged obstacles and barely missed trees.

Tiger held his breath a few times, thinking the Jeep wouldn't clear between thick trunks a few times. One of the side mirrors didn't make it when it slammed into a tree, exploded from the impact, and Tiger heard paint scraped off the side of the door.

"Don't drive out into the open when we get there. We'll sneak up behind them and take them out. They won't hear us with all that racket."

"Fuck that. I'm hoping to draw them away from her." Slade snarled the words, too enraged to care what happened to them as long as they fired at him instead of at Trisha. "I want them after me instead."

"They are humans," Tiger growled. "They don't fight that way. We won't draw them off, at least not all of them. Listen to me. I know you are enraged but do what I say. You aren't rational."

Slade nodded, knew his friend spoke the truth, but he couldn't seem to think past the fear of Trisha getting hurt or killed. He knew he'd left rational behind at the first sound of the gunfire when he'd driven off the road.

"Fine."

\* \* \* \* \*

Trisha watched Harley flinch, jerk back and grab his bloody arm when a bullet struck him. He didn't stop firing his gun though. He just gripped his injury for a few seconds before he ignored it.

She wanted to help him but knew it would be suicide to try to reach him. Bullets struck the cabin repeatedly and holes opened up along the wall by the door in a sudden flurry but Harley threw himself down at the last second. He crawled, cursed, and moved to a new location. He stood and began firing again. More bullets tore through the cabin walls as the men outside returned fire. A framed picture hanging on the wall near where the couch had been shattered from a bullet, sending glass raining down.

Trisha turned her head to check on Brass, who leaned against a thick support beam while he fired outside. He'd obviously guessed accurately that some of the men would try to sneak up along the back. Trisha heard a noise and stared at the kitchen as the countertop Brass had wedged against the window came crashing down. It hit the sink and slid to the floor. Trisha saw movement as the long barrel of a gun entered from where someone had obviously gotten the window open.

"Kitchen window," Trisha yelled.

Brass dived for the floor and slid across it a few feet on his belly until he could see the kitchen. He twisted onto his side, gun in hand, and aimed. Brass shot the intruder in the head when a man attached to the barrel of the gun climbed through the window.

The body jerked before he collapsed with half of his body slung over the sink. Brass turned and blinked at Trisha before he dumped an empty clip from the handgun and shoved in a new one. He lunged to his feet to reach his post by the support beam again. His gaze peered out the window he guarded.

"Tell me if you see anyone else, Trisha," Brass ordered. "Don't look away. You're our eyes."

Trisha mutely nodded but remembered he wasn't looking at her. "I've got your back." Her voice came out shaky but she knew he heard her when he didn't repeat the order.

She stared in horror at the body draped through the window. Blood ran down the cabinet under the sink and pooled on the floor. She forced her attention away from the red and the grotesque sight of what was left of his head where pieces were missing. She focused on the window opening instead. If someone used it to enter the kitchen they would be able to shoot at Brass and Harley. Their sole focus needed to be on the outside.

The shooting stopped suddenly and Trisha held her breath. She was afraid to look away from the window and she didn't. The lives of men she cared about depended on her keeping a steady visual.

"They are reorganizing," Brass growled. "How you doing, Harley?"

"Two hits but just grazes on my arm and lower leg. I'm good to stand."

"Moon?"

"Still here and fine. I've gotten six of them for keeps and winged two more. They are staying behind the trucks or sneaking through the woods to circle around. Right now they are huddled, probably trying to come with a plan to rush us. I don't have a good shot from the back. The porch roof blocks my view."

Brass lowered his voice to a whisper. "Ammo?"

"I'm good," Moon called from above.

Harley hesitated. "Low."

"Moon? Cover the front." Brass kept his voice soft to prevent it from being heard by the men outside.

"Got it."

"Harley, trade positions with me after you resupply. Hold the back while I fix the problem inside the kitchen."

Trisha watched Harley limp to the bags on the floor. He shoved ammo clips into his pockets along the legs of his pants. She stared with worry at the blood trail he'd left when he walked. She wanted to tend to him. Brass hesitated inside the kitchen, swept his gaze around it, and crouched. He reached the dead man, grabbed him by his collar, and dragged him totally inside the cabin. He even took a second to check for a pulse. He shoved the body where the stove had once stood to put it out of the way.

He stayed low to the floor when he grabbed the broken countertop and used it for a shield in front of his body when he rose and slammed the heavy piece back over the window. He turned, examining the kitchen. Brass moved, a loud noise sounded, and she watched as he turned, gripped the cabinets that housed the dishes and ripped them from the wall. There were three of them hooked together but he dumped the entire section of cupboards on top of the sink as though it weighed nothing. He studied it before spinning around to meet her gaze.

"How are you doing?" Brass moved toward her.

"I'm fine. Can I look at Harley? He's losing a lot of blood."

"You stay put." He glanced at the bloodstained floor, lifted his gaze to where Harley stood against the back window and frowned. "Harley? Walk to Trisha." Brass' gaze returned to her. "You can treat him sitting on your ass right there. You don't move from that spot."

Brass headed for the back window. Harley limped to Trisha. She shoved the table out of the way and she focused on the bleeding area. He'd been hit just under his knee on the outer side of his leg. Her fingers shook as she hooked the material of his pants with her fingers where the bullet had torn it open and widened the hole enough to see his bloodied skin. The bullet had grazed him but it was a deep cut.

Harley had a knife strapped to his thigh. She glanced at it first before she met his gaze. He watched her silently.

"Hand me your knife, please."

He didn't hesitate to pass it over, handle first. Trisha looked down her body, realizing she didn't have a lot of clothes on. She gripped the bottom of her shirt and began to slice it. She took off four inches of the bottom and made a large strip and held up the knife, handle first, to Harley. He instantly reclaimed it.

"I would have shot Moon if I had known you'd cut off your clothes if one of us got shot."

"I heard that," Moon called out from above.

Trisha laughed as she wrapped the strip around his leg and tied it tightly. "That should hold it enough to slow the bleeding but it needs stitches."

"It feels better already."

"Let me see your arm."

Harley crouched and twisted his big body to turn his shoulder her way. She quickly tore the thin material of his shirt to see the wound. It was a bloody mess. She hesitated.

"I need to feel to see how deep it is and it's going to hurt."

He nodded, not looking at her. "We have great pain tolerance. Go for it."

Even though Trisha hated to do it, she eased her fingers into the ragged wound that was bleeding badly and instantly touched something there. *Crap.*

"I feel a bullet. I thought you said it was a graze."

"I lie sometimes."

Trisha used her fingertip to dig out the damaged bullet after realizing it hadn't gone deep, feeling lucky that the projectile had gone through the cabin wall before it had struck Harley. It had slowed the bullet down significantly to prevent it from tearing completely through his body. She feared a big vessel had been nicked by the amount of blood seeping down his arm. She had to stop the bleeding and she knew he wouldn't lie down flat for her to apply pressure until help arrived.

She could try to cauterize it but dismissed that idea. She asked for his knife again and cut off more of her shirt until the material was just under her breasts. She locked her teeth together, hating how she would have to hurt him.

"I'm packing the wound and afterward, I'm going to tie it off. The pressure from the filler will stop or greatly slow the bleeding but it's going to hurt."

"Do it but just hurry, Trisha. I need to be on my feet. They will open fire on us again at any time. They aren't just going to go away as much as we wish they would."

Trisha balled up a small piece of her shirt and packed it into the hole. It was extreme but she didn't have a choice. She studied it, saw a decrease in the bleeding, and wrapped a strip tightly around his arm to hold it in place, before tying it off. Long seconds ticked past while she watched the bandage but the bleeding seemed to have stopped.

"Try to keep that arm as immobile as you can. This isn't exactly a fix but more of an emergency temporary patch."

He nodded, stood, and shoved the side table back in front of her to shield her from stray bullets. "Thanks."

Harley retook his position by the front door while Brass stood by the back wall. Suddenly Brass and Harley chuckled.

"What's so funny?" Trisha glanced between them, wondering if the stress of the situation had finally gotten to them.

Brass looked relieved when he glanced her way. "We have company. The neighbors are on their way to welcome our guests. I can pick up their scents."

"At least four." Harley inhaled. "And Valiant is one of them."

"Poor bastards," Moon chimed in from above. "This is going to be interesting."

Trisha just wanted it to be over. She wished she could see what was going on outside but bullets suddenly tore through the cabin again.

"Full frontal assault," Moon yelled. "They are going for one of the trucks."

"Trisha," Harley yelled, running for her. "Get out of there!"

Trisha shoved at the table and knocked it aside. Bullets struck the wall near Brass as he loudly cursed. Harley suddenly gripped Trisha's arm as she struggled to get to her feet and yanked her toward the stairs. He kept his body between hers and the front of the cabin. Bullets tore through the room from the front of the cabin, embedding in walls and glass shattered.

"Get up there," Harley snarled.

He released Trisha at the bottom of the stairs. She ran and reached the top before she realized Harley hadn't followed her. She turned and saw him lying on the floor at the bottom of the stairs. Brass rushed the fallen man, grabbed him with both hands, lifted and dumped him over his shoulder to pound up the stairs.

"Trisha, get on the bed," Brass snarled at her, tossing Harley's limp form on it first. "Get behind him and stay flat."

Trisha heard the distinct sound of an engine seconds before an explosion of noise boomed through the cabin so loudly it hurt her ears. She threw herself onto the bed next to Harley. The cabin shook as though an earthquake had hit—one sharp jolt of movement. She screamed, terrified, as wood snapped and groaned. More glass shattered and crunched from somewhere below them on the first floor. The sound of an engine seemed super noisy, as if it were next to Trisha.

"They breached the front wall," Moon roared.

"Breached it hell," Brass snarled back. "That truck is parked inside the living room now."

Trisha saw that Brass took position at the top of the stairs where he'd thrown his body flat onto his stomach. He started firing at something below and gunfire became deafening to the point that Trisha covered her ears. She couldn't look away from her friend though, too worried for him.

"Keep your head down, Trisha," Moon yelled at her.

The engine died and someone screamed from below as Brass kept firing. He dropped a clip, snapped another one in and continued shooting after a pause of only seconds. Moon fired his weapon from the window.

Trisha's heart pounded. Those men had driven a truck through the front of the cabin. Bullets tore up the floor by the bed where Trisha watched holes appear in the wood and continued on through the roof. Debris rained down. Trisha turned in to Harley's still form and she grabbed him, clinging, until she realized her hand felt wet and warm on Harley.

*Blood. He's bleeding.* She opened her eyes to stare in horrified shock at Harley, sprawled on his back. Her hand over his heart on his chest lifted and it was covered in blood. All hell broke loose around her as men yelled, guns were fired and the cabin continued to be riddled with bullets. Trisha hated feeling helpless as she stared at her bloodied hand, knowing if she sat up she'd be of no use to him with bullets slamming into her as well.

A loud roar sounded over the shouting, the gunfire, and the cabin being sliced apart by bullets. Trisha had heard that ear-splitting roar before. It sounded as if Valiant had entered the cabin.

# Chapter Eighteen

ಐ

Trisha felt hot tears running down her face when the gunfire ceased. She heard another roar, closely followed by something similar to a wolf's howl. She lifted her head and watched Brass shove up from the floor. Moon hovered by the window grinning.

"You should see this. There's about ten of ours out there now and they have the assholes. One son of a bitch is trying to run from Valiant. Oops. He thought he could flee from Valiant. Now he's a flying...ouch. He was doing a bird impression but now he's part of a tree. Well, he was until his body hit the ground. Now he's dead." Moon chuckled. "That had to hurt. It seems the last thing on his mind was bark."

Trisha fought her way to her knees to stare down at Harley, realizing he wasn't moving at all and instantly reached for his neck. A sob tore from her throat when she didn't find a pulse. She frantically gripped his shirt and tore it open to examine a gaping wound on the left side of his chest.

"Oh no," Brass gasped.

Trisha moved. It was hard to do on the soft mattress but she got beside Harley and she tilted his head to open up his airway. Trisha leaned over him, gripping his nose with one hand, supported him with the hand behind his neck, and covered his mouth to start breathing for him. She blew in air, shifted her gaze to watch his chest rise, and sat up. She released him to press her hands together over his chest above the wound. She counted in her head as she did compressions.

"Trisha?" It was Slade's voice and he was close.

"Get help," she gasped in air and blew into Harley's mouth. She forced air into his lungs again. She did more chest compressions. "Life flight. Nearest trauma center. Hurry."

"Trisha?" Slade was very near, almost as if he were on the bed behind her. "He's gone."

Trisha forced air into Harley's lungs again. "No!" She refused to give up. He'd used his body to shield her to reach the stairs. He'd taken bullets protecting her and the baby. No way would she give up on him. She'd saved patients with worse wounds before.

She kept going until she stopped, checked his pulse, and nearly collapsed with relief. "I've got a heartbeat." She stared at his face to make sure he continued breathing. Relief swept through her as he took a breath on his own and then another. His pulse was weak but there.

Trisha studied his chest to discover it was a sucking wound, telling her that his lung had been compromised. "Someone get me something plastic, now. A baggy, anything. Hurry. His lung will collapse."

Someone handed her a new, folded trash bag and she went to work while Harley kept breathing on his own. She put pressure on the bleeding wound over his chest. She just had to be careful not to put too much weight down for fear of collapsing the injured lung. Forever seemed to pass as Trisha knelt over him until she finally heard a helicopter.

Arms gripped Trisha around her waist. "Help is here. They can't see you, Doc. No one can. Let him go. Moon will hold that in place for you." Slade held her, speaking softly against her ear. "Come on, sweet thing. You've done all you can do. They aren't our people inside that helicopter, they are yours, and if you stay there will be too many questions."

"Take her out the back window," Brass ordered softly.

Trisha twisted her head to stare at Slade. "I'm the New Species doctor and he needs me."

Slade hugged her harder against his body. "Think of the baby, Trisha. They can do for him what you could." He lifted her completely away from the bed and hurried toward a back window.

Brass kicked out what was left of the window. Bullets had broken it mostly out but sharp, jagged corners had remained. Brass stepped through the window first and onto the porch roof, only to disappear over the edge. Slade gripped Trisha, turned her inside the cradle of his arms and bent. They barely fit through the opening but then they stood on the roof. Slade walked to the edge to peer down.

"Harley needs me. Put me down, Slade." She frantically wiggled, trying to get a look at the bed and caught a glimpse of her friend laying still with Moon huddled over him. "Please? I'm a doctor!"

Slade seemed to be ignoring her as he spoke to someone else. "Can you catch her?"

"I can," Valiant growled. "Drop her."

*Drop me?* Trisha's eyes widened as she stared at Slade, pulled from her frantic need to monitor Harley's condition. Slade's grim expression didn't reassure her.

"Freeze just the way you are, sweet thing." He lifted her out away his body to dangle over the edge of the porch roof and let go.

Trisha had a horrible sense of falling and grunted when two strong arms caught her around her upper back and behind her knees. Slade had dropped her about seven feet down into Valiant's waiting arms. She stared in shock at the ferocious New Species. He spun and bolted into the woods with her clutched close to his massive chest. Panic hit her hard when he sprinted away with her. They reached a thicker part of the woods far from the cabin but he kept going.

"We're far enough," Brass stated, running alongside them.

"Take me back," Trisha demanded. "I need to help Harley. I could do things a medic can't during the flight." She could still hear the sound of the helicopter. They'd probably have a hard time stabilizing him and she wasn't sure where the nearest trauma center was located. "I need to monitor him and—"

"Shut up," Valiant snarled.

Trisha's fear overrode her outrage at being taken away from her patient. She sealed her lips as the guy kept going with her held inside his massive arms, taking her farther from the cabin.

Valiant finally slowed and glanced down at Trisha, frowning. "You should eat." He looked away, peering at their surroundings.

Trisha was thrilled to see Slade jog out of the woods behind them. He grinned. "Clean getaway." He approached Valiant and opened his arms. "I'll take her. Thanks."

Trisha met his gaze. "Harley needs—"

"The humans have him and you're not going back." Slade's dark gaze narrowed. "You can argue with me but it won't change anything. You saved him and now it's up to them to make sure he survives. Our priority is you and the baby. Harley knew it would be dangerous when he took the job and accepted the risks."

Tears spilled down her cheeks. She wanted to protest but realized as she heard the helicopter growing fainter that they'd already scooped him up and transported him away. She couldn't do anything more for him. She just had to hope that the life-flight crew were top notch and that his lung didn't collapse. His heart could stop again. A hundred other things that could go wrong began to filter through her head until she pushed them back. She couldn't do anything more for him and worrying about all the "what ifs" wouldn't do anyone any good. She was a professional and knew she needed to let it go until she heard news from the hospital.

Valiant transferred her from his arms into Slade's. "Those men destroyed the inside of my house." Valiant growled in anger. "I was out hunting and smelled them. They were gone by the time I reached my home but I followed them this way."

"I'm sorry." Slade watched him. "Thank you for the help."

"She's one of ours."

Slade nodded. "Mine specifically."

Valiant arched an eyebrow. "It now makes sense why you threatened to kill me for touching her. You should feed her more. She's too skinny. You should at least be breeding a bigger one if you are going to be mounting a human. I can feel all her bones."

"I'm not skinny," Trisha protested softly, using one hand to wipe her face. She sniffed and her anger stirred. It may have been the stress and trauma but she felt insulted. "I needed to drop ten pounds before I got pregnant. I eat plenty too. You're making me feel as though I'm not taking care of myself. I'm healthy to the point of having excess weight I could lose."

Slade cleared his throat. "Where? I'm partial to your breasts and I love your ass just the way it is."

"You know I'm going to get bigger, a lot more so, in a few months, don't you?"

Slade nodded. "I can't wait to see you fat."

"I won't be fat," she sputtered. "Pregnant is not fat."

"Where should we take her?" Brass moved closer.

"You can take her to my home," Valiant sighed. "Just for one day." He shot Slade a warning look. "Only one."

"Thank you. Your place is the closest and I need to stash her until darkness falls. I want to move her to my house unseen. It's going to be a mess out there right now after this happened. In a few hours things will calm." Slade shifted her in his arms. "I want her under cover quickly."

Valiant nodded. "Even better. Let's go."

"You can put me down," Trisha informed Slade.

He shook his head. "You are barefoot. Just wrap your arms around my neck and relax." He suddenly grinned. "Unless you want me to put you on my back again."

She wound her arms around his neck, remembering their time after the SUV crash and how the muscles of her thighs had ached for days afterward from clinging to him. Valiant led the way with Slade following and Brass trailing behind.

"Where's Moon?" Trisha twisted her head, searching but she didn't see him. "Is he okay? He wasn't shot too, was he?"

"He's unharmed. He planned to stay with Harley." Brass answered. "He'll guard him while he's inside the human hospital."

"Will someone let us know how Harley is doing?" Trisha met Slade's gaze. "Please? I'll worry until I hear if he made it."

He nodded. "I'll make sure you're updated as soon as I have news on his condition."

"Thank you." She knew he would keep his word.

* * * * *

Valiant lived inside a large two-story house. Trisha stared at it, surprised. It was an old Victorian, in pretty good shape. Someone had lovingly restored the place unless it had been built to mimic an older house. Either way it appeared authentic and impressive.

"This is land we bought adjoining the old resort," Slade explained. "An old woman lived here but her son had died. She was all alone and not doing so well. Now she's in a retirement center with a full-time staff to care for her. We were able to buy up a lot of properties in the area that surrounded the resort. We paid them nearly twice the market price to make them happy."

Valiant walked up the wide porch steps. The double doors were broken and Trisha winced. One of the stained-glass doors had been smashed and she knew it would be impossible to replace. Brass used his foot to sweep the glass to the side as Valiant ushered them inside his home.

Trisha stared at the beautiful woodwork inside the nice entryway and at the hand-carved banister that led to the second floor. Her doubts of the real age of the home vanished. The beautiful woodwork shone with love and pride, craftsmanship that no longer existed except for the very rich. Valiant led them through double doors into a large living room. Trisha stared in horror.

"They wrecked most of the house," Valiant growled. He walked to the overturned couch and straightened it. "Put her down there. Between the three of us we should be able to make her more comfortable."

"I'm so sorry," Slade told him sincerely. "We'll help you replace what was destroyed." He gently eased Trisha down to the couch before he moved away.

Trisha watched quietly while the men righted furniture. She was grateful no one had taken a knife to the antique furniture. Valiant left to retrieve a broom and a dust pan. It didn't take the men long to clean up.

"Can I use your phone?" Slade glanced at Valiant.

"They didn't damage the one in the kitchen. Use it."

Slade disappeared. Brass took out trash. Valiant studied Trisha grimly as she watched him back.

"I saw what you did for Harley. I heard you say you are a doctor."

She nodded. "I work at Homeland."

"Did you ever work for Mercile Industries?" Anger made his exotic, cat eyes a scary sight.

"No. I never saw a New Species until after you'd all been freed. Slade was brought to my emergency room directly from the testing facility he'd been rescued from."

He relaxed. "You look too young to be a doctor."

"I started medical school at fourteen. I've always been kind of smart."

"You really work at Homeland?"

"Yes."

Valiant smiled, all traces of his anger disappearing. "You are attracted to Slade? He's kind of gruff."

She smiled. "He has his moments."

"I hear some of our women are kept at Homeland. Do you take care of them too?"

"When they need me."

"Will you do me a favor when you return there?"

"Yes," she agreed instantly. He'd helped save her life.

His cat-like golden eyes narrowed. "Don't you want to know what I want from you before you answer?"

"You helped save my life and I owe you. What do you need from me?"

He hesitated. "I want a mate. Will you talk to the women and see if anyone is interested? It gets lonely out here. I want a big, sturdy woman. I'd prefer a feline mixed species but as long as she's tough I wouldn't be picky." He paused. "I frighten most of my own kind. Our women don't scare easily since they were raised in testing facilities. I bred with a feline female once inside while in captivity and she didn't scream at the sight of me or beg the men who brought her into my cell to take her away. All the others refused me. Primates were especially terrified when were introduced to me."

Trisha had to swallow and remember to keep her mouth closed. He wanted her to find him a girlfriend? She swallowed again.

"I can talk to them. There are about three dozen New Species women living in Homeland dorms. I'm just not sure how many of them are feline but I've seen some."

He nodded. "I had heard that. Talk to them for me and tell them I am not as scary as I appear." He suddenly stood. "Are you hungry?"

"A little."

"I'll get you some good food. Pregnant women should eat often and you need to do that more than most. You are too skinny." He stalked out of the room.

Trisha hugged her waist and let the conversation settle into her thoughts. Valiant was one big man. If someone took her into his cell and asked her to have sex with him, she probably would freak out too.

She shook her head in disbelief. He seemed nice once he calmed and wasn't snarling. Maybe one of the New Species would be interested in him but she didn't envy that woman. He was just too big and ferocious. She didn't believe he'd hurt anyone he was with but just the sight of him angry would be enough to scare the hell out of anyone dating him if he lost his temper.

Slade returned alone and sat on the couch inches from her. "I spoke to Moon. Harley made it to surgery and he's holding his own. All the men who attacked you have been taken care of but most of them died. The three who survived are being transferred to human authorities and will be questioned." He studied her. "How are you holding up, sweet thing? Since you involved yourself with my kind your life hasn't seen too many dull moments, has it?"

She hesitated. "I didn't work for New Species when I met you the first time. You made me curious enough to want to send my résumé into Justice so I blame you."

He smiled. "Really?"

"Yes."

"You'd think it would be the opposite. I grabbed you when I woke and pulled you into my bed. I pinned you under me and told you what I planned to do to you."

She could feel heat warm her cheeks. "Yeah, well, maybe that's what got me interested."

Slade's smile widened and he reached for her. His hand slid across her thigh to rub her leg. "What part interested you? I know I was sure I wanted to keep you under me for days."

"That part kept me up nights, wondering what it would have been like if you'd had your way with me."

He inched closer. "I haven't had the opportunity to do that yet, sweet thing. I want to spend days with you under me."

"You won't pin her there on my couch," Valiant growled.

Slade sprang back and his hand released Trisha. He smiled at Valiant. "Sorry. I didn't hear you enter the room."

"You were too concentrated on the female." Valiant handed Trisha a soda and a banana-nut muffin. "It amazes me how soft our kind have grown since we were freed. Once, no one would have been able to creep up on you before you were aware of them."

"Once we were chained to walls and slept on mats on the floor. Once we were prisoners. Once is over."

Valiant nodded. "True enough."

"I have to go handle the fallout of what has happened." Slade gave Valiant an intense look. "Is it okay if I leave her and Brass here with you?"

"Fine but remember you said you were going to take her out of my home tonight."

Slade stood and his gaze met Trisha's. "You're safe here and I'll be back in a few hours when the sun goes down. I'm going to take you to my house. Get some rest."

"Okay. Hurry back."

Slade smiled. "I will. I'll come for you soon."

Trisha cringed. She'd heard him say that to her before yet he'd never returned. Instead he'd avoided her by accepting a job overseeing Reservation. She watched him go, realizing she had to learn to trust him or she would always be afraid every time he walked away from her. She didn't want to live that way.

"Don't look so fearful. You are safe here with me. You're too skinny to draw my sexual interest, Slade has claimed you, and I'm too angry at what was done to my home to be aroused by your tempting female scent. He'll be back for you." Valiant growled low. "He knows I'd kick his ass if he left a human with me for more than a day. I have some cleaning to do. Relax. Sleep. Just don't leave. There is a bathroom by the front door in case you need it. The intruders who breached my domain didn't damage it. Brass is going to help me right everything."

"I am?" Brass stood in the doorway.

Valiant nodded. "I'm bigger and I say you will help me."

"Works for me." Brass winked at Trisha. "I'm going to go help the large feline clean up."

"I'll be right here resting and not helping," Trisha teased.

Brass chuckled before he turned and followed Valiant out of the living room. Trisha finished her muffin and lay down on the comfortable couch until she realized her hands were still bloody from Harley's wounds. She'd been so distracted by all that had happened, she hadn't noticed it before.

She stared at the dried blood and fought the urge to be sick. She stood and went in search of the bathroom, knowing it was a losing battle. Her stomach heaved and she barely made it in time before she lost her snack. Ten minutes later she stretched out on the couch. Exhaustion helped her fall asleep quickly.

\* \* \* \* \*

"I'm glad to hear it." Slade hung up the phone, his gaze meeting Tiger's, and he blew out a deep breath. "Harley survived surgery. Justice sent a human team to back up Moon. Guard him with a few more of our men. He'll be safe."

"We've heard from the authorities. They wanted permission to go to the crime scene but Justice is handling it with Fury's help. We can't allow them to go into the wild zone and I had one of our males sent to retrieve all of the doctor's belongings. We don't want any trace of her left there in case the police manage to talk Justice into allowing them to see where the attack took place."

"Thanks." Slade leaned back in his chair. A hand lifted to run through his hair. "I could have lost her. Again."

"But you didn't. This is why I don't envy you for having a human."

"One day you might meet one you can't resist."

"Don't make threats." Tiger glared.

A grin curved Slade's lips. "It's not so bad."

"You're going to be a father. You're biased. Your woman has given you a miracle."

That reality kept making Slade's heart race. "I am, but she is one to me before I ever learned of the baby that grows within her. I'm happy but worried. She's not Species. Humans aren't as tough as our women. I think of all the things that could go wrong."

"Stop. She's a strong female of mind, if not of body. That matters."

"She is pretty tough."

Tiger snorted. "You should see your face."

"What?"

"Nothing. It's just obvious that you care deeply for her. You look proud and happy." Tiger stood to pace the office. "They are never going to leave us alone and just allow us to live in peace."

Slade knew Tiger meant the humans who hated them. "I know but we can hope. I've been told that people fear what they don't understand. Perhaps with time they will learn more about us and see that we aren't their enemy. We've even segregated our lives from theirs for the most part to assure them they are safe. A lot of them fear we're unstable or that we'd attack them without provocation."

"Perhaps that is the problem. Maybe setting up our own living environments wasn't the best way to have them accept us."

"I don't know but think of all the lives that would have been taken if they could attack and pick us off one by one. It may not be the best way to get them to accept us but it's the best way for us to survive. They don't seem ready to be our neighbors just yet. At least not all of them. Time is something we need to learn how to live with each other. Some Species hate humans. Remember the reason Reservation is necessary." He blew out a deep breath. "I'm glad I don't have Justice's job. Mine is to finish Reservation, to make it a safe haven for our people and to protect Trisha. Anything beyond that is more than I want to think about right now. Trying to handle our own people is difficult enough without trying to deal with the humans too."

"We're going to have to tighten security again. I don't know how we're going to do it. Our men are already tired and overworked. We're overrun with humans who may not be here just to do construction. Those males who attacked the cabin purposely took jobs seeking an opportunity to kill some of us. Justice is going to switch some of our men out to give them a rest. I'll just be happy once we're fully functional here and can close the gates to restrict which humans enter."

"It won't be too much longer."

"I know." Tiger leaned against the wall. "I'm just grateful your doctor wasn't harmed and that she was able to save Harley. That was amazing. It would have destroyed you to lose her and hurt all of us if we'd lost him. Where are you on the whole issue of you being a danger to her? Do you still believe that you claiming her as your own will put her life more at risk?"

"I've learned that she's in danger whether I'm a part of her life or not. She chose to work with us. She's dedicated. I'm just happy that she's decided to give me a second chance. I won't let her down again."

"I know you won't." A grin curved Tiger's features. "Did you ever think you'd revolve your entire life around a human? Or a woman at all, for that matter?"

"No." Slade grinned back. "But this time I'm happy that I was wrong. This is the good kind of surprise that life threw my way."

"Don't dump all the work on me." Tiger growled. "I know you won't want to leave her side but Brass did a fine job protecting her and I can't finish Reservation without you. We're a team. You can protect her and our people."

Slade nodded. "Securing Reservation will secure her safety. It's one and the same now."

# Chapter Nineteen

ဆာ

"Doc?"

Trisha didn't have to look to know it was Slade who rubbed her arm. She opened her eyes and he smiled.

"Hi. Did you have a good nap?"

She couldn't resist reaching up to cup his face. The guy warmed her in every way just by looking at him and appreciating his pure masculine appeal. She smiled back at him.

"It would have been better if you'd been sleeping with me and we were naked."

Slade's smile turned into a flat-out grin.

"I didn't need to hear that," Valiant growled.

"Crap," Trisha sighed. "We're not alone, are we?"

"Nope," Brass stated.

Trisha's hand dropped away from Slade's face. "I'll sit up if you move to give me room."

Slade inched away, straightened and held out his hand to help her up. "It's dark outside now."

She glanced around the living room, remembering she was in Valiant's home. The home's owner sat on a chair not too far from her and Brass had stretched out on a lounge chair in the corner with his long legs spread out. Slade pulled her to her feet.

"Thank you for the hospitality and for helping save me." She addressed Valiant.

"I'd say any time but I still have a lot of cleaning to do before my house is livable." He did smile at her. "It was nice killing humans."

She just blinked. "I'm glad?" *What can I say to that?* She wasn't sure. She hoped she passed muster on comebacks and figured she had when Valiant appeared amused. She turned her head and peered up into Slade's face. "I'm ready to go."

He insisted upon carrying her since she didn't have shoes and Brass followed them to a waiting SUV parked outside. Brass opened the back door for Slade to deposit Trisha on the back seat. Both men climbed into the front.

"You need to crouch down when we drive closer to the main areas," Slade ordered softly. "I'm going to park inside the garage when we arrive at my house. You can't go near any windows or outside once we reach it. No one is to see you."

"But—"

"No buts," Brass growled. "You are to stay hidden. You trust us with your life and we both agree that would be the safest. No one is to know where you are."

"Fine," she conceded, too shaken to argue the point. "Has there been any word on Harley?"

"He's in critical condition but he's tough and made it through surgery," Slade informed her softly. "Moon is sure he'll pull through. You saved him, Doc."

"Good work, Trisha. I was sure he was gone." Brass gave her a grateful look. "I would have been devastated losing my friend. He's a brother to me in my heart."

Trisha leaned back and relaxed, thrilled that her friend would survive. "He's tough and we all know how tough all you guys are." Her stomach chose that moment to grumble. She chuckled. "I'm starving."

"We'll get you fed when we get to Slade's house." Brass turned on the seat to continue to watch her. "We won't be able to get your clothes to you immediately. The cabin is a total loss and I've been informed that they removed your stuff but it is damaged or dirty. I'm afraid you will have to wear Slade's until we can get you more or have yours cleaned."

"Loss is right," Slade sighed. "Tiger sent a man out to pull the truck out of the living room and a large portion of the loft totally collapsed. The entire structure is unstable. Those assholes driving a full-sized work truck through the front of it just made more construction nightmares for me. It's going to have to be leveled and another one built."

"Is there anywhere else I'll be stashed or will I be staying at your house for a while, Slade?" Trisha hoped he'd keep her close.

"You're going to be living with me. The house is far enough away from the hotel area and the new buildings being put up that there's no reason for anyone to come there. We just don't want you peeking out windows or stepping outside just in case anyone gets nosy. At night we can take you for short walks outside to give you a break from being contained. We remember how it is to long to be outside. Brass is going to stay with you when I'm at work and Moon should be returning sometime in the next few days. Justice will send a replacement for him to the hospital soon. We didn't want to bring in a new guard for you since the less people who know about your pregnancy, the better."

"But all my guards will be New Species, right? So that's totally safe. They wouldn't leak any information about the baby."

"True," Brass agreed. "But Justice is playing it safe. You're important to us, Trisha. You are our first conceiving female."

She frowned, not liking the term. "You make me sound as if I'm a horse."

Brass turned to face forward in his seat. He mumbled something that made Slade laugh.

"What? That's not fair. You know I couldn't hear that! Come on, guys. Play nice with me."

Slade cleared his throat. "He said something to the effect that with our dicks it wasn't a bad analogy."

Brass laughed. Trisha rolled her eyes and shook her head. "Some people are full of themselves."

Slade glanced back at her and his teeth flashed when he grinned. "Want a reminder when we get to the house? Maybe you're forgetting my size and you need a visual reminder."

"I've seen horses when I worked for a veterinary hospital. You wouldn't be getting near me if you actually resembled one from the waist down." She paused. "But you are larger than anyone else I've ever been with. Does that sooth your manly pride?"

Slade growled. Brass chuckled. Trisha grinned from the back seat until she was ordered to crouch down. It was dark outside, she didn't see the reason for hiding, but she didn't want the men to growl at her, something New Species seemed to love to do when they were irritated or emotional. Slade pulled into his garage and she heard the automatic garage door come down. He was the one to open the back passenger door.

"Are you going to sleep there or are you going to come inside the house?"

She flipped him off and sat up. Trisha glanced around the garage. It was a double garage and a Jeep sat on the other side of the SUV. It was a tight squeeze to get out until the door closed as Slade led her into the house.

"Oh. My. God," Trisha gasped.

Slade spun around to face her. "What?"

She gawked at the kitchen. "You're a slob!"

Trisha curled her lip at the piles of dirty dishes in both sides of the sink. The stove... She forced her gaze away from it, guessing that would need to be power washed. The floor... Her feet were bare and she could feel the dirt. Her gaze flew to Slade's, realizing he just watched her silently, frowning.

"You *are* a slob," Brass groaned softly. "Ever hear of soap and water, man?"

"I've been working sixteen hours a day and sleeping six for the three weeks I've been here. Give me a break." Irritation flashed on his face. "There's not someone to hire to clean my house. I don't get days off to do it myself."

"Wow. You did this in just three weeks?" Trisha shook her head. "I can't wait to see the rest of the house." She hoped her sarcasm wasn't too noticeable.

"You could sleep in the woods," Slade teased. "At least there's not a truck sitting inside my living room. You only lasted in the cabin for what? Twenty-four hours? It has to be torn down it's in such bad shape. At least mine just needs cleaned."

"Kiss my ass." Trisha stuck her tongue out at him.

He suddenly grinned and his gaze raked slowly over her body. "I'd love to, Doc." He snapped his sharp teeth at her.

Brass chuckled when Trisha backed up.

"Keep those babies away from my backside." She shook her head. "It wasn't an actual request."

"I don't know how you sleep with humans," Brass chuckled. "Way too fragile. One of our women would love being bitten."

Slade nodded but he kept the grin in place. "I know but she's cute. What could I do? She wanted me badly."

"Stress on the word wanted." Trisha shot him a dirty look and walked past him through a dining room.

"Uh-oh," Brass chuckled. "Someone's in the dog house."

"I don't have one." Slade laughed.

The dining room was obviously not a room Slade ever used since it was basically clean, minus the dust issue. The living room was another story. It might have been a nice coffee table if she could see the surface but dirty dishes, empty beer and soda cans and an overflowing ashtray littered it. She frowned, studying Slade.

"You smoke?"

He shrugged. "Sometimes I do when I have a few beers. I've been trying to get past the horrible taste of them. Human male bonding seems to demand we drink some of them together after work and smoke too."

"Well, please don't while I'm here. The smell of cigarettes will make me sick."

"I won't smoke inside the house."

"Smart man. It's really bad for you."

She glanced at the living room before she moved on. The downstairs contained a full bathroom, a family room that wasn't used and an office that was. She opened her mouth but closed it after noticing every surface covered with papers or discarded drinks. It amazed her that a man owned so many dishes. She headed for the stairs when the main floor tour ended.

"Are we going to go look at every room?" Slade followed behind her.

"Yes. I want to know where I'm living and what I'm dealing with. I'm starting to miss the seventies."

Brass laughed.

"What does that mean?" Slade glanced at them.

"I'll explain later." Brass snorted.

There were two bathrooms and three bedrooms on the second level. One of the bathrooms opened from the hallway. The second bathroom was located inside the master bedroom. It was a large room with a twin bed. She frowned at the small mattress and turned to glance at Slade but said nothing. She checked out the other two bedrooms next. One room had nothing more than a twin bed and a dresser. A weight set and a treadmill dominated the last room. She closed the door and met Slade's gaze.

"So where are you going to sleep? Brass gets the spare room and you only have a twin bed. I'm not sleeping on the floor. I guess you could sleep on the couch or on your weight bench." She put her hands on her hips.

Slade blinked a few times, a confused look on his features. Brass chuckled and Slade shot him a dirty look before frowning at Trisha.

"I'm sleeping inside my room on my bed and you are sleeping on my bed with me. I know it's small but we'll fit. Trust me."

Her gaze roamed his body. She hesitated. "I'm not sleeping on the bottom. The only way we're both going to share that bed is if one of us sleeps on top of the other. You'll crush me."

Slade suddenly moved. "Let me show you how it will work. Good night, Brass. Make yourself at home. There's plenty of food in the fridge."

"Hey," Trisha protested when Slade grabbed her. He ignored her objection as he scooped her into his arms. "What about dinner? I'm hungry."

Slade growled. "I'm hungry too." He walked into his master bedroom and kicked the door closed behind them. He strode to the narrow bed and gently lowered Trisha on top of it.

Trisha watched as Slade bent over, staring at her. She loved the passion that flared in his eyes. He did look hungry but it wasn't for food. He wanted her. He tore off his shoes and socks before he dragged his shirt over his head. Trisha's gaze slowly took in the sight he posed, appreciating his muscular arms and broad chest.

Slade growled at her again and yanked at the front of his pants to get them open. "You could undress."

"I could but I'd miss the show."

His hands stilled for an instant but then he jerked his pants down his hips to kick free of them. He stood in his black underwear until he reached for the last item of clothing on his body. Trisha watched him shove the material down and bit her lip. Slade's cock was thick, engorged with blood to an impressive size that most men would envy, and his need for her was unmistakable.

He reached for Trisha's shorts. She heard the material tear in his haste to tug them down her hips and legs. He threw them over his shoulder and just ripped her shirt open. It had already been destroyed when she'd cut pieces from it earlier to make strips for Harley's injuries. She wasn't wearing a bra and it caused a grin to spread across Slade's rugged features.

"No underclothing, Doc? I'm shocked but really turned on."

"I was taking a shower when those men arrived. Brass yanked me out and tossed clothes at me. My underwear and bra weren't in the pile he shoved into my arms."

Slade's grin died. "He saw you naked?" He growled as anger seemed to darken his eyes.

"He was saving my life. I'm sure he didn't even notice."

"Trust me when I say he noticed." Slade grabbed her ankles and tugged her down the bed until her ass stopped at the very edge. "Anyone would note every exposed inch of you."

"Thank you." She smiled and tried to sit up, wanting to kiss him.

He used his hand, placed between her breasts, and pushed her flat onto her back. His hand slid down her belly, over her hip, and then both gripped her thighs to push them up. He spread them wide to gaze at the sight of her pussy. He knelt at the end of the bed to get a better look, licked his lips, and growled softly. Trisha looked down their bodies to stare at Slade's aroused cock straining straight up inches from her pussy.

"Aren't you even going to kiss me before you take me?"

"Yeah, sweet thing. I'm going to kiss you before I fuck you." He pushed her legs wider apart and his heated gaze studied her body stretched out before him.

Trisha tried not to feel embarrassed over his intense interest in every inch of her, especially when he lingered while staring at her exposed pussy. He scooted back to lower his head and gripped the inside of her thighs to hold them open. His hands shifted enough that Trisha realized what he planned to do. His breath was hot against her thigh right before his tongue teased her clit with strong licks before his mouth closed over the bundle of nerves, sucking with firm tugs. She came unglued.

"Oh God," she moaned.

His mouth withdrew from her sensitive flesh. "I told you I was going to kiss you."

"I thought you'd aim for my mouth."

He tilted his head, regarding her. "Do you want me to stop? I have to admit I don't want to. I've been dying to taste every inch of you. Don't deny me, sweet thing."

"Do you want to die? That's what will happen if you do stop. Please continue."

He chuckled a second before his mouth and tongue returned. Trisha moaned louder as her fingers dug into the bedspread just for something to cling to while she arched her back. She thought she could handle the amazingly good sensations he created throughout her body with his mouth. That was right up until his tongue started to flicker over her clit rapidly and he started to growl deep enough to vibrate against it. Trisha tensed, wasn't even sure if she was breathing anymore, and she came—screaming.

Slade lifted his head quickly, gripped her hips, and pulled her toward him. His thick cock pressed against her pussy and he entered her slowly while she still reeled from the aftermath of the climax he'd just licked her into. She moaned as he pushed his broad shaft into her deeper, enjoying the feel of having her body stretched in a delicious way that left her feeling full and taken by the man she loved. His big cock felt amazing to her still-climaxing body.

Slade thrust into Trisha fast and deep, driving her over the edge of bliss again within minutes and caused her to cry out his name. Slade growled deep, pounded into her faster and threw back his head. She watched him bare his sharp teeth as he began to come inside her, swelling to the point of near pain, and he shouted out. His body jerked against her as he poured his heated release inside her.

Trisha smiled when she opened her arms to Slade and he collapsed over her chest. They both panted while Trisha wrapped her legs around the back of his thighs and her fingers ran through his silky hair where his head rested between her breasts. His heavy breathing tickled her skin a little but she loved holding him too much to complain or ask him to turn his head enough to make it stop.

"I told you a twin bed would work," he chuckled.

"Sure works for me in this position but I'm not sure how you're going to sleep on your knees that way."

Slade turned his head a little and moved. He flicked his tongue over the side of her breast, causing Trisha to shiver. Her breast responded instantly, the tip growing taut. Slade opened his mouth, covered her nipple, and allowed his sharp teeth to scrape over it. Trisha arched against him. The erotic feel had her passion igniting all over again. He released her nipple and lifted his head to grin down at her.

"Want to go again, Trisha?"

"I do but I need food. How about we eat and pick up right here afterward?"

Slade laughed. "Let me run you a bath. You soak while I make us something for dinner."

"Wait a minute. I've seen that kitchen. Maybe we should order takeout."

Slade straightened. He twisted his hips a little and it lifted Trisha's ass from the bed. His hand slapped her ass hard enough for make her flinch but wasn't painful.

"I won't poison you and we don't have takeout food anywhere near Reservation. We also couldn't trust them to prepare our food since we aren't sure if they are friendly to us. I have plans that involve you being very much alive and healthy." He grinned. "I think I can withdraw without hurting you now that the swelling is down somewhat. Come on, Doc. Bath and food, in that order."

Her legs clamped around his hips when he tried to withdraw his cock from her body. She glared at him. "Remember the rule? You're inside me so calling me Doc isn't acceptable. What's my name, lollypop?"

He shook his head at her but grinned sheepishly. "Sorry, Trisha."

"Lollypop?" Brass shouted from down the hall. They heard laughter.

Heat flooded Trisha's cheeks. "He heard everything we just said and did, didn't he?"

Slade shrugged. "It's our hearing, *Trisha*." He stressed her name. "It's not really his fault, though he should have just laughed without making a comment."

"Sorry," Brass yelled from the spare bedroom. "Lollypop."

Slade groaned as he gently withdrew his cock completely from Trisha. He stood and pulled her to her feet. "I'm going to have to kill him if he keeps calling me that."

# Chapter Twenty

ઓ

Trisha looked around at the kitchen as Brass put away the last clean dish. Trisha sighed, rubbing her aching lower back with her hands.

"It's finally clean."

Brass frowned. "I told you to lie down two hours ago. You're carrying a child. Slade would have helped clean this with me after he comes home tonight if you'd just waited."

"I couldn't stand it," Trisha admitted as she opened the fridge and grabbed a soda and an iced tea, handing the soda to Brass. "Look on the bright side. He'll be surprised when he gets home."

"Or kick my ass for allowing you clean so much. Did we have to do the entire house in one day? You need to take it easy. Slade is going to blame me if something happens to you or that child."

"Well, you couldn't very well tackle all this alone and you did all the tough grunt work. You are the one who did all the scrubbing and heavy lifting."

"You're holding your back. Is it hurting?"

"A little." She turned and suddenly sprinted away.

She could almost feel Brass on her ass when she ran for the downstairs bathroom. She slammed the door, hoping it didn't hit him in the face. She barely dropped to her knees before her lunch came up.

The door opened behind her. "I warned you, woman. You're sick now."

She couldn't talk while that whole throwing her guts up thing stopped her. Brass gently gripped her hair and his other hand rubbed her back. She finally stopped when there was nothing left inside her stomach.

"Don't follow me into a bathroom," she groaned. "This is so embarrassing."

"You are carrying a child. Morning sickness happens."

"Not this early."

"Maybe you are sick because you worked too hard today. Do not do it again, Trisha. I forbid you to lift another finger. Let this be a lesson."

"That or I'm experiencing early morning sickness because nothing about this pregnancy is going to be ordinary. I wish some New Species women had given birth so I'd have an idea of what to expect. Maybe it's normal to get morning sickness at this early stage while carrying a New Species baby."

"I'm going to help you up. Are you done with being ill?"

She nodded. "I need a toothbrush and toothpaste."

Brass helped her to her feet by supporting her weight. "I'll go get the things Slade brought for you this morning. I saw those things inside one of the bags. Are you going to be okay while I go retrieve them?"

"I'm fine. Thanks."

She turned and studied her reflection in the mirror after Brass left her alone. She looked pale and drawn. *Maybe I did overdo it today.* She'd just wanted to clean the house. If she didn't know better, it almost seemed as if she had an uncontrollable nesting urge, something common that some pregnant women experienced. She also tended to clean when she was nervous or worried—both emotions she experienced.

Brass returned and opened up a new toothbrush and a tube of toothpaste. He stood there, refusing to leave, as Trisha scrubbed her entire mouth. She hated being sick. When she was certain she didn't have bad breath or a lingering smell, she washed her face. Brass handed her a towel, acting as though he were a lady in waiting. She grinned at that amusing concept, dried her face, and handed the towel back to Brass.

"Thank you."

He nodded but suddenly bent, scooped her into his arms and straightened to walk toward the stairs.

"Put me down. I can walk."

"You have outdone it and I'm taking charge. You'll follow my orders."

"I will not. Come on, Brass. I'm fine."

"Shut up."

"Kiss my ass."

"I'm ready to spank it."

"You don't ever touch her ass," Slade snarled. "What is going on here? Why are you carrying her?"

Brass turned with Trisha in his arms, staring at Slade, who glared at him. Brass tensed.

"She wanted to clean your house. I told her I would do it alone but she wouldn't listen. She felt the need to help me. She just suffered morning sickness and I'm taking her to your room to rest."

Slade's anger faded and his gaze softened when it met Trisha's. "Are you all right?"

"I'm fine. Can you have him put me down? He won't listen to me. He thinks I can't walk or something."

Slade dropped the briefcase he carried and kicked the front door closed behind him. He approached Trisha and opened his arms. "I'll take her."

"She's all yours." Brass handed Trisha over.

"I'm so lucky." Slade laughed.

Trisha put her arms around Slade's neck. "I'm not helpless, you know. I can walk and everything."

"Shut up."

"Kiss my ass."

"And this is where you walked in," Brass snickered. "See why I was threatening to spank her?"

"Yes," Slade said, nodding, still staring at Trisha. "I'll spank your ass and then kiss it."

She laughed, not expecting him to be playful with her. She was glad he wasn't angry that she'd cleaned the house and had probably overdone it. "That sounds kinky."

He smiled and climbed the stairs. "Brass, will you please make dinner?"

"Sure."

"I'm going to shove her into the bathtub and try not to drown her for being so stubborn."

"Good luck with that." Brass laughed.

Trisha glared at Slade. "That's not funny."

"Sure it is." He carried her into their bedroom. He finally put her down on the bathroom counter. "And next time you decide to clean the house while you're pregnant I might not be joking about shoving you under the water."

She watched him turn on the faucets, loving Slade's bathtub. He had a garden tub and a separate shower. Slade tested the water and then turned toward her while the tub filled.

"How was your day, honey?" Trisha batted her eyelashes at him.

He grinned. "Fine, sweet thing. I'd ask how your day was but I already know. Do you feel better now that the house is clean?"

"Tons, minus the whole tossing my guts up part."

He winced. "I'm not kissing you."

"I brushed my teeth."

He stared at her mouth. "Let me rephrase that. I'm not kissing your mouth. Let's get you out of those sweats if you want a kiss." His gaze lowered. "Those seem really big on you. Are those rolled at the waist?"

"You're hugely tall and I can't help it if you have really long legs. I would wear my shorts but someone tore them last night." She lifted her shirt to show him the waist of the pants she'd had to manipulate to fit her body better.

He smirked. "You could just go without clothes."

She smirked right back at him. "Sure. I could do that. Of course, I'm sure Brass would get to see a whole new side of me. Two of them, actually."

His eyes narrowed and his mouth tensed, not liking that thought at all. "Wear any of my clothes you want."

"I thought that's what you might say." She grinned.

"Rolled sweatpants look very sexy on you. In fact, I insist that you wear them all the time when you're not with me inside our bedroom. I really love it when you wear my clothes."

Slade edged her off the counter until she stood and lifted the large T-shirt over her body. His hands brushed her breasts, which instantly responded to his touch. He knelt in front of her, smiled, and gripped the waist of the sweats.

"I've been waiting all day to see this." He tugged down the pants.

Trisha burst into laughter at the shocked expression on Slade's face seconds later. "You waited all day to see me wearing your boxers?"

His eyebrows rose. "You're even wearing these?" Two of his fingers hooked the fly of them and wiggled them inside the parted material against her skin. "I guess there are advantages."

"Stop that." She yanked at his hand, pulling his fingers out. "I would have sewn that closed if I'd found a needle and thread. It seems you don't own either."

His eyes widened. "Those are mine. Don't mess with my boxers. What would I do when I wear them if you sew all of them closed?"

"Pull them down."

He laughed, shaking his head. "I have to get you clothes."

"And here I thought you were trying to get me naked."

He gripped the boxers and slid them down her legs. "Thanks for reminding me. Get into the tub."

"But I thought there would be touching and kissing and…"

He stood and reached for his shirt. "There will be but inside the tub."

She glanced at the bath and grinned. "Oooh!"

Slade laughed as Trisha climbed into the tepid water as the tub filled. She turned her head and watched as Slade started to remove his clothes. She loved seeing him naked and enjoyed watching as he stripped everything off with a big grin on his handsome face.

"Want to turn the water off, Doc? It will overflow soon if you don't."

She twisted the faucets and had to move out of the way to make room for Slade to climb inside the tub. It was a tight fit as he sat down behind her. Slade opened his knees and lifted Trisha back until she sat snug between his thighs. She leaned back against his chest.

"This feels great but not really conductive to kissing and more."

"I'm sorry. Let me fix that."

She turned her head and looked at him to find him grinning again. He reached up and grabbed a bottle of baby oil from a built-in shelf on the wall.

"Baby oil?"

He laughed. "I usually put it on my skin to soften it while I soak. I get a lot of calluses naturally on my hands." He showed her his fingertips. "But that's not the use I have for it right now."

Trisha watched him pour baby oil over his fingers before they slipped under the water. She gasped as they slid between her parted thighs and moaned when his fingers spread her, rubbing her clit. A louder moan came from her when he stopped to breech her pussy with one of his digits.

"Slade."

"Doc."

She elbowed him.

Slade chuckled before his hands caressed her body until he gripped her hips. He lifted her and she bit her lip as he eased her down onto his stiff cock until he filled her pussy. She sank deeper as her body lowered all the way until she sat completely over his lap.

"Better, Trisha?"

"You're such an asshole."

He thrust up into her. "You're a doctor. Did you fail a test on anatomy? That's not where I am."

"Fuck you," she moaned.

"No, Trisha. That's what I'm going to do to you."

He gripped her hips and thrust up into her hard and fast. Water sloshed over the edge of the tub but Trisha ignored that while she moaned. Slade shifted them and gripped her hips a little lower, proving his strength. He lifted her up and down on him, his hands easily manipulating her weight, and set a faster pace that left her mindless with ecstasy.

Slade's entire body tensed as he came and began to swell inside her. She was so close to climaxing but Slade slowed moving her over him as he growled viciously. He jerked before his body stilled.

"Sorry," he growled.

*Crap.* Trisha nodded, sexually frustrated, as Slade suddenly moved his legs and forced her thighs open wider. Her body ached with the need to climax but she tried to ignore it until she watched Slade grab the baby lotion again. He poured it on his fingers a second time before they dipped under the water. Trisha moaned when he teased her clit.

"Tell me if I hurt you," he ordered softly. "I am still really swollen."

She didn't care. The pleasure became too overpowering from what his fingers were doing to her as he played with her swollen bud, rubbing circles and coaxing moans from her. Slade moved inside her gently, not withdrawing far, and just fucked her deep. The pressure she experienced from his swelling and the feeling of his fingers manipulating her sex had her shouting his name when she threw her head back against him. Sheer rapture tore through her as the climax gripped her. Slade growled.

"Forget me hurting you." He gripped her hips, holding her very still. "You're killing me, sweet thing. God, you clamp around me so hard it hurts. That will teach me to let you come first."

"Sorry." She didn't mean it in the least.

He chuckled. "It's a good way to go." His lips brushed her neck. "Relax, Doc."

She elbowed him. "You're inside. What's the rule?"

"Ouch. Sorry, Trisha."

"Stop calling me Doc."

"But it's what you are."

Trisha turned enough to see his face and clenched her muscles. Slade winced.

"I give. I'll stop calling you Doc. You're squeezing me to death. Swelling, remember?"

She smiled and relaxed against Slade. "Now you get to hold me. I really love that whole swelling thing."

"So did I until you nearly squeezed me to death."

Trisha grinned and reached for the washcloth. "I'll make it up to you."

\* \* \* \* \*

Trisha couldn't look away from a smiling Slade as she grinned back. Brass sighed loudly.

"Is this how it's going to be until that baby arrives? You two will make me lose this fine turkey sandwich dinner. I know you keep rubbing her thigh under the table, Slade."

Trisha turned her gaze on Brass. "It is a great sandwich. Thank you for making them. I love the bacon you added."

"Yes," Slade chuckled. "We're going to be having lots of sex until and after the baby arrives. I love to touch her and I plan on doing it often."

The phone rang. Slade winked at Trisha and rose to retrieve the phone. He turned his back to the table, talking quietly.

"Are you feeling better now? No more sickness?" Brass gave her a concerned stare.

"I'm good." She took a bite of her sandwich. "I mostly feel sick in the afternoons."

"I thought it was morning sickness."

She shrugged. "Tell it to the baby."

Brass laughed. "It won't listen."

"Exactly my point."

Slade hung up and sighed as he returned to the table. Trisha's smile died at the irritated expression he wore.

"What is it?"

Slade sat. "There are just more problems to deal with. I can't wait until we can close Reservation to workmen and actually secure it."

"More troubles?" Brass stopped eating. "Something else has happened?"

"You could say that." Slade stood again and left the dining room to enter the kitchen. Seconds later he returned with a soda. He popped the top and took a sip as he retook his seat. "The three attackers who survived yesterday are claiming to be part of a new branch of a human hate group who've sworn to make us sell the land and leave the area. They are boasting that yesterday just marked the beginning of the trouble we will endure if we stay. We still have a lot of construction to finish and we need the workers to complete it. Any of them could be members of this new group."

"Was their intent yesterday to kill a few of us or did they have bigger plans than attacking the cabin?" Brass growled the words.

"Their objective, according to one of them, was to destroy any remote structures and kill any of our kind they came across. They knew they'd be attacked if they targeted the bigger structures such as the hotel with all of our security in place. We know they succeeded with the cabin. One of the human males knew the old woman who used to live in Valiant's house. I guess since Valiant never removed all the woman's belongs, when they reached the second floor, he decided the woman must still live there and they left. Otherwise they were going to torch the place. They were stopped before they could find more homes to attack."

"That Victorian is such a beautiful house." Trisha shook her head. "What jerks."

"I'm more pissed about their attack on you." Slade looked grim. "They could have killed you. Every hour I had some of our men do a head check on the humans but now we have to do it every half hour. They had over twenty minutes to cause trouble before we noticed they were gone. I'm also going to have to put tracking systems on all vehicles that enter Reservation and have them monitored. They smuggled guns past our security, which alarms me too. We see a lot of vehicles coming in with building supplies and tools. That's going to slow things down since we have to check every inch of anything coming through the gates now. Our people are already exhausted."

"Tell Justice you need more men." It sounded simple enough to Trisha.

"We're stretched thin already." Slade leaned back in his chair. "He's put as many men here as he can without weakening the defenses at Homeland. We're already using double the manpower that we'll actually need when we're up and running because we have to monitor so many humans."

Trisha held out her hand and waved it to get their attention. "Uh, what about the women?"

"The women?" Slade stared at her with a frown. "What about them?"

"There are at least three dozen New Species females that I know about at Homeland. Why don't you bring them here?"

Slade shook his head. "They are to be protected. Our females are few."

She frowned at him. "Did anyone ask them what they wanted? Have you seen some of your women? I think they are more than capable of handling the job of counting some humans and doing some of the security work. I saw cameras so I assume you have a monitoring room? How many of your men have to do that? Put the women there if you don't want them manning the gates or having direct contact with the construction workers."

"It's a good idea," Brass stated.

Slade hesitated. "It's a great idea." He smiled at her. "Let me see if Justice is agreeable to it and if the women would be interested in helping out here."

"What about housing?" Brass stared at Slade. "Where would we put them?"

"The top floor of the hotel has been finished. There are ten suites up there with two sleeping rooms in each of them so that's about twenty bedrooms."

"Would it be safe?" Trisha remembered that Brass hadn't wanted to put her there when Slade had suggested it.

"I don't see why not. Those men didn't attack it before due to how many people are present and how tight security is around the larger structures with the ongoing construction." Slade paused. "There isn't any other option."

"I don't know," Brass hedged. "Setting fire to the hotel would be a good way to do it if the humans want to cause trouble. It's the biggest structure at Reservation. I would worry our females could be trapped in a fire if we put all of them on the top floor."

"You're right." Slade agreed. "It was a good idea but we just can't house them, Trisha. We can't put them in harm's way if there is even a risk of danger. As much as I need the help, I can't exactly ask them to room with the men."

"You could bring in a few motor homes." Trisha shrugged. "Women don't mind sharing with each other usually and you'll have them working in shifts, right? Maybe park them inside the wild zone and ask Valiant and the others keep an eye on them. Just scrap the rebuilding of the cabin. That way none of the construction workers have any reason to be out there."

Slade smiled at her. "Do you want my job? You seem to be better at it than I am. I never would have thought of asking our women to help out."

"She's a doctor," Brass chuckled. "She's much smarter than we are."

"I don't know." Slade grinned at Brass. "She couldn't tell an asshole from—"

"Shut up," Trisha laughed, cutting him off, and kicked him under the table. "I know the difference."

Both men smiled at her while Trisha shook her head at them. "Don't you have some calls to make, Slade? You should ask Justice before he goes to bed and give him time to talk to the women before they are snoozing too. The faster a decision gets made, the faster you could have extra help here." She flashed him a grin.

Trisha looked at the other man. "And you, Brass. There's laundry that needs to be done. You said you wanted to do it all so I didn't have to. Hop to! It's not going to get done by itself."

"I said I'd clean. I never said anything about laundry." Brass stood. "I hate sorting and folding clothes." He groaned. "But I'll do it so you don't."

"I'm going to go lie down. Good night!"

"She's so bossy." Brass chuckled.

"I know but she's got a great ass." Slade chuckled too. "When she yells at me and gets demanding, she always storms away after. I watch her ass as she leaves and I just can't seem to care anymore that she's domineering."

Trisha stopped on the stairs and laughed. She shook her head and retreated to the bedroom.

# Chapter Twenty-One

ഌ

Trisha tried to hide her horrified and stunned reaction. She kept a forced smile firmly on her mouth until the muscles in her cheeks ached. Brass' highly amused expression was obvious but he didn't chuckle. Slade didn't show any restraint when he bent over, held his stomach, and laughed until tears dampened the corners of his eyes.

Valiant growled. "Why is he so amused?"

"I have no idea," Trisha lied. "I think sometimes he's socially challenged."

Slade stopped laughing instantly as his gaze flashed to hers and narrowed dangerously. He sent her a look that promised he'd get even with her soon. Trisha glanced away with a grin, hoping he'd attempt to lick her to death, but her amusement died quickly as she caught sight of the table again.

She tried not to gawk at the big hunk of raw meat wrapped inside plastic that Valiant had just placed in the dining room. She wasn't sure what it was but it looked big enough to be a body. *God, I hope it's an animal.*

"That was so kind of you to bring us...so much. It will last us a good week." *Or a month*, she added silently. She forced her attention away from the wrapped meat and smiled wider at Valiant. "What is the occasion?"

"Slade informed me that you were the one who thought up asking our women to come here. Twenty of them arrived yesterday. I have seen some of them from afar and am very pleased with the selections. I asked you to find me one female but you brought many for me to meet. I wanted to say thank you. I knew it would be bad form to just bring the entire carcass so I skinned and gutted it for you. I even removed the limbs and head." He motioned to the large thing on the table. "I wrapped it to prevent blood from dripping on your carpet."

"That was so very kind," Trisha got out, trying hard to be polite, despite her shock. She stepped closer to him but then stopped. "May I have a hug to say thank you?"

He frowned. "Why would you want to hug me? You just said thank you."

"It's a human thing." Brass grinned. "They seem to hug each other. Just deal, Valiant. She harasses me if I don't allow her do that to me sometimes. It's nice."

Valiant sighed deeply. "I guess I should get used to being touched since I want a mate." He opened his arms. "Go ahead." He looked completely disgusted.

Slade suffered another fit of laugher but Trisha ignored him. She had to stretch up on tiptoe to put her arms around the huge man. Valiant held still while Trisha gave him a quick squeeze around his waist before she stepped back.

"That wasn't so bad, was it?"

"No. You smell nice." Valiant shrugged. "It wasn't bad."

"Thank you." She glanced at the wrapped hunk of meat before flashing her gaze to Slade. "Why don't we have a barbeque? You and Brass can cut it up, freeze what we don't use, and we'll have some of that for dinner."

Slade smiled at the big lion-like man. "That sounds great. Thank you, Valiant. Do you want to stay for dinner?"

Valiant shook his head. "I have women to meet and a mate to find." He fled the house.

Trisha pointed at the plastic that blood stained from the inside and whispered in case Valiant remained within hearing range. "What is it?"

"Hell if I know." Slade shrugged.

"I'm guessing deer," Brass whispered. "There are a lot of them out by his place. Deer steaks do sound good." He stepped closer to the table. "Let's get this into the kitchen."

"Use the back porch, please," Trisha instantly corrected. "That way you can hose the deck off after you cut it up."

"Yeah." Slade grinned. "That way you can hose off the deck once you cut it up, Brass."

"You're helping," Brass growled at Slade. "I'm not a butcher."

"Neither am I."

"Well, don't look at me." Trisha frowned when both men turned to stare at her.

"You are a doctor and should be good at cutting things apart." Slade flashed a hopeful grin.

"No way. Nu-uh. I'd be so sick. I'm the pregnant one, remember? I feel morning sickness coming on just at the thought of doing that." She put her hands over her stomach and batted her eyelashes at Slade. "You are the big predator, after all. Isn't that what you always tell me? So go…hunt up a knife and get busy."

"So bossy," he groaned.

Trisha laughed. "Want to watch me storm away?"

Brass chuckled. "You look at her ass and I'll find some sharp knives and freezer storage bags."

Trisha turned, presented her backside to Slade, and smiled at him over her shoulder. "Call me when you're done. I'm going to go get naked and take a bath. Thank you!"

"Tease."

Trisha strolled toward the stairs. "You got that straight. Call me when dinner is ready. You're the best."

"Keep walking," Slade growled. "Shake it a little, sweet thing."

Trisha walked into the master bedroom still feeling highly amused. Some of her clothes had been returned to her that morning. Someone had salvaged them from the damaged cabin. She pulled out a summer dress and underthings from the dresser then moved into the bathroom.

She studied her naked body in the mirror, seeing that she'd already starting showing her pregnancy despite the early stage of it. It worried her a little, no one knew what to really expect, and it could be dangerous. She had already experienced morning sickness, which marked the pregnancy as odd right from the beginning.

Slade had sneaked her into the new medical facility earlier that morning before dawn where they had an ultrasound machine. The facility wasn't up and running yet but the equipment had arrived. The baby measured bigger than normal. It made her wonder how large a New Species baby would be at birth. The baby seemed to be developing at an accelerated rate as well. The way Slade had grinned at the sight of his child had warmed her heart. She had no doubt he wanted the baby as much as she did.

Slade was mixed with canine and their pregnancy cycles were far shorter than a human's. She worried that the baby might grow and develop faster with Slade's altered DNA. She'd have to keep a very close eye on the baby's development to figure it out and try to estimate a due date. She'd talked to Justice by phone and asked if he would order more medical equipment to do just that. He'd readily agreed to get whatever she wanted.

"What's that look for?"

Slade entered the bathroom and walked up behind her. His hands slid around her waist to gently cup her slightly rounded belly. Their gazes met in the mirror while his hands caressed her stomach. He kissed the top of her head.

"What look?" She leaned back against him.

"You're worried."

She smiled. "I am a little. I don't want anything to happen to our baby or anything to go wrong."

"You're alarmed because he's bigger than he should be and you're advancing in your pregnancy stages faster than normal."

She nodded. They'd had this conversation when she'd noted her discoveries at the clinic. "Yes. Stop calling the baby a 'he'. What if it's a girl? You'll give her a complex. I couldn't get a clear picture of the sex yet."

He laughed. "I will not give our baby a complex. You just get annoyed when I say we're having a boy. It's a shame his legs were up and together so you couldn't get a view of his sex."

"It should be too early to tell but the baby is measuring at almost a twelve-week gestation. I don't really care what sex it is as long as our baby is healthy."

"Me neither." Slade hugged her against his chest a little tighter. "It's going to be fine, sweet thing. You're an amazing doctor and Justice will get you anything you request. He's looking for a trustworthy, excellent doctor to assist you who specializes in high-risk pregnancies. You can stay on top of this. You stated the baby looks perfect and has a strong heartbeat despite the anomalies with his size."

"I know. I just worry."

"I know that." Slade grinned. "I could spend the next hour up here distracting you."

She suddenly laughed. "Aren't you supposed to be helping Brass cut up that meat?"

"I came up here to change clothes but I didn't hear the water running. Please allow me to distract you. Then I can tell Brass you were upset and needed me." He winked. "He will get stuck doing all the butchering."

Trisha wiggled and gripped his arms around her waist. "Oh no. He'll growl at me and burn my dinner. Let go, Slade. I'm fine. I'll take a bath and you go change your clothes."

He turned her inside his arms and his smile died. "Are you really all right, Trisha? I want you to always confide in me. I want to be here for you."

"I'm fine. I'm going to worry but I'm also going to keep a close watch on our baby. Sometimes I just fret a little too much."

"SLADE!"

Trisha grinned. "You're being bellowed at."

He groaned. "Please let me stay?"

She pushed at him. "Go help him."

"But I want to kiss you all over and keep you under me for days."

"Tease."

"Not if I barricade the bedroom door to prevent Brass from coming after me."

"I love you but I'm not going to save you from cutting up all that meat. I'm hungry and I want deer steaks."

Slade's smile died and his beautiful eyes widened. "You love me?"

She stared at him. "You know I love you."

"You never told me that before."

"I haven't? Well…" She rose up on tiptoe and her arms wound around his neck. "I love you, Slade. I love you with my whole heart."

Slade lifted her a little higher until their faces were level. "I love you too, sweet thing. You're everything to me. Now we have to make love. Too bad for Brass."

"I heard that," Brass yelled. "Make love to her later. Only an idiot wouldn't know you two are madly in love with each other so it shouldn't come as a surprise. Get your ass out of the bathroom and help me with this deer."

Trisha let her face fall onto his chest when she lowered down his body and groaned against his shirt. "God, I can't wait until we can actually have a conversation without someone overhearing it."

Slade laughed. "I'll build him a dog house outside that he can sleep in."

She grinned, lifting her head to meet his gaze. "Promise?"

"Don't do it," Brass yelled. "I'm not sleeping in a dog house."

"It's almost as though we already have a child, isn't it?" Slade groaned while he eased away from her a few inches.

"Almost. He bellows at bad moments and he's keeping us from making love because he wants attention." She laughed. "Yeah. It's almost as if we're already parents."

"You take your bath. I'll go deal with the deer and Brass. We'll eat soon." His gaze raked down her, allowing his passion to show. "Then I'll get him shitfaced drunk until he passes out and we'll make sure he can't interrupt us from having lots of sex tonight."

Trisha's mouth opened to agree.

"Sounds like a good plan," Brass yelled.

Trisha backed up and blew a kiss to Slade. She turned her back on him, bent, and turned on the water. She heard a sexy growl and turned her head to peer at the man she loved over her shoulder. Slade stared at her naked ass.

Trisha pointed to the door. "Out. I'll bend over for you later. I promise."

"Bossy."

"But I have a nice ass."

"No. You have an amazing ass."

"So do you."

"So do I," Brass yelled. "Now, can we cut up this deer?"

## Also by Laurann Dohner

ɛꙩ

### eBooks:

***Print Books:***
Cyborg Seduction 1: Burning Up Flint
Cyborg Seduction 2: Kissing Steel
Zorn Warriors 1 & 2: Loving Zorn
Zorn Warriors 3: Tempting Rever
Zorn Warriors 4: Berrr's Vow

## About the Author

℅

I'm a full-time "in-house supervisor" (sounds *much* better than plain ol' housewife), mother and writer. I'm addicted to caramel iced coffee, the occasional candy bar (or two) and trying to get at least five hours of sleep at night.

I love to write all kinds of stories. I think the best part about writing is the fact that real life is always uncertain, always tossing things at us that we have no control over, but when you write, you can make sure there's always a happy ending. I *love* that about writing. I love to sit down at my computer desk, put on my headphones and listen to loud music to block out the world around me, so I can create worlds in front of me

℅

The author welcomes comments from readers. You can find her website and email address on her author bio page at www.ellorascave.com.

## Tell Us What You Think

We appreciate hearing reader opinions about our books. You can email us at Comments@EllorasCave.com.

# Why an electronic book?

We live in the Information Age—an exciting time in the history of human civilization, in which technology rules supreme and continues to progress in leaps and bounds every minute of every day. For a multitude of reasons, more and more avid literary fans are opting to purchase e-books instead of paper books. The question from those not yet initiated into the world of electronic reading is simply: *Why?*

1. *Price.* An electronic title at Ellora's Cave Publishing runs anywhere from 40% to 75% less than the cover price of the exact same title in paperback format. Why? Basic mathematics and cost. It is less expensive to publish an e-book (no paper and printing, no warehousing and shipping) than it is to publish a paperback, so the savings are passed along to the consumer.

2. *Space.* Running out of room in your house for your books? That is one worry you will never have with electronic books. For a low one-time cost, you can purchase a handheld device specifically designed for e-reading. Many e-readers have large, convenient screens for viewing. Better yet, hundreds of titles can be stored within your new library—on a single microchip. There are a variety of e-readers from different manufacturers. You can also read e-books on your PC or laptop computer. (Please note that Ellora's Cave does not endorse any specific brands.

You can check our website at www.ellorascave.com for information we make available to new consumers.)

3. *Mobility.* Because your new e-library consists of only a microchip within a small, easily transportable e-reader, your entire cache of books can be taken with you wherever you go.

4. *Personal Viewing Preferences.* Are the words you are currently reading too small? Too large? Too... ANNOYING? Paperback books cannot be modified according to personal preferences, but e-books can.

5. *Instant Gratification.* Is it the middle of the night and all the bookstores near you are closed? Are you tired of waiting days, sometimes weeks, for bookstores to ship the novels you bought? Ellora's Cave Publishing sells instantaneous downloads twenty-four hours a day, seven days a week, every day of the year. Our webstore is never closed. Our e-book delivery system is 100% automated, meaning your order is filled as soon as you pay for it.

Those are a few of the top reasons why electronic books are replacing paperbacks for many avid readers.

As always, Ellora's Cave welcomes your questions and comments. We invite you to email us at Comments@ellorascave.com or write to us directly at Ellora's Cave Publishing Inc., 1056 Home Avenue, Akron, OH 44310-3502.

MAKE EACH DAY MORE *EXCITING* WITH OUR

# ELLORA'S
# CAVEMEN
## CALENDAR

WWW.ELLORASCAVE.COM

ELLORA'S CAVE
Romanticon

Annual convention
for women who
refuse to behave

*Discover for yourself why readers can't get enough
of the multiple award-winning publisher
Ellora's Cave.*

*Whether you prefer e-books or paperbacks,
be sure to visit EC on the web at
www.ellorascave.com*

*for an erotic reading experience that will leave you
breathless.*